Vibrant Allure

June Hale

Published by June Hale, 2024.

This is a work of fiction. Similarities to real people, places, or events are entirely coincidental.

VIBRANT ALLURE

First edition. October 20, 2024.

Copyright © 2024 June Hale.

ISBN: 979-8227456953

Written by June Hale.

Chapter 1: The City of Dreams

The rhythmic clatter of my suitcase wheels on the cracked pavement creates a symphony of anticipation in my ears, punctuated by the honks of yellow cabs weaving through the labyrinth of traffic. Each sound, each smell, draws me deeper into the pulsing heart of Manhattan, where dreams and reality blur in a dizzying dance. I glance up at the buildings, their glass façades reflecting the endless sky, and a shiver of exhilaration courses through me. This is it. This is the canvas for my aspirations, each sidewalk a runway, each passerby a potential muse.

I find myself standing in the midst of a thrumming crowd outside a bustling café, its windows fogged with warmth and the sweet scent of pastries. The words "Welcome to New York" hang in the air, and for a fleeting moment, I feel that welcoming embrace wrap around me like a cozy blanket on a chilly night. I push through the crowd, my heart racing with every step, as though the very pavement beneath my feet is a launchpad for my future.

Inside, the café is alive with chatter and laughter, the rich aroma of roasted coffee beans mingling with freshly baked croissants. I squeeze past tables filled with patrons deeply engrossed in conversations and the clinking of cutlery. A glance at the barista reveals a flurry of movement, a whirlwind of energy behind the counter, his tattooed arms dancing as he crafts drinks with the precision of an artist. It's chaotic, yet there's a harmony to it, a rhythm that I crave in my life.

I order a cappuccino, the foam expertly shaped into a delicate heart that almost makes me giggle with delight. Settling into a corner table, I pull out my sketchbook, the pages still crisp and empty, awaiting the first strokes of my creative vision. As I sip the warm, frothy drink, I can't help but let my gaze wander to the other patrons. There's a couple sharing a slice of cake, their laughter mingling with the soft clattering of plates, and a group of friends animatedly discussing their next big project, the ambition in their voices palpable.

With every sip, I can feel my confidence blossoming, and I begin to sketch, the pencil gliding over the page as my imagination takes flight. I envision bold silhouettes and playful fabrics that swirl and twirl with the movement of their wearers, each design a reflection of the vibrant city outside. This is the beginning of something magical, a journey that I have fought for with every ounce of my being.

Suddenly, the bell above the café door jingles, and in walks a whirlwind of color. She's wearing a flamboyant, oversized jacket that looks like it belongs in a fashion magazine, her hair a riot of curls bouncing with each step. She radiates energy, her presence commanding attention like the spotlight on a stage. I can't help but stare, a mix of awe and envy surging through me. As she approaches the counter, she shoots the barista a dazzling smile, and I can't resist leaning a little closer to catch snippets of her conversation.

"Two shots of espresso, please!" she exclaims, her voice a melody over the café's background noise. "And make it extra strong. I've got an army of fabrics to tame today!"

Her exuberance is infectious, and I find myself chuckling softly at her enthusiasm. As she turns to scan the room, her gaze lands on me, and for a heartbeat, the world fades away. Her eyes, a vibrant shade of green, light up with mischief, and I wonder if she can see my thoughts swirling around like confetti in the air.

"Hey! I love your sketches," she calls out, startling me from my reverie. I blink, caught off guard, but she's already crossing the room, her energy crackling like static electricity. "I'm Bella. Mind if I join you?"

"Uh, sure!" I manage to reply, excitement bubbling up inside me. As she slides into the seat across from mine, I can't help but notice the way her jacket drapes effortlessly over her frame, the fabric flowing like water.

"First day in the city?" she asks, her eyes twinkling with genuine curiosity.

I nod, suddenly feeling the weight of my own journey. "Yeah, just moved from Meadowbrook. I'm here to pursue fashion design."

"Meadowbrook? That sounds... quaint," she replies, a teasing smile playing on her lips. "So, what's the first thing on your New York bucket list? A fabulous gallery opening? A rooftop party overlooking the skyline?"

"Actually, I'm just hoping to find my footing here," I admit, a hint of vulnerability creeping into my voice. "I have a few designs I want to showcase, but I'm not quite sure how to break into the scene."

"Breaking in? You'll barge through that door, darling! You've got to be bold!" Bella's enthusiasm is like a shot of espresso, firing me up. "Let me show you around. You'll meet the right people, and I know just the place where you can start!"

Before I can respond, she's already leaning over my sketchbook, her fingers dancing over the pages. "These are amazing! I can see the city in your designs—colorful, fierce, and unapologetically you. You have to let me help you make your mark here."

I can hardly process her words, my heart racing at the thought of diving headfirst into this vibrant world with someone so vibrant herself.

With a sudden flair for drama, she leans back in her chair, a mischievous glint in her eye. "Trust me, Lila. If you want to thrive in this city, you need to embrace its chaos, wear it like a badge of honor. It's the only way to survive, and I have a feeling you're destined for greatness."

The weight of her words lingers in the air, an unexpected twist in my otherwise ordinary day. With Bella's enthusiasm igniting a fire in me, the possibilities of this city suddenly seem endless, an invitation to step beyond my comfort zone.

The sun begins its slow descent, casting a warm golden hue across the city, transforming the stark glass and steel into a canvas of vibrant possibilities. As I sip the last dregs of my cappuccino, Bella's energy seems to wrap around me like a cozy scarf against the cool evening air. "We're hitting the streets, Lila. Time to see what this city is made of!" she declares, her eyes sparkling with mischief.

With a quick flick of her wrist, she gathers her oversized jacket around her, and I can't help but feel a twinge of envy at her effortless style. I follow her out of the café, my heart racing with a mixture of excitement and trepidation. We plunge into the lively crowd, the energy thickening like the city's famous humidity, wrapping around us as we push deeper into the urban fabric.

"Welcome to the epicenter of creativity!" Bella proclaims, gesturing dramatically at a group of street performers who are drawing an enthusiastic crowd. Their wild rhythms and colorful costumes add a pulsating backdrop to the scene, each note vibrating through the cobblestones beneath our feet. "These are the real artists of the city, unafraid to throw their talents out into the world. You should take notes!"

"Notes? I'm struggling to keep up," I laugh, trying to match her pace as she weaves through the throng. The streets pulse with life, and I feel as if I've stepped into a vibrant painting, each person a stroke of genius against the canvas of Manhattan.

"Just let the city take you where it wants," Bella advises, her tone half-serious. "You'll be amazed at where you end up. Trust me; I once met a Broadway producer while I was searching for a bathroom."

"Broadway? Now that sounds like a twist," I reply, caught up in her whirlwind of excitement. "But right now, I'd settle for finding a good fabric store."

"Ah, but that's where you're wrong! You're in New York! Fabric stores are just the beginning. You need inspiration first!" Bella declares, leading me past the tantalizing scents of street food vendors. The air is rich with the mingled aromas of sizzling skewers and buttery pretzels, and my stomach grumbles in agreement.

We stop at a food cart adorned with a gaudy sign proclaiming, "The Best Tacos in New York!" Bella insists we try them. "I've been here long enough to know that this city serves up creativity on every corner, including the food!" She places an order, and while we wait, I observe the bustling interaction between the vendor and the customers, a lively exchange filled with laughter and playful banter.

"Here," she says, handing me a taco overflowing with vibrant toppings. "Eat! Let it fuel your creativity. Every bite is a burst of flavor, just like the city."

I take a bite, the flavors exploding in my mouth, and I can't help but smile. "Okay, you're right. This is amazing."

"Of course, I'm right! I'm Bella!" she teases, her voice dancing above the street noise. Just then, a skateboarder zips past, narrowly missing us. Bella doesn't flinch. Instead, she chuckles, "Welcome to the jungle, my friend."

After finishing our impromptu feast, we continue down the bustling street, the atmosphere thick with artistry and chaos. Bella leads me to a quirky thrift store, its windows cluttered with an eclectic mix of vintage garments and bold accessories. "This is where creativity comes to life! You'll find gems here, Lila. Just wait!"

Inside, the dim light creates a warm cocoon, and the smell of old leather and fabric is intoxicating. I wander through the racks, fingers grazing over textured fabrics, each piece whispering stories of the past. Bella dives headfirst into a pile of sequined tops, her laughter ringing like chimes. "You have to help me find something outrageous! I need a statement piece for tonight's gala."

"Gala?" I ask, momentarily distracted from my exploration. "You didn't mention a gala!"

"Surprise!" she exclaims, emerging from behind a curtain of shimmering fabrics, a sequined top precariously balanced on her head. "It's an exclusive fashion event. The city's elite will be there, and you're coming with me!"

"Wait, what? I don't have anything to wear!" Panic starts to creep in, but Bella simply waves her hand dismissively.

"You're a designer! You can work magic with anything! Trust me, just channel your inner diva." She flings a vintage fur coat around her shoulders and strikes a pose, her playful bravado a comforting balm against my nerves.

As I sift through a particularly striking dress—a bold crimson that practically sings to me—I can feel my heart begin to race with the idea of stepping into a world I've always admired from afar. The fabric is soft against my fingers, and the thought of wearing it to a fashion gala sends a thrill through me.

I catch Bella watching me with an approving nod. "See? This is the spark! You have it in you. Now, let's get this piece, and you can wear something fabulous for the event tonight!"

"Alright, I'm in," I say, my voice tinged with both excitement and dread. "But if I trip and fall, I'm blaming you."

She bursts into laughter, and her joy is infectious. "You won't! Just follow my lead. And if you do, we'll make it a runway fall. Embrace the drama, darling!"

With a final flourish, she drapes the dress over my arm, and together, we head back onto the streets, ready to transform the evening into something memorable. The sun has dipped below the horizon, and the city lights start to twinkle like stars, each one a reminder of the magic waiting just beyond my reach.

Bella and I navigate the streets, her lively chatter filling the air as she shares her latest escapades. As she describes her outlandish adventures, I can't help but feel a sense of belonging unfurling within me. In this chaotic, vibrant city, I feel like I'm finally finding my place.

Just as we round the corner, a sudden commotion draws our attention. A street artist, paint splattering across the sidewalk, is passionately crafting a mural, the vibrant colors mesmerizing. We stop, captivated, as the artist's brush dances with life, creating a vivid world that feels like it might just come alive any second.

"See, Lila? Inspiration is everywhere," Bella whispers, nudging me forward. "Take it all in. This is where your dreams begin."

As I stand there, watching the paint swirl and merge on the pavement, I realize that this city, with all its unpredictability, is exactly where I'm meant to be. A whirlwind of colors and creativity awaits me, and I'm ready to dive in.

With each passing moment, the energy of the city seeps into my very being, igniting a fire I didn't know I possessed. Bella leads me through the streets, her laughter bubbling up like champagne as we weave past tourists and locals alike. The cacophony of voices, the clatter of heels on the pavement, and the occasional shout of a street vendor all blend into a lively symphony that makes my heart race.

We arrive at a gallery nestled between a chic café and a trendy boutique, its white walls contrasting sharply with the vibrant chaos of the street. The sign outside announces an exhibition titled "Raw and Unfiltered." Bella pushes the door open, and I'm immediately enveloped by a hush, the atmosphere shifting as though we've crossed an invisible threshold into a world where creativity reigns supreme.

Inside, the space is a stark contrast to the bustling streets, with dim lighting casting an intimate glow over the displayed works. Each piece tells a story, and I'm drawn to the bold colors and daring shapes, each one echoing the vibrant energy of the city outside. I glance at Bella, who is already lost in the art, her eyes sparkling with delight.

"Look at this one!" she calls, pointing to a striking installation made from recycled materials. "It's chaos turned into beauty. Just like us, right?"

I chuckle, drawn into her infectious enthusiasm. "Right. We're practically art in motion!"

"Exactly! Now, come on! We need to mingle!" Bella takes my hand and pulls me toward a group gathered around an abstract painting, their animated discussion filling the room.

As we approach, a tall man with tousled hair and a paint-splattered apron catches my eye. He's passionately explaining the symbolism behind his piece, his voice smooth like silk, drawing everyone in with an effortless charm. "This piece represents the struggle between conformity and individuality," he declares, sweeping his arm toward the painting. "In a city where everyone is trying to stand out, we often forget the beauty of our shared experiences."

Bella leans in closer, her curiosity piqued. "What's your name, artist?"

"Julian," he replies, flashing a grin that could light up the darkest alleyways. "And you are?"

"Bella, and this is my friend, Lila. She's an aspiring designer, fresh off the bus from the suburbs," she teases, giving me a nudge.

"Ah, the wilds of Meadowbrook," he muses, his eyes twinkling with mischief. "What do you think of the city so far?"

"It's—" I start, but the words escape me. How do I encapsulate this whirlwind of colors, sounds, and opportunities into a single phrase? "It's exhilarating. I feel like I'm finally where I'm meant to be."

"Then you're already ahead of the game," Julian replies, his gaze steady and encouraging. "Embrace the chaos. It will inspire you more than you can imagine."

A few more guests gather around us, and soon the conversation spirals into a lively debate about art, life, and everything in between. I find myself laughing, my earlier anxieties melting away like ice under the sun. Bella expertly navigates the group, her charm pulling everyone into our orbit, and for the first time, I feel a flicker of hope that maybe this new chapter will be filled with everything I've longed for.

As the evening wears on, I can't help but steal glances at Julian, who seems to effortlessly command attention. His passion for his craft radiates, igniting something deep within me. I want to ask him about his process, about the moments of doubt that accompany creation, but before I can find the courage, the lights flicker, and the room hushes.

A figure steps forward, her silhouette sharp against the vibrant backdrop of the art. It's a woman, striking in a fitted black dress, her hair a glossy cascade that gleams under the soft lighting. There's an air of authority about her, and I can feel the energy in the room shift as she addresses us.

"Welcome, everyone! Thank you for being here to celebrate the creativity that flows through our veins in this city." Her voice is smooth yet commanding, drawing everyone's attention. "Tonight is not just about art; it's about community and collaboration. I'm thrilled to announce that we will be hosting a fashion showcase next month, featuring emerging designers. If you're interested in participating, please see me after."

My heart skips a beat, the words sending a wave of adrenaline rushing through me. A fashion showcase! This could be my chance to step into the spotlight and present my designs to the world. I exchange a glance with Bella, whose eyes widen with excitement, her smile electric.

"I can't believe it!" I whisper, barely able to contain my enthusiasm. "This could be my shot!"

"Absolutely! You have to go talk to her!" Bella urges, nudging me forward. "You can do this!"

I take a deep breath, steeling myself. I've never been great at approaching strangers, especially not in this bustling, vibrant world. But this opportunity is too tantalizing to pass up. With a mixture of nerves and excitement coursing through me, I make my way through the crowd, my heart pounding in time with the music playing softly in the background.

As I reach the front, I gather my thoughts, ready to speak with the woman who could change everything for me. But just as I open my mouth to introduce myself, a loud crash reverberates through the gallery, startling everyone into silence.

I spin around, my eyes darting to the source of the noise. A figure is sprawled on the floor, a piece of art clutched tightly in their arms, the remains of a shattered glass display scattering like confetti around them. Gasps fill the air, and my stomach twists with anxiety.

"What just happened?" Bella whispers, her eyes wide with shock.

The woman in the black dress moves swiftly, her composure unwavering, but the tension in the room thickens like fog. As the crowd murmurs, I catch snippets of conversation, the words "disaster" and "expensive" slicing through the uncertainty.

Just then, Julian steps forward, his demeanor shifting from relaxed artist to focused leader. "Everyone, please remain calm. Let's see if we can help."

As he approaches the fallen figure, I strain to see who it is, the uncertainty making my heart race. The crowd parts slightly, revealing a familiar face. My heart sinks—it's someone I didn't expect to see here, someone from my past who I thought I had left behind.

A jolt of recognition floods through me as I lock eyes with Sarah, my old friend from Meadowbrook, the one I had shared dreams with and who had always kept me grounded. But now, she looks lost and frantic, her expression a mix of embarrassment and fear.

"Sarah?" I call, my voice barely rising above the hushed whispers surrounding us.

In that moment, our eyes meet, and the world narrows down to just the two of us. The chaos around us fades, and all I can think is that the city of dreams has suddenly become a tangled web of memories and unresolved emotions. What was she doing here, and why did she look so troubled?

I take a step closer, the energy in the room crackling with tension, the stakes suddenly higher than I ever expected. With every heartbeat, I can feel the world shifting, and I realize that this evening has only just begun to reveal its layers.

Chapter 2: Unexpected Roommates

The first time I spotted Ivy Carter, she was orchestrating a spectacle with nothing more than a couple of paintbrushes and a half-empty coffee cup. The tiny café in Greenwich Village was buzzing with the usual mid-morning chaos—caffeine-fueled conversations clashing with the hiss of the espresso machine. I had settled into my usual corner, a cozy nook that seemed to cradle me like an old friend, when I noticed her. Her fiery red hair practically screamed for attention, spilling down her shoulders like a waterfall of flames. As she laughed, a bright, throaty sound that cut through the noise, the world around her faded, and I couldn't help but be drawn in.

"Did you just order a side of existential crisis with that?" she quipped, her laughter spilling over into a grin that could light up the dimmest of rooms. I couldn't help but chuckle, even though I had been trying to eavesdrop on the philosophical debate occurring two tables over.

With my latte untouched and the steam curling up like lazy thoughts, I leaned forward, intrigued. "Only if it comes with extra whipped cream," I shot back, waving my cup like it was a trophy for cleverness. The spark in her emerald-green eyes suggested she was all too willing to engage in this unexpected banter.

Over the next hour, we slid into conversation as if we had known each other for years, trading tales of dreams and disappointments, aspirations and the occasional dose of reality. Ivy was a whirlwind of creativity, her words painting vivid images of her latest projects—colorful murals that sprawled across building walls like wildflowers breaking through concrete. In contrast, my own life felt like a series of neatly stacked boxes, each labeled with responsibilities and expectations, a bit too rigid for my taste.

The world outside the café buzzed along, but inside, it was just us, weaving a tapestry of laughter and shared dreams. I watched as she sketched on a napkin, her fingers dancing across the surface as if the paper was a canvas begging for color. I could see the raw passion in her strokes, a glimpse of the vibrant world she created in her mind, and it sparked a longing in me to break free from my self-imposed constraints.

"You know, we should totally be roommates," she declared suddenly, her eyes sparkling with mischief. The boldness of her suggestion struck me like a bolt of lightning. I didn't have time to mull over the practicality of the idea; something about her enthusiasm was infectious. "I mean, think about it! You with your organization and me with my chaos—it could be a beautiful disaster."

"Or a chaotic mess," I replied, half-joking, though the thought settled into my mind like an unexpected gift. What if?

That evening, over greasy slices of pizza, we hashed out the details, a tentative plan blossoming between us. Ivy's apartment was barely more than a shoebox—a charming little space crammed with canvases leaning against every available surface and paint splatters brightening the faded floors. She described it as a 'work-in-progress,' and it was clear she adored it despite its quirks. I found myself enchanted by her vision, a space bursting with potential, as if it were waiting for someone to breathe life into its walls.

"Don't worry, I'm basically an expert at cozying up small spaces," she reassured me, her voice lilting with a hint of mischief. "Just throw in a couple of potted plants, and voila! Instant jungle."

As our laughter mingled with the sounds of the bustling city outside, I realized I was more than ready to take the plunge. The chaos of Ivy's world was intoxicating, a sharp contrast to the predictable rhythm I had adhered to. I felt a sense of adventure stirring within me, a yearning to explore the uncharted territory of spontaneity and creative freedom.

A week later, I stood outside the apartment, the door creaking open to reveal Ivy in all her disheveled glory, paint-streaked and grinning. The living room overflowed with mismatched furniture—an eclectic mix of thrift store finds and her own creations. Each piece had a story, a history that resonated with the vibrant energy Ivy poured into her art. It felt like stepping into a dream, a place where chaos and creativity coexisted harmoniously.

"Welcome home!" she exclaimed, flinging her arms wide as if to embrace me and the entire universe all at once. I stepped inside, inhaling the mingling scents of fresh paint, coffee, and something sweet that I later discovered was the result of her latest culinary experiment—a questionable batch of blueberry muffins that didn't quite rise.

As the days turned into weeks, our personalities danced around each other, sometimes colliding, sometimes harmonizing in a beautiful, if chaotic, rhythm. Mornings were filled with Ivy's boisterous laughter and her attempts at experimenting with breakfast recipes that often ended in a puff of smoke. I found myself taking on the role of a reluctant sous-chef, slicing fruit and attempting to salvage her culinary disasters while stifling giggles.

In the evenings, as the sun dipped behind the skyline, we transformed the cramped living room into an art studio. I watched Ivy throw herself into her work, the way her hands moved as if possessed, capturing the essence of the world around her on canvas. Her passion became contagious; I found myself sketching alongside her, exploring my own artistic inclinations that had long been buried beneath layers of practicality.

But as much as we flourished in our shared space, there were moments when our differences erupted like a pot boiling over. Ivy's carefree spirit often clashed with my penchant for order. The clutter that surrounded us sometimes felt overwhelming, like an artist's palette gone rogue. I would take a deep breath, stepping over a pile of brushes and paint tubes, reminding myself that chaos was just another form of creativity, albeit a messier one.

"Why do you insist on folding everything?" Ivy would laugh, a teasing glint in her eyes as she watched me tidy up. "The world isn't meant to be tidy! It's messy and beautiful and unpredictable!"

"And yet, I find solace in tidiness," I countered, unable to suppress a grin. "Besides, someone has to keep us from being swept away in this whirlwind."

With every playful argument, every shared laugh, our bond deepened, transforming from mere roommates to partners in a wild and unpredictable adventure. Each day in that cramped apartment was an exploration—of art, of life, and of ourselves. Together, we navigated the unpredictable landscape of our dreams, a vibrant tapestry woven from both our spirits, interlacing chaos and creativity into something beautifully unique.

Every day in that little apartment felt like we were crafting our own version of a rom-com, minus the predictable plot twists and sappy resolutions. Our mornings began with an orchestra of sounds: Ivy belting out the lyrics to songs that danced through her head while I sipped my coffee, trying to summon the will to tackle the day. Her version of Adele was often a little off-key, but the way she sang with unrestrained passion transformed the ordinary into something extraordinary. I'd find myself laughing, a warm glow settling in my chest as I joined her for the occasional duet, both of us pretending to be rock stars in our caffeine-fueled reverie.

One morning, as she rummaged through a disarray of paint tubes that had become our kitchen's avant-garde decor, I noticed the light streaming through the window, catching the dust particles like tiny fairies in a sunbeam. "You know," I said, reaching for a half-empty jar of coffee grounds that was acting as a makeshift vase, "this place could really use some plants. It feels like it's missing a pulse."

"Plants?" Ivy looked up, her eyes sparkling with mischief. "Or maybe I could just paint a jungle on the wall. More permanent, don't you think?"

"Sure, if you want our living room to look like a botanical garden exploded." I raised an eyebrow, unable to stifle my laughter.

"Just think of the inspiration! Every brushstroke a reminder of how life is messy, just like us!" She flashed a grin that was too contagious to resist.

It was this banter, this easy flow of conversation punctuated by laughter, that forged our friendship. As weeks melted into each other, the vibrant chaos of Ivy's life became a part of my own. I often found myself swept away in her whirlwind of color and creativity. We spent late nights sprawled on the couch, debating the merits of various artistic movements, our discussions morphing into late-night strategy sessions about our futures. Ivy had a knack for turning even the most mundane moments into grand adventures.

One such evening, as the city hummed beneath the backdrop of a velvet sky, Ivy burst into our living room, her arms overflowing with an assortment of discarded canvases she had salvaged from a local gallery's dumpster. "Look what I found! It's like a treasure trove of inspiration!"

I peered at the canvases with mild skepticism. "And how many of those are likely to turn out... less than masterpiece-worthy?"

"Don't be a pessimist! It's art! The beauty lies in the imperfections!" She arranged the canvases like trophies, her eyes gleaming with excitement. "We'll create something breathtaking. Just you wait."

I couldn't help but admire her boundless enthusiasm. In her presence, I often felt like a timid butterfly ready to emerge from a cocoon. She had a talent for pushing me out of my comfort zone. That night, we painted under the flickering light of our living room lamp, creating an explosion of colors that filled the walls with a vibrant energy that mirrored our ambitions. I surprised myself, losing track of time as I immersed myself in the rhythm of the brush against the canvas, each stroke a catharsis.

But not every day was filled with inspiration. There were moments when our contrasting styles collided, creating tension that felt as sharp as the scent of acrylic paint. One evening, after Ivy had transformed the kitchen into a chaotic blend of half-finished paintings and paint splatters that would make a seasoned artist cringe, I finally snapped.

"Ivy! This place looks like a tornado of creativity hit it! I can't even find my cereal without stepping in paint!" My voice rose in exasperation, the pent-up frustration spilling over like the milk I'd just fumbled.

"Oh come on, just embrace the chaos! It's art, not a museum!" She stood there, paintbrush in hand, eyebrows raised in challenge.

"Yes, but even chaos needs a little order! There's a fine line between 'creative genius' and 'total disaster,' you know!"

"Disaster is in the eye of the beholder," she countered, a teasing smirk playing on her lips. "And I see potential here."

Rolling my eyes, I couldn't help but feel a small tug of amusement at our contrasting viewpoints. Still, I felt a gentle twinge of guilt creeping in for losing my cool. "Maybe I just need a little more coffee," I muttered, my tone softening.

Ivy chuckled, the tension dissipating like morning fog under the sun. "I'll help you clean up—if you promise to let me paint your room in something whimsical. You need a little whimsy in your life!"

Her plea made me pause. "Whimsy? Like polka dots or unicorns?" I raised an eyebrow, unable to contain my grin.

"Exactly! Picture it: you wake up every morning to a burst of color and magic. Isn't that what life should be?"

As I gazed at her, it dawned on me that Ivy embodied everything I had suppressed within myself—an unyielding spirit, a desire for adventure, a thirst for life beyond the mundane. "Fine," I relented, holding up my hands in mock surrender. "But only if you promise to limit the unicorns to just one."

"Deal!" She exclaimed, clapping her hands together in delight, and just like that, our truce was sealed with a burst of laughter.

The following weekend, as she painted the walls of my room in a kaleidoscope of colors, I realized I had stepped far beyond my comfort zone. I had embarked on an adventure without knowing the destination, and it felt exhilarating. Ivy's laughter floated through the apartment, a melody woven with the scent of fresh paint and the sounds of the bustling city outside.

Yet, amid the bursts of joy, the shadows of uncertainty lurked at the edges. The art world was a fickle mistress, full of dreams yet riddled with the harshness of reality. Ivy's talent was undeniable, yet she struggled with the kind of self-doubt that could topple the tallest of dreams. I could see the flicker of uncertainty in her eyes whenever she spoke of her aspirations, her fierce exterior sometimes crumbling beneath the weight of expectation.

"Do you ever worry?" I asked one night, as we lounged on the floor surrounded by drying canvases. "About not being good enough, or the future, or... everything?"

Her expression shifted, a vulnerability breaking through the vibrant facade. "All the time," she admitted, her voice softening. "But what's the alternative? Not trying at all?"

It was a profound moment, one that echoed through the dimly lit room. We shared stories of our dreams, our fears, the paths we longed to carve out of the chaos. It felt like we were sculpting our futures together, the chisel of our words shaping the raw stone of uncertainty into something beautiful and resilient.

As the city lights blinked to life outside our window, illuminating the dim corners of our new life, I felt a surge of gratitude for Ivy's presence in my world. With her by my side, every day became a new canvas, a chance to color outside the lines, and I was ready to embrace it all, imperfections and chaos included.

The apartment was a riot of color, an ever-evolving canvas that reflected not just Ivy's artistic flair but also the delightful chaos of our lives together. Each morning began with the same routine: Ivy's exuberant singing wafting through the air, followed by the sizzling of her experimental breakfast creations. "If I can't be a renowned artist, I can at least be a renowned brunch chef!" she'd declare, usually just before setting off an accidental culinary explosion.

On one particularly ambitious morning, she concocted a smoothie bowl that somehow managed to erupt like a volcano, splattering bright green liquid across the kitchen walls. I stared, half-awed, half-horrified as Ivy surveyed the scene with wide eyes, her mouth agape. "Well, that's one way to get your greens!" she quipped, unable to contain her laughter as she dabbed a finger in the gooey mess and tasted it.

"Delicious!" she exclaimed, and I couldn't help but chuckle. Her childlike enthusiasm made even the messiest situations feel like grand adventures.

As the days blurred together in a delightful tapestry of color and chaos, our lives intertwined more deeply. We transformed our living space into a refuge for creativity, and soon it became a meeting ground for aspiring artists, writers, and dreamers. Every Thursday, we hosted a little soirée we affectionately called "Artistic Chaos Night," where the apartment filled with eclectic souls eager to share their work, their stories, and the occasional glass of wine that somehow found its way into the mix.

One Thursday, as I arranged a few extra chairs, Ivy burst in, her cheeks flushed with excitement. "You'll never believe what just happened! I got invited to showcase my work at the new gallery on Bleecker Street!"

I dropped the chair I was holding, the clatter echoing through the cramped space. "Ivy, that's incredible! This is what you've been dreaming about!"

"I know! But here's the catch," she continued, a sudden seriousness washing over her features. "It's next month, and I need to present my best pieces. I'm already stressing about what to show."

"Let's go through your collection! You have so many stunning pieces. You just need to choose the ones that truly represent you," I encouraged, stepping closer to her, eager to share in her excitement and alleviate some of her anxiety.

As we sifted through her vibrant artworks, a mixture of emotions swept over me. I could see the fear in her eyes, the doubt creeping in like a shadow. "What if they don't like my work? What if it's not enough?"

"Hey, stop that right now," I said, crossing my arms. "You are more than enough. You have a unique voice that deserves to be heard. Remember that time you painted that mural in the park? People were stopping to take pictures! You have talent, Ivy!"

Her expression softened, and for a moment, I saw the flicker of her spirit reigniting. "You really think so?"

"I know so," I affirmed, feeling the warmth of our shared dreams wrap around us like a comforting blanket. "Now, let's get to work on making your presentation as spectacular as your art."

The next few weeks turned into a whirlwind of creativity and collaboration. Ivy poured her heart into her work, and I became her sounding board, helping her refine her pieces and prepare for the gallery opening. Each evening, we'd huddle together, surrounded by paints and canvases, and the apartment would pulse with our shared energy.

One night, after we had spent hours working, Ivy leaned back against the couch, paint smudged across her cheek and a tired smile on her lips. "I couldn't have done this without you. You've been my anchor in this storm of creativity."

"And you've been the color in my otherwise black-and-white life," I replied, chuckling. "Who knew I could unleash my inner artist while surviving your culinary catastrophes?"

As we laughed, the tension that had built up over the weeks started to ease. I could sense a shift within both of us; Ivy was transforming into the artist she had always aspired to be, and I was discovering my own voice amid the colorful chaos. Yet, beneath the surface, a lingering unease nestled itself in my chest. I could feel Ivy's mounting pressure, the weight of expectation pressing down on her shoulders like a heavy blanket.

The day of the gallery opening arrived, and Ivy was a bundle of nerves, her vibrant red hair seemingly brighter against the stark backdrop of her carefully chosen pieces. I stood by her side, watching as people drifted in, their eyes wide with curiosity. Ivy's art hung proudly on the walls, each piece a fragment of her soul laid bare for all to see.

As the evening progressed, compliments flowed like the wine we had strategically placed in the corner, but I could see her heart fluttering between pride and fear. When a renowned local art critic wandered in, my breath hitched. I could feel the tension in the room as Ivy's eyes darted to me, searching for reassurance.

"Just breathe, Ivy. You've got this," I whispered, giving her hand a reassuring squeeze.

But the critic's gaze swept through the room with the practiced air of someone who had seen it all. I could feel Ivy's anxiety building like a balloon stretched to its limit. Then, as if sensing the collective tension in the air, the critic paused before one of Ivy's paintings—a vivid explosion of colors swirling together like a tempest.

Ivy held her breath, her knuckles white as she gripped my hand. Time slowed, the gallery around us fading into a blur as the critic leaned in closer, scrutinizing every brushstroke.

After what felt like an eternity, the critic turned, his expression unreadable. "This piece has potential," he stated, and I felt Ivy's breath catch. "But it lacks cohesion. It feels disjointed."

My heart sank as I watched the color drain from Ivy's face. "No," I breathed, feeling a wave of frustration wash over me. How could anyone not see the beauty and depth she had poured into her work?

Before I could think, I stepped forward, my voice tinged with fierce protectiveness. "It's not disjointed; it's a reflection of the chaotic beauty of life. It tells a story—her story!"

The room fell silent, a collective gasp echoing around us. Ivy's eyes widened, a mix of horror and surprise etched across her features. I hadn't meant to speak up, but the words had escaped before I could rein them in.

"Excuse me?" the critic raised an eyebrow, clearly taken aback by my outburst.

Realizing I had just turned the evening into a battleground, I faltered, the weight of my impulsive words pressing down on me. Ivy shot me a look that was half mortified, half grateful, and I could feel my heart racing.

"Umm... I didn't mean to interrupt," I stammered, feeling the heat rise to my cheeks. "But you must understand that art isn't just about perfection; it's about the emotion behind it. It's about breaking free from conventions."

The air crackled with tension, and for a moment, I feared I had jeopardized everything for Ivy. Just then, Ivy stepped forward, her voice steadier than I expected. "I appreciate your feedback, truly," she said, her tone almost soothing. "But my art reflects my journey, my struggles, and it is indeed a little chaotic. That's life, isn't it?"

The critic blinked, clearly caught off guard by Ivy's newfound confidence. "Perhaps," he replied, his tone shifting, "but chaos can also alienate an audience if it's not grounded."

"Or it can invite them in," Ivy countered, a glimmer of defiance lighting up her emerald eyes. "Art is subjective, and my work is an invitation to explore my world. If you don't like it, that's okay. Not every piece has to resonate with everyone."

The tension in the room shifted, and I felt a surge of pride for Ivy. There she stood, unwavering, owning her narrative even in the face of criticism. As the critic pondered her words, the gallery buzzed with murmurs of appreciation and interest.

And just when it seemed that Ivy had turned the tide, a voice pierced through the chatter, sharp and unexpected. "But isn't that the point?" A woman stepped into view, her demeanor cool and calculated. "To challenge norms, to create discord? What if that's exactly what the world needs? The chaos, I mean."

My breath hitched. I recognized her—a successful gallery owner who had been a part of Ivy's dream landscape. As the room fell into a hush, I felt the stakes heighten, the air thick with anticipation. Ivy's eyes met mine, a mixture of uncertainty and hope flickering within them, while the critic's expression shifted from skepticism to intrigue.

It was a moment suspended in time, a climax of emotions hanging delicately in the balance. With every heartbeat, I could sense Ivy teetering on the edge of either triumph or despair, and the gallery seemed to hold its breath, waiting for the next stroke of destiny to unfold.

Chapter 3: The Spark of Attraction

The gallery buzzes with a palpable energy, a symphony of laughter and clinking glasses that reverberates off the high ceilings, adorned with vibrant art pieces that seem to dance under the dim lights. I step through the archway, my heels clicking rhythmically against the polished wood floor, feeling a rush of excitement mingled with anxiety. My fingers brush against the smooth silk of my dress, a deep emerald green that feels both flattering and a little too daring, much like my current state of mind.

It's not just the art that captivates me; it's the thrumming heartbeat of the room—the scent of rich coffee mingled with the delicate hint of freshly popped popcorn wafting from a nearby stall. I scan the crowd, my heart racing as I spot Ivy, her laughter ringing out like a bell, clear and bright. She's holding court by a particularly striking piece—a swirling canvas of blues and golds that seems to capture the essence of the ocean. I wave, and she beams back, her smile so infectious that I can't help but feel my own worries wash away.

But it's not Ivy who draws my attention in a way that makes my heart flutter and my palms clammy. No, it's Nathaniel, standing slightly apart, his presence magnetic. He's dressed impeccably in a tailored navy suit, the fabric hugging his broad shoulders and tapering perfectly at the waist. His hair, a tousled mess of chestnut waves, catches the light as he turns, revealing a profile that could have been carved by a master sculptor. He stands with an air of effortless confidence, engaging with a small group, his voice smooth as honey, each word laced with a charm that seems to hypnotize those around him.

As I catch his gaze, our eyes lock, and the world around us blurs into a hazy backdrop. It's as if time pauses, the noise of the gallery fading to a whisper. My breath hitches, the moment stretching into something tangible—a silent invitation crackling in the air. He raises an eyebrow, a playful challenge sparkling in his deep brown eyes, and I feel a flush creep up my neck. What is this? A dare? An unwritten rule between us that defies logic and reason?

I break the spell first, forcing myself to look away, my heart pounding with an exhilarating mix of desire and trepidation. After all, he's Ivy's brother. The brother who has always seemed larger than life, a figure of suave sophistication that could make anyone feel small. But there's an undeniable allure in the way he leans into the conversation, how his laughter rings out like music, inviting everyone in, yet keeping a part of himself hidden—mysterious and enticing.

The thought of Ivy's friendship looms over me like a storm cloud, threatening to rain on this unexpected thrill. I shake my head slightly, as if that will clear away the distraction. Instead, I grab a glass of sparkling water from a passing tray and take a moment to breathe. This isn't just an art show; it's a minefield of emotions, and I can't afford to step on the wrong one.

"Hey, are you okay?" Ivy appears beside me, her brow furrowed in concern. "You look like you've seen a ghost."

"Just... overwhelmed, I guess," I reply, forcing a smile that feels more like a grimace. "This place is so vibrant. I'm just trying to take it all in."

She nods, but her gaze drifts to Nathaniel, who is now holding court with a couple of art enthusiasts, effortlessly weaving between topics of design and aesthetics. "He's pretty amazing, isn't he?" Ivy remarks, a hint of pride lacing her words.

I nod, attempting to keep my tone light. "Yeah, he certainly knows how to command a room." The double meaning doesn't escape me; command is the last thing I want him to do with my heart.

A teasing smirk spreads across Ivy's lips. "You're blushing, and I'm pretty sure it's not just the wine. Are you crushing on my brother?"

"Hardly! I mean, he's... charming, but it's not like I'm planning a romantic getaway with him or anything," I stumble over my words, my mind racing as I contemplate the absurdity of even considering it.

Ivy's laughter is light, airy. "You're adorable when you're flustered. Just know, if you ever need me to distract him so you can make your move, I'm your girl."

"Not a chance, Ivy!" I retort, a mixture of flattery and panic swirling within me. "He's your brother, and I'm just—"

"Just what? A girl who deserves to have a little fun?" Ivy interrupts, her tone teasing yet sincere. "Besides, he's single, and he could use a distraction."

I can feel the heat rising in my cheeks as Nathaniel glances our way, catching the tail end of our conversation. He smirks, a knowing expression crossing his face, and my heart skips. The tension coils tighter in my chest, a mix of intrigue and reluctance. Suddenly, a cacophony of laughter erupts from the group around him, and he tilts his head back, his eyes sparkling with delight.

"See? He's having fun," Ivy nudges me, her eyes dancing with mischief. "You should at least say hi."

"Hi?" I echo, incredulous. "That's your grand plan?"

"Trust me," she whispers, winking at me before leaving to greet a friend across the room, leaving me alone with my swirling thoughts.

As Nathaniel strides toward me, I feel my pulse quicken, like a drumbeat echoing through my veins. His approach is casual, yet there's an undeniable intensity in his gaze that sends my heart racing. Just as I brace myself for our encounter, he stops in front of me, that charming smile plastered on his face.

"Enjoying the art?" he asks, his voice smooth and warm, wrapping around me like a cozy blanket.

"Definitely," I manage to reply, my voice a touch higher than usual. "It's... captivating."

"Just like you," he replies effortlessly, his tone teasing yet sincere, leaving me momentarily speechless. I feel as though I've been dropped into a world where nothing exists but the two of us, the room fading into an irrelevant blur.

"Flattery will get you everywhere," I retort, trying to maintain some semblance of composure.

His laugh is genuine, a delightful sound that makes my heart flutter. "Good to know. I'll keep that in mind. I'm Nathaniel, by the way."

"I know," I reply, my cheeks warming as I extend a hand. "I'm—"

"Claire," he finishes, his grip firm and warm, sending an electric jolt up my arm. "I've heard so much about you. Ivy talks about you like you're some kind of superhero."

"Superhero?" I chuckle, surprised by the compliment. "More like a sidekick at best."

"Every superhero needs one," he quips, his eyes glinting with mischief. "What's your superpower?"

I hesitate, trying to think of something clever. "Hmm... making awkward situations even more awkward?"

"Impressive," he replies, his grin widening. "I think you just found your calling."

The playful banter flows between us, a dance of wits that ignites a thrill in the air, a spark that promises the kind of connection I've longed for. Yet, as the laughter continues, I can't shake the sense of impending consequence lurking in the shadows. I glance around the room, half-expecting Ivy to emerge and pull me back from the edge of this exhilarating precipice.

But Nathaniel doesn't seem to notice. He leans in slightly, his voice low and conspiratorial. "So, what do you think of the exhibit? Any favorites?"

I glance at the art pieces that surround us, my mind racing between admiration and the strange sense of danger in this moment. "There's something about the abstract pieces—like they're hiding secrets just out of reach."

"Ah, the allure of mystery," he muses, his gaze never leaving mine. "It's often where the real beauty lies."

Our conversation continues to flow effortlessly, punctuated by laughter and light-hearted teasing, the room around us blurring into an intimate bubble. But in the back of my mind, I know this isn't just a chance meeting; it's a crossroad. The path before me is lined with choices, and each one feels like a leap into uncharted territory.

As the evening unfolds, I can't help but feel the intoxicating mix of thrill and dread coursing through my veins, a reminder that while the spark between us is undeniable, the consequences of igniting that flame could alter the delicate balance of my world.

The night hums with a palpable tension, an electric current sparking between Nathaniel and me as we navigate the crowded gallery. Our conversation flows like a well-composed symphony, each note resonating with a playful banter that pulls me closer to him. The art surrounding us seems to fade into the background, a mere backdrop to the intricate dance we're performing—his gaze steady and intense, mine flickering between excitement and apprehension.

"So, tell me, what do you do when you're not charming art enthusiasts?" I ask, my playful tone mirroring the warmth radiating from his presence. It feels thrilling to banter with him, the words tumbling from my lips as if they've always belonged there.

"I design buildings that make people swoon," he replies, a teasing glint in his eyes. "Or at least that's the hope. What about you? What kind of superpowers are you hiding?"

"Mostly I just rescue stray cats and awkward situations," I quip back, trying to keep my tone light. "It's a busy job."

He laughs, the sound low and rich, sending an unexpected flutter through my chest. "You know, I might need a superhero on my next project. All that meowing could drive the clients mad."

"Just let me know when your architectural dreams need saving, and I'll be there, cape and all," I respond, relishing the easy flow of our exchange. The tension still simmers beneath the surface, a thrilling reminder of the risk I'm taking with every flirtatious remark.

As we continue to talk, I find myself gravitating closer, the space between us shrinking until it feels like a cocoon, just the two of us against the world. My mind races with thoughts of Ivy, the nagging reminder of our friendship sitting like an anchor in my chest. This shouldn't feel this good—this connection shouldn't be this effortless. Yet here I am, captivated by every smile, every shared laugh, and the way his eyes light up when he talks about his work.

"Have you ever thought about the stories behind the art?" Nathaniel suddenly asks, his expression turning serious, his brow furrowing in a way that makes my heart skip a beat. "Like, what drove the artist to create? What was happening in their lives?"

I consider his question, the weight of it surprising. "I suppose it's a little like us, isn't it? We all have our layers, our complexities that influence how we present ourselves to the world."

He nods, his gaze steady and thoughtful. "Exactly. Each piece is a snapshot of a moment, a feeling. Just like every encounter we have is shaped by our pasts. It's fascinating."

Before I can respond, Ivy returns, her enthusiasm cutting through our moment like a knife. "There you are! I thought I'd lost you two to the art forever," she exclaims, her eyes sparkling with mischief. "What were you two discussing? The secrets of the universe?"

Nathaniel shoots me a quick glance, a hint of amusement dancing in his eyes. "Something like that. Claire was just sharing her superhero aspirations."

"Oh, I knew it!" Ivy beams, her smile wide. "She's already been my sidekick in many a social venture. It's only fitting she claims the title."

My laughter bubbles up, mingling with Nathaniel's as we exchange knowing looks. There's a moment of unspoken understanding, a bridge formed between us, as Ivy gestures for us to follow her deeper into the gallery.

As we move from one stunning piece to the next, Ivy excitedly shares anecdotes about the artists, her passion infectious. Yet, as she speaks, I can't help but steal glances at Nathaniel, who seems to soak up every word with genuine interest, his attention unwavering. Each time our eyes meet, the spark flickers to life again, igniting that familiar tension that both excites and terrifies me.

"Did you know that the artist of that sculpture over there once spent a year living in a tent to inspire his work?" Ivy says, pointing toward a colossal metal structure that twists and spirals into the air.

"Wow, that's commitment," Nathaniel replies, his voice warm with admiration. "I can't imagine what that must have been like—isolated and inspired all at once."

"Some might call it madness," I interject, my tone teasing. "But maybe it's just the price of genius."

Ivy laughs, and we continue moving through the gallery, but the thrill of Nathaniel's presence lingers in the air, crackling like static electricity.

"I was thinking," Ivy says suddenly, her voice dropping slightly as she glances between us, "we should plan a gallery crawl next weekend. Hit up a few more openings. What do you think?"

"Sounds like a blast," Nathaniel replies, his eyes shining with enthusiasm. "I could definitely use some inspiration."

I feel my stomach twist, the excitement mingling with unease. "Sure, that could be fun," I manage to say, but inside, my mind races. A gallery crawl means more time with Nathaniel, and while the thought is intoxicating, the implications weigh heavily on my heart.

"Great! Let's make it happen," Ivy declares, her excitement palpable. "We'll need to coordinate our schedules. It'll be like an artist's tour, complete with snacks and drinks."

The idea of spending more time with Nathaniel sends a thrill through me, but it's accompanied by a sense of dread. How can I reconcile my budding feelings with my commitment to Ivy?

As we drift through the gallery, I try to focus on the art, but each piece feels like a reminder of the precarious tightrope I'm walking. Nathaniel's laughter echoes in my ears, a haunting melody that pulls me in while pushing me away. My thoughts swirl, a cacophony of desire and caution that threatens to overwhelm me.

Finally, we reach a small alcove, where a striking painting captures my attention—a riot of colors swirling together, each stroke telling a story that feels familiar yet foreign. I lean in closer, tracing the lines with my eyes, feeling the emotion radiating from the canvas.

"It's beautiful," Nathaniel observes from beside me, his voice low, reverberating through the air between us.

"It is," I reply, momentarily lost in the painting. "There's something about it that feels... alive."

"Maybe it's the artist's spirit," he muses, and I can't help but notice the way his gaze lingers on me, the intensity making my heart race.

"I'd like to think that every piece of art carries a piece of the artist," I say, allowing my thoughts to spill out. "Like it becomes a part of their legacy."

"Or a reflection of their truth," he counters, his eyes deepening with understanding.

I turn to him, the connection between us feeling almost tangible. "It's a beautiful thought. Maybe we should all aspire to leave behind a bit of our truth in everything we do."

He nods, the warmth in his gaze sending shivers down my spine. "If that's the case, I think you're well on your way."

Before I can respond, Ivy jumps back into the conversation, her voice a burst of enthusiasm. "Okay, enough of this art chat! Let's grab some drinks and mingle! I see the bar across the room."

"Lead the way," Nathaniel replies, and I follow them, feeling the tension shift slightly, though it lingers like an uninvited guest.

As we make our way to the bar, Ivy's chatter fills the space, but my thoughts remain tangled with Nathaniel. I can't shake the feeling that our connection is blossoming into something more than just flirtation, something deeper that threatens to unravel the carefully woven fabric of my friendship with Ivy. The looming possibility of heartbreak hangs in the air, a specter I can't seem to shake.

As Ivy orders drinks, I catch Nathaniel watching me, a thoughtful expression on his face. "Are you okay?" he asks, his tone suddenly serious, concern etched in his features.

"Yeah, just... processing," I admit, the honesty slipping out before I can reel it back.

"About the art?" he prompts gently, leaning in, his presence grounding.

I shake my head, feeling the weight of my emotions. "More about us, I think. This—whatever it is, it's complicated."

His gaze sharpens, the corners of his mouth twitching into a soft smile. "Complicated can be good, you know. Sometimes it leads to the best stories."

"Or the worst endings," I counter, the reality of my situation crashing down on me.

He studies me for a moment, his expression earnest. "But wouldn't you rather experience it fully than wonder what could have been?"

Before I can answer, Ivy returns, drinks in hand, her energy infectious. "Cheers to new adventures and late-night art debates!" she exclaims, raising her glass high.

Nathaniel and I exchange a glance, the unspoken question lingering between us, the moment slipping away like sand through my fingers. I clink my glass against theirs, trying to shake the weight of uncertainty. The night is still young, and though I can feel the pressure building, a part of me is desperate to see where this thrilling journey might take me.

The night unfolds like a carefully orchestrated performance, each moment a delicate brushstroke on the canvas of my emotions. Ivy's laughter bubbles around us, mingling with the chatter of the gallery guests, but my focus remains tethered to Nathaniel. He stands beside me, the warmth of his presence radiating like a beacon, and the way his laughter dances through the air sends delightful shivers down my spine.

As we sip our drinks—mine a tart cranberry concoction, his a dark and sophisticated whiskey—I find myself captivated not just by his charm but by the intelligence that glimmers behind his playful banter. "So, Claire," he says, leaning slightly closer, his voice dipping into a conspiratorial whisper that wraps around me like a silk scarf. "What's the wildest thing you've ever done at an art gallery?"

I consider his question, the wheels in my mind spinning as I recall past escapades that pale in comparison to the thrill of this moment. "Let's see... I once tried to climb a giant sculpture, thinking it would make for a fantastic Instagram post," I confess, a wry smile curling my lips. "I ended up getting yelled at by security and had to apologize profusely while blushing like a tomato."

Nathaniel bursts into laughter, the sound rich and infectious. "I can only imagine! What were you thinking? 'Climbing art is the new viewing art?'"

"Hey, it was a moment of inspiration," I reply, feigning offense. "Art should be interactive, don't you think?"

He raises his glass in mock salute. "To interactive art! And to climbing our way to new heights—both in creativity and in awkward encounters."

Just then, Ivy returns with an eager grin, her presence bringing a surge of energy. "I just overheard some insiders talking about a secret after-party. Apparently, it's at an exclusive rooftop bar downtown!"

My heart leaps, the prospect of the night morphing into something more thrilling. "Sounds like a perfect adventure," I reply, my pulse quickening. But I glance at Nathaniel, whose expression is a mixture of intrigue and hesitation.

"Rooftop bars can be a bit cliché," he remarks, his tone teasing yet thoughtful. "But if there's one thing I've learned about clichés, it's that they often turn into the best stories."

"Exactly!" Ivy interjects, her excitement palpable. "Come on, let's go make some memories!"

Nathaniel looks at me, and I can see a hint of uncertainty in his eyes. The tension between us hangs thick like the humidity before a storm, and I can't help but feel that this night could take a turn I'm not fully prepared for. Yet, a part of me is desperate to plunge into the unknown, to embrace the thrill of what could be.

"Alright," I say, summoning courage I didn't know I had. "Let's do it."

We navigate through the crowd, Ivy leading the way with a buoyant spirit, while Nathaniel walks close beside me, the warmth of his body radiating a comforting heat. The conversation flows easily, our laughter punctuating the air, yet my mind races with the consequences of our growing connection.

As we step outside, the crisp night air washes over me, refreshing and invigorating. The city sprawls before us, twinkling lights dancing in the darkness like a blanket of stars fallen to earth. I take a deep breath, the adrenaline coursing through my veins as Ivy pulls us toward the waiting cab.

"I can't believe we're doing this!" she exclaims, excitement bubbling in her voice as she squeezes into the back seat, her enthusiasm infectious. "This is going to be epic!"

As the cab whisks us away, I steal glances at Nathaniel, who seems contemplative, a hint of a smile still playing on his lips. "What are you thinking?" I ask, breaking through the comfortable silence that has settled between us.

He turns to me, his expression softening. "Just how unpredictable life can be. One moment you're at a gallery, sipping overpriced drinks, and the next you're heading to a rooftop party. It's exhilarating."

"True, but unpredictability can also lead to chaos," I reply, my heart racing as I consider the implications of that chaos. "Sometimes, it feels safer to stick to the known."

He leans closer, his gaze steady. "But where's the fun in that? Sometimes you have to embrace the chaos and see where it takes you."

His words hang in the air, a challenge and an invitation all at once. I want to embrace that chaos, to throw caution to the wind, but the thought of risking my friendship with Ivy looms large in my mind.

When we arrive at the bar, the atmosphere is electric, the sounds of laughter and music spilling out into the street. Ivy bounds out of the cab, her energy infectious, and I follow, heart pounding with both excitement and apprehension.

The rooftop is adorned with twinkling lights and lush greenery, a secret garden under the stars. Laughter mingles with the gentle clinking of glasses, and the ambiance envelops us in its warmth.

"This place is stunning!" I marvel, taking in the view of the city skyline that stretches infinitely before us.

"I knew you'd love it," Ivy beams, her eyes sparkling as she takes in the scene. "Let's grab drinks and mingle!"

As we make our way to the bar, Nathaniel sidles closer, his voice low and playful. "What's your drink of choice, superhero?"

I smile, feeling emboldened by the surroundings and his presence. "Surprisingly, I tend to stick to fruity cocktails. I mean, who wouldn't want a drink that tastes like summer?"

"I can get on board with that," he replies, his eyes dancing with mischief. "Let's get you a summer cocktail then."

With drinks in hand, we weave through the crowd, Ivy leading the charge as she greets familiar faces. I find myself drifting back to Nathaniel, the connection between us pulsating like a heartbeat.

"Okay, serious question," he says, leaning closer, the intensity in his eyes making my breath hitch. "If you could design your own dream art installation, what would it look like?"

I think for a moment, imagining the vibrant colors and sweeping lines. "It would be immersive—a space where people could walk through different worlds. Each section would tell a story, filled with sound and light."

His eyes widen, clearly intrigued. "Now that sounds incredible. I'd love to see it come to life. Maybe we could collaborate? An architect and a superhero artist?"

The flirtation hangs in the air like an unspoken promise, sending a thrill coursing through me. "I'd like that," I say, my voice barely above a whisper.

As the night deepens, the atmosphere shifts, laughter blending with the pulsing music, creating an intoxicating blend of energy.

I notice how Nathaniel's hand inches closer to mine, the subtle movement igniting a fire in my chest. Just as I'm about to lean in, a commotion at the edge of the rooftop catches my attention—a sudden burst of shouting that slices through the revelry.

My heart races as I turn, my pulse quickening with anxiety. Ivy, oblivious to the chaos, continues to mingle, but Nathaniel's eyes darken, and he grabs my wrist gently. "Stay close," he murmurs, his voice steady but urgent.

The noise escalates, and my stomach drops as I spot a small group arguing fiercely, their voices rising above the music. It's a jarring reminder that the night's lightness could turn dark in an instant.

Suddenly, a glass shatters, sending shards sparkling like stars against the night, and my breath catches in my throat. I look up at Nathaniel, panic swirling in my chest, uncertainty clawing at the edges of my thoughts.

"We should get Ivy," I say, my voice barely audible over the ruckus.

But before he can respond, a figure shoves through the crowd, eyes wild and frantic. "Get out of the way!" they shout, and in that instant, the world tilts on its axis.

Chaos erupts as people begin to scatter, and a primal instinct kicks in. Nathaniel pulls me closer, shielding me with his body as the crowd surges around us. I can feel the heat radiating from him, the intensity of the moment igniting something deep within.

"Stay behind me," he urges, his eyes fierce and protective.

My heart races as the adrenaline floods my system, but it's not just fear—I can't shake the feeling that this night has transformed from a delightful escapade into something far more perilous. Just as the chaos swells, an unsettling thought slithers through my mind: maybe the unpredictable nature of this evening is more than just a thrill.

And as we find ourselves caught in the whirlwind of confusion, one question gnaws at me, even as my heart pounds in my chest: what if this chaos is only the beginning?

Chapter 4: Secrets and Shadows

The café hummed with the gentle buzz of conversation, a warm oasis tucked between the relentless pace of the city. I settled into my usual corner, the one with the oversized armchair that swallowed me whole, wrapping me in its plush embrace. The scent of freshly brewed coffee mingled with the sweetness of pastries, creating an intoxicating aroma that felt like home. As I stirred my vanilla latte, the frothy swirls danced in the cup, mirroring the whirlpool of thoughts in my mind. Nathaniel's face floated before me—those deep, contemplative eyes and that easy smile that could brighten even the gloomiest of days.

Yet, today was different. Today, the air crackled with unspoken tension. Ivy was late, and with every tick of the clock, my heart drummed a little harder against my ribs. I sipped my drink, forcing the rich flavor down as I tried to shake off the anxious thoughts swirling in my head. Ivy was my anchor, my steadying force in the chaotic sea of life. Without her, I felt adrift, as if I were a ship without a sail.

The door swung open, and Ivy burst in, her presence illuminating the dim space. She wore her usual ensemble: a floral dress that clung to her curves and a cascade of curls that danced around her face, framing her features like a halo. But something was off; the bounce in her step seemed muted, and the light in her hazel eyes flickered like a candle threatened by a breeze.

"Hey!" she chirped, sliding into the chair across from me, her smile wide but lacking its usual sparkle. "Sorry I'm late. Traffic was a nightmare."

I wanted to brush off her excuse, to poke fun at her typical tardiness, but I could sense a heaviness lurking beneath her cheerful façade. "No worries," I replied, forcing a smile of my own. "I've just been—well, waiting."

Ivy stirred her coffee, eyes darting around the room as if searching for something that wasn't there. The playful banter we usually exchanged hung in the air, stifled by an invisible weight. I wanted to reach out, to shake her from her reverie, but I didn't know how to breach the unspoken divide.

Finally, she leaned in, her voice dropping to a whisper, "I've been thinking a lot lately."

The casual tone felt like a prelude to something more significant. My pulse quickened. "About what?"

She hesitated, biting her lip. "About... well, about life. You know, things from the past."

A chill slithered down my spine, the kind that prickles the skin and makes the hairs stand on end. I leaned closer, trying to draw her into my warmth, to shield her from whatever shadows lurked behind her eyes. "Ivy, you can tell me anything. You know that, right?"

With a deep breath, she finally let the words tumble out, raw and unfiltered. "I struggled with anxiety for years, and I've never really talked about it. And there was this guy... he wasn't good for me. Not at all. It was toxic, and I—I didn't realize how much it affected me until it was too late."

My heart sank as I processed her confession. Ivy, the vibrant spark of our friendship, had been carrying a burden that was heavier than I could ever imagine. "Ivy, I'm so sorry. Why didn't you tell me sooner?"

"Because I didn't want it to define me," she admitted, her gaze dropping to the table, tracing the grain of the wood as if searching for answers within its lines. "I wanted to be the fun, carefree person everyone loved. But underneath, it felt like I was drowning."

My chest tightened, and a mix of empathy and helplessness washed over me. I reached across the table, my fingers brushing against hers. "You're so much more than your past. You're brave for sharing this with me."

Her eyes lifted, shimmering with unshed tears. "I've always been scared that if people knew, they wouldn't look at me the same way. But I trust you, and I guess I'm just tired of hiding."

The confession settled between us, a fragile thing that needed careful handling. I could see the chasm that had formed not just from her past, but also from the reality of my growing feelings for Nathaniel. How could I juggle the complexities of love and friendship when shadows loomed so large?

As I opened my mouth to speak, the door swung open again, and in walked Nathaniel, all tall and striking, his presence commanding the room. He spotted us immediately, and a smile broke across his face like the first rays of dawn. "There you two are! I thought I'd never find you."

Ivy straightened, her smile returning but not quite reaching her eyes. I felt the weight of the moment shift, an unspoken tension clinging to the air as Nathaniel approached. "What's going on?" he asked, oblivious to the emotional storm brewing just beneath the surface.

"Just some girl talk," I replied, hoping to deflect his curiosity. But the moment felt fractured, the cracks widening with every heartbeat. How could I embrace my burgeoning feelings for him when Ivy's past cast such a long shadow over our lives?

"Mind if I join?" he asked, sliding into the empty seat, his easy charm infusing the space. I could feel Ivy's pulse quicken, a flicker of something—maybe hope?—passing between them.

"Of course!" I said, forcing cheer into my voice as if it could disguise the tension. The chatter resumed, but in the back of my mind, Ivy's revelations echoed relentlessly. Trust was fragile, a delicate tapestry woven from the threads of our shared experiences, and now, those threads felt frayed, tugged by the weight of unspoken fears.

As Nathaniel launched into a light-hearted story about a mishap at work, my gaze drifted to Ivy. I could see her masking her emotions behind a practiced smile, a dance I was all too familiar with. I wanted to pull her close, to shield her from the world that had hurt her, but my heart also ached with the possibility of what could be with Nathaniel.

The coffee shop buzzed around us, oblivious to the tempest brewing at our small table, where love and friendship mingled uneasily. The dance of trust and uncertainty began, and I knew that no matter how carefully I treaded, the shadows of Ivy's past would weave through my emotions, complicating the path ahead.

As Nathaniel launched into an amusing anecdote about a client who mistook a stapler for a fancy new tech gadget, I couldn't help but notice how easily his laughter filled the room, enveloping us like a warm blanket. Ivy leaned in, her smile widening as she enjoyed his tale, yet a flicker of uncertainty lingered in her gaze. I felt the familiar tug-of-war in my heart: my affection for Nathaniel blossomed like spring flowers, but Ivy's vulnerability loomed like a storm cloud threatening to rain on our budding connection.

The more Nathaniel spoke, the more I realized how effortlessly he wove his charm, pulling both Ivy and me into his orbit. His animated gestures and expressive face could command a room, and there was a sincerity in his voice that made even the most mundane stories feel like grand adventures. Yet, the laughter echoed with a hollow note for me, resonating with the knowledge of Ivy's hidden pain. I wanted to bask in the light of this moment, yet a part of me couldn't shake the fear that the shadows of her past would eventually consume our friendship and my budding romance.

"Wait, wait—let me get this straight," I interjected, trying to lighten the mood, "he tried to return a stapler because it didn't have Wi-Fi?" My eyes twinkled as I played along with the absurdity, and Nathaniel chuckled, grateful for the opportunity to elaborate.

"Exactly! He insisted it was a technological oversight. Apparently, he was really looking forward to 'connecting' with it." His laughter was infectious, and Ivy joined in, the tension in her shoulders loosening just a bit.

But as the banter flowed, I couldn't help but glance at Ivy, searching for signs that she was truly with us, not just putting on a brave face. The sparkle in her eyes dimmed when Nathaniel looked away, and for a brief moment, I saw the shadow of her past flicker behind her smile—a ghost of pain that had been tucked away like a forgotten heirloom.

As the afternoon sun cast golden rays through the café windows, illuminating the dust particles dancing in the air, I felt a pressing need to ensure Ivy knew she was not alone. "You know, Ivy," I began carefully, "Nathaniel's quite the storyteller. We should do this more often—get out and share some laughs. It can be therapeutic, right?"

Ivy shot me a grateful look, but I could see the conflict brewing beneath her composed exterior. "Yeah, definitely. I think I could use a little therapy in the form of caffeine and chaos," she replied, her tone light but her eyes betraying a deeper apprehension.

Nathaniel, ever the attentive listener, turned his attention back to Ivy. "Chaos? Now that's a word I can get behind. What kind of chaos are you envisioning?" His playful tone coaxed a smile from her, but I could sense the undercurrents of tension still weaving between us like a fraying thread.

"Just the usual," Ivy shrugged, her voice breezy. "Like those surprise dance parties you see in movies. You know, one minute you're sipping coffee, and the next, you're cha-cha-ing on a table." She laughed, but I could see her struggle to keep the mood light, as if the weight of her past were an anchor pulling her deeper into the ocean of her thoughts.

"Table dancing, huh?" Nathaniel raised an eyebrow, a teasing glint in his eye. "I'll have to remember that for our next coffee date.

Although, I should probably consult my lawyer first. I don't think I can afford to pay for any broken furniture."

I joined in the laughter, but my mind whirred with the complexities of our dynamic. I wanted to support Ivy, but my heart ached for the growing connection with Nathaniel. Would my feelings for him diminish the space I wanted to create for her healing? I leaned forward, determined to ground our conversation back to the solid earth of camaraderie. "How about a game night? Just the three of us? I promise to keep my competitive spirit in check—mostly."

Ivy brightened at the suggestion, nodding enthusiastically. "That sounds perfect! We can have snacks, games, and maybe I can show off my dubious skills at charades."

"Charades? Bring it on!" Nathaniel leaned in closer, his grin contagious. "I'm ready to crush you both. Just don't be surprised when I nail the entire animal kingdom in under thirty seconds."

"Oh please," I laughed, "Ivy could probably act out a lion better than you. She's got the ferocity down."

But beneath the surface of our light-hearted exchanges, a tension simmered, unresolved and thick. I knew I had to address Ivy's past and the weight it held over her—over all of us.

As the café's ambient noise swelled around us, I took a deep breath. "Hey, Ivy, if there's ever a time you feel like talking about anything—anything at all—I'm here for you. You know that, right?"

She froze for a heartbeat, and I could practically see her weighing her options, her vibrant personality contorting into something guarded. "Thanks," she replied, her voice barely above a whisper. "I appreciate it. Really. But I think I'm okay for now."

That one statement pierced my heart; I could tell she was trying to reassure me, but the underlying uncertainty was palpable. I wanted to scream that it was okay not to be okay, but the fear of pushing her too hard kept my mouth shut. The trust between us felt tenuous, stretched thin like an overused rubber band. I wondered how long it would take before it snapped.

Just then, a shrill ring broke the moment, and Ivy's phone buzzed against the table. She glanced at the screen, her expression shifting from light-heartedness to trepidation as she read the message. "It's... it's my therapist," she stammered, her voice faltering. "I, uh, need to take this."

"Of course," Nathaniel said, his gaze shifting to me, concern flickering in his eyes. "Do you want us to wait?"

"No, no, it's fine," Ivy insisted, standing up. "I'll be right back."

As she walked away, my heart sank. The weight of the unspoken hung heavily in the air, and I turned to Nathaniel, searching for reassurance. "Do you think she's really okay?"

Nathaniel sighed, his brow furrowing slightly. "It's hard to say. People can wear a mask, you know? Sometimes the ones who seem the happiest carry the heaviest burdens."

His words hit me like a gust of wind, stirring up the storm inside my heart. "I just wish she'd open up to me," I admitted, feeling the vulnerability seep through the cracks of my confidence. "I want to help her."

He nodded, understanding etched on his face. "Being there for someone means more than just saying the right things. It's about giving them the space they need to be themselves. And sometimes, that means letting them figure things out in their own time."

"Easier said than done," I replied, crossing my arms. "It's hard to watch someone you care about struggle."

"True," Nathaniel said, his voice low and thoughtful. "But the fact that you care speaks volumes. Just remember, you can't carry her pain for her. She has to want to share it."

Before I could respond, Ivy returned, her expression a mix of relief and determination. "Sorry about that," she said, sliding back into her seat. "Just needed to check in."

"Everything okay?" I asked, my concern creeping back in.

"Yeah, just the usual. You know how it is." Her words were casual, but I could see the flicker of something deeper in her eyes.

Nathaniel leaned forward, a playful smile breaking the tension. "How about we order dessert? That'll lighten the mood, right?"

Ivy perked up, and I smiled, grateful for his ability to steer the conversation back to lighter waters. But in the back of my mind, the shadows loomed large. The road ahead felt uncertain, fraught with the complexities of friendship and burgeoning romance. And as we sat there, the three of us ensconced in laughter, I couldn't shake the feeling that the shadows would eventually demand their reckoning.

The dessert menu arrived, and I couldn't help but feel a spark of anticipation. Nathaniel was flipping through it with the enthusiasm of a kid in a candy store, while Ivy and I exchanged a glance, both of us knowing it was time to lighten the mood after the heaviness of earlier.

"Okay, hear me out," Nathaniel began, his voice dropping to a conspiratorial whisper. "What if we order every single dessert on this menu and turn it into a sugar-fueled taste test? We can rank them, make it a competition. Winner gets to pick our next game night theme."

"Are you sure that's a good idea?" I quipped, leaning in as if sharing a secret. "I'm pretty sure I could eat my body weight in chocolate cake, but I'm not sure my stomach would agree with that plan."

"Oh, come on! Think of the glorious chaos!" he urged, his enthusiasm infectious. "Imagine the sugar rush and the hilarious sugar crashes afterward. We'd need to take dance breaks to shake it all off. That's content for Instagram right there."

Ivy's laughter rang like a melody, brightening the dim café, and I felt my heart lift. "Okay, I'm in! But only if we get a giant slice of that triple chocolate cake. You can't have a sugar-fueled taste test without it."

"Perfect! Triple chocolate cake it is!" Nathaniel declared, gesturing to the waitress. "And everything else. We're going full-on dessert buffet!"

As the waitress scribbled down our orders, I felt a momentary sense of normalcy wash over us, a reprieve from the emotional weight of Ivy's past. Yet, the undercurrent of tension still threaded through my mind, nagging at me like an itch I couldn't quite reach.

"I'll help you two rank everything," Ivy said, her eyes twinkling with excitement. "But I'm warning you, I'm a professional taste tester."

"Is that what your therapist told you?" I teased, raising an eyebrow, eager to bring back the playful banter we thrived on.

"Actually, it was more about embracing my inner child," she shot back, grinning. "And if my inner child wants dessert, who am I to deny her?"

"Good point," I conceded, clapping my hands together in mock seriousness. "Your inner child is wise beyond her years."

As our desserts began to arrive, plates stacked high with sugar-laden indulgence, I felt a warm rush of gratitude. The laughter flowed freely, with Ivy and Nathaniel both chiming in with playful jabs and outrageous claims about their sweet-tasting prowess. Yet, as I watched them, the gnawing anxiety about Ivy's revelation refused to leave me.

Between bites of rich chocolate cake, I leaned closer to Ivy. "You know, if you ever feel like talking again, I'm right here. No pressure, but I want you to know that."

"Thanks," she replied, her smile softening, though a shadow flickered across her features. "It's just... hard sometimes, you know? It's easier to keep everything bottled up."

Nathaniel caught the moment, his expression shifting to one of understanding. "I get it. I have my own stuff I don't always share. Sometimes it's about finding the right moment, the right people. But you both have to promise me you won't hide behind your masks around me. That's a promise, right?"

"Deal," Ivy said, and I nodded in agreement, both of us trying to anchor the promise in the air between us, hoping it would hold.

The laughter resumed, but every now and then, I caught glimpses of Ivy's guarded expressions, the cracks in her vibrant facade. It was a strange sensation, watching her flit between genuine joy and a lingering shadow of sadness.

As the sun dipped lower in the sky, painting the café in warm hues of amber and gold, the conversation shifted to our plans for the upcoming weekend. "What do you think about a hike?" Nathaniel suggested. "There's a beautiful trail not far from here. The views are incredible, and I promise there's a waterfall that will make all the sweat worth it."

"I can get behind that!" I exclaimed, picturing the clear, cool water cascading down the rocks. "Count me in!"

"What about you, Ivy?" Nathaniel asked, his gaze steady. "Think you could brave a few hours in nature with us?"

Her expression faltered for just a moment, and I could see the conflict flickering behind her eyes. "I love the idea, but I'm not sure... What if I have a panic attack or something?"

"Hey, it's just a hike," I said gently, leaning forward. "We'll take it slow, and if you need to sit and breathe, we'll do that. I'll have a water bottle ready, and maybe we can even bring a little picnic to enjoy at the waterfall. No pressure, just a day outside."

Nathaniel added, "And if all else fails, we'll turn it into a comedy show. You can laugh at my terrible hiking skills."

Ivy chuckled at that, and the spark of excitement returned to her gaze. "Okay, you guys have convinced me. I'm in!"

With the decision made, the conversation shifted again, filled with playful debates over hiking gear, whether backpacks were cooler than fanny packs (clearly, they were not), and whether or not trail mix could be considered an acceptable meal replacement.

But just as the atmosphere lightened, Ivy's phone buzzed again, slicing through our laughter like a cold knife. She glanced down, her expression shifting to one of alarm. "I have to take this," she said, her voice suddenly serious.

"Of course," Nathaniel replied, sensing the shift. "We can wait."

Ivy stood up, retreating to a quieter corner of the café, her back turned to us as she answered the call. I exchanged a worried glance with Nathaniel, who furrowed his brow, concern creeping into his features.

"Do you think everything's okay?" he asked quietly, the previous levity in his voice now overshadowed by the uncertainty that hung in the air.

"I hope so," I murmured, unable to shake the gnawing feeling in my gut. "But it's clear there's more she hasn't told us. I just wish she'd trust us enough to share."

Nathaniel nodded, his eyes still fixed on Ivy. "It's not easy to open up about the past, especially when it still feels so close. But she's strong. I believe she'll come around."

Just as those words left his lips, Ivy spun around, her face pale and drawn, a storm brewing behind her eyes. I felt my heart race as she rushed back to our table, her breath shallow.

"I have to go," she said, urgency coloring her tone.

"Wait, what?" I exclaimed, startled. "I thought we were just getting started with dessert!"

"It's—" She hesitated, glancing back over her shoulder as if someone were following her. "I just... I can't stay. I need to take care of something."

"What's going on?" Nathaniel asked, his brows knitting together.

"I'm sorry! I'll call you later, I promise!" she said, already retreating toward the door, her figure almost a blur in the fading light.

I reached out, feeling a surge of panic. "Ivy, wait! What about our hike? What about everything we just talked about?"

But she was already gone, the door swinging shut behind her. The café fell silent, the weight of her absence pressing down on us like a sudden winter chill.

"Did she seem... off to you?" Nathaniel asked, his voice barely above a whisper.

I nodded, dread pooling in my stomach. "I don't know what just happened, but that didn't feel like a casual goodbye."

We exchanged another look, both of us aware that something deeper was at play. As the last rays of sun slipped beneath the horizon, leaving us in the gathering dusk, I knew the shadows were closing in. And they weren't just Ivy's shadows anymore.

Chapter 5: A Broken Heart

A warm breeze danced through the open window, carrying the sweet scent of blooming lilacs and freshly baked pastries from the café across the street. I was settled in my favorite armchair, a patchwork of colors worn soft from countless hours of reading, daydreaming, and sometimes, hiding. It was a sanctuary, that chair, in a studio filled with the cacophony of clinking paintbrushes, the rhythmic tapping of Ivy's fingers on her laptop, and the distant hum of a city that never truly slept. I should have been focused on the preparations for Ivy's upcoming art exhibit, a culmination of her heart and soul, but the cacophony of thoughts in my mind drowned out the sounds of our little haven.

I had been working alongside Ivy for months, nurturing her burgeoning talent while simultaneously wrestling with my own ambitions. It was a delicate balance, one I often felt was slipping through my fingers like sand. The vibrant canvases she painted depicted her struggles and triumphs, each stroke a testament to her resilience. In contrast, I found myself paralyzed, oscillating between fervent dreams and paralyzing self-doubt. My heart raced with excitement for Ivy, but it also fluttered with a sense of impending loss. I was caught in the undertow of my own insecurities, and then came the moment that would turn the tide completely.

Nathaniel's voice floated in from the other room, rich and warm like freshly brewed coffee. I was accustomed to his presence, the way he filled a space not just with his physicality but with an energy that crackled like a summer storm. I had been balancing on the precipice of something extraordinary with him—late-night conversations that stretched into dawn, laughter echoing through our shared space, and an unspoken promise of what could be. But that promise felt tenuous, like a threadbare tapestry.

"I just can't pass it up, Ivy," he said, his tone both excited and heavy with the weight of the decision. "Chicago is a once-in-a-lifetime opportunity. I'd be a fool to let it slip away."

My heart plummeted. I was a fool, I realized, for letting myself believe that something so beautiful could withstand the relentless march of reality. There was a harshness to his words that rattled my very core. Chicago. The name reverberated through my mind like a clanging bell, marking the beginning of the end. I had envisioned us, together, navigating the maze of this city, but now the dream felt like a fleeting mirage in the desert of my hopes.

Ivy's voice broke through my reverie, laced with a blend of support and trepidation. "You have to do what's right for you, Nate. But... what about us? What about here?"

There it was. The unsaid question that hung heavily in the air, mingling with the scent of fresh paint and unfulfilled dreams. I leaned closer, desperate to catch every word, my breath hitching in my throat. The delicate threads of my own ambitions, once woven tightly with Nathaniel's, began to fray. What if he took that leap and I remained anchored here, lost in the shadows of my own uncertainty?

"We can make it work, Ivy. I know we can," he replied, but there was a fleeting hesitation in his voice, a crack in the façade of confidence he wore so well. The realization hit me like a lightning bolt; I was no longer just an observer of their conversation. I was a participant in a narrative that threatened to spiral out of my control.

As Nathaniel's words sank in, an unexpected surge of frustration coursed through me. Why did everything feel so precarious? Why was I left teetering on the edge while he danced off into the sunset? I rose from my chair, my heart racing not with excitement but with a tumult of emotions I couldn't quite name—jealousy, fear, and a profound sense of loss.

The weight of it all hung like a storm cloud in my chest as I glanced around the studio. Ivy's paintings stared back at me, vibrant and alive, yet I felt as if I were drowning in a sea of muted colors. Each brushstroke was a reminder of her strength, her determination to rise above her struggles, while I felt shackled by mine. What was I doing? Where was my voice in this chaotic symphony of ambition and desire?

"Ivy," I said, my voice steady but barely masking the tremor beneath, "what if I can't keep up? What if I end up losing everything—Nathaniel, my dreams... everything?"

She turned to me, her eyes softening, holding a depth of understanding that made my chest tighten. "You won't lose everything. You have to believe in yourself, in your art, in what you can create here. You're more capable than you know."

Her words were a balm, yet they felt insufficient against the gnawing doubt that had burrowed itself deep within. I had watched her fight her way through a world that often seemed intent on crushing her spirit. But in that moment, I was reminded that I, too, had battles worth fighting.

The vibrant city outside continued its relentless hustle, each passerby a reminder of dreams pursued and lives lived. I had found joy in Nathaniel, in his laughter and passion for life. But if he chose Chicago, could I truly remain here, isolated in my insecurity? Or could I harness this moment, this pain, and turn it into something powerful?

As I stood there, the weight of the world on my shoulders, I felt the first stirrings of resolve bubbling up from within. The heart may be fragile, but it also has an incredible capacity to heal, to adapt, and to forge new paths in the aftermath of loss. And perhaps, just perhaps, this moment of despair could be the catalyst for something new and extraordinary.

The morning light crept hesitantly through the gauzy curtains, draping the studio in a gentle glow that felt almost too warm for the tempest brewing inside me. The echoes of Nathaniel's words from the previous night lingered like a stubborn stain, refusing to wash away. Chicago. The word hung in the air, dense with unfulfilled promises and the weight of unspoken fears. I had tossed and turned, battling a whirlwind of emotions, from panic to resentment, each wave crashing harder than the last.

With a determined sigh, I swung my legs over the side of the bed, my feet landing on the cool wooden floor, grounding me in this moment. I needed to channel this restless energy, to find a way to reclaim my narrative. As I prepared for the day, I threw on a paint-splattered shirt that had seen better days, a talisman of sorts, reminding me of the passion that had once ignited my own artistic ambitions.

The studio was alive with anticipation as Ivy flitted around, adjusting the last of her exhibit preparations. She had transformed our shared space into a vibrant gallery, every corner radiating with colors and emotions. "What do you think?" she asked, stepping back to admire her latest piece, a swirling canvas that seemed to capture the very essence of chaos and beauty intertwined.

"It's stunning," I replied, my heart swelling with pride for her. "You've poured everything into this."

Her eyes sparkled, but I could sense a shadow lurking just beneath the surface. "It feels like the last hurrah before everything changes," she mused, her voice barely above a whisper. "I hope people see the struggles behind the beauty."

"Of course they will. Your art speaks volumes," I assured her, but the irony stung. How could I inspire her to believe in herself when I felt like a walking contradiction? As I grabbed a brush and began to layer paint on my own canvas—a half-finished landscape that echoed my internal disarray—I felt Ivy's gaze on me, probing and gentle.

"You're avoiding something," she said, her tone teasing yet tinged with concern. "What's going on with you?"

I shrugged, feigning nonchalance as I mixed vibrant blues and greens, the colors swirling together like the emotions inside me. "Nothing. Just the usual artist block."

"Come on, don't feed me that line. You look like a deer caught in headlights. Is it Nathaniel?"

My heart dropped. "I overheard him talking about moving to Chicago," I admitted, my voice cracking slightly. "It's a big opportunity, and I... I can't help but feel like he's slipping away."

Ivy stepped closer, her expression shifting from playful to serious. "You know that doesn't mean you have to lose yourself in the process. You can chase your dreams too. You've just got to decide what you want."

What did I want? The question hung in the air, heavy and challenging. I had spent so much time supporting Ivy, championing her journey, that I had neglected to even consider my own aspirations beyond the shadows of her brilliance. Did I want to be an artist, to step out of her light and into my own? Or was I destined to remain a supporting character in someone else's story?

As if sensing my hesitation, Ivy nudged my shoulder gently. "Listen, you've got a week before my exhibit opens. We'll make a pact. I'll help you find your vision, and you help me with the last of mine. We'll both step into our greatness together."

"Greatness?" I scoffed, but her enthusiasm was infectious. "More like a glorious disaster."

"Exactly! What's the worst that could happen?" she challenged, her grin wide and infectious. "We fall flat on our faces? Please. We'll just pick ourselves up and paint over the mistakes."

I chuckled at the image of us, two artists in a heap of paint and disappointment. Perhaps Ivy was right; maybe the pressure to create something extraordinary was just the catalyst I needed. I could feel a flicker of hope igniting, a spark that urged me to explore the uncharted territories of my own ambitions.

The day unfolded like a canvas, full of possibilities. We spent hours immersed in our work, our laughter mingling with the sounds of the bustling city outside. As we took breaks to sip on coffee that turned cold while we were lost in conversation, the heaviness in my heart began to lift, if only slightly.

But the specter of Nathaniel's impending move loomed large, reminding me that even amidst the chaos of creativity, there was an impending storm waiting to unleash its fury. Just as I began to settle into a rhythm, my phone buzzed with a text, shattering the fragile calm.

It was Nathaniel. "Hey, can we talk? I want to share something important."

A lump formed in my throat. A part of me wanted to ignore it, to wallow in my newfound resolve. But the other part, the one that still yearned for his presence, urged me to respond.

"Sure. When?" I typed, my heart racing as I hit send.

Ivy glanced at me, her brow raised. "You're not thinking of just letting him go, are you?"

"No," I replied, though the uncertainty danced in my chest. "But I need to know what he's really thinking. If he's ready to jump ship, I can't just sit here and wait."

When Nathaniel arrived, the air felt charged, thick with anticipation and unspoken words. He stepped into the studio, a familiar sight that sent my heart into a frantic beat. He wore that same worn-out leather jacket, the one I adored, its fabric cradling memories of our late-night escapades and shared dreams. But today, there was an edge to him, a tension that made the room feel smaller, the walls closing in as I awaited the conversation that would change everything.

"Thanks for meeting me," he said, his eyes searching mine, trying to decipher my thoughts. "I know I've thrown a lot at you."

"You could say that," I replied, my tone laced with a mix of jest and genuine hurt. "So, Chicago?"

"Yeah," he said, running a hand through his tousled hair. "It's a huge opportunity. But it means leaving everything behind—us included."

The room seemed to hold its breath, the air heavy with our unspoken connection. "What if I don't want to lose you?" I finally whispered, my heart aching with the truth of my words.

His gaze softened, but the distance between us felt like an insurmountable chasm. "You won't lose me. But I can't pretend this isn't happening. I need to know if you'll be okay with it."

A flood of emotions surged within me, a tempest of fear and longing. "How can I be okay with something that feels so wrong?"

He stepped closer, the warmth of his presence washing over me. "You're stronger than you think. And I believe in you, even when you don't."

In that moment, amidst the chaos of dreams and decisions, I knew this was a crossroads, a moment that would either tether us together or set us adrift in our separate currents. And perhaps, just perhaps, it was time to take that leap into the unknown, not just for him, but for myself.

The lingering tension in the air was palpable as Nathaniel and I stood together, our unspoken words swirling around us like autumn leaves caught in a gust of wind. I could see the conflict written all over his face, the fine line between ambition and affection stretching taut between us. With each passing second, the stakes rose higher, and I could feel the world around us fade into a blur, leaving only the two of us suspended in this fragile moment.

"I don't want to lose you," I finally said, the words spilling out before I could second-guess myself. It was a truth that felt both liberating and terrifying, as if I were unearthing a hidden treasure only to realize its value could cut deeper than any knife. "But I can't just wait around for you to decide what you want. I need to know if this is worth fighting for."

He opened his mouth, then closed it again, frustration flickering in his eyes. "You make it sound so black and white. It's not that simple. I'm trying to build a future, and I don't know how to fit you into that picture right now."

The sting of his words hit me like a slap, and I forced myself to take a step back. "So that's it? You're just going to up and leave?" My voice wavered, betraying the hurt that threatened to engulf me.

"I'm not abandoning you. I'm trying to make something of myself!" he shot back, the raw edge of his emotion mirroring my own. "What do you want from me, exactly? You're acting like I'm making a choice to hurt you."

"No, Nathaniel, it's not about that," I countered, my heart racing as I tried to regain control of the conversation. "It's about whether you want to include me in your future or if I'm just a chapter in your story that you're ready to close."

Silence fell, heavy and suffocating. I could see the gears turning in his mind, the way he wrestled with his thoughts, and I knew I was pushing him to a breaking point. My chest tightened with the realization that this was our defining moment, one that could shift the very course of our lives.

Finally, he let out a slow breath, his shoulders sagging slightly as if the weight of the world rested upon them. "I wish it were easy. I wish I could say I have it all figured out, but..." He hesitated, the words hanging in the air like the last note of a fading song.

"I get it," I whispered, desperately trying to mask the cracks forming in my resolve. "You want to chase your dreams, and I want to support you. But I can't be your fallback plan."

His gaze softened, and for a moment, the distance between us felt smaller, almost bridgeable. "You're not a fallback plan. You're the one thing that keeps me grounded. I just don't know how to balance it all."

"Maybe we don't have to balance anything. Maybe we just need to be honest about what we want," I replied, my heart hammering as I offered him a way out of the turmoil.

He nodded slowly, the tension in his expression easing just a fraction. "Okay, let's be honest. I'm scared. Scared of leaving you behind, scared of failing in Chicago. But I'm also terrified of getting stuck here, doing the same thing forever."

I held his gaze, searching for a glimmer of hope amid the uncertainty. "So what do we do?"

"Let me take the job. But let's not close the door on us just yet. I want to see how things unfold," he suggested, his voice steadying. "Let's try to make this work, even if it's messy."

I wanted to believe him. I wanted to grasp onto that glimmer of hope, to paint a future where distance didn't matter and love was enough to bridge any gap. But something deep within me whispered that it wouldn't be that simple. "What if it doesn't work?" I asked, my voice barely above a whisper. "What if we drift apart?"

His eyes flickered with the vulnerability I had come to cherish. "We won't know until we try. I'll make it work, I promise. And if it doesn't, I'll come back. I will."

As he stepped forward, I felt the warm brush of his fingers against my skin, and for a brief moment, the world around us faded again. I leaned into him, savoring the connection we shared, even as uncertainty loomed. But the comfort of his embrace was tainted with an underlying dread that whispered all the things we were not saying—every unsaid fear and lingering doubt.

"Okay," I finally said, trying to mask the tremor in my voice. "We'll try."

His smile was like a balm, spreading warmth through the frigid air that had encased us. But beneath the surface of that smile, I sensed the unspoken reality we were both tiptoeing around: change was inevitable, and love, while powerful, often came with the threat of loss.

As the days slipped by, Ivy's art exhibit loomed ever closer. The gallery was alive with preparation, an intricate tapestry of vibrant canvases and eager chatter. Yet, beneath the excitement, I felt like a ticking time bomb, emotions brewing just below the surface. I was determined to pour my heart into supporting Ivy, to be there for her as she unveiled her work to the world, even if my own dreams felt increasingly nebulous.

The night of the exhibit arrived, cloaked in anticipation and tinged with an electric buzz that hummed through the air. The gallery was abuzz with the clinking of glasses, the soft rustle of dresses, and laughter that echoed against the walls adorned with Ivy's masterpieces. Each canvas was a portal into her soul, an intricate dance between darkness and light. As I stood beside her, watching the crowd admire her work, I felt an overwhelming swell of pride.

"I can't believe it's finally happening," Ivy breathed, her voice trembling with excitement.

"You deserve this," I replied, giving her arm a gentle squeeze. "Look at how far you've come."

But as the night wore on, I found myself glancing at the door more often than I cared to admit, the anticipation for Nathaniel's arrival battling with the quiet dread that accompanied his impending move. Would he show? Would this be the last time I'd see him, and if so, would it feel like a goodbye or just an extended pause?

The moment finally came when he stepped through the door, the crowd parting like the Red Sea, and for a heartbeat, the world around me ceased to exist. He looked good, too good, with that familiar, crooked smile lighting up his face. But there was a tension in his posture, a tightness around his eyes that hinted at the internal struggle I had come to recognize.

"Hey," he said, approaching me with an ease that belied the chaos swirling in my gut. "You look amazing."

"Thanks, you too. How's Chicago?" I asked, trying to keep my voice light despite the heavy weight of everything unsaid.

"Just as bustling as I imagined," he replied, his gaze drifting to the canvases around us. "But I think I'd prefer to be here, with you."

His words ignited a flicker of hope, but before I could respond, Ivy appeared beside me, her eyes sparkling with excitement. "Nathaniel! I'm so glad you made it! Come see my latest piece."

As Ivy ushered him toward the canvas that depicted her own tumultuous journey, I felt the air thicken with unexpressed feelings. They chatted animatedly, and I stepped back, allowing them their moment while grappling with my own heart's tumult.

But as the night continued, the sharp pangs of reality returned. I watched as people admired Ivy's work, as Nathaniel complimented her with genuine awe. And in that moment, amidst the laughter and warmth of the gallery, the weight of uncertainty hung heavily on my shoulders.

What if this was the last night we shared like this? The last night before he left, potentially leaving me behind, questioning everything? My heart raced, and the familiar knot of anxiety twisted tighter within me.

Suddenly, the gallery door swung open, and a gust of chilly air swept through the room. I turned, half-expecting to see another familiar face, but instead, my heart dropped. A figure stepped inside, someone I hadn't seen in years—my ex-boyfriend, Matt, looking more dashing than ever, with a confident smirk that sent a ripple of discomfort through the crowd.

What was he doing here? My stomach twisted, the realization hitting me like a punch to the gut. The fragile balance of my evening shattered as he scanned the room, locking eyes with me across the sea of guests.

Just as Nathaniel turned to follow my gaze, I felt a rush of panic coursing through me. Everything that had been carefully woven together in this moment felt suddenly tenuous, unraveling before my eyes.

"Nate, I—" I began, but the words caught in my throat, leaving me stranded between the past and an uncertain future, surrounded by a gallery filled with dreams and the specter of a life I thought I'd left behind.

And as I stood there, heart racing, the tension in the air palpable, I realized I had to make a choice. Would I embrace the love that had just begun to bloom, or would I allow the ghosts of my past to pull me back into the shadows?

But before I could figure it out, Matt took a step forward, a determined glint in his eye, and I knew that whatever happened next would change everything.

Chapter 6: Decisions in the Dark

The neon lights of Manhattan flickered like stars caught in a perpetual dance, illuminating the restless streets that pulsed with energy. Each corner beckoned with the allure of a new adventure, a fresh start. I wandered aimlessly, my heart still heavy with the weight of Ivy's words. The memory of our confrontation clung to me like a damp coat, the chill of her accusations echoing in my mind. In moments like these, I sought refuge in the city's embrace, where anonymity and excitement intertwined like lovers at a midnight rendezvous.

As I drifted past a line of eager patrons outside a vibrant club, the thumping bass of music seeped through the walls, wrapping around me like a warm hug. I stepped inside, letting the chaos engulf me, the intoxicating mix of laughter, conversations, and rhythmic beats overwhelming my senses. The dim lights created an intimate atmosphere, where secrets danced just out of reach, and the promise of oblivion loomed temptingly.

At the bar, I ordered a drink, the bartender's deft hands moving with a fluidity that caught my eye. His hair was dark and tousled, as if he'd just rolled out of bed after a night spent chasing shadows. When he turned to face me, his smile was a beacon in the haze, sharp and inviting, revealing a confidence that made my heart skip. "What's a girl like you doing in a place like this?" he asked, his voice low and smooth, blending effortlessly with the ambient noise.

"Trying to forget," I replied, attempting a nonchalant shrug, but the vulnerability slipped through my facade like water through a sieve. He raised an eyebrow, intrigued.

"Good luck with that. The city has a funny way of making you face your demons." He poured a drink, the amber liquid catching the light as he slid it toward me. "I'm Leo, by the way."

"Lila," I offered, clinking my glass against his as I took a sip. The drink was both bitter and sweet, much like the night I found myself in. "Cheers to distractions."

"Distractions are my specialty." He leaned in closer, the warmth of his presence washing over me. "Tell me what's haunting you, Lila. I'm a great listener."

I hesitated, the words caught in my throat like a stubborn fish refusing to be reeled in. Instead, I opted for a lighter approach. "What about you, Leo? What's your story?"

"Ah, the classic bartender line. You know, we're trained to ask the questions and serve the drinks while keeping our secrets locked behind the bar." He grinned, a playful glint in his eyes. "But since you're here, I might indulge you a little. Let's just say I'm not a fan of the nine-to-five grind. I prefer the unpredictability of nights like this."

"Sounds liberating." I glanced around, noticing the diverse crowd—the carefree dancers, the couples lost in their own worlds, the solitary souls nursing their drinks, each lost in their own stories. "But isn't it lonely?"

"Only if you let it be." He gestured to the thrumming heart of the club. "You can find connection anywhere, even in a place like this."

His words lingered in the air between us, a spark igniting a sense of camaraderie that felt both exhilarating and terrifying. I leaned closer, drawn in by the warmth of his presence. "So, tell me, do you always play the therapist for the girls at the bar?"

"Only the interesting ones." He flashed a charming smile, and I felt my pulse quicken. "What's your poison? Because I have a feeling this isn't your usual scene."

"Not usually, no. But tonight I'm in the mood for something different." I could feel the edges of my worries starting to soften, the pulsating music and Leo's teasing banter weaving a cocoon around me, sheltering me from the storm I had left behind.

"Then how about a little adventure?" Leo leaned back, an enticing sparkle in his eye. "I can show you the city that never sleeps—after my shift, of course."

"Isn't that a bit risky? I mean, what if you turn out to be an axe murderer?" I raised an eyebrow, unable to resist the thrill of the unknown.

He chuckled, the sound rich and warm, washing away the shadows of my earlier confrontation. "Trust me, if I were an axe murderer, I wouldn't be standing here with you, charming you with my wit."

"Fair point." I took another sip, the drink emboldening me. "All right, let's make this a night to remember. But only if you promise not to kill me."

"Scout's honor." He placed a hand over his heart, mock solemnity in his expression, and I found myself laughing—a sound I hadn't realized I missed until that moment. The laughter felt like a breath of fresh air, a reprieve from the chaos that had clung to me all evening.

As the night unfurled, we shared stories that wove an invisible thread between us, drawing me deeper into the allure of the moment. Leo's laughter became a balm, soothing the jagged edges of my worries, each exchange a delightful distraction from the chaos awaiting me outside this sanctuary of sound and light. I lost track of time, the rhythm of the night becoming a comforting lullaby that wrapped around us like a warm blanket, shielding me from the reality waiting just beyond the door.

But beneath the surface of this newfound camaraderie, a knot of uncertainty twisted in my stomach. Every laugh, every teasing remark felt like a flirtation with danger. The exhilaration was intoxicating, but I couldn't shake the feeling that with every moment I spent with Leo, I was delaying the inevitable—a confrontation with my own demons that awaited me in the shadows of the night.

Yet, for now, I was content to indulge in the thrill of the present, to let the music guide me deeper into the heart of the city, to let Leo's laughter drown out the echoes of Ivy's accusations, if only for a little while longer. In that dimly lit bar, surrounded by the frenetic energy of Manhattan, I found solace in the arms of an enticing stranger, knowing that at some point, the real world would come knocking, demanding its due. But for now, I would revel in the embrace of distraction, if only to gather the strength to face whatever lay ahead.

The bar buzzed with life, an electric energy that thrummed through the air like a secret waiting to be unveiled. I leaned against the polished wood, letting the warmth of the crowded room seep into my bones, a stark contrast to the chill of my earlier encounter. Leo had just finished pouring a cocktail that shimmered with hues of blue and silver, the result of an artful mix that seemed too pretty to drink. "Here's to new beginnings," he said, presenting the drink with a flourish that made it feel like a precious gift.

"To new beginnings," I echoed, raising the glass to my lips, the cool liquid sliding down my throat like a refreshing promise. The taste was bright and tangy, a playful reminder that life could still hold surprises, even when darkness loomed.

As I sipped, Leo leaned closer, his presence warming the space between us. "So, what's a girl like you running from, really?" He didn't pry; it was more a gentle nudge, an invitation to dive deeper if I dared. I hesitated, caught in the crossroads of honesty and the comforting veil of distraction.

"Let's just say I had a bit of a family meltdown before I walked in here." My words tumbled out, wrapped in a chuckle that didn't quite hide the sorrow. "The kind that leaves you questioning every choice you've made."

Leo's eyes softened, the intensity of his gaze urging me to continue. "Family drama is like a twisted novel, isn't it? You think you know the plot, and then boom! A twist you never saw coming."

I laughed, a genuine sound that surprised me. "Exactly! And just when you think you're turning the page to something better, the next chapter throws you a curveball."

He nodded, understanding. "I get it. But sometimes you have to write your own ending. Are you ready for that?"

The question hung in the air, heavy yet liberating. I swirled the drink in my glass, contemplating my next words as the music pulsed around us, wrapping us in a cocoon of sound. "I don't know if I'm ready, but I'm definitely tired of running."

"Then why not take a break? Just for tonight?" He flashed that enigmatic smile again, the corners of his lips curling in a way that felt like an invitation to step into the light, to shake off the shadows clinging to my heart.

"Okay, Leo. Let's say I take your advice. What does 'taking a break' look like in a city that never sleeps?" I raised an eyebrow, challenging him.

He leaned back, a playful glint in his eye. "Well, it starts with me showing you my favorite spots in Manhattan. No tourist traps, just the good stuff. And, of course, a drink or two to fuel the adventure."

"I'll need a solid drink if I'm going to face whatever night you have in store." I smirked, the idea of letting go of my burdens for a few hours igniting a spark of excitement within me.

"Perfect! But remember, no regrets," he said, holding up his glass in a mock toast. "You might just find that the world is bigger than the one you've been trapped in."

And with that, the night unfolded like a dream. Leo, the captivating bartender turned impromptu tour guide, led me through the labyrinthine streets of the city, the glow of neon lights illuminating our path. We strolled past hidden gems—tiny art galleries tucked between towering skyscrapers, cozy cafes where the smell of freshly brewed coffee mingled with laughter, and street performers pouring their souls into music that echoed down the sidewalks.

As we wandered, our conversation flowed like the river that cut through the heart of the city. He shared snippets of his life—a childhood spent in a small town, a leap of faith to pursue his dreams in Manhattan. I found myself captivated not just by his stories, but by the way he told them, each word punctuated with emotion and enthusiasm.

"What about you, Lila?" he asked, suddenly serious, pausing on a corner as the streetlights flickered around us. "What's your story?"

I hesitated, the weight of my reality settling on my shoulders like an unwelcome guest. "I grew up in a picture-perfect family," I began, my voice barely above a whisper. "But behind closed doors, everything was... different. The kind of different that makes you question everything you know. Ivy—she's my sister—she's been through a lot, and I thought I could help her. But tonight, I just messed it all up."

"Families are messy. It sounds like you care a lot, though." His gaze was steady, unwavering, as if he could see right through the armor I wore.

"I do. But sometimes I feel like I'm drowning, you know? Like I'm losing myself in trying to save someone else." The admission left a bitter taste on my tongue, a cocktail of guilt and helplessness.

"Maybe you need to find out who you are first before you can help anyone else," Leo suggested, his voice gentle yet firm. "It's not selfish to prioritize yourself. It's necessary."

We resumed our stroll, and with every step, I felt the weight of my burdens begin to lift, the lightness of the evening sparking a flicker of hope deep within. As we reached the edge of a small park, a sudden wave of laughter caught my attention. A group of people gathered nearby, celebrating under the glow of fairy lights strung between trees.

"Let's crash this party!" Leo declared, pulling me toward the vibrant scene.

Before I knew it, we were amidst the laughter, the warmth of the crowd enveloping us like a well-worn blanket. I watched as Leo effortlessly blended into the group, his charm drawing everyone in. He introduced me as his partner in crime for the evening, and I felt a thrill at the word—partner, not just in distraction, but in the unfolding adventure.

The energy was infectious, laughter mingling with the sounds of clinking glasses and playful banter. In this moment, surrounded by strangers who felt like friends, I let the night wash over me. The heaviness in my heart began to dissolve as we danced under the stars, the music pulsing through my veins, inviting me to forget, if only for a little while.

Leo caught my eye, his expression both mischievous and warm as he twirled me into the throng. "See? This is what I meant about connection. You just have to be willing to dive in."

As we spun and swayed, I felt a surge of exhilaration, an unexpected release that felt foreign yet thrilling. Maybe this was what it meant to truly live, to let the world swirl around me while I anchored myself in the present. The laughter, the music, the flickering lights all blended together in a glorious tapestry of joy, and for a moment, I dared to believe that I could reshape my own narrative.

But just as I began to feel invincible, the familiar weight of my worries crept back, an uninvited reminder that reality awaited me, lurking in the shadows. As the night wore on, I found myself torn between the intoxicating thrill of distraction and the lingering chaos that awaited my return. In the midst of this vibrant celebration, I realized that while escapism was enchanting, the heart of the matter still awaited my attention—a tangled web of emotions that refused to stay hidden, waiting for me to face it head-on.

As the music swelled and laughter danced through the air, I lost myself in the moment, letting the vibrant chaos of the night envelop me. Leo spun me around, our bodies moving instinctively to the beat, and for the first time in ages, I felt a spark of something that resembled joy. The weight of Ivy's confrontation drifted away like the smoke curling from the fingers of a distant street performer, and I surrendered to the rhythm of the night.

"See? You've got moves!" Leo shouted over the pulsating bass, his voice playful, yet tinged with an admiration that made my cheeks warm. "Maybe you should join me behind the bar!"

"Only if I get to mix drinks as colorful as you!" I shot back, my laughter bubbling over as I twirled away, losing myself in the laughter of strangers who felt like friends.

Leo's presence was intoxicating, his easy confidence infectious, and I was swept along in the current of this impromptu celebration. We danced and drank, the world outside fading into a blur of muted colors, worries slipping through my fingers like grains of sand. I was still Lila, but tonight, I was also a thousand possibilities wrapped in glitter and rhythm.

At one point, we found ourselves perched on the edge of a low wall surrounding the park, taking a break from the frenzy. The city lights sparkled like diamonds scattered across velvet, and the chill of the night air sent a delightful shiver down my spine. Leo pulled out a small flask from his pocket, the metal gleaming under the moonlight. "Here's a little something to keep the adventure alive," he said, offering it to me.

"What are we drinking?" I asked, eyeing the flask with a mix of curiosity and caution.

"Just a little homemade whiskey. It's smooth and packs a punch," he replied, a cheeky grin on his face. "Trust me, it'll warm you right up."

I took a swig, the liquid burning pleasantly as it slid down my throat. "Wow, this is definitely smoother than my family drama," I laughed, handing it back to him.

"Family drama is overrated," he declared, tilting the flask to his lips and gulping down a generous mouthful. "Let's focus on having a great night, shall we?"

"Agreed! Here's to not being haunted by the past." I raised my hand, pretending to clink glasses with the flask. He laughed, and that sound—so genuine and warm—wrapped around me like a security blanket.

Just then, the distant sound of sirens echoed through the streets, a stark reminder of the real world lurking at the edges of our little oasis. My heart sank, the thrill of the evening suddenly tinged with the familiar sense of dread. I brushed it off, refusing to let it ruin the moment. "Let's go find some street food," I suggested, desperate to keep the mood light. "I hear the hot dog carts here are life-changing."

"Hot dogs it is!" Leo exclaimed, hopping off the wall with the energy of a kid at a carnival. I followed suit, the two of us weaving through the crowd like a pair of dancers in a world of color and sound.

As we strolled, Leo shared stories about his favorite food stalls, his voice animated, painting pictures of mouthwatering treats that made my stomach grumble. We passed a taco truck that smelled like heaven, but Leo insisted we save room for the legendary hot dog cart just a few blocks away.

"Trust me," he said, his eyes sparkling with mischief. "It's worth the walk."

"Okay, Mr. Hot Dog Connoisseur," I teased, nudging him playfully. "I'm counting on you to deliver on this promise."

He shot me a sidelong glance, the corners of his mouth quirking up. "Don't worry; I never break a promise—especially not one that involves food."

Just then, the atmosphere shifted. A tension cut through the air, and I felt a prickling at the back of my neck. I turned, scanning the street, but all I saw were happy faces and the glow of neon lights. "Did you feel that?" I asked, frowning.

"Feel what?" Leo replied, glancing around, too. "The magic of the city? Because it's palpable right now."

"No, like... something's off." I shook my head, dismissing my own unease. Maybe I was still feeling the aftereffects of the whiskey. "It's probably just me being paranoid."

"Paranoia is the city's second language," he joked lightly, but I could see the flicker of concern in his eyes. "Let's get those hot dogs and see if they make everything better."

We continued our journey, laughter bubbling up between us, but the nagging feeling of discomfort persisted. The hot dog cart came into view, a quaint little setup bathed in warm light, and as we approached, the friendly vendor greeted us with a broad smile. I glanced at Leo, who was already animatedly discussing the toppings.

"Do you want the works or are you a plain girl?" he asked, winking at me.

"Definitely the works," I replied, the need for indulgence suddenly overwhelming. "If I'm going to have a night of distraction, I might as well go all in."

After placing our orders, we stepped aside to wait, and just as I turned to Leo, a commotion erupted behind us. A group of men emerged from the shadows, their voices raised in anger. My heart raced as the atmosphere shifted again, the joyous night turning ominous.

"Leo..." I whispered, my unease morphing into fear. "What's going on?"

He turned, his brow furrowing as he assessed the situation. "Stay close to me," he instructed, his demeanor shifting from playful to serious in an instant. The tension in the air thickened, and I felt a cold sweat prickling at the back of my neck.

Before I could respond, a loud crash erupted from the nearby alley as one of the men shoved a trash can to the ground. The noise drew attention, and suddenly, everyone was turning to see what was happening. My breath hitched in my throat as Leo stepped forward, instinctively positioning himself between me and the approaching chaos.

"Leo, we should go," I urged, grabbing his arm.

"Just a second," he said, his eyes scanning the crowd, his protective instinct flaring to life. "I need to make sure everyone is okay."

But as I watched him, a gut feeling twisted within me—a realization that this night, which had felt like an escape, was unraveling at the seams. The laughter and music faded, replaced by raised voices and shouts. I could see the men moving closer, their intentions unclear but definitely threatening.

Then, as if in slow motion, one of the men took a step toward us, his expression dark and determined. I felt Leo tense beside me, and before I could process what was happening, everything changed. A shout pierced the air, and suddenly, the world around us erupted into chaos, with people scattering, voices rising, and the unmistakable feeling of danger looming like a thundercloud ready to burst.

In that moment, my heart raced with uncertainty. I grasped Leo's hand, our fingers entwined, my mind racing with questions. Just when I thought the night might deliver a well-deserved escape, it brought with it a darkness I hadn't anticipated. And as the tension escalated, I realized that this was a pivotal moment—one that would force me to confront not just the chaos of the night but the chaos within myself.

Chapter 7: Love's Reckoning

The gallery buzzed with an electric energy, a swirling tapestry of laughter, vibrant colors, and the unmistakable scent of expensive wine that clung to the air like an uninvited guest. I stood amidst the whirlwind of the opening night for Ivy's exhibit, feeling both a participant and an observer in a beautifully chaotic world. The art hung like whispers on the walls, each piece a window into Ivy's soul, capturing fragments of her wild imagination and effortless charm. Her paintings, full of swirling colors and daring strokes, seemed to pulse with life, just as the crowd around them did.

I clutched a delicate crystal glass, the cold rim biting into my fingers as I navigated through clusters of guests, all swathed in silk and sophistication. Ivy's laughter rang out like a siren's call, drawing me closer. She was surrounded by admirers, her brilliance illuminating the space, but I was fixated on one person—the man who stood slightly apart, a brooding figure against the backdrop of creativity. Nathaniel.

His eyes, a deep forest green, scanned the room with a quiet intensity, taking in the beauty of the art and the beauty of those around him, yet always returning to rest on Ivy with an almost palpable admiration. The world seemed to fade around us as our gazes locked, an electric pulse igniting between us that sent warmth flooding through my veins. I had spent countless hours pondering this moment, rehearsing the lines I would deliver, the emotions I would reveal, yet now, with the room thrumming around us, my courage wavered.

"You're lost in thought, or are you just captivated by my masterpiece?" Ivy teased, a playful glint in her eye as she sidled up beside me. She had an uncanny ability to read me like a book, her perceptiveness sharpening the weight of my secret.

"More like captivated by the artist," I replied, forcing a lightness into my tone, though the heaviness of my own heart nearly dragged me down. "You've outdone yourself. This is breathtaking."

"Wait until you see the one that's hidden in my studio. It'll knock your socks off," she winked, completely unaware of the tempest brewing within me. I opened my mouth, ready to confess my feelings for Nathaniel, to weave our destinies together like threads in her vibrant tapestry, but just then, the air shifted. The gallery doors swung open, letting in a gust of cool night air that carried with it the faintest hint of a storm, and my phone buzzed violently in my pocket.

I instinctively reached for it, the screen illuminating my face with a soft glow. The name flashing across it made my heart drop: Mom. My breath hitched as I swiped to answer, the warmth of my earlier resolve quickly turning icy.

"Anna," her voice was taut, frayed at the edges. "We need to talk. It's about the shop."

Panic surged through me like an electric current, snapping my attention away from Nathaniel. "Is everything okay? You sound... tense."

"We're not okay," she said sharply, the words slicing through the atmosphere like a knife. "The bakery is on the verge of collapse. If we don't act fast, we'll lose everything. I need you back here."

The noise of the gallery dulled into a muffled backdrop, the vibrant colors around me dimming like the flickering lights before a storm. "What do you mean? Can't we find a way to fix this without me? I have my work here, my life..." I stammered, feeling a rush of resentment bubble beneath the surface.

"I need you, Anna. You're the only one who can help. It's always been you," she pressed, her voice now a mix of urgency and desperation.

As the weight of her words sank in, a flood of memories rushed back—baking cookies on snowy afternoons, the warmth of the oven mingling with the smell of fresh bread, the laughter of my little brother echoing through our cramped kitchen. Our family business was not just a bakery; it was the cornerstone of our lives, the embodiment of our love and effort. But here, amid the vibrant canvas of Ivy's creations, I felt torn between the life I had crafted for myself and the demands of my past.

I looked up at Nathaniel, who was watching me now, concern etching lines across his brow. His presence felt like a beacon amidst the chaos, and for a moment, I considered running into his arms, letting him anchor me in the storm. But my mother's voice pulled me back.

"Anna?" she asked, the quiver in her tone reminding me of the stakes involved.

"I'll be home as soon as I can," I said, resolve hardening within me. The words tasted bitter, a stark reminder that dreams often lay crumbled at the feet of reality. I hung up and turned back to the gallery, my heart aching as the vibrant colors swirled around me like a dizzying whirlpool. I caught Nathaniel's gaze, and the warmth in his eyes was an antidote to the cold reality I faced.

"What's wrong?" he asked, stepping closer, his voice low and steady, slicing through the din around us.

"Family business," I replied, forcing a smile that felt more like a grimace. "I need to go home. There's... a crisis."

"Crisis?" His brow furrowed, concern knitting his features into a tapestry of worry. "Can I help?"

"Just... it's complicated." The words hung heavy between us, laden with unspoken promises and the weight of everything I wished to share with him.

Before I could stop myself, I reached for him, fingers brushing his arm as I drew a deep breath, the moment stretching between us, a fragile thread of connection amid the chaos. "I wish I could stay," I confessed, my voice barely above a whisper.

He stepped closer, closing the gap, and the heat of his body radiated toward me like a lifeline. "You will, Anna. You have to take care of your family, but we can figure this out." The sincerity in his voice wrapped around me like a warm embrace, urging me to lean into the moment, even as the storm of my responsibilities loomed overhead.

But just as I dared to believe in the possibility of us, reality crashed back in, a relentless tide that threatened to pull me under. With every heartbeat, I felt the mounting pressure of obligation press against my chest, forcing me to confront the painful truth that weighed heavily on my heart. The future I had envisioned, intertwined with Nathaniel, felt more like a mirage, slipping further from my grasp with each passing second.

The vibrant atmosphere of the gallery now felt like a distant echo, a cacophony of laughter and music fading into a solemn reality. Nathaniel stood before me, a lighthouse in a storm, but the winds howled, pulling at my resolve. I forced myself to smile, but it felt brittle, a fragile veneer over the tumult of emotions roiling within.

"I can't just leave," I said, more to convince myself than him. "Not now, not when Ivy's dream is finally taking flight. It's everything we've worked for."

"I get that," Nathaniel replied, his voice steady as a warm embrace. "But Ivy's success shouldn't come at the cost of your family. You need to take care of what matters to you."

The sincerity in his eyes caught me off guard, a stark contrast to the swirling chaos in my mind. I had built my life here, surrounded by vibrant canvases and the hum of creativity, yet my roots clung tightly to the small-town bakery where my family poured their heart and soul. I glanced toward Ivy, her laughter a melody of triumph, and felt a pang of longing to share in that joy. But deep down, the gnawing responsibility weighed heavily, a constant reminder of what lay waiting for me back home.

"Anna, you're not just abandoning your dreams by going home," Nathaniel continued, his gaze unwavering. "You're facing them. And that takes real courage."

His words sparked something within me, a flicker of understanding that warmed my chest. "Courage," I echoed softly, contemplating the word. What did it mean to be courageous? To chase dreams or to face the reality of obligation?

Just as I was about to respond, a figure emerged from the crowd—a tall, elegantly dressed woman with a sharp bob and an air of authority that practically radiated. She made her way toward us, heels clicking against the polished floor like a metronome, each step a reminder of the world outside our little bubble.

"Anna! There you are!" she called, her voice smooth yet commanding, cutting through the haze of emotion. "I've been looking for you." It was Melissa, a well-respected art dealer with a reputation for spotting talent. My heart sank slightly. She was known for making demands, and I didn't have the energy to deal with her right now.

"Hi, Melissa," I greeted, forcing my voice to remain light, despite the weight on my chest. "What's up?"

"I wanted to discuss potential collaborations for future exhibits. Your input would be invaluable, especially given how well Ivy's opening has gone." Her gaze shifted to Nathaniel, lingering just long enough to assess him, before returning to me. "I think you could play a significant role in bringing a fresh perspective to our next show."

"Oh, um, that sounds great, but—" I began, feeling the pressure of her expectation pressing down like a vice, but Nathaniel interjected, his tone warm yet firm.

"Anna has some pressing matters to attend to," he said, a protective edge to his voice that made my heart flutter unexpectedly. "Maybe she can get back to you after the dust settles?"

Melissa's perfectly manicured eyebrows arched, surprise flickering across her features. "Oh, of course! Family obligations can be... challenging." Her voice dripped with a honeyed condescension, leaving a bitter aftertaste. "I just hope you don't let this opportunity slip away. They don't come around often."

As she turned on her heel and glided back into the crowd, Nathaniel let out a breath he hadn't realized he was holding. "Wow, she really knows how to throw shade," he said, a lopsided grin breaking across his face. "But seriously, Anna, don't let her get to you. This is your moment, too."

"You make it sound easy," I countered, the tension in my shoulders knotting tighter. "I don't even know if I want to keep pursuing this. It feels selfish to even think about my dreams when everything is crumbling back home."

Nathaniel stepped closer, the warmth of his presence enveloping me like a soft blanket. "Caring about your family doesn't mean you have to sacrifice everything you want. You can do both. You're strong enough to juggle it all." His voice was steady, like an anchor pulling me from the stormy sea of uncertainty.

"But what if I can't?" The vulnerability crept into my words, a chink in my armor that I had always kept tightly sealed. "What if I fail? What if I go home and the bakery is gone?"

"Then you rebuild," he replied, his confidence a soothing balm against my frayed nerves. "You're resourceful and talented. You've always been the one to hold everything together. Just because the world is asking you to choose doesn't mean you have to let go of your dreams."

The sincerity in his voice sank into my bones, warming me from the inside out. I took a breath, considering his words. Could I really juggle both worlds? It felt daunting, yet with him beside me, the idea didn't seem entirely impossible.

"I guess I just don't want to disappoint anyone," I admitted, feeling the weight of expectations settle on my shoulders once more.

"Disappointment is part of life," Nathaniel said, leaning in closer, his voice low and soothing. "But you have to live for yourself. Nobody else can do that for you."

I searched his eyes, finding a wellspring of understanding, a depth of connection that sent warmth flooding through me. The chemistry between us crackled in the air, as palpable as the music pulsing around us.

"Can I ask you something?" I said, my voice barely above a whisper.

"Anything," he replied, his expression open and inviting.

"If I go back home and face this... what if I don't come back?" I knew it was a question steeped in fear, the kind that lurked in the corners of my mind like a shadow. "What if I lose this—us?"

He took a step closer, his gaze unwavering. "You won't lose us unless you let fear dictate your choices. I want you to chase your dreams, Anna, but I also want you to know that I'm here. I'm not going anywhere."

A warmth blossomed in my chest, kindling a flicker of hope. The tension that had coiled tightly around my heart began to unravel, giving way to a sense of possibility. "You really mean that?"

"Absolutely. I'm rooting for you, always." His voice was steady, a promise that both thrilled and terrified me.

Just then, Ivy reappeared, her face flushed with excitement and her arms laden with a cluster of fresh flowers she had just received from a guest. "You two look deep in conversation," she said, an unmistakable sparkle in her eye. "Plotting world domination, or just strategizing how to handle my brilliance?"

I chuckled, grateful for the lightheartedness she brought. "A bit of both, actually."

"Well, whatever it is, I'm sure it's more interesting than the flower bouquet I just snagged. Just wait until you see this arrangement; it's practically a masterpiece!" Ivy waved the flowers around with a flourish, her infectious energy reinvigorating the space.

As she chatted animatedly about the exhibit, I glanced at Nathaniel, who smiled back, a shared understanding passing between us. In that moment, with Ivy's exuberance swirling around us, I felt a renewed sense of determination rising within me. The path ahead was uncertain, and the weight of responsibility loomed, but with Nathaniel by my side, I was ready to face whatever came next. Life would require balance, a delicate dance between my dreams and obligations, but I knew I wouldn't have to do it alone.

The gallery buzzed around us, a lively celebration of art and life, yet I felt trapped in a bubble of my own making. Ivy's laughter rang like a bell, a sweet reminder of the joy she spread, while Nathaniel stood beside me, his presence both a comfort and a challenge. I was acutely aware of the paths diverging before me, one leading back to the comforting chaos of family obligations and the other promising the thrill of chasing my own dreams.

"Are you sure you don't want to join in the festivities?" Ivy called, her voice brimming with excitement as she floated to our side, her bright dress swirling around her like petals in a breeze. "You look like you've just been handed the last piece of a jigsaw puzzle and don't know where it fits."

"Just a little distracted," I admitted, forcing a smile. "I was thinking about home."

Nathaniel leaned closer, his warmth igniting the space between us. "Home can wait," he murmured, his voice low enough that only I could hear. "You deserve to enjoy this moment."

I glanced at Ivy, who was now chatting animatedly with a group of patrons, their eyes wide with admiration as she pointed out details in her paintings. She was the embodiment of success, a radiant figure I had always admired, yet my heart felt heavy, caught between the exhilaration of her triumph and the dread that clung to me like a shadow.

"Let's grab a drink," Nathaniel suggested, tilting his head toward the bar where a line of crystal glasses glimmered invitingly. "We can toast to Ivy's brilliance and forget about everything else for just a moment."

"Good idea," I agreed, needing the distraction. As we moved toward the bar, the chatter of guests washed over us, blending with the melodic strains of a jazz trio playing softly in the corner. The music was lively yet soothing, wrapping around us like a warm embrace, but I couldn't shake the anxious flutter in my stomach.

"What's your poison?" Nathaniel asked, leaning against the polished wood of the bar, his easy smile easing the tension in my shoulders.

"Surprise me," I replied, grinning back at him. It felt good to tease, to let the weight of the world slip from my shoulders, even if just for a moment.

As he ordered two glasses of a sparkling rosé, I stole glances around the gallery, observing the vibrant crowd that had gathered to celebrate Ivy's success. I felt a pang of envy mixed with pride, realizing that the life Ivy had built was the very one I longed for—freedom, creativity, and passion. But as I looked back at Nathaniel, his dark hair catching the light just so, I wondered if it was worth pursuing if it meant leaving everything behind.

"Here's to Ivy, and to you," Nathaniel said, lifting his glass as he turned back to me. "May your dreams always be as vivid as her paintings."

"To us," I said, clinking my glass against his. The bubbly liquid shimmered like sunlight caught in a web, and for a heartbeat, I allowed myself to revel in the moment, letting laughter and conversation wash over me.

But as I took a sip, my phone buzzed insistently in my pocket, breaking the spell. I frowned, my heart sinking as I fished it out. A text from my mother flashed on the screen, and my stomach twisted into knots as I read her words: I need to see you. It's urgent.

"What's wrong?" Nathaniel asked, his gaze narrowing as he noticed my sudden shift in mood.

"It's my mom," I murmured, the cheerfulness around us dimming like the last rays of sunset. "She wants to see me... urgently."

He nodded, concern flooding his features. "Do you need to go?"

"I don't know. I want to be here, but..." My voice trailed off, the weight of expectation pressing against me like a heavy fog.

"Let's find a quiet corner," he suggested, and I followed him, my heart racing. The gallery was filled with joyful laughter, but my thoughts were far away, racing toward home and the impending crisis.

We found a small alcove tucked away from the bustling crowd, the soft glow of fairy lights creating an intimate cocoon. "What's really going on?" Nathaniel asked, his tone gentle but probing.

I ran a hand through my hair, feeling the tension tighten around my temples. "It's the bakery," I admitted, my voice barely a whisper. "Mom said it's on the verge of collapse. I don't know how to help her or if I can even go back. I feel like I'm being pulled in two different directions."

Nathaniel's expression softened, his eyes reflecting an understanding that made my heart ache. "You're strong, Anna. You'll figure it out, but don't let the fear of what could happen dictate your choices."

"I know," I said, biting my lip. "But what if I leave and things only get worse? What if I lose everything I've built here?"

"Sometimes you have to take risks," he replied, stepping closer, the warmth of his body radiating toward me. "You can't control every outcome. Just because you're afraid doesn't mean you shouldn't try."

His words resonated within me, a rallying cry for my tangled thoughts. I took a deep breath, considering the delicate balance between duty and desire. "What if I go back, and I can't find my way back here?" I murmured, vulnerability spilling over as I met his gaze.

"Then I'll help you find your way," he said, sincerity etched in every line of his face. "You don't have to do this alone."

Before I could respond, the distant sound of Ivy's laughter floated toward us, reminding me of the vibrant world just beyond our sanctuary. It pulled at me like a forgotten song, and as I prepared to step back into the celebration, a sudden flash of movement caught my eye.

Across the gallery, a figure loomed, dark and imposing, eyes fixed intently on me. I felt a shiver dance down my spine. The stranger moved closer, pushing through the crowd with an urgency that sent my heart racing. A cold twist of dread coiled in my stomach as recognition washed over me.

"Nathaniel," I whispered, fear tightening my throat. "Do you see that person?"

His eyes followed my gaze, the warmth evaporating from his expression as he stiffened, a shadow crossing his features. "Yeah. Who is that?"

"I think it's... it can't be..." My voice faltered as the figure drew nearer, and a chill settled over the vibrant gallery, the colorful world around us suddenly muted. The stranger's eyes locked onto mine, an unsettling familiarity sending my pulse racing.

"Anna!" Ivy's voice broke through the tension, and I turned just in time to see her approaching, excitement radiating from her like sunlight. "You've got to see this! There's someone here who wants to meet you—"

But before she could finish, the stranger stepped into the light, a smirk curving their lips as they pointed directly at me. The words that escaped their mouth sent a jolt of disbelief coursing through me, pulling the ground from beneath my feet.

"Guess who's back in town?" they taunted, the familiar voice ringing out like a bell, filling the air with the sharp tang of unresolved pasts and unheeded warnings.

In that moment, everything came crashing down, the laughter and light of the gallery fading into a distant memory as I stood frozen, heart pounding, caught between the worlds of dreams and reality, torn from one moment into the impending storm.

Chapter 8: Fractured Bonds

A chill swept through the air, sharp as a freshly broken promise, as I stood on the doorstep of my childhood home, the familiar scent of pine mingling with the faintest hint of autumn's decay. The leaves had begun their slow transformation, painting the trees in shades of gold and crimson, but I felt more like a dull shade of gray, caught in the maelstrom of my own conflicting choices. Inside, the echoes of laughter that once filled these walls were now replaced with the muted tones of strained conversations and unspoken grievances.

Ivy's face flashed through my mind, her expression a whirlwind of hurt and disappointment. My heart twisted at the thought. Confiding in her had felt liberating in the moment, like shedding a heavy coat in the warmth of spring sunlight. But now, standing in the shadow of my family obligations, I was left feeling exposed and vulnerable. I could still hear her voice, edged with disbelief, questioning how I could prioritize my family's needs over our friendship. It gnawed at me, a relentless reminder that I had crossed an invisible line.

"Are you coming in, or are you just going to stand there all day?" My mother's voice cut through the haze, an invitation laced with exasperation. She stood at the threshold, arms crossed, her gaze sharp as a hawk's. I felt like I was back in high school, nervously fidgeting under her scrutiny, trying to convince her I was more than a wayward child.

"I'm coming," I replied, forcing a smile that felt more like a grimace. The door creaked open, and I stepped inside, the familiar creak of the floorboards beneath me a haunting reminder of the countless times I had run through these halls, blissfully unaware of the complexities waiting just beyond childhood.

As I entered the living room, I was greeted by the comforting yet suffocating aroma of my mother's baking. Her famous apple pie was cooling on the counter, a sweet distraction from the chaos looming just below the surface. I could almost hear Ivy's teasing laughter, the way she would roll her eyes when I declared it the best in the world. But today, that memory was bitter, tainted by the growing distance between us.

"Your father will be home soon," my mother announced, her tone shifting to one of expectation, as if I were a puzzle piece she was trying to fit into a larger picture. "He's been asking about you. You know how worried he gets."

Worry. It was a word that hung in the air like a dark cloud, an omnipresent weight. My father's well-intentioned concern often felt like a noose tightening around my throat, choking the life out of my independence. I could see it now, the way he would lean against the doorframe, his brow furrowed, as he attempted to probe the depths of my mind and heart, searching for the missing pieces of me.

"I'm fine, Mom. Really," I said, forcing a lightness into my voice that felt foreign. "Just been busy with work."

"Busy with work?" she repeated, a hint of disbelief slipping through. "You've barely been home this month. Is it work or something else?"

The question hung between us, electrifying the air. I could feel the pressure building, the unspoken words ready to burst forth, but I swallowed them down, unwilling to expose the fragile thread that connected me to Ivy and the gnawing guilt that consumed me.

"Just work," I insisted, a little too firmly, and the momentary flicker of concern in her eyes deepened into a frown. I wished I could tell her everything—the fracture in my friendship, the pressure of my family's expectations, the shadow of uncertainty that Nathaniel cast over my heart. But how could I? Each revelation felt like a stone added to the burden I was already carrying.

The door swung open, and my father stepped inside, his presence filling the room like the first rays of sunlight after a storm. "There she is!" he boomed, his voice buoyant. "I was starting to think you'd forgotten how to come home."

I forced another smile, my heart a chaotic symphony of emotions. His warmth wrapped around me, but it only deepened the chasm of guilt gnawing at my insides. I was both there and not there, present in body but absent in spirit, my mind racing with thoughts of Ivy and the choices I had made.

"I was just chatting with your mother about how busy you've been," he said, settling into the armchair as if it were his throne. "You're working too hard, you know. You need to take time for yourself. We have dinner plans with the Thompsons tonight; you remember them, right?"

I nodded, though I couldn't shake the unease curling in my stomach. The Thompsons were lovely people, but tonight, they represented everything I was trying to escape—their perfect family dynamics, their perfect little lives, and the unspoken expectations that loomed like storm clouds overhead.

"I'll be fine," I said, my voice a mix of determination and reluctance. "It'll be good to see everyone."

Yet, as I feigned enthusiasm, all I could think about was Ivy's face, the hurt etched on her features as I'd chosen my family over her. Each laugh shared over dinner would be a reminder of the fracture between us, a reminder of my choices and the ever-widening rift that had begun to unfurl beneath me.

The evening passed in a blur of smiles and small talk, the Thompsons' banter almost a musical backdrop to my internal monologue. I played my part, laughing and nodding, but inside, I felt like a ship adrift, lost in a fog of my own making. Nathaniel's supportive words echoed in my mind, a siren call urging me to be honest, to confront the brewing storm within me. But the thought of diving into those turbulent waters was daunting, as if I were standing on the edge of a precipice, unable to decide whether to leap or retreat.

And then, as if summoned by my restless thoughts, Nathaniel's text vibrated against the table, a beacon of light piercing through the gathering gloom. "Hey, thinking of you. Want to talk later?"

In that moment, I was caught between the familial comfort surrounding me and the flickering flame of connection I felt with him. My heart raced, caught in the tumult of loyalty and desire, the line between duty and personal happiness increasingly blurred.

I stole a glance at my parents, engrossed in conversation, and a part of me craved the sanctuary of Nathaniel's understanding, the way he always seemed to peel back the layers I carefully constructed around myself. With a swift tap of my fingers, I replied, "Yes, I'd like that." The promise of that conversation felt like a lifeline, but it also tightened the knot of uncertainty deep within me, each word pulling me further into the storm I was trying so desperately to avoid.

The evening air was thick with the fragrance of spiced apple cider and cinnamon, an inviting scent that clung to my clothes as I made my way down the narrow street toward the café where Nathaniel and I had arranged to meet. The golden light spilling from the windows cast playful shadows on the pavement, illuminating the world in a way that felt almost surreal. The bustle of the city was alive with chatter and laughter, yet I felt oddly detached, as if I were moving through a dreamscape where everything was vivid and bright, yet entirely out of reach.

As I pushed open the door, the soft jingle of the bell above announced my arrival, pulling me into a realm of warmth and camaraderie. The café was charming, adorned with mismatched furniture and eclectic artwork that created an atmosphere as inviting as a hug from an old friend. I spotted Nathaniel at a corner table, his familiar silhouette framed by the soft glow of the overhead lights, a half-empty mug of steaming coffee before him. He looked up as

I approached, a smile breaking across his face that made my heart flutter in unexpected ways.

"Hey there, light of my life," he teased, his eyes sparkling with that mischievous glint I adored. "Did you swim through a sea of family obligations to get here?"

"Something like that," I replied, sinking into the chair opposite him. "I was almost swallowed whole by my parents' expectations, but I managed to escape." The weight of my earlier encounters was still heavy, and while I attempted to appear lighthearted, I could feel the undercurrent of tension crackling between us.

"I'm glad you did," he said, leaning forward, his expression shifting from playful to serious. "I wanted to check in. You seemed... well, you seemed a bit overwhelmed the last time we spoke."

His concern pierced through my facade, and I felt my heart twist uncomfortably in my chest. "It's just family stuff, you know? They're trying to make sense of me, and I'm trying to make sense of everything—life, choices, Ivy... it's a lot."

Nathaniel's brow furrowed, and I could sense the gears turning in his mind. "And Ivy? Is she still angry?"

I sighed, the sound escaping me like a balloon deflating. "Yeah, she is. I get it, though. I've put her in a tough position, and I don't know how to fix it. I'm caught between wanting to be there for her and feeling this pull back to my family, who seem to need me now more than ever."

"Friendships shouldn't feel like a tug-of-war," he said, his voice gentle but firm, as if he were trying to anchor me to a solid ground amidst my swirling thoughts. "You deserve to find a balance that allows you to breathe, not suffocate under pressure."

The words struck me, a truth I had been unwilling to face. "What if there is no balance?" I countered, my voice barely above a whisper. "What if I end up losing both my family and my best friend in the process?"

"Then we figure it out together," he replied, his tone resolute. "You're not alone in this, you know. You're allowed to lean on me."

I felt a rush of warmth wash over me at his words. Nathaniel always had this uncanny ability to make me feel safe, like I could unravel all my tangled threads without fear of judgment. Still, an echo of guilt lingered in my mind, a voice that reminded me of Ivy's hurt. "What about us?" I asked, the question hanging between us like an uninvited guest. "Are you okay with all this? With me being so preoccupied?"

He hesitated, his expression turning contemplative. "I'm here because I want to be, not because I have to be. But I can't help but wonder if you're fully committed to what we have."

I felt a sharp sting at his words, a defensive wall rising instinctively within me. "How can you question my dedication? I'm here, aren't I? I've always been here!"

"Being physically present doesn't always mean you're emotionally available," he countered gently, his voice steady but insistent. "I just need to know you're choosing us, too."

The way he phrased it made me feel like I was on the edge of a precipice, peering into an abyss that could swallow me whole. "I don't want to choose," I said, my voice quivering as I fought to hold back the flood of emotion threatening to spill over. "I want to have both, but it feels impossible."

"Sometimes the impossible becomes possible when you're willing to face the truth," he said softly, his eyes locked onto mine with an intensity that made my pulse quicken. "What truth do you need to face, really?"

I inhaled sharply, the words lodged in my throat like shards of glass. "That I can't be everything to everyone. That I can't fix this mess without losing something along the way."

"That's brave to admit," he said, a hint of admiration coloring his tone. "But losing something doesn't mean you lose everything. It means you're making space for what truly matters."

We shared a moment of silence, the weight of our conversation wrapping around us like a warm blanket, yet heavy with unspoken fears. I wanted to scream at the unfairness of it all—the way life twisted and turned, leaving us grappling with choices that felt impossibly tangled.

"I wish it were simpler," I murmured, breaking the silence, the wistfulness in my voice betraying my longing for clarity.

"Life isn't meant to be simple; it's meant to be lived," Nathaniel said, his tone lightening again, an attempt to diffuse the tension that had settled like a storm cloud. "But I can promise you this: I'll always be here, right in the eye of the storm, ready to weather it together."

His words struck a chord deep within me, resonating with a flicker of hope. "And what if the storm doesn't end?" I asked, the vulnerability creeping back into my voice.

"Then we find shelter, my dear," he said, his smile reappearing like sunshine breaking through clouds. "And if that shelter happens to be a cozy café with pie, so much the better."

I couldn't help but laugh, the sound bubbling forth like a refreshing spring after a long winter. "Is that your way of suggesting we get some pie, or are you offering to be my emotional support dessert?"

"Both," he replied, grinning. "A two-for-one special. Now, let's conquer those calories together."

As I felt the tension ease and warmth settle in my chest, I realized that in this moment, I wasn't just navigating the turbulent waters of my life alone; I had a partner ready to face the chaos beside me. But just as I began to settle into that comforting thought, my phone buzzed again, a notification that pulled me back into the reality I had tried to escape.

I glanced at the screen and felt my heart plummet. Ivy's name lit up the display, her message a tidal wave crashing over my fragile sense of calm. "We need to talk. It can't wait."

My stomach twisted, a knot tightening around the uncertainty swirling in my mind. "I'll be right back," I said, the lightness of our earlier banter evaporating in an instant as I stood to take the call, my heart racing with a mix of dread and anticipation. I didn't know what awaited me on the other end, but I could feel the storm brewing, ready to burst forth, and I was powerless to stop it.

I glanced at the screen, my heart racing as Ivy's message blinked like a warning light, bright and insistent. My pulse quickened, an unwelcome rush of anxiety flooding through me. The weight of the world shifted on my shoulders as I took a breath, steeling myself for whatever storm was about to erupt. I had hoped that maybe, just maybe, our friendship could weather the turbulence of my decisions. But the dread pooling in my stomach suggested otherwise.

"Is everything okay?" Nathaniel's voice cut through my swirling thoughts as I turned slightly away from him, trying to absorb Ivy's words. "You look like you just saw a ghost."

"Not a ghost, but it might as well be," I replied, forcing a smile that felt more like a grimace. "It's Ivy. She wants to talk, and I think I know what it's about."

"You want me to go?" he offered, concern lacing his tone.

I shook my head, the thought of him leaving felt like casting away my lifeline. "No, stay. I might need the support."

Nathaniel nodded, but his brow remained furrowed, a silent acknowledgment that the road ahead wouldn't be easy. I tapped Ivy's message open, the words jumping out at me with a harsh clarity. "We need to talk. It can't wait." I could almost hear the frustration behind those words, sharp as a knife.

With a deep breath, I dialed her number, the ringing in my ear punctuating the silence in the café. Nathaniel leaned back in his chair, watching me intently, and I could feel his gaze like a warm embrace. Ivy picked up on the second ring, her breath hitching as she answered.

"Why did you ghost me?" Her voice was raw, edged with an emotion that sent a pang of guilt through me.

"I didn't ghost you, Ivy," I replied, trying to keep my tone even, though my heart raced. "I just... I've been overwhelmed."

"Overwhelmed? You're telling me you're overwhelmed while I'm over here feeling completely abandoned?" Her words hit hard, each syllable dripping with disappointment.

"I know, and I'm sorry. I didn't mean to make you feel that way," I said, desperation creeping into my voice. "It's just that my family needs me right now, and I'm trying to balance everything."

"Balance? That's rich coming from you, who seems to have tipped the scales toward family without a second thought," Ivy shot back, her frustration igniting like a spark in dry grass. "What about us? What about our friendship?"

"I want to be there for you," I pleaded, feeling the walls closing in. "But I can't just ignore my family's needs. They're going through a tough time."

A heavy silence settled over the line, thick and suffocating. I could practically hear her heart break, and it was a sound that reverberated in my chest, each thud a reminder of what I was risking. "You know what? Maybe I don't want to talk about this right now," she finally said, her voice trembling slightly. "I just can't believe you'd choose them over me."

"I didn't choose them over you!" I nearly shouted, drawing a few glances from nearby tables. Nathaniel raised an eyebrow, his expression a mix of concern and curiosity. "I just need some time to sort things out. I thought you'd understand."

"Understand?" Ivy laughed, but there was no joy in it—only bitterness. "I'm starting to think you don't understand anything about our friendship, about how much you mean to me."

"I do! I just..." My voice faltered. I couldn't find the words to articulate the mess I was in. "I'm scared, Ivy. Scared that I'm losing you and scared that I'll regret not being there for my family."

"Maybe it's already too late," she whispered, the weight of her words crashing down on me like a tidal wave.

The call ended with a soft click that echoed in my ears, a finality that felt like a slap. I dropped the phone onto the table, staring into space, while Nathaniel reached across the table, his hand enveloping mine. The warmth was grounding, yet it couldn't chase away the chill creeping into my heart.

"Are you okay?" he asked, his voice low, filled with concern.

"No," I admitted, tears prickling the corners of my eyes. "I just made it worse."

"Hey," he said gently, lifting my chin with his fingertips so I met his gaze. "You haven't lost her yet. You're both just in a rough spot. Talk to her, and be honest about everything. You're trying to balance a lot, and it's okay to acknowledge that."

I took a shaky breath, the tension in my chest shifting slightly at his words. "What if she doesn't want to talk? What if I've ruined everything?"

"Then you fight for it," he replied, squeezing my hand. "Friendships are worth fighting for. Just like relationships. Just like us."

His confidence was reassuring, a glimmer of hope amid the swirling chaos of my emotions. But the truth gnawed at me: even if I fought for Ivy, what would that look like? And how would I reconcile my obligations to my family with the fissures forming in my friendships?

"Let's talk to Ivy together," Nathaniel suggested, as if reading my mind. "Maybe having both of us there will help. If she sees you're not alone, she might feel more inclined to listen."

I hesitated, my heart racing at the idea. "Do you really think she'd want to see you?"

"If she doesn't, that's her choice. But I think she'll appreciate the effort. It shows you care."

The resolve in his voice ignited a flicker of determination within me. "Okay, let's do it," I said, the adrenaline coursing through my veins. "But where? I don't think she'll want to meet at the café, and I can't face my house just yet."

"Let's take a walk," Nathaniel suggested, his eyes lighting up with the thrill of a plan. "There's a park nearby. It's quieter and might give you both space to breathe."

As we stood up, I felt a mix of dread and hope swirling within me. The park loomed before us, an expanse of greenery that held the potential for clarity—or chaos. We stepped out into the cool evening air, the sky painted with strokes of pink and purple, a canvas stretching out like a promise.

As we approached the park, I felt the familiar weight of anxiety settle in my stomach again. The possibility of encountering Ivy felt like an impending storm, dark clouds gathering overhead. I didn't know how this would unfold or if I could face the reality of our fractured bond.

Suddenly, my phone buzzed again, a jolt that nearly made me jump. I pulled it out, my heart racing as I glanced at the screen. Another message from Ivy, and my stomach dropped at the urgency behind it: "I'm at the park. We need to talk. Now."

Panic set in as I exchanged a glance with Nathaniel. "She's here," I breathed, my throat suddenly dry. "What if she's decided she's done with me?"

"Then you'll have to convince her otherwise," he said, his grip reassuring as we approached the park entrance. But as we stepped inside, I caught sight of Ivy standing near the fountain, her back turned to us, the fading light casting a halo around her figure. She looked fragile, a lone statue amid the chaos of the bustling park.

And then, in that instant, I realized something was off—something felt wrong. As I took a step closer, my heart thundered, a sense of foreboding wrapping around me. Ivy's body stiffened, and before I could reach her, she turned, her expression unreadable, the tension between us palpable as the weight of our choices hung in the air.

"Can we just talk?" I started, but before I could finish, I saw the look in her eyes—a mix of fear and resolve. "I don't think I can do this anymore."

The world around me faded, and all that existed was that moment, the knife-edge of her words slicing through the air. The cliff I had been teetering on suddenly crumbled beneath my feet, and as the ground fell away, I was left grasping for anything solid to hold onto.

Chapter 9: A Leap of Faith

The room buzzed with laughter and the clinking of glasses, a symphony of joy and celebration that enveloped me as I surveyed the vibrant gathering in Ivy's cozy living room. Twinkling fairy lights draped from the ceiling like captured stars, casting a warm glow over the scene. Tables laden with homemade cakes, pastries, and colorful balloons danced above our heads in a jubilant display. In one corner, Ivy's niece and a couple of giggling friends took turns attempting to blow out the candles on a cake decorated with too many sprinkles and not enough finesse, while Ivy herself radiated the kind of joy that only a birthday could bring.

I stood there, clutching a glass of punch that had long since lost its chill, my thoughts swirling like the colorful streamers floating above us. Just days ago, I had felt a sense of clarity; I knew what I wanted, yet now, a tide of uncertainty threatened to drown me. It wasn't just the raucous laughter that made my heart race; it was the uninvited tension that hung in the air like a fog. The kind that signals a storm is brewing, just out of sight.

As I drifted toward the snack table, I noticed Ivy across the room, her laughter pealing like a bell, each chime vibrant and rich. She was so radiant, drawing everyone in, unaware of the weight I carried. She was my best friend, my anchor, and here she was celebrating another trip around the sun, blissfully ignorant of my swirling tempest of feelings. I should have been wholly absorbed in her happiness, yet the gnawing sensation of what lay unaddressed crept back.

"Another punch?" came a voice, smooth as silk, snapping me back to reality. I turned, and there he was—Nathaniel. Just as handsome as I remembered, with tousled hair that hinted at too many late nights and a charming smile that could disarm even the most formidable of foes. His presence sent a jolt through me, like a thunderclap on a calm day. How had I forgotten how effortlessly he could command a room?

"Thanks, but I think I've had enough sugar for one evening," I replied, attempting a nonchalant smile while my insides did cartwheels. "The punch is basically liquid sugar at this point."

"Just like Ivy," he quipped, gesturing toward her with a playful roll of his eyes. "Too much sweetness for one night can lead to chaos."

"Isn't that the truth?" I chuckled, finding solace in the familiarity of his banter. "But it's her birthday. Chaos is practically mandated."

His gaze turned serious for a moment, probing, as if trying to read the chapters unwritten on my face. "How have you been?"

The question, simple yet layered, hung between us like a taut string ready to snap. The last time we'd spoken, I had poured out my heart, my fears laid bare like an open book, and yet here we stood, the echoes of that conversation looming over us. My answer danced on the tip of my tongue, but the truth was slippery, like trying to catch smoke with bare hands.

"I've been—adjusting," I finally replied, choosing my words with care. "You know, just figuring things out."

"Figuring things out," he echoed, nodding slowly as if he could decipher my hidden meanings. "That sounds... precarious."

"Like walking a tightrope," I joked, though my voice held a tremor that betrayed the façade of lightness. "One misstep, and who knows what'll happen."

The corners of his mouth quirked upward. "Or you could find the balance and make it to the other side. You've always been good at that."

His words wrapped around me, a bittersweet comfort as I recalled moments spent together, balancing between the safety of friendship and the thrill of something more. A knot tightened in my stomach, not from fear but from the realization of how much I still cared for him, how much I craved to leap off that precipice into the unknown. But what would that look like? What would I lose and gain?

"Come on!" Ivy's voice pierced through the haze, rallying everyone for the traditional birthday circle. "It's time for presents and speeches!"

The crowd shifted, and I felt a pull toward the growing energy, yet my heart remained anchored to the conversation I had just begun with Nathaniel. He stepped closer, the distance shrinking until I could smell the faint trace of his cologne, fresh and inviting.

"Are you going to join us?" he asked, his eyes sparkling with mischief. "Or do you plan to keep dodging the spotlight?"

"Spotlight?" I scoffed, rolling my eyes as the tension thickened like molasses. "I'd rather be the ghost in the corner."

"Ghosts have their charm," he replied, a playful challenge dancing in his tone. "But I think it's time you claimed your space."

His encouragement, so deceptively simple, ignited something deep within me—a flicker of bravery hidden beneath layers of doubt. I had spent too long tiptoeing around my own desires, pretending they were trivial when, in truth, they felt monumental. As the call for speeches rose like a tide, I felt the swell of determination swell with it. Maybe this was the moment I had been waiting for, the catalyst that could propel me into the unknown.

"Let's do this," I whispered under my breath, more to myself than anyone else. The rush of anticipation coursed through me as I stepped into the circle, heart pounding like a drum. Ivy looked at me expectantly, her smile a beacon, and I knew it was time to cast off the chains of hesitation. It was time to leap.

As I stepped into the circle, the warmth of the gathered crowd enveloped me like a soft embrace, filling the gaps that doubt had carved into my heart. Ivy's beaming face was a lifebuoy in the swell of my uncertainty, urging me forward. The room was a tapestry of anticipation, faces lit with eager curiosity, friends and family leaning in, hungry for my words. I could feel Nathaniel's gaze, a steady presence at my back, a silent support that made me bolder than I'd ever thought possible.

"Okay, everyone," Ivy declared, her excitement palpable, "let's hear from our guest of honor. This is not just my party; it's a moment for all of us to celebrate life!"

I could hear the laughter bubbling beneath her words, a blend of nostalgia and joy, but my heart thudded like a restless drum. "Well, I wouldn't call myself a guest of honor," I said, attempting a light-hearted tone. "Unless that means I get to eat cake first."

The laughter that rippled through the crowd provided a momentary cushion against the weight of the moment. Yet, I could feel a deeper current beneath the surface—a surge of expectation. I swallowed hard, knowing I had to go beyond the punchline and step into the truth I had avoided for too long.

"Alright, I'll make it quick," I said, gaining momentum. "I just want to say how much I admire Ivy. She's the kind of friend who makes you feel like you can conquer the world, even on days when you can barely get out of bed."

Ivy's eyes sparkled with pride, and my heart swelled. "And if we're being honest," I continued, allowing a smile to tease the corners of my mouth, "having a birthday means you're one year closer to being an even more fabulous version of yourself, which is terrifying for the rest of us."

Laughter erupted, and I felt myself relax, but the urge to dive deeper lingered like an itch I couldn't scratch. I looked around the circle, locking eyes with familiar faces, each one carrying a history that felt both comforting and suffocating. The laughter faded as the weight of my unspoken truth settled back in.

"I think we all have dreams and aspirations," I ventured, voice steadying as I held Ivy's gaze. "But sometimes, we're too afraid to chase them. We hold back because we fear what others might think or what might happen if we fail." I felt the collective breath of the room, every eye now fixated on me, drawn into the sincerity of my words. "I've spent too long being afraid. Afraid to ask for what I want, afraid to leap."

The silence that followed was pregnant with tension, as if everyone was holding their breath. Ivy leaned closer, her smile now a beacon of encouragement. "What are you saying?" she whispered, a playful challenge in her tone.

"I'm saying I'm ready to leap, Ivy. I'm tired of tiptoeing around my own desires. I want to pursue my passion for art, to finally show my work, even if it means facing rejection." I took a deep breath, the words spilling out as if they had been waiting, bound and silenced, for this very moment. "I want to paint and create, even if it scares me."

A murmur ran through the crowd, a blend of surprise and support, the air thickening with unspoken solidarity. It was exhilarating and terrifying all at once. I could see the expressions of my friends shifting, and in the corner, Nathaniel's gaze sharpened with intrigue.

"Now, wait a minute," he interjected, stepping forward as the crowd began to whisper among themselves. "You're saying you want to pursue art? As in, exhibit it? Like, put it out there for the world to see?"

"Yes," I said, surprised by the fierce conviction that surged through me. "I want to share my work. I've been holding back for far too long, hiding behind excuses. It's time I put myself out there."

The weight of those words settled around me like a warm blanket, enveloping my fear in a tender embrace. Nathaniel's expression shifted, and I couldn't tell if it was concern or admiration. "That's a huge step," he said carefully, a spark of admiration lighting up his eyes. "What's holding you back, then?"

My breath hitched as I thought of all the missed opportunities and quiet evenings spent painting in solitude, yearning for validation but shying away from the spotlight. "I guess... I'm scared. Scared of what people will think, scared of failing, of being judged."

"But what if you soar?" he challenged, the gentle teasing in his voice buoying my courage. "What if you create something magnificent that brings you joy and others, too? Isn't that worth the risk?"

His words hung in the air, resonating deeply within me. The conversation shifted as Ivy chimed in. "Exactly! Life is all about taking chances. This is your time to shine. No more hiding in the shadows!"

With the cheers of encouragement from my friends filling the room, I felt the warmth of their belief wrapping around me, pushing away the shadows of doubt that had lingered for too long. "So, let's make a toast," Ivy declared, raising her glass high, her enthusiasm infectious. "To leaps of faith and chasing dreams!"

Glasses clinked together, laughter bubbling up as the atmosphere transformed into a heady mix of joy and hope. I looked around at the faces I cherished, knowing I had ignited a spark that would push me further into my own journey.

"Okay, I'll take that leap," I declared, voice ringing with newfound strength. "I'll start by submitting my work to local galleries. One step at a time, right?"

The collective support surged around me, but just as I felt the warmth of that newfound courage settle in, a thought flickered like a candle flame in the wind. What if I failed? What if I put my heart on display and it was met with indifference? But I quashed the fear, knowing that I had to let go, had to dive into the chaos and embrace whatever came next.

"Here's to embracing chaos and finding magic in the unexpected!" I toasted, raising my glass, determination swelling in my chest. As the cheers erupted around me, the world felt vast and open, a canvas waiting for my brush. The night, once cloaked in uncertainty, now shimmered with potential. I had taken the first step, and I felt a thrill ripple through me. It was time to paint my destiny with bold strokes, no matter where the journey led.

As the laughter faded and the remnants of my toast hung in the air, I felt an exhilarating rush of energy coursing through me. The crowd began to disperse, eager to dive into the cake and the bounty of snacks, but I stood rooted, heart racing with the thrill of what I had just declared. Around me, conversations sparked, vibrant and lively, yet my thoughts drifted to the quiet anticipation in Nathaniel's eyes.

"Impressive," he said, leaning closer as if sharing a secret. "You really went for it. I didn't know you had it in you."

"I didn't either," I admitted, a nervous laugh escaping my lips. "But it felt right. Terrifyingly right."

"Terrifying can be good," he replied, a playful smile teasing the corners of his mouth. "It means you're pushing boundaries. What's your first move, then? When do you start your campaign for world domination?"

"World domination might be a bit ambitious," I shot back, the banter flowing easily. "I was thinking of starting with a local gallery. I have a few pieces I've been hiding."

"Sounds like the perfect first step. Just don't let your nerves talk you out of it," he cautioned, the seriousness in his voice grounding me. "You owe it to yourself to try."

His words wrapped around me like a warm blanket, igniting a flicker of determination in my chest. "You know what? You're right. I should start working on my portfolio tomorrow."

"Tomorrow, huh? Living on the edge, I see," he teased, arching an eyebrow. "A whole day of procrastination before diving in."

"Hey, even artists need a little time to prepare for greatness," I shot back playfully, grateful for the levity he brought into the moment.

As the party swirled around us, a familiar sense of camaraderie wrapped around me, a safety net of shared dreams and laughter. I glanced over at Ivy, who was busy unwrapping presents, her delight contagious. It was hard to believe that I had almost shied away from this, from the joy of being surrounded by people who believed in me, who cheered for my ambitions.

"Alright, enough about me," I said, turning my focus back to Nathaniel. "What about you? What grand plans are you hatching these days?"

He hesitated, a shadow flickering across his features. "Actually, I'm thinking of taking a leap myself."

"Really? You?" I teased, unable to suppress the grin that spread across my face. "What could possibly intimidate the great Nathaniel?"

He chuckled, running a hand through his hair, an endearing habit I remembered well. "I'm not as invincible as I appear, you know. I've been considering starting my own design firm."

"Now that's a leap worth taking!" I exclaimed, excitement bubbling in my chest. "What's stopping you?"

His gaze darkened, the momentary lightness giving way to something heavier. "A lot of things, actually. Mainly fear. Fear of failing, fear of leaving a secure job. You know how it is."

"Maybe we both need to hold each other accountable," I suggested, my heart racing at the thought of embarking on this journey together. "You help me with my art, and I'll help you get your business off the ground."

"Deal," he said, his smile returning, and it felt like a pact, a silent agreement that bonded us in our shared uncertainties.

But as the evening wore on, a new tension threaded itself into the fabric of the party. I caught snippets of conversation drifting my way—snatches of gossip that felt oddly pointed. "I heard she's finally going to show her work." "I can't believe he's thinking of going solo." The words danced in the air, prickling at the edges of my confidence.

"Hey, did you hear that?" I whispered to Nathaniel, nodding toward a small group of Ivy's friends clustered near the snack table, their laughter a little too sharp, their glances a little too curious.

"Let them talk," Nathaniel replied, his tone dismissive, yet his expression betrayed concern. "They don't know what it takes to create something from nothing. It's not their journey."

"Right," I said, though doubt curled in my stomach like a viper. "But what if they're right? What if I'm not good enough?"

"Stop that," he said, his voice firm yet gentle. "You've spent too long in your own head. Remember, this is your time. Don't let the noise drown out your voice."

I nodded, but the knot of anxiety tightened as I glanced back at Ivy, who was now beaming at a particularly glittery present, her joy illuminating the room. It felt wrong to let my insecurities overshadow her happiness.

"I need a moment," I said suddenly, needing space to gather my thoughts. Nathaniel nodded, concern etched on his face, but I waved him off, knowing I needed to step away from the swirling energy for just a moment.

I slipped outside onto the small balcony, the cool night air washing over me like a balm. The stars glittered overhead, and for a moment, I allowed myself to breathe deeply, inhaling the scents of fresh grass and blooming jasmine. But as I leaned against the railing, a feeling of unease crept back in.

Was this really the right decision? What if I exposed myself only to face harsh criticism? I needed to embrace my path, to push beyond the fear. But as my thoughts spiraled, I heard footsteps behind me.

"Hey," Nathaniel's voice broke through the darkness, smooth and calming. "You okay?"

"Just needed some air," I replied, forcing a smile. "It's a little overwhelming in there."

"Want to talk about it?"

"No, I think I just need to remind myself of why I'm doing this," I said, staring into the night, attempting to find my footing again. "I can't let fear win."

"Good," he said, stepping beside me. "Fear can be a slippery slope, but I know you can overcome it."

As I turned to meet his gaze, I felt a wave of gratitude wash over me. Before I could respond, a sudden noise startled me—a sharp crack, like the sound of something breaking. We both turned, eyes wide, to see a figure emerging from the shadows, stepping into the flickering light of the porch.

"Nice party you've got here," came a voice, dripping with mockery, the shadow looming larger as it stepped into view. My heart raced, recognizing the face that haunted my past, and with it came an overwhelming rush of uncertainty.

Chapter 10: Threads of Memory

Dust motes danced lazily in the sunbeams that spilled through the sheer curtains of my childhood bedroom, casting a warm glow over the faded photographs sprawled across my mother's floor. Each snapshot whispered stories long tucked away, nudging at my heart with both tenderness and melancholy. I crouched down, my fingers brushing the glossy surfaces, each one a portal to another time—a time when laughter echoed through these walls like a sweet melody, before the world outside pulled me away.

In one photograph, I was a wild-haired child, perhaps six or seven, wearing a bright pink dress that my mother had lovingly sewn. My curls were a glorious mess, framing my face as I beamed at the camera, a balloon clutched tightly in one hand and a piece of chocolate smeared across my cheek. The memory of that day flickered back to me, the summer air warm against my skin, the taste of chocolate a delightful treasure as I ran through our backyard, pretending to be a princess, a dreamer, a star.

Time played cruel tricks on memory; those innocent days seemed to glow with an unattainable brightness. Now, as I flipped through the collection, each photo seemed to shimmer with a bittersweet glow, reminding me of the price I paid for the dreams I chased. The bustling streets of New York, with their kaleidoscope of sights and sounds, felt so distant from the peace of Meadowbrook. With every turn of a page, I could almost hear the soft rustle of fabric and the murmur of voices whispering dreams in my ear, a reminder of the ambitious teenager who used to sketch designs on napkins in the local café.

The thought made me chuckle, yet there was a tightness in my chest that wouldn't let go. The friends who once swirled around me in a whirlwind of creativity had faded into the background, each pursuing their own paths in a world that didn't wait for anyone. But as I lingered over the smiling faces, I found myself aching for those connections—the shared dreams, the laughter echoing in empty halls, the late-night talks that lingered over mugs of tea.

Tucking a strand of hair behind my ear, I pulled out a small, worn journal from the depths of a cardboard box. Its cover was marred with creases and stains, evidence of years spent wedged between the clutter of teenage aspirations. I opened it carefully, half-expecting the pages to crumble under my touch. Instead, they opened like a portal to my past, revealing a treasure trove of sketches and notes that once sparked joy and excitement.

The first page depicted a flowing dress, whimsical and ethereal, the kind of creation I had dreamed of seeing on the runways of New York. I could almost hear the faint strains of a fashion show in my mind, the rhythm of heels clicking against polished floors, the gasp of an audience captivated by the artistry. It wasn't just about fabric and stitches; it was about crafting a narrative, breathing life into a vision. As I traced the lines of the sketch, a flicker of my old passion ignited deep within me, fierce and unyielding.

This journal was not just a collection of sketches; it was a map of dreams, a reminder of who I once was and who I yearned to become again. I could feel the determination brewing in my veins as the memories wrapped around me like a familiar shawl. I had traded the promise of my dreams for the perceived safety of a more traditional life, yet the longing for that vibrant world still pulsed within me, relentless as the tide.

The more I flipped through its pages, the more I felt the threads of my past pulling me back to New York, urging me to reclaim the pieces I had lost. I could picture myself walking those bustling streets again, the wind tousling my hair as I confidently navigated the cityscape, each corner a canvas waiting for my touch. I longed to stand in a room filled with fabric swatches and sewing machines, surrounded by kindred spirits who shared my relentless pursuit of beauty.

Yet, that image was quickly tempered by the weight of uncertainty. What if the dreams I had once held so dearly were merely fleeting fantasies, illusions wrapped in the silk of nostalgia? The thought gnawed at me, dragging me back to the present moment, the clutter of my mother's house closing in like a warm embrace tinged with the sorrow of lost time.

"Hey, are you planning to move back or just daydream?" my mother's voice broke through the haze, pulling me out of my reverie. She stood in the doorway, arms crossed, a half-smile playing on her lips, curiosity dancing in her eyes.

"Maybe a little of both?" I replied, unable to suppress a grin. "I found something that might just be a sign."

Her brows raised, interest piqued. "A sign, you say? Should I be worried?"

"Not at all," I laughed, the sound bubbling up as I held up the journal. "More like an old friend reminding me of who I used to be. It's just... I need to figure out how to weave all these threads together again."

My mother stepped into the room, the familiar scent of her lavender-scented lotion enveloping me. She leaned against the doorframe, studying me with a knowing gaze. "Sometimes, you have to revisit the past to find your way forward, you know. Just promise me you won't lose yourself in it."

"Promise," I said, though the uncertainty loomed large, a shadow at the edge of my renewed determination. As I watched her nod, her expression softening, I felt a flicker of hope. Perhaps returning to New York wouldn't mean severing ties with my past but weaving them into something new, something vibrant and alive.

The journal lay open in my lap, its pages fluttering gently as a breeze slipped through the half-open window. Each flicker of paper felt like a whisper, a call to rekindle the fire that once burned so brightly in my heart. My mother leaned against the doorframe, arms crossed, a smile playing on her lips as if she could sense the shifting tides of my thoughts.

"Do you need to grab a designer's degree or just a few more naps before you head back?" she quipped, her teasing tone breaking the weight of nostalgia that threatened to envelop me.

"Both, maybe," I shot back, laughter bubbling up. "But I'm pretty sure the naps can wait. You know I work best on a caffeine high."

"Ah yes, the secret of creativity: coffee and delusions of grandeur." She stepped inside, her hair catching the light like spun gold, and settled onto the floor beside me, peering at the sketches with a mix of pride and curiosity.

"What is this one?" she asked, pointing to a particularly ambitious drawing of a gown that spiraled out like a blooming flower. The fabric seemed to shimmer under her gaze, as if it could leap off the page and twirl into existence.

"That," I began, brushing my fingers over the delicate lines, "was my attempt at creating something magical for a charity gala. I wanted it to embody hope, you know? A bit of whimsy with a touch of elegance."

"Looks like it's got your signature flair. You've always had a knack for the dramatic." Her voice was light, but I could hear the underlying seriousness in her tone. "What happened? Why did you stop?"

The question hung in the air, a delicate thread waiting to be tugged. I hesitated, aware of the thin veil of vulnerability that loomed. "Life happened, I guess. Responsibilities, expectations... I got caught in the spiral of what I should be rather than what I wanted to be."

She nodded, her gaze thoughtful. "It's easy to lose sight of ourselves in that whirlpool. But look at you now—rooting through your past, reclaiming what's yours. You're not a lost cause, dear."

Her encouragement flickered through me, igniting a warmth I hadn't realized I craved. Maybe I didn't need to shoulder the weight of that 'should.' Perhaps I could simply be.

With renewed determination, I set the journal aside, my heart racing as a plan began to unfurl within me. "You know what? I think I will go back to New York. Not just for me, but for all those dreams I've stuffed into this house."

My mother's smile widened, a glimmer of excitement in her eyes. "And what's the first step in this grand adventure?"

"Finding a studio," I declared, the words spilling out with an eagerness I hadn't felt in years. "I need a space where I can create, a sanctuary where inspiration flows like a river."

"I assume you're not looking to house-hunt in Meadowbrook?" she teased.

"Meadowbrook has its charms, but I think my art is a bit too unruly for its quaintness. New York is where the chaos breathes life into creativity."

Her laughter chimed, filling the room with a sweetness that felt like home. "Then let's start looking! But first, how about we celebrate your grand return to the art world with some of my famous lemon bars? They might just give you the zing you need for inspiration."

The offer brought a smile to my face as I nodded enthusiastically. "Yes, please! If they can spark creativity as they do joy, I might just design a whole line after them."

As she bustled off to the kitchen, I couldn't help but feel a surge of hope. I turned my attention back to the journal, flipping through the pages as if they held the key to a treasure chest of ideas waiting to be unleashed. Each sketch, every note carried the essence of my younger self, the dreamer who wasn't afraid to reach for the stars.

A few moments later, the unmistakable scent of freshly baked lemon bars wafted into the room, tangy and sweet, urging me to embrace the nostalgia. My mother returned, her arms laden with a plate piled high, and I couldn't help but laugh as she set it down like an offering.

"May these fuel your imagination," she said dramatically, her eyes twinkling with mischief.

"Perfect! Just what I need to dream up something fabulous." I plucked a bar from the plate, the warm, sticky glaze shimmering under the light. With the first bite, the tartness burst in my mouth, a jolt of brightness that made me grin like a fool. "Delicious! Who knew inspiration could taste so good?"

She took a seat beside me, mirroring my expression as she bit into one herself. "I think we've discovered the secret to creativity. You should market that."

"Lemon bars: the true muse of the artistic soul," I mused, my mind swirling with possibilities. "I can see it now: 'For every sketch, a slice.'"

As we laughed, I felt the warmth of home wrap around me like a favorite sweater, yet there was an undercurrent of tension thrumming beneath it all. The leap back into my dreams felt exhilarating, yet the thought of New York's cold embrace loomed in the background, a reminder that dreams often come with their own challenges.

"Do you think anyone will take me seriously?" The question slipped out before I could stop it, tinged with doubt.

"Absolutely," my mother said firmly, her voice steady. "But remember, it's not just about being taken seriously. It's about being true to yourself. That's what will draw people in—your authenticity."

Her words lingered in the air, filling the room with a clarity that felt like fresh air. "You really think so?"

"Without a doubt. You've always had a unique voice, a perspective that's yours alone. Don't dilute it for anyone. Not the critics, not the judges, and certainly not yourself."

Her unwavering belief in me was like a lifeline, and I clutched it tightly as I envisioned the bustling streets of New York, the rhythm of life pulsing around me like an electric current. Each corner held the promise of new encounters, new adventures, and perhaps a bit of chaos—just the way I liked it.

"Okay then," I declared, determination blooming anew. "Let's plan this out. I'll need a portfolio, a list of studios, and definitely a few contacts."

"Now you're talking! And I might just have a few ideas to get you started."

With my mother's laughter surrounding me and the lemon bars sweetening my resolve, I felt the cobwebs of doubt begin to lift. The threads of my past were weaving into a tapestry of possibility, vibrant and alive, each strand leading me closer to the world I had longed for. In that moment, I realized that the journey ahead would be anything but predictable, but that unpredictability was exactly what I craved. The road back to myself had just begun, and I was ready to embrace every twist and turn along the way.

The late afternoon sun bathed the kitchen in a golden hue as I and my mother plotted my return to New York, fueled by enthusiasm and lemon bars. The warmth radiated not just from the sun but from the bond we shared, rekindled over shared dreams and freshly baked treats. As we sat side by side, flipping through the journal, I could feel the tentative strands of hope weaving into something tangible, something real.

"You know, if I'm going to make this happen, I'll need to reconnect with the right people," I mused, tapping my finger on a particularly elaborate sketch of a gown that twirled like a dancer. "I mean, the last time I was in the city, I barely had time to grab a coffee, let alone network."

"Then it's time to change that," my mother said, a twinkle in her eye. "Let's make a list of people you might know—friends, acquaintances, anyone from those design programs you did."

I felt a flutter of excitement at the thought. "Oh! What about Mia? She was always so supportive. And she's a stylist now, right?"

"Exactly! And don't forget your cousin Alex. He's got connections in the fashion industry. He might even have an in with some designers," she said, her voice laced with encouragement. "What do you think you'll say to them?"

"Probably something along the lines of, 'Help me! I'm drowning in ambition and need a lifebuoy!'" I laughed, but beneath the humor lay a kernel of truth that made my heart race.

"Maybe ease into it with something less dramatic. 'Hi, it's me! Remember all those dreams I had? Well, I'm back, baby!' might be a better opener." She nudged me playfully, her laughter infectious.

We spent the next hour crafting messages that danced between casual and enthusiastic, our words punctuated by laughter and the sweet aroma of lemon zest. It felt good to plot a course toward my ambitions, to visualize the next steps rather than dwell on the past.

Once we settled on a game plan, I stood and stretched, energized. "Okay, so what's next? Do I jump into the fashion scene like some sort of fabric-clad superhero?"

"Maybe just don your cape of creativity and strut confidently into your old stomping grounds. You never know who might be watching," she said with a wink.

"Or who might be judging my 'heroic' sense of style," I quipped, a grin tugging at my lips. "If they were to witness my usual ensemble of sweatpants and a T-shirt, I might not be invited back."

"True, but you could always charm them with your personality. And let's be honest, who doesn't love a good underdog story?"

Feeling buoyed by her words, I decided to treat myself to a little pre-New York shopping spree. "You know what? I'll buy myself a fabulous outfit for my return. Something that says, 'I'm here, I'm fierce, and I definitely know what a sewing machine looks like!'"

"And a cape, don't forget the cape," she called after me as I headed toward the hallway, the scent of lemon bars still hanging sweetly in the air.

That evening, after a series of excited exchanges with Mia and Alex, I flopped onto my childhood bed, the journal resting beside me like a trusted ally. I could hardly contain my excitement as I imagined my first steps back into the city—each one a deliberate declaration of my resurgence.

But that night, sleep eluded me, my mind a whirlwind of thoughts and ideas. I could practically hear the city calling my name, an intoxicating symphony of horns, chatter, and creativity swirling together, promising adventure and opportunity. Yet, beneath that excitement lingered a darker note of anxiety. What if I wasn't ready? What if I stepped into my old world and found it had moved on without me?

The following day dawned bright and crisp, the kind of morning that hinted at fresh starts. With my mother's encouraging words echoing in my mind, I donned a pair of chic yet comfortable shoes and a stylish, vibrant blouse—my version of a superhero costume, ready to reclaim my dreams.

"I'm off to the mall!" I called to my mother, who was busily tending to her garden outside. She looked up and flashed a thumbs-up, her face beaming with pride.

As I drove to the mall, I couldn't shake the nagging feeling in my gut—an amalgamation of anticipation and dread. The streets leading to the mall were familiar, yet they felt like a prelude to a grand performance, the tension building with each turn.

Once inside the mall, I was enveloped by the soft hum of chatter and the tantalizing scent of freshly brewed coffee. I darted between stores, slipping into boutiques with eager anticipation, my fingers trailing over fabrics as I imagined the outfits I would create for myself—pieces that would express the essence of my rebirth.

After a few hours of trying on everything from whimsical dresses to structured jackets, I finally landed on a stunning red jumpsuit that made me feel like I could take on the world. It hugged my curves perfectly, a bold statement piece that whispered promises of confidence and charisma.

As I admired myself in the mirror, a familiar voice sliced through my reverie. "Wow, look who's back and ready to take names!"

I turned to see Mia, her vibrant personality shining through her layered ensemble. "Mia! It's so good to see you!" I exclaimed, enveloping her in a warm hug.

"You look incredible! That jumpsuit is to die for! I didn't realize you were coming back to the city. When did you get in?"

"Just yesterday. I've been sifting through memories and plotting my grand comeback," I said, my excitement bubbling over. "I'm actually meeting up with Alex later. I want to dive back into the fashion scene."

"Perfect! You'll be a sensation. We need to catch up! There's a new café I want to show you. They have the best pastries and..."

Before she could finish, a sharp ring pierced the air. I fished my phone from my pocket, glancing at the screen. It was Alex.

"Speak of the devil," I said, a grin plastered on my face as I answered the call. "Hey, Alex!"

"Hey! Are you at the mall? I need to talk to you. It's kind of urgent." His voice was tight, a note of tension threading through it.

"Urgent?" I repeated, my heart quickening. "What's going on?"

"Meet me at the coffee shop down the block from the mall. You'll want to hear this in person."

"Okay, I'll be there in five," I said, a wave of unease crashing over me.

I hung up and turned to Mia, her brows knitted in concern. "What was that about?"

"I'm not sure, but it sounded serious."

"Do you want me to come with you?" she offered, genuine concern lighting up her face.

"No, I think I need to handle this on my own." I forced a smile, trying to mask the nerves bubbling beneath the surface. "But let's meet up after—I'll fill you in on all the juicy details."

"Okay, but you better spill every single one!" she called as I turned to leave, her voice fading into the mall's din.

My heart raced as I navigated the familiar streets, the coffee shop looming ahead like a stage set waiting for the drama to unfold. The door chimed as I entered, and I spotted Alex at a corner table, his expression grave as he tapped his fingers nervously against the surface.

"Alex!" I greeted, sliding into the seat across from him. "What's going on?"

He leaned in, his voice low. "I've been hearing things, and you need to be careful. The fashion industry is shifting, and not everyone is happy about new talent entering the scene."

A chill slithered down my spine. "What do you mean?"

"There are whispers about established designers feeling threatened by fresh faces, especially those who used to have a name in the business. I just want you to be cautious."

Before I could respond, a figure brushed past me, sending a shiver through the air. I turned to look, my heart pounding, as a familiar silhouette vanished into the crowd, leaving behind a swirl of uncertainty.

"Do you know her?" Alex's voice cut through my thoughts, but I was already lost in the haze of recognition, a mixture of dread and exhilaration swelling within me.

"What just happened?" I whispered, my pulse racing as the door swung shut behind the figure.

The lingering sense of déjà vu twisted through my mind, pulling me deeper into the uncharted territory of what lay ahead. I had thought I was stepping back into a familiar world, but as the door closed and the air thickened with tension, I couldn't shake the feeling that something far more complicated was waiting just beyond the surface, ready to unravel everything I had hoped to reclaim.

Chapter 11: Crossroads of the Heart

The city buzzes like a live wire, an intricate tapestry of laughter and clinking glasses weaving through the sultry summer night. The rooftop bar, a hidden gem perched above the bustling streets, cradles us in its warm embrace. Flickering string lights dangle like stars plucked from the sky, casting a gentle glow that dances across the faces of patrons lost in their own worlds. The scent of grilled seafood mingles with the salty breeze, creating an intoxicating perfume that draws me deeper into this vibrant tableau.

I lean against the wrought-iron railing, the cool metal a stark contrast to the heat radiating from the street below. From this vantage point, the city stretches out in all its neon glory, each light a heartbeat pulsing with energy. Yet here I stand, tethered to the ground by the weight of unmade decisions that feel like a noose tightening around my heart. I sip my wine, the rich flavor enveloping my senses, but it does little to quell the storm brewing within me. My thoughts spiral like the wind whipping through the skyscrapers, reminding me of the obligations that call me home—a family legacy that feels more like a chain than a gift.

As I scan the crowd, my gaze lands on Nathaniel, his figure a beacon amid the sea of faces. He stands out not just for his tall frame or the way the light plays off his tousled hair, but for the way he makes the ordinary seem extraordinary. With every shared smile, every fleeting touch, the air between us crackles with something electric, something profound. Yet here, at this very moment, I feel a chasm yawning wide beneath us, the enormity of my internal conflict spilling over like the half-finished bottle of wine between us.

"Nate," I say, my voice barely rising above the chatter, "it's amazing up here, isn't it?" The words sound hollow to my own ears, but he turns to me with that lopsided grin that makes my insides flutter.

"Almost as amazing as you," he quips, a playful glint in his eyes. "But I think we both know the real star of the show is the view." He gestures expansively, and I can't help but laugh, the tension in my chest easing just slightly.

We share stories that flit between light and deep, an effortless back-and-forth that feels as natural as breathing. Yet as the night wears on, the gravity of our conversations shifts, drifting toward the uncharted territory of our relationship. I can feel the weight of his gaze, steady and probing, as if he can read the unsaid words swirling around us.

"I want this to work, you know," Nathaniel finally says, his voice low and sincere, the playful banter replaced by a raw intensity that makes my heart stutter. "You and me." The words hang heavy in the air, swirling with the scent of the wine and the salty breeze, beckoning me to lean into them.

My stomach tightens, a visceral response to the beautiful vulnerability of his admission. The notion is intoxicating, yet it strikes a chord of fear deep within me. "I want that too," I whisper, my throat dry as the realization sinks in. "But—"

"There's always a 'but,' isn't there?" He interjects, his tone teasing yet underlined with an unmistakable seriousness that sends a shiver down my spine.

"It's just... my family. They have these expectations, you know? There's this whole world waiting for me back home, a life that's already scripted. I'm scared of what stepping away from that would mean." I clutch my glass tighter, feeling its cool surface ground me as my words tumble out. Each syllable feels like a confession, laying bare my fears under the open sky.

Nathaniel's expression shifts, concern etching lines on his handsome face. "You're not a puppet, you know. You can't let their dreams dictate your life. You deserve to chase your own happiness, even if it means shaking things up a bit."

His words strike a chord, but the weight of familial obligation clings to me like an unwelcome shadow. "It's not that simple," I reply, frustration bubbling up like a volcano threatening to erupt. "There are sacrifices. I've worked so hard to get to this point, and walking away feels like throwing it all away."

"Sometimes, the best things in life require a leap of faith," he counters, his eyes locked onto mine with a fierce intensity. "Don't let fear hold you back from something incredible."

I want to believe him, to shed the layers of doubt that shroud my heart, but the path forward feels like a treacherous tightrope suspended above a chasm of uncertainty. The weight of my family's expectations hangs in the air, a palpable force that threatens to pull me back into the safety of the known.

As I sip my wine, trying to quiet the tumult in my mind, a figure catches my eye—a familiar silhouette cutting through the crowd. It's my brother, Alex, a whirlwind of energy and spontaneity, always one to lighten the mood. He waves, his enthusiasm infectious, but my heart sinks as I remember his recent words of caution about love. The air thickens with tension, and suddenly, the world feels too small, too confined, as if every decision I've ever made has led me to this exact moment.

"Look, I need to—" I start, but Nathaniel's hand finds mine, the warmth of his skin igniting something deep within me, something I'm not ready to confront.

"Just think about it," he says, his voice a soothing balm. "You don't have to decide right now. Just promise me you won't close yourself off from what could be."

I meet his gaze, the intensity of his blue eyes holding me captive. The laughter and music of the bar fade into a distant hum, leaving only the two of us suspended in a moment of possibility. Yet just as I begin to lean into that promise, Alex arrives, throwing open the door to this fragile world we've crafted, and I know the crossroads of my heart are about to collide with the reality of my life.

As Alex strides toward us, his presence disrupts the delicate equilibrium Nathaniel and I have just begun to forge. The excitement of his arrival is tinged with a knot of tension in my stomach. "Hey! You guys look cozy!" he exclaims, his voice buoyant, cutting through the soft strains of music. He sidles up to the table, a wide grin plastered across his face, completely oblivious to the whirlwind of emotions swirling between me and Nathaniel.

"Cozy like a couple of cats on a windowsill," Nathaniel replies, his tone playful, though I catch the flicker of discomfort in his eyes. I can see him brace himself for the inevitable disruption my brother's presence brings.

"More like two lost souls trying to navigate a storm," I murmur, but the comment barely escapes my lips before Alex grabs the bottle of wine, pouring himself a generous glass. His carefree nature always has a way of seeping into the atmosphere, making it hard to maintain any serious thread of conversation.

"So, what's the plan for tonight?" Alex leans back in his chair, eyes sparkling with mischief. "Are we having a philosophical discussion about the meaning of love, or are we throwing caution to the wind and dancing like fools?"

"Why not both?" Nathaniel chimes in, raising an eyebrow at me, his playful tone laced with a challenge. I can't help but smile at the way he effortlessly matches my brother's energy, a skill I've always admired.

"Let's save the deep stuff for later," I say, grateful for the reprieve. "For now, let's just enjoy the evening."

And so we do. Laughter floats between us like a sweet melody, and for a while, I let the worries slip away, focusing instead on the moment—the carefree banter, the way Nathaniel's eyes crinkle when he laughs, and the infectious energy Alex brings to the table. The tension of earlier fades into the background, replaced by a camaraderie that fills the air with warmth.

As the sun dips below the horizon, painting the sky in hues of orange and pink, I find myself wishing for a more permanent escape from the dilemmas awaiting me at home. But the night rolls on, and with it comes the weight of reality, creeping back into my thoughts like an unwelcome guest. I glance at Nathaniel, who seems to sense the shift in my demeanor. His gaze holds mine for a moment too long, a silent conversation passing between us that I can't quite decipher.

"Let's dance!" Alex suddenly shouts, leaping up and pulling me from my chair. Before I can protest, he drags me toward the small dance floor, which is alive with other patrons twirling under the canopy of lights. The music pulses around us, a vibrant heartbeat that quickens my pulse.

"Come on, don't be a party pooper!" he calls over his shoulder, already moving to the beat, his carefree spirit urging me to join in. I can't help but laugh, surrendering to the rhythm as I sway alongside him, my worries momentarily forgotten.

Nathaniel watches us from the edge of the dance floor, his hands shoved into his pockets, his smile warm yet tinged with something more profound—an emotion I can't quite place. I catch his eye, and my heart stutters at the intensity there, a magnet pulling me back to the edge of that emotional precipice.

"See? This is what life is about!" Alex shouts, spinning me around, my laughter mingling with the music. "You need to let loose more often!"

"I'm not sure 'letting loose' involves spinning in circles until I'm dizzy!" I giggle, though the lightness in my chest is undeniable. I'm reminded of carefree summer nights spent dancing with friends, where nothing mattered except the music and the moment.

But as the song shifts, and the beat slows, I feel that familiar tension coil back into existence. The rhythm of the music mirrors the thudding of my heart, each beat echoing the internal struggle that has now risen to the surface. Alex finally retreats to the sidelines, leaving Nathaniel and me standing in the center of the swirling crowd, the lights dimming around us as the world seems to recede.

"I didn't think I'd have to rescue you from your own brother," Nathaniel murmurs, stepping closer, the warmth of his body radiating towards me. "He can be quite persuasive, can't he?"

I chuckle softly, the sound caught somewhere between amusement and apprehension. "You have no idea. He's got a knack for turning every situation into a spectacle."

"Maybe that's what we need—more spectacle and less seriousness." His voice drops to a softer timbre, the playful edge slipping away as he searches my eyes, the weight of our earlier conversation hanging between us like a thread ready to snap.

"Perhaps," I concede, the reality of his words settling over me like a comforting blanket, but the undercurrents remain turbulent. "But it's hard to see the spectacle when I'm drowning in responsibilities."

He tilts his head, studying me with an intensity that makes my breath hitch. "What if you didn't have to drown? What if you could swim?"

His words hang in the air, a tantalizing promise wrapped in the guise of a question. I bite my lip, considering the notion, the appeal of shedding my burdens to dive into the unknown with him at my side. "That's a pretty big 'what if.'"

"Sometimes the biggest leaps come from the smallest shifts in perspective," he replies, his gaze unwavering. The vulnerability in his voice draws me in, sparking a glimmer of hope amidst my uncertainty.

The world around us blurs, the music fading into the background as my heart races in response to his unwavering conviction. "I just—"

Before I can finish, a loud crash echoes through the bar, pulling my attention away from the moment. A commotion stirs near the entrance, voices raised in shock, and I catch a glimpse of chaos spilling into our carefully curated night. My heart sinks as I recognize familiar figures stepping through the door—my parents, flanked by a few family friends, their expressions a mixture of disbelief and disappointment.

"Great. Just what I needed," I mutter under my breath, the swirling weight of obligation crashing down on me once again. The warmth of Nathaniel's presence feels distant, like a dream slipping through my fingers.

"Are you okay?" he asks, concern etched across his features.

I force a smile, though it feels brittle. "Yeah, just peachy." But the tension in my voice betrays me, the chasm widening once more between my desires and my reality.

As my parents weave through the crowd, searching, I know the moment of reckoning is near, and with it, the crossroads of my heart that I've been so desperately trying to navigate will soon erupt into chaos.

As my parents make their way through the bar, their expressions morph from confusion to recognition, and my heart sinks further into my stomach. The joyous buzz around us fades, replaced by the pounding of blood in my ears. Nathaniel shifts beside me, his presence warm and grounding, yet I can feel the tension radiating off him as he instinctively draws closer.

"Speak of the devil," I mutter, barely loud enough for him to hear. "They weren't supposed to be here."

"Do you want to run?" he offers with a teasing glint in his eyes, but the weight of my parents' expectations hangs heavily in the air, the joking suggestion not quite hitting the mark.

I can't help but laugh softly, though it's tinged with panic. "As tempting as that sounds, I think running might attract more attention."

"Let's not make a scene then," he says, leaning closer so only I can hear. "Just act natural."

"Natural? Right. Because that's my forte." I plaster on a smile that feels more like a grimace as my parents approach. My father's brow furrows, his lips pursed in a disapproving line, while my mother's eyes sparkle with an unsettling blend of pride and concern.

"Look who we found!" Alex's voice cuts through the tension, his tone jovial, completely unaware of the storm brewing at our table. "I was just showing your daughter how to dance like no one's watching."

"Oh, were you?" My mother's gaze narrows slightly, her instincts sharp as she scans the scene. "How lovely to see you, Nathaniel."

"Mrs. Thompson," he replies, his voice steady, though I can see the way his hands fidget at his sides. "Always a pleasure."

"Is it? Because it seems like every time I see you, it's at some sort of gathering that could be considered a little... questionable." My mother's eyebrow arches, her tone laced with unspoken judgments. I can almost hear the unvoiced question: What are your intentions with my daughter?

Nathaniel takes a measured breath, unfazed by her scrutiny. "I assure you, Mrs. Thompson, I have only the best intentions."

"Do you?" she replies, her voice soft but sharp enough to cut through the lighthearted atmosphere. "Because your intentions might just be the crux of my concern."

"Mom!" I interject, the protest tumbling out before I can reel it back in. "This isn't the time or place." My heart races, torn between the desperate urge to defend Nathaniel and the reality of my family's expectations.

"It's fine," he says, brushing off my discomfort with a calmness that only intensifies my admiration for him. "I'm happy to clarify my intentions. I want to be a part of her life, not as a fleeting shadow but as someone who genuinely cares."

"That's sweet," my mother replies, her tone still laced with doubt. "But love isn't just about feelings, it's about commitment, responsibility."

"And what if those commitments come with a hefty price?" Nathaniel counters, his eyes blazing with conviction. "What if they ask her to sacrifice her happiness for a dream that's not her own?"

The air between us thickens, charged with unspoken tension, and I feel the weight of my parents' expectations loom larger, threatening to crush this moment of budding intimacy.

"Let's sit down, shall we?" my father suggests, gesturing toward the empty chairs at our table. "We should talk."

"Talk?" I echo, panic bubbling up in my chest. The last thing I want is for this discussion to unfold in front of Nathaniel. The path ahead, already riddled with uncertainty, feels as if it's about to collapse under the weight of family obligations.

"Yes, talk," my father insists, his voice firm. "Your mother and I are concerned about the decisions you've been making lately. You've been distant, lost in a world that doesn't seem to be your own."

"Distant?" I scoff, incredulous. "You have no idea what's been going on in my life, Dad. This is the most alive I've felt in ages."

"You think running around with your brother and this boy is going to solve your problems?" he asks, his tone sharp and dismissive, like a seasoned prosecutor about to deliver a closing argument.

Nathaniel's hand brushes mine, a reassuring gesture, and I feel a flicker of warmth in the storm raging around us. But it's fleeting, overshadowed by my father's intensity.

"Maybe you should consider what's really important. Your family needs you, and you've got responsibilities waiting for you at home."

"Responsibilities," I hiss, the word a bitter pill in my mouth. "Is that all you think I am? A pawn in some grand scheme?"

"Not a pawn, a daughter," my mother interjects, her voice softer yet firm. "We just want what's best for you. What's wrong with wanting you to follow the path we've laid out? We've sacrificed so much."

"Sacrificed? Or controlled?" I bite back, feeling the walls of the bar closing in, the lights blurring into a hazy glow. "Do you even hear yourselves? All this talk about responsibility, yet you refuse to see what I want."

"Maybe you don't even know what you want!" My father shoots back, frustration flaring in his eyes. "You're caught up in this fantasy. It's not real!"

"And you think this," I gesture to the crowded bar, "is any more real? You're living a script that doesn't leave room for anyone else."

The tension escalates, my heart pounding like a drum as I glance at Nathaniel, who watches the exchange with a mixture of concern and empathy. The fierce determination in his gaze sparks something within me, an ember of defiance burning brightly against the looming darkness of my family's expectations.

"Maybe I don't have to choose," I say, my voice steadier than I feel. "Maybe I can have a life that's mine while still honoring what you've done for me."

My father's face hardens, and I brace myself for the inevitable storm of anger, but instead, it's my mother who steps forward, her expression shifting from anger to something softer, more vulnerable. "We're just worried, sweetie. We've seen so many people get lost in their dreams, only to be crushed when reality hits."

"Reality?" I scoff again, unable to mask the bitterness in my tone. "Maybe reality isn't what you think it is. Maybe it's about taking risks and discovering what life truly means."

Just then, a loud crash echoes through the bar once more, this time accompanied by panicked shouts. My heart races as the atmosphere shifts abruptly, and the crowd around us stirs with unease. I glance toward the entrance, where a small group of people is now spilling into the bar, their faces pale with fright.

"What is happening?" Alex asks, instinctively moving closer to me as the tension thickens like fog.

"Stay close," Nathaniel murmurs, his grip on my hand tightening. The fear in his voice sends a shiver down my spine as I catch a glimpse of what's unfolding—a confrontation, a clash of emotions playing out under the soft glow of the bar's lights.

Before I can react, a figure bursts through the crowd, moving straight toward us, and the world around me blurs into chaos. My heart races, the throbbing pulse of the music replaced by an ominous silence, and in that split second, the reality of everything I've been grappling with crystallizes. I'm standing at the edge of something monumental, and the ground beneath me feels dangerously unstable.

"Emily!" the figure shouts, their voice a mix of urgency and desperation, cutting through the haze of noise. The name hangs in the air, pulling me back, grounding me, even as the tempest of my heart begins to swirl once more.

Chapter 12: The Art of Vulnerability

The gallery buzzed with an electric energy, a vibrant pulse that coursed through the air like the beats of a drum. Ivy's art exhibit had transformed the once-quiet space into a veritable carnival of color and creativity. I stepped through the entrance, the scent of paint mingling with a hint of jasmine from the floral arrangements that adorned the room. The walls were alive with her work, each piece a visceral exploration of emotion that made my heart race. I could see the threads of her soul woven into every brushstroke, and it took my breath away.

She was there, surrounded by admirers, her laughter ringing out like the tinkling of delicate chimes. I paused for a moment, hidden behind a large canvas, absorbing the scene. Ivy was a force of nature, radiating warmth and charisma. Her honey-colored hair fell in soft waves over her shoulders, catching the dim light in such a way that it seemed to glow. I couldn't help but smile, her enthusiasm infectious even from a distance. This was the Ivy I knew—an artist unafraid to bare her soul, yet still wrapped in a cocoon of uncertainty that she fought to escape.

As she spotted me, her face lit up, and she waved enthusiastically. The crowd parted like the Red Sea, and suddenly I was swept into her orbit. "You made it!" she exclaimed, pulling me into a hug that felt like coming home. "What do you think? Isn't it incredible?"

"It's like stepping into a dream," I replied, my voice barely above a whisper. "You've turned this place into a whole new world."

She beamed, a blush creeping onto her cheeks. "Thanks! I really wanted to capture something raw, something real." Her gaze flickered around the room, drinking in the admiration of others. "But enough about me. I've been thinking..."

"Oh no," I interrupted playfully, my eyes widening. "When Ivy starts with that phrase, I know I'm in for it."

She laughed, a musical sound that danced through the air. "I want us to collaborate on a piece. Something that reflects our journey as friends. I think it could be cathartic for both of us."

The idea hit me like a splash of cold water. My stomach tightened, a swirl of excitement and dread crashing together. Collaborating meant laying my soul bare, risking vulnerability, and exposing the rawest parts of myself. I had spent years building walls, perfecting the art of hiding behind a smile. "Ivy, I don't know..."

"Come on," she prodded, her eyes sparkling with mischief. "It'll be fun! We'll paint late into the night, listen to bad music, and share secrets. You can't tell me that doesn't sound like a good time!"

I hesitated, the ghosts of my past whispering doubts in my ear. Yet something deep within me stirred, yearning for the connection I had long denied. "Okay," I agreed, my voice stronger than I felt. "Let's do it."

The following week, we transformed my cramped apartment into a makeshift studio, our laughter echoing off the walls as we filled the space with chaos and creativity. I could hardly keep track of the paint splatters that dotted the floor, but it didn't matter; it was a sign of our progress, our shared energy.

"What color do you think represents friendship?" Ivy mused one night, her brow furrowed in concentration as she swirled her paintbrush through a palette of vibrant hues.

"Definitely not beige," I quipped, causing her to giggle. "I mean, that's practically the absence of color. Maybe a deep green? It feels nurturing, like a hug from the earth."

"Hmm, green it is!" she declared, dabbing the brush against a canvas that was beginning to come alive. "And how about dreams? What color embodies that?"

"Blue, I think," I said, the word tumbling out before I could second-guess myself. "Not just any blue, though—like the kind you see at twilight when the world is quiet, just before the stars start to twinkle."

Ivy nodded, her expression thoughtful. "Perfect. We'll blend them together, our colors intertwining just like our stories."

As we painted, I felt walls crumbling, each stroke of the brush forcing me to confront emotions I had buried deep. We painted our childhood memories, weaving them into the fabric of our piece. I shared stories of my awkward teen years, the heartbreak of lost friendships, and the burden of expectations. Ivy listened, her eyes wide with understanding, her presence a soothing balm.

"Why didn't you ever tell me this before?" she asked, her voice soft yet inquisitive.

"Because it's easier to hide behind smiles than to reveal the mess beneath," I admitted, a lump forming in my throat. "I've always thought of myself as the strong one, the one who holds it all together. But it's exhausting."

"Strength isn't just about holding everything in," Ivy replied, her words wrapping around me like a warm blanket. "It's about having the courage to let it out. That's the beauty of vulnerability."

Those words echoed in my mind as we continued to create. I discovered the power of honesty, the freedom that comes with letting go. Each splash of paint became a release, a way to transform pain into beauty.

On the final night of our collaboration, the piece stood before us, a vibrant tapestry of colors and textures, a testament to our journey together. It symbolized resilience, our shared laughter, fears, and dreams merged into a single expression of our friendship.

As I stared at our creation, I felt a shift within me. I was no longer just the girl hiding behind a façade; I was a canvas of my own, ready to embrace the messy, beautiful strokes of life.

The night of the gallery opening arrived, and the air was thick with anticipation, crackling like electricity before a storm. Ivy had transformed the space into a sanctuary of art and emotion, each piece telling a story of its own, yet all intertwining like threads in a larger tapestry. I stood off to the side, clutching a glass of something fizzy and bright, watching as the crowd moved in and out of the dim light, their laughter spilling over like champagne bubbles. Ivy had outdone herself, and the pride swelling in my chest felt almost painful.

I could see her at the center of it all, animated and radiant, her eyes dancing as she spoke to a couple of patrons who were clearly enamored by her work. She had always had that effect on people, a gravitational pull that drew them into her orbit. It struck me that this was not just her moment; it was ours. The piece we'd created together—a swirling explosion of blues and greens—was tucked away in a corner, awaiting its grand reveal.

As the crowd moved and swayed, I felt a tickle of nerves dance in my stomach. What if our piece fell flat? What if they couldn't see the layers of meaning we'd poured into it? Ivy was my best friend, but the idea of exposing our work to the world was a different beast altogether. I took a deep breath, reminding myself that art was subjective. Maybe vulnerability would resonate with someone else just as it had with us.

"Hey, Earth to you!" Ivy's voice pulled me back from the precipice of my spiraling thoughts. She appeared before me, her cheeks flushed with excitement, her hair a halo of chaos. "You're looking a little lost. Did you find a secret exit or something?"

"Just contemplating the depth of my life choices," I replied with a grin, raising my glass in mock toast. "You know, the usual."

She rolled her eyes playfully. "Stop that! You're going to make me question my life choices too, and I can't afford that right now. Tonight is about celebration!"

"Celebration! Right!" I echoed, shaking my head to clear the clouds of doubt. "So, what's next? Are we unveiling our masterpiece soon?"

"Soon, my friend. Soon," she promised, her eyes twinkling with mischief. "But first, let's do some schmoozing. You know how much I love the art of mingling."

"Oh yes, the 'art' of mingling," I said, sarcasm lacing my words. "Nothing says 'authenticity' like forced small talk over a plate of overcooked hors d'oeuvres."

She laughed, a sound that sparked warmth in the chilly air. "You're not wrong, but we can make it fun. Just remember to smile and nod, and maybe drop a few art terms. People love that."

"Art terms, right. I'll just casually mention the 'juxtaposition of post-modern existentialism' while holding a crab puff," I quipped, trying to match her infectious enthusiasm.

With a wink, Ivy grabbed my hand and led me toward a small cluster of guests who were deep in conversation, gesturing animatedly. As we approached, Ivy turned on her charm like a switch, sliding into the group with practiced ease. I trailed behind, attempting to blend into the background, but the moment she introduced me as her collaborator, I found myself thrust into the spotlight.

"What was your inspiration for that stunning piece in the corner?" a woman in an emerald dress asked, her gaze penetrating. "It's so... vibrant."

Ivy looked at me expectantly, and I felt my throat tighten. "Um, well, we wanted to capture our friendship and the journey that brought us together," I said, feeling like I was reciting lines from a play. "The colors represent..."

"Vulnerability and resilience," Ivy chimed in, finishing my sentence with a smile that made me feel like I could breathe again.

"We painted late into the night, sharing secrets and laughter, and it all just... flowed."

The woman nodded, intrigued. "That's beautiful. It reminds me of my own friendships—how they shape who we are."

Before I could respond, a tall man with tousled hair and an air of confidence stepped into the conversation. "I must say, I found the piece to be a fascinating commentary on modern relationships. There's a certain chaos in it that speaks to the unpredictability of human connections."

I glanced at Ivy, who was struggling to stifle a giggle. "You should see her in action," she whispered to me. "He could probably discuss the life cycle of a paintbrush and make it sound riveting."

I rolled my eyes, though I couldn't help but smile. The man continued to elaborate, his voice rich and smooth, while I found myself zoning out. I was used to hearing my own thoughts, and listening to him felt like staring at a beautiful painting but failing to understand the strokes that made it whole.

"Sorry, but can you pause for a second?" I interjected, a cheeky grin spreading across my face. "Are we talking about relationships or paintbrushes? Because I'm not sure I'm ready for either."

The group erupted into laughter, the tension in my shoulders easing. "I appreciate your refreshing honesty," the man said, his smile widening. "Not enough people are willing to say what they really think. It's refreshing."

Ivy nudged me playfully. "See? You're a natural. You could charm the socks off a statue."

Before I could respond, an art dealer I recognized from previous events, a tall woman named Claudia, approached us. She exuded confidence, her tailored suit accentuating her sharp features. "Ivy! What an impressive collection you have here," she said, her eyes narrowing as they scanned the room. "And this piece... it's truly exceptional."

Ivy straightened, her excitement palpable. "Thank you! I'm really proud of it. My friend and I collaborated on this one."

Claudia's gaze shifted to me, and I felt a flicker of apprehension. "Ah, the mysterious collaborator. How lovely to finally meet you." Her tone was almost predatory, and I fought the urge to step back.

"Just here to provide comic relief," I replied, attempting to ease the intensity with humor. "And maybe some questionable paint choices."

"Art is meant to provoke," she said, her lips curling into a smirk. "I can see you both have a unique chemistry. I'd love to discuss a possible exhibition. This kind of work deserves more exposure."

Ivy's eyes widened, her excitement evident. "Really? That would be amazing!"

Claudia nodded, her gaze steady. "I think we could create something spectacular together."

As they exchanged business cards, I felt the room shift around me. My heart raced, caught between pride for Ivy and a creeping sense of uncertainty. What did it mean to expose ourselves more fully to the world? The evening unfolded like a delicate origami, revealing layers I hadn't anticipated, and all at once, I knew our journey was just beginning.

The gallery hummed with excitement, a living organism pulsating in rhythm with the vibrant personalities milling about. Ivy, radiant in her element, basked in the glow of her success. The energy surged around us, infectious and exhilarating, as conversations mingled with the clinking of glasses. I couldn't shake the feeling of standing on the precipice of something extraordinary—and terrifying.

"Did you see Claudia's eyes light up when she talked about our piece?" Ivy gushed, her cheeks flushed. We stood close, the noise around us fading to a soft murmur as we took a moment to catch our breath amidst the whirlwind of compliments and questions. "This could be the start of something huge."

"Sure, if by 'huge' you mean completely terrifying," I teased, nudging her shoulder playfully. "What if we're just riding a wave of enthusiasm that crashes down the moment someone discovers we used glitter instead of actual talent?"

She laughed, but I could see the gears turning in her mind. "Come on, we're not just glitter! We've got depth. That piece is layered—just like us."

"More like an onion," I replied, raising an eyebrow. "One minute you're crying, and the next, you're peeling back another layer to reveal something stinky."

"You're ridiculous," Ivy said, shaking her head, but the smile on her face was unmistakable. "What's wrong with a little complexity?"

"Complexity is great. Just as long as we don't start trying to explain ourselves to art critics who revel in dissecting every brushstroke."

Her laughter bubbled over, momentarily drawing the attention of nearby guests. I took a sip of my drink, the tangy citrus dancing on my tongue, and glanced at our piece once more. It stood there, a kaleidoscope of colors and textures, telling our story without needing words.

Just then, a voice broke through my reverie. "Excuse me, is this the infamous collaboration I've been hearing about?"

I turned to find a woman who looked like she had stepped out of a fashion magazine, complete with a sharp blazer and a keen eye. Her confidence radiated, drawing Ivy and me into her orbit. "I'm Eleanor," she introduced herself, extending a hand. "I've been captivated by your work."

"Thanks!" Ivy replied, her enthusiasm bubbling over. "We're so proud of it."

Eleanor tilted her head, her gaze assessing. "Proud, yes. But you should be ambitious too. I could see this piece in a major gallery. You have something special here, but you'll need to push boundaries if you want to make waves."

"Push boundaries? Is that the polite way of saying we should get more avant-garde?" I asked, half-joking.

"Precisely," Eleanor responded, a glimmer of mischief in her eyes. "You need to challenge yourselves, to dig deeper. People want authenticity, raw emotion. The world is craving connection—especially in art."

I felt a familiar flutter of anxiety creep into my chest. "But what if we get it wrong?"

"Wrong is subjective," she countered with a sly smile. "What matters is that you're willing to take the risk. Just imagine—if you can expose your vulnerabilities, people will connect with your story. There's power in that."

"Power, yes. But also potential disaster," I muttered, glancing at Ivy. "I like the idea of people connecting, but I'm not sure I'm ready to take a sledgehammer to my emotions."

"Ah, but there's the beauty of it," Eleanor said, her voice lowering conspiratorially. "You won't just be revealing your weaknesses; you'll be redefining them. And who knows? You might discover something new about yourself in the process."

Ivy's eyes sparkled with excitement, her creative spirit clearly ignited. "What if we create a series? We could explore different themes, different aspects of our lives—vulnerability, joy, pain..."

"Exactly!" Eleanor clapped her hands, her enthusiasm palpable. "Let's talk details. I want to help you showcase this to the right audience."

I felt like I was being swept into a current I couldn't control. "And by 'details,' you mean exposing all our secrets to the world? What a lovely thought."

Ivy shot me a look that was half exasperated and half amused. "Come on, don't be a wet blanket. This is an opportunity!"

"An opportunity that could leave us bare," I shot back, my playful tone wavering slightly. The thought of vulnerability gnawed at me, each second stretching into eternity as I wrestled with my doubts.

"Art is about taking risks," Ivy said softly, her voice a balm against my turmoil. "I believe in us. We can do this."

A flicker of warmth ignited in my chest. She was right; we had been through so much together, and if anyone could do this, it was us. "Okay, let's do it," I relented, the words tumbling out before I could second-guess myself.

"Great! We'll brainstorm tomorrow," Ivy said, bouncing on her toes. "Let's make it a late-night session—just like old times."

"Ah, the good old days of paint-covered pajamas and half-baked ideas," I replied, a smile creeping across my lips. "I'll bring the snacks."

"Only the finest!" she declared dramatically, raising her glass in a mock toast.

Just then, a commotion erupted at the entrance, a sharp contrast to the celebration enveloping us. The room fell silent, heads turning toward the disturbance. A tall figure pushed through the crowd, their presence commanding and intense. I squinted, trying to make out the features of the newcomer.

"Is that...?" Ivy began, her voice trailing off.

Before she could finish, the figure locked eyes with me—deep, penetrating eyes that sent a shockwave of recognition rippling through my body. My breath caught in my throat as a cascade of memories flooded back, each one sharp and vivid. The warmth of summer nights, shared laughter, the heartbreak that followed. It felt as if time had collapsed, pulling me back to moments I had tried so hard to forget.

"Hello, stranger," he said, a crooked smile playing on his lips as he stepped closer, the crowd parting like waves before him. "Long time no see."

A chill swept through me, a mix of excitement and dread. What was he doing here, now, of all times? I could feel the atmosphere shift, the air thickening with unspoken words and unresolved tension. The night, once bursting with possibilities, suddenly felt like a delicate bubble teetering on the edge of bursting.

Chapter 13: Ties That Bind

The gallery hummed with life, a vivid tapestry woven from laughter, whispers, and the soft clink of champagne glasses. Each corner of the room was awash with the kaleidoscope of Ivy's art, her vivid brushstrokes a reflection of her vibrant spirit. I stood by her side, a proud companion in the symphony of colors that surrounded us. The air was thick with the scent of fresh paint and polished wood, a heady mix that made my heart race with anticipation and a tinge of apprehension.

Ivy was a force of nature, dressed in a flowing emerald gown that seemed to dance with her every movement. Her hair, a cascade of fiery curls, framed her face like a living halo, accentuating her infectious smile. She was in her element, the gallery lights highlighting the gleam in her eyes, and I couldn't help but marvel at her ability to capture the essence of life on canvas. As she welcomed guests, her laughter was like music, wrapping around me and lifting my spirits. Yet, the closer I stood to her brilliance, the more my own insecurities gnawed at the edges of my consciousness. I felt like a pale shadow beside her, a mere flicker in the blaze of her talent.

I glanced at the crowd, taking in the art enthusiasts, critics, and friends who had gathered to celebrate Ivy's success. Their admiration for her work was palpable, and I couldn't shake the feeling that I was an outsider peering into a world I was desperately trying to be a part of. As I sipped my champagne, the bubbles tickling my nose, I couldn't help but wonder if my own ambitions were as lofty as I wanted them to be, or if I was merely drifting along in Ivy's wake.

Just then, Nathaniel entered the room, and time seemed to pause. He was a striking figure, his tall frame exuding confidence and an effortless charm that drew the eye of everyone around him. With tousled dark hair and a dapper navy suit that fit him like it was tailor-made, he looked every bit the art aficionado, though I knew him to be more than that. His eyes, warm and inviting, scanned the room before locking onto mine. A smile broke across his face, and in that instant, the noise around me faded, leaving only the electric connection between us.

"Isn't it incredible?" he said, stepping closer, his voice a smooth blend of admiration and intrigue. He gestured toward Ivy, who was currently enveloped in a group of admirers, her laughter ringing out like a bell.

"It really is," I replied, unable to hide my awe. "She's going to be the talk of the town after tonight."

Nathaniel's gaze flicked back to Ivy, then returned to me. "And what about you? How do you fit into all of this?" His question caught me off guard, stirring the insecurity bubbling within. What was my place in this world of color and ambition?

"I'm just here for support," I said, forcing a smile that I hoped masked the tumult inside. "Ivy's the star of the show."

"You're far too humble," he countered, his expression thoughtful. "You should take some credit for her success. Every artist needs a muse, after all."

"Muse?" I echoed, the word tasting strange on my tongue. The thought of being a source of inspiration for someone as talented as Ivy felt absurd. Yet, Nathaniel's gaze held a sincerity that made my heart flutter, igniting a flicker of hope. Perhaps there was more to my role than I had realized.

As we stood there, a gentle tension began to weave between us, a thread of unspoken words and potential. I could feel the warmth radiating from him, like sunlight breaking through a canopy of clouds, and I couldn't help but lean into it. But just as I was beginning to bask in the glow of his attention, whispers of doubt crept into my mind. Was I really worthy of his interest? What if I was merely a temporary distraction in his world, a fleeting moment of intrigue that would soon fade?

The night wore on, the gallery alive with energy. I watched as Ivy navigated through the crowd, her laughter echoing off the walls, a melody of pure joy. I felt a tug of longing for that same lightness, that ability to draw people in effortlessly. It was a feeling that had always eluded me, and as I stood there, I felt my shoulders tighten beneath the weight of comparison.

Nathaniel turned to me again, his eyes glimmering with curiosity. "What do you do when you're not playing cheerleader for your best friend?"

"Ah, well, I dabble in a bit of writing," I replied, the words tumbling out before I could stop them. "Mostly short stories and some poetry. Nothing worth showcasing, really."

"Nothing worth showcasing?" he echoed, his brow furrowing slightly. "I refuse to believe that. I'd love to read something you've written."

His interest sparked a warm rush of surprise, but I quashed it quickly, afraid to let it blossom. "It's just for fun. I don't really take it seriously."

"Why not? Everyone should take their passions seriously, especially if they're good at them." There was a challenge in his tone, and it made my pulse quicken.

I shrugged, trying to play it off. "Maybe I'm just not that ambitious. I'm more of a behind-the-scenes kind of person."

"Behind the scenes?" he said, tilting his head slightly as if assessing a puzzle. "I can't help but think you're selling yourself short. What if you stepped out from behind the curtain?"

The air between us thickened with possibilities, and I felt myself drawn to him, yet a part of me hesitated. What if I was more like a shadow than a star, destined to linger in the periphery? A fleeting image, never quite defined, always just out of focus.

As Ivy continued to hold court among her admirers, I sensed that the night was far from over, and the unexpected twists and turns awaited us. The gallery buzzed, but I stood there, a reluctant participant in my own story, wondering if I had the courage to step into the light.

As the evening progressed, the gallery transformed into a living organism, pulsating with conversations and creativity. Ivy glided through the throng, her laughter mingling with the clinking of glasses and the hum of compliments. I found myself at a crossroads, torn between the magnetic pull of the crowd and the comforting yet disquieting presence of Nathaniel beside me. His engaging manner made it easy to lose myself in our dialogue, yet the undercurrent of my insecurities surged as I compared myself to Ivy's vibrant persona.

"I've got a wild idea," Nathaniel said suddenly, his voice cutting through my musings. "How about you and I take a break from this cacophony? Let's escape to the balcony for a breath of fresh air."

His suggestion sparked a thrill of anticipation, the thought of being alone with him causing a rush of warmth to color my cheeks. I nodded, trying to suppress the excitement bubbling up inside me. We slipped away from the revelry, the distant sounds of laughter and applause fading as we stepped outside into the cool evening air. The balcony offered a stunning view of the city, twinkling lights stretching out like a blanket of stars beneath the inky sky.

"Ah, much better," he said, leaning against the railing, his silhouette framed by the glowing horizon. "I needed this."

I joined him at the railing, taking a deep breath of the crisp air that seemed to wash away the noise of the gallery. "Me too. It's easy to get lost in all that excitement."

"Easy to get lost in Ivy's shadow, you mean." His words hung in the air, direct yet gentle, and I felt the weight of them settle over me like a mist.

I turned to him, surprised. "I didn't think you noticed."

"Of course I noticed. You're too talented to let yourself fade into the background," he replied, his gaze piercing yet encouraging. "What are you so afraid of?"

The question hung between us, heavy with unspoken fears. I struggled to find the right words, grappling with the truth that felt too raw to share. "I guess I worry that my dreams are too small. I'm not as... ambitious as Ivy. She's a whirlwind, and I'm just... me."

"Just you?" He laughed lightly, but there was no mockery in it, only warmth. "You underestimate yourself. It's not about being a whirlwind. It's about finding your own way to create, whatever that looks like. Have you ever thought that maybe your stories have the power to inspire, just as much as Ivy's paintings?"

The way he said it struck a chord, igniting something deep within me. "In theory, yes. But when it comes down to it, I hesitate. I'm not sure my words could ever resonate in the same way."

"Your hesitation is a monster you've created in your mind," he said, leaning in closer. "You write from your heart, and that's the most important part. Authenticity trumps all else. Besides, everyone loves a good story. Just look at Ivy!"

The moonlight reflected off his eyes, a pool of warmth that invited honesty. I took a moment to gather my thoughts, feeling vulnerable yet strangely empowered by his belief in me. "I don't know if I can do that," I admitted, my voice barely above a whisper. "What if I'm not good enough?"

"Who defines 'good enough'? It's a subjective standard, and it changes with every person who reads your work. You can't let that hold you back." He paused, his expression thoughtful. "You have a unique voice, and it deserves to be heard."

Just then, a shout from inside the gallery drew our attention, and Ivy burst onto the balcony, her cheeks flushed with excitement. "There you are! I was looking for you two. Come back in! There's something I want you to see."

With a shared glance of amusement, Nathaniel and I followed Ivy back inside, the warmth of the gallery embracing us like a familiar blanket. As we stepped back into the lively atmosphere, I couldn't help but notice the spark of competition flaring in Ivy's eyes. It was as if she had conjured a vision of grandeur and was determined to share it with us.

"Look!" she exclaimed, pulling us toward a corner where a large canvas was covered with a satin sheet. The murmurs of the crowd faded into the background as she lifted the fabric, revealing a breathtaking piece—a landscape bathed in the soft hues of twilight, the sky painted with streaks of lavender and gold. "This is my favorite! It's a tribute to our hometown."

The painting was exquisite, capturing not just the physical beauty of our shared memories but also the emotions tied to those places—the laughter, the sorrow, the fleeting moments of joy. I felt a swell of pride for her talent, but an echo of doubt whispered through me again.

"Wow, Ivy," I said, forcing a smile as I studied the canvas. "It's beautiful. You've really captured it."

"Thank you! But I need your help. Nathaniel, I want to know what you think. You have that discerning eye for detail." Her request seemed innocent enough, yet I sensed the competitive edge laced within it, a test of my own worthiness.

"I think it's stunning," he replied, his eyes glimmering with appreciation as he stepped closer to examine the brushstrokes. "But I also think it could use a bit of—"

"See?" Ivy interrupted, her tone bright yet challenging. "This is exactly what I need. Someone who isn't afraid to critique me, to help me grow. You know, not everyone has that ability to see what needs to change."

The air around us thickened with tension, and I felt my heart race, caught between admiration for Ivy and a growing frustration. It felt like a game, a subtle duel for Nathaniel's attention and validation. Did she know how easily her words could undermine my growing confidence? Or was this simply Ivy being Ivy, fiercely competitive yet unaware of the consequences?

Nathaniel's gaze flickered between us, sensing the undercurrent of unspoken words. "Ivy, it's already amazing. But I think every artist has room for growth, and that's part of the process."

I caught the edge of sarcasm in his tone, but Ivy simply smiled, ever the optimist, brushing off any potential tension. "That's true! I just need to know how to take it to the next level. And who better to help than two brilliant minds?"

As she said it, I could feel my pulse quickening, the weight of expectation pressing down on me. Did I have the ability to contribute anything meaningful? Could I really step into the light, or was I destined to linger in the shadows? The night felt charged with possibilities and pressures, and as I stood there, the once-vibrant colors of Ivy's world began to swirl around me like an unpredictable storm, pulling me deeper into the whirlwind.

The energy in the gallery swirled like a tempest, every conversation tinged with enthusiasm and a hint of rivalry. Ivy was captivating, effortlessly drawing admiration from everyone around her, while I stood slightly apart, my heart racing as I grappled with the mixed emotions swirling within me. Nathaniel remained close, his presence like a steady anchor amidst the chaos, yet I felt the unyielding tug of my insecurities threatening to pull me under.

"Let's add a touch of mystery to this party," Ivy said, her voice laced with excitement as she surveyed the crowd. "Who doesn't love a good dramatic reveal? Nathaniel, how about you be my official critic? I could use a bit of constructive criticism, and you're perfect for the role."

Her request hung in the air, a spark igniting tension between us. I glanced at Nathaniel, who raised an eyebrow, clearly intrigued yet cautious. "A critic, huh? I'm not sure I can live up to that title. I'm more of a casual observer, really."

"Nonsense!" Ivy waved her hand dismissively, a spark of mischief in her eyes. "You have an artist's eye. And besides, who doesn't want to share their opinions when surrounded by art? Think of it as an opportunity to lend your expertise."

"Or a trap set for me to stumble into," he replied with a smirk, but the tension in the air was palpable. Ivy's determination mixed with Nathaniel's playful reluctance created an atmosphere charged with unspoken challenges. I could feel my heart thudding in my chest, torn between wanting to support Ivy and fearing that my own voice would be drowned out in the cacophony of her brilliance.

"Come on," Ivy insisted, her enthusiasm infectious. "Just think of the wonderful things you can say! Or perhaps something a little edgy, to keep everyone on their toes." She leaned closer to him, a conspiratorial glint in her eye. "Let's shake things up a bit."

As the words fell from her lips, I sensed an unease coiling in my stomach. Ivy was so driven, so confident, and here I was, tethered to her like a balloon, afraid of what would happen when she let go. I wasn't certain how to voice my discomfort without sounding petty or insecure.

"Alright, you win," Nathaniel conceded with a chuckle. "But just know, I'm not responsible for the chaos that ensues."

"Perfect! I thrive on chaos," Ivy declared, her laughter bright and clear. "Let's give these people a show!"

As she turned to address the crowd, I felt Nathaniel's gaze linger on me, a curious look playing across his features. "You okay with this?" he asked softly, stepping closer. "I know Ivy can be a bit overwhelming at times."

I shrugged, forcing a smile even as a knot twisted in my stomach. "I'm fine. I just... I want her to shine. This is her night, after all."

His eyes held mine, a flicker of understanding passing between us. "You matter too, you know. Don't let anyone else's brilliance dim your light."

I nodded, but the words felt like empty promises. The spotlight on Ivy was so intense, it cast long shadows over my own aspirations. Still, I couldn't deny the thrill of being part of something so alive, the electricity of the crowd fueling a fire within me that I hadn't acknowledged before. Perhaps there was still a way for me to shine, even if it wasn't the way I envisioned.

As Ivy took her place at the center of the gallery, the room quieted, anticipation hanging thick in the air. "Welcome, everyone!" she called out, her voice rising above the soft murmur. "Thank you for being here tonight to celebrate not just my work but the very essence of our community—our history, our memories, and the beauty we all contribute to the world."

A ripple of applause surged through the crowd, and I felt a swell of pride for her, momentarily pushing my insecurities aside. Nathaniel leaned in, whispering, "She's got them wrapped around her finger."

"Just wait," I replied, my voice barely audible over the growing applause. "This is just the beginning."

Ivy continued, her energy infectious. "Tonight, I want to give you a glimpse into my creative process. But first, I need a little help. Nathaniel!" she called, gesturing him forward with an exaggerated flourish. "Would you grace us with your keen observations?"

The crowd turned their attention toward Nathaniel, the collective breath held in eager anticipation. He stepped forward, a playful smile tugging at his lips as he took his place beside Ivy. "Well, I suppose I'm here to sprinkle some wisdom, but don't hold your breath. I'm just a humble admirer of art, after all."

With that, Ivy stepped aside, leaving Nathaniel in the spotlight, a confident grin on his face as he began to share his thoughts on her work. The way he spoke was magnetic, drawing the audience in as he painted vivid pictures with his words. I watched as he animatedly described Ivy's piece, bringing it to life with his keen observations and spirited commentary.

Yet, as he spoke, I felt a strange sense of detachment, a disconnect growing as I stood on the sidelines. The more Nathaniel engaged with Ivy's art, the more I felt like an observer in my own life. Was I truly supportive, or merely a spectator clinging to the edges of their brilliance?

A tension crept back in as Ivy's laughter mingled with Nathaniel's compliments, a delicious concoction of flirtation and admiration. My heart twisted in a way that felt both familiar and unsettling. I wanted to be happy for her, for them, but the feelings of inadequacy rushed back like an unwelcome tide.

Then, unexpectedly, Ivy turned to me, her expression shifting as she caught the glimpse of my unease. "You should join us!" she exclaimed, her eyes sparkling. "Your perspective would add so much!"

I hesitated, the lump in my throat growing. "I'm not sure I can—"

"Nonsense! We all need to hear from the brilliant writer in the room," Nathaniel interjected, flashing me a smile that sent a warm shiver down my spine. "Let's hear your take. I'm dying to know how you interpret this masterpiece."

The pressure mounted, the eyes of the gallery now turned toward me, and I felt the air thicken with expectation. A thousand thoughts collided in my mind, fear battling with the glimmer of possibility. Was this the moment I'd been waiting for, or would I crumble under the weight of my own self-doubt?

I took a deep breath, steeling myself for the challenge ahead. "Okay," I finally said, my voice surprisingly steady as I stepped forward. "But just remember, I'm not responsible for any chaos that ensues."

Laughter erupted in the crowd, breaking the tension, and as I joined Ivy and Nathaniel at the front, I realized I was ready to step into the light, ready to face whatever awaited me. The moment was electric, and the weight of my fears seemed to lift slightly.

But just as I began to speak, the gallery doors swung open, and a gust of cold wind swept through the room, silencing the crowd. All eyes turned toward the entrance as a figure stepped inside, and the atmosphere shifted dramatically, tension rippling through the air like a live wire.

The newcomer was a striking silhouette, their presence commanding attention, and I felt my heart skip a beat. What was going to happen next? The gallery buzzed with murmurs, anticipation electrifying the air as the figure moved closer, obscured by shadows, leaving us all on the edge of something we couldn't yet define.

Chapter 14: The Other Side of Trust

The gallery hummed with life, a swirling canvas of laughter, clinking glasses, and murmurs of admiration. I stood at the edge of the room, soaking in the moment—the culmination of months spent curating a collection that had come to feel like an extension of my very soul. Each piece spoke a story, a fragment of someone else's life splashed with color and emotion, yet here I was, feeling anything but vibrant. My fingers traced the smooth edge of a sleek, dark sculpture as I turned my gaze to the crowd, watching strangers revel in the beauty of my curated chaos. But just as the evening felt like it was mine, my phone buzzed insistently in my pocket, shattering the illusion of a flawless night.

I fished it out, heart skipping a beat as I saw my mother's name flash across the screen. The urgency in her messages often came wrapped in worry, and as I read the words that followed, the glow of celebration dimmed. "We've hit another snag with the shop," it read. "Can you come home? We need you." My stomach twisted, the familiar weight of duty pressing down harder than the silk dress clinging to my frame. The family business, a quaint little bookstore that had seen better days, felt like an anchor pulling me away from the horizon I so desperately wanted to reach.

I glanced up, hoping to find solace in the crowd, my friends, and Nathaniel's steady presence, but the moment felt heavier. Nathaniel stood across the room, sharing a laugh with Ivy, who seemed to light up every space she occupied. Their shared joy contrasted sharply with the storm brewing inside me. The warmth of their friendship was inviting, yet it felt like an unwanted reminder of all the ways I was tethered to the past. I took a deep breath and approached them, the tension coiling tighter in my chest with each step.

"Everything okay?" Ivy asked, her eyes narrowing with concern as I approached.

"It's... complicated," I managed, the words sticking to my throat like dry bread. "Mom needs me at the store. Another setback."

Ivy tilted her head, a flicker of understanding crossing her face. "You should go. You know you can't ignore your family."

But it wasn't that simple. I had spent years building a life, a dream that sparkled just out of reach, one that was too precious to abandon at the first sign of trouble. "It's just... I finally feel like I'm getting somewhere here. Like I belong."

"Belonging doesn't mean you have to sacrifice everything," Nathaniel interjected, his voice low and steady, filled with an earnestness that stirred something in me. "You have to follow your heart, but you can also be there for your family."

His words washed over me, tinged with a warmth I craved but feared. Nathaniel was the kind of man who seemed to embody the calm after a storm, the kind of person who made the mundane feel extraordinary with just a smile. I felt a pull toward him, a connection that transcended the chaos surrounding us, yet the shadows of my past lingered just out of reach, whispering warnings of betrayal and disappointment.

"I'll be fine. I can handle it," I replied, though even I could hear the tremor of uncertainty in my own voice. "I just don't want to let anyone down."

Ivy stepped closer, a soft determination etched on her face. "You're not letting anyone down by taking care of yourself too. Just think about it, okay?"

As I nodded, the reality of my situation sank deeper. The memories of my father's disappointment when I'd first dared to dream outside the confines of our little shop surfaced unbidden. I could still hear his voice, thick with disbelief, as I declared I wanted to curate art instead of selling books. It felt like ages ago, and yet, those moments haunted me still. I swallowed hard, battling the resurgence of that old wound.

"Let's not dwell on the past," I said, forcing a smile that didn't quite reach my eyes. "Tonight's about celebrating the gallery."

Just then, the gallery's lights flickered, casting playful shadows across the floor. The laughter in the room momentarily faded as an artist stepped up to the mic, ready to share a few words. I took a step back, allowing the spotlight to shift away from me, grateful for the distraction. As I watched him, I couldn't shake the feeling that the universe was playing some sort of cruel joke, testing my resolve.

A shift in energy surged through the crowd, and I felt Nathaniel's warmth radiate beside me. He leaned in, his voice barely above a whisper. "You're incredible, you know that? All this—" he gestured to the gallery, "—this is a testament to your hard work. Don't let anything dim that light."

The sincerity in his words wrapped around my heart like a gentle embrace, but I still felt the tug of my mother's plea. In that moment, I realized it wasn't just about the gallery; it was about trust—trust in myself, in my dreams, and in the people I let in. The memories of betrayal were like tendrils wrapping around my heart, squeezing it tight.

As the artist spoke, I found myself lost in thought, swirling emotions clashing inside me like paint on canvas. The choice ahead felt like a tightrope walk over an abyss of uncertainty. Would I choose to step into the light, pursuing what my heart craved? Or would I return to the familiar, the safe, where expectations loomed like heavy shadows?

A murmur rippled through the gallery as the artist concluded his speech, and I could feel the energy of the room shift once again. The applause erupted, reverberating through the walls like an echo of a thousand dreams, and yet, my heart felt like a lead weight in my chest. Nathaniel's gaze lingered on me, those deep-set eyes reflecting the light of the gallery, pulling me into a world where ambition and desire danced in tandem. I wanted to savor this moment—this night that had been so painstakingly crafted. But the reminder of my mother's distress clawed at my insides, demanding my attention like a toddler throwing a tantrum in a crowded café.

I took a step back, creating a small island of space between us. "I just need a moment," I said, my voice steadier than I felt. I needed to process, to decide if I would tether myself to the familiar or leap into the unknown. The taste of anticipation mingled with the bittersweet pang of obligation, and it left a sour note in my mouth.

"Hey," Nathaniel called, his voice slicing through the sea of chatter. I turned to see him pushing through the crowd, his brows knit together in concern. "You okay?"

"Yeah, peachy," I replied, forcing a smile that felt more like a grimace. "Just contemplating the meaning of life in a gallery full of art."

His lips quirked up, the playful glimmer in his eyes momentarily distracting me from my internal chaos. "Well, if you figure it out, let me know. I could use some life advice over a pint later."

The light banter flickered briefly, like a candle fighting against the wind. I wanted nothing more than to lose myself in his charm, but the reality of the situation pulled me back like a threadbare safety net. I turned my gaze to the vibrant paintings that adorned the walls, each canvas bursting with emotion, begging for attention. But all I could think of was the dimming glow of the bookstore, and the fear that maybe, just maybe, I was destined to disappoint.

"Do you ever feel like you're standing at a crossroads?" I asked, my voice dropping to a whisper. The noise around us faded into a dull hum as I searched his face for understanding. "Like every choice you make has the potential to change everything?"

His expression softened, and for a moment, I could see the gears turning in his mind as he processed my question. "Every day," he replied, a hint of vulnerability coloring his tone. "It's like trying to decide between a pizza place and that fancy new vegan restaurant everyone raves about. One leads to comfort; the other, an adventure. Sometimes, I just want to flip a coin."

I chuckled lightly, appreciating his humor even in this weighty moment. "So, pizza is your safe space?"

"Absolutely. You can't go wrong with cheese."

As his lightheartedness wrapped around me, I felt the tension ease slightly. "But what if I've already committed to a different menu?" I asked, my voice barely above a murmur.

"Then maybe it's time to re-evaluate your order," he suggested, his gaze steady and earnest. "You're not obligated to stick to something just because you've always had it. Life's too short for stale bread."

His words struck a chord deep within me. The tension coiled in my stomach loosened, and I began to see my dilemma in a new light. Perhaps my mother's plea for help was not a chain around my neck but rather a choice—one that could lead me back to a passion I had long neglected.

"Can I ask you something?" I blurted out, suddenly aware of the gravity of the moment.

"Anything."

"What if I don't trust myself anymore?"

He didn't hesitate. "Then you need to remind yourself of everything you've achieved. You curated this gallery, you built a life here—trust in the journey you've taken to get to this moment."

The sincerity in his voice sent a warm surge through me. I studied his face, searching for any hint of insincerity, but found none. He was a beacon of light, standing firm while I felt like I was lost in a swirling fog. I thought about my past, the betrayals that had cut deep, and how every scar felt like a reminder of my inadequacies. But standing here with Nathaniel, I felt something shift—a flicker of hope igniting beneath the layers of doubt.

As we stood there, the applause for the artist crescendoed around us, the crowd swelling with excitement. I could hear the jubilant laughter mixing with the music that filled the air. It was intoxicating, and for the first time that evening, I felt the tension between my dreams and my responsibilities begin to thaw.

"Maybe," I began, the words tumbling out, "maybe I can go home for a bit, help Mom, and then come back here. I could strike a balance."

"Now you're talking." His smile was bright enough to chase away any lingering shadows. "You don't have to abandon your dreams; just find a way to juggle them. I mean, look at us—art and family can coexist, right?"

I nodded slowly, considering the possibility. A small seed of defiance sprouted within me, mingling with the warmth of determination. Perhaps I didn't have to choose one over the other; I could embrace both.

As the night progressed, laughter and conversations danced around us, but I felt a newfound sense of clarity emerging amidst the chaos. I would go home and support my family, but I wouldn't let that decision eclipse my aspirations. Nathaniel's presence beside me was a grounding force, reminding me that I wasn't alone in this journey.

"Let's toast to choices," Nathaniel declared, raising his glass toward me, the light reflecting off the surface like a promise. "To balancing dreams and responsibilities. And to pizza, obviously."

I chuckled, clinking my glass against his, feeling the warmth of the moment swell within me. "To pizza," I echoed, allowing the laughter to wash over me like a balm.

But as I raised my glass, I felt the echo of my mother's plea resonating within me, reminding me that this journey was far from over. The road ahead was uncertain, but for the first time in a long time, I was ready to embrace it, trusting myself to navigate the complexities of love, ambition, and the tangled threads of family ties.

The laughter from the gallery echoed like distant music, soft yet insistent, reminding me that life danced on despite the chaos brewing inside. Nathaniel and I stood amidst the ebb and flow of art enthusiasts, each conversation swirling around us like vibrant brush strokes on a canvas. I could feel the pulse of the evening, the way it wrapped around my heart, urging me to stay a little longer, to embrace this newfound clarity.

"Want to take a stroll?" Nathaniel suggested, his voice laced with that casual charm that made it feel as though the world had narrowed down to just the two of us. "The view from the terrace is worth a million gallery lights."

The idea struck me as a welcome escape from the emotional maelstrom swirling in my chest. "Lead the way," I replied, allowing him to guide me through the throng of attendees, weaving past small clusters of chatter and laughter. As we stepped onto the terrace, the cool night air enveloped us, offering a refreshing contrast to the warmth of the gallery.

I inhaled deeply, savoring the crispness of the night, while the city sparkled below like a tapestry woven from dreams. The stars hung above, twinkling with an invitation to share secrets and dreams alike. I leaned against the railing, feeling the smooth metal against my palms, the city lights reflecting in my eyes as I attempted to untangle the thoughts that had clung to me like ivy.

"Nice view, isn't it?" Nathaniel's voice broke through my reverie, grounding me. I turned to find him standing beside me, the soft glow from the gallery framing him in an ethereal light, making the moment feel almost surreal.

"Beautiful," I replied, my gaze drifting back to the sprawling landscape before us. "It's like a living painting."

"Just like you." His words slipped out effortlessly, and I felt a rush of warmth wash over me. I turned to meet his gaze, and for a heartbeat, the air between us crackled with something electric.

"What, me? A piece of art?" I teased, raising an eyebrow, a playful smile dancing on my lips.

"Definitely. You've got layers, depth, and the ability to surprise," he shot back, the corner of his mouth lifting in a smirk that made my heart flutter.

I couldn't help but laugh. "You might need to get your eyes checked if you think I'm anything close to a masterpiece."

"Oh, trust me, I've seen plenty of masterpieces, and none of them compare." His tone turned sincere, earnest. "You're extraordinary in a way that makes you feel like home, but with an adventure waiting to happen."

The weight of his words settled around us, drawing me in. In that moment, I wanted to lean into that connection, to explore what lay beneath the surface of our playful banter. But a sharp reminder of my obligations clawed at my consciousness, dragging me back into the fray of family duty.

"I've been thinking," I started, hesitating as uncertainty gnawed at my confidence. "About going home, helping my mom at the bookstore. It feels right, but... it also feels like giving up."

He turned to face me fully, his expression serious now, eyes piercing through the veil of my uncertainty. "You're not giving up; you're just expanding your horizons. Helping your family doesn't mean abandoning your dreams. Sometimes, they can coexist beautifully."

I looked out at the cityscape, pondering his words. I wanted to believe that I could juggle both worlds without losing myself. The thought of returning home felt heavy, but perhaps it also offered an opportunity to reconnect with my roots.

VIBRANT ALLURE

Just then, the gallery door swung open, and Ivy emerged, her face flushed with excitement, as if she had just sprinted a marathon. "You won't believe it!" she exclaimed, her breathless enthusiasm infectious. "The artist you were raving about earlier is here! And he's looking for you!"

The moment hung in the air, charged with promise. A knot of anticipation twisted in my stomach. The artist—a visionary, a genius—had been an elusive shadow in my plans for the gallery. "He's here?" I echoed, trying to suppress the mix of anxiety and thrill.

"Yes! He wants to meet the curator behind this incredible collection." Ivy gestured animatedly, her eyes sparkling with excitement. "This could be a huge opportunity for you."

I felt the ground shift beneath me, the once-clear path of my evening suddenly tangled with the sudden influx of possibilities. I glanced at Nathaniel, whose expression mirrored my own mixture of excitement and apprehension.

"Are you going to take it?" he asked, his voice low but firm, a gentle encouragement.

"I... I should," I replied, uncertainty lacing my tone. The idea of meeting him was intoxicating, yet the thought of leaving Nathaniel felt equally daunting.

"Go on, I'll be right here," he assured me, a slight smile playing on his lips. "I'll just be admiring the view."

I took a deep breath, stepping back from the railing. "Okay, I'll be quick," I promised, and with one last glance at Nathaniel, I turned and hurried back inside, my heart racing with the dual thrill of excitement and trepidation.

The gallery buzzed with energy, a whirlwind of color and sound. I scanned the room, searching for the artist, my heart pounding in rhythm with the laughter and conversations. And then I saw him—a tall figure standing in the corner, surrounded by a small crowd of admirers, his presence magnetic.

As I approached, I caught fragments of his conversation. He spoke passionately about inspiration, the dance between chaos and creation. I couldn't help but be drawn in, my pulse quickening with each word. This was it—the moment I had been waiting for, a chance to step into a world that felt vibrant and alive.

But as I finally reached the edge of the crowd, ready to introduce myself, the unmistakable sound of my phone buzzing in my pocket cut through the atmosphere. I hesitated, torn between the tantalizing opportunity before me and the nagging urgency of my family's needs.

With a quick glance at the screen, my heart sank. It was my mother. The message read: "We need to talk. It's urgent."

The room around me blurred into insignificance, the chatter fading as the weight of that message settled in my stomach like a stone. A chasm of doubt opened up beneath my feet, threatening to swallow me whole. I glanced back at the artist, standing in all his brilliance, an opportunity that felt just out of reach.

But the thought of my mother waiting, desperate and uncertain, tugged at my heartstrings. As I stood there, caught in this web of conflicting emotions, I realized that the decisions I faced were more than just about art or family; they were about trust—trusting myself to navigate the murky waters ahead.

"Hey," Ivy's voice broke through my thoughts as she joined me, her brows furrowed in concern. "You alright? You look like you've seen a ghost."

"I'm not sure what to do," I confessed, the urgency of my mother's message weighing heavily on my heart. "I really want this, but..."

"Then go to her," Ivy urged gently, her eyes wide with understanding. "You can't ignore family when they need you.

Opportunities will always be there, but you can't get back these moments."

The conviction in her voice anchored me, yet I felt that deep yearning to break free, to grasp the opportunity that lay before me. "But what if I lose everything?"

"You won't," Ivy assured me. "Trust yourself."

Just then, the crowd around the artist began to shift, and before I could respond, he turned and locked eyes with me. There was an intensity there, a recognition that sent a thrill racing through my veins. My heart leaped in my chest, and I suddenly felt paralyzed by the choices before me.

And then, as if the universe had decided to toy with my fate, the lights flickered ominously, plunging the gallery into a momentary darkness. Gasps erupted around us, and the moment shattered like glass, leaving me teetering on the edge of decision.

In that instant, with my mother's message echoing in my mind and the artist's piercing gaze holding me captive, I realized that I was at a crossroads, standing on the precipice of everything I had ever wanted. And as the lights flickered back to life, I faced a choice that would change everything.

Chapter 15: Shattered Expectations

The café was one of those charming little spots that seemed to thrive on an air of effortless elegance. Located at the corner of a bustling street, it was adorned with delicate fairy lights that twinkled like stars against the dusky sky, giving the space a magical glow. The aroma of freshly brewed coffee wafted through the air, mingling with the sweet scent of pastries, creating a heady concoction that teased my senses. I settled into a small table by the window, my heart racing, a restless energy crackling within me.

Nathaniel arrived moments later, his tall figure cutting through the crowd like a lighthouse beam in a storm. The way he moved was both graceful and determined, but that evening, his usual confident stride was overshadowed by a palpable tension. As he approached, I caught the flicker of apprehension in his deep brown eyes. I couldn't help but feel a magnetic pull, even as anger simmered just beneath the surface.

"Hey," he said, sliding into the chair opposite mine. His voice held a mixture of warmth and uncertainty, a combination that usually sent shivers down my spine. Tonight, however, it did nothing to quell the whirlwind of emotions swirling inside me. I leaned forward, my hands clasped tightly, fighting against the urge to push them into fists.

"Why didn't you tell me?" The words slipped out before I could rein them in. The question hung heavy between us, punctuated by the soft murmur of the café and the clinking of ceramic cups.

"I didn't think it was necessary," he replied, his brow furrowing slightly as if my confrontation took him by surprise. "It was just a conversation."

"A conversation?" I echoed, incredulity lacing my tone. "You've been talking to my mother about the family business, Nathaniel.

That's not just a conversation. It's a decision that involves me whether you like it or not."

His gaze dropped to the table, tracing the rim of his coffee cup as if it contained the answers we both sought. "I thought it might help. I thought..." He paused, collecting his thoughts. "I thought you might want to know what she has in mind."

I laughed, the sound bitter and hollow. "Help? You think talking to her behind my back is helpful? I can't even process how you thought that was a good idea."

"Evelyn," he began, but I cut him off, the rawness of my emotions spilling out like a dam bursting.

"I don't want to hear excuses. You've stepped into my life, into this messy situation with my mother, and I feel like I'm the last to know everything. Why did you feel like you had to hide this from me?"

His expression shifted, a mixture of frustration and hurt flashing across his face. "I didn't want to burden you. You've already got so much on your plate with everything that's happening."

I shook my head, disbelief washing over me. "You think keeping secrets is protecting me? You don't get to decide what's a burden for me, Nathaniel. You're not my savior; you're supposed to be my partner."

He inhaled deeply, his shoulders tensing as if preparing for a storm. "You're right. I should have told you. But I didn't want to complicate things, especially now that we're..."

"Now that we're what?" I challenged, the heat of the moment sparking an intensity that crackled like electricity in the air between us. "In a relationship? You think that's enough to justify keeping secrets?"

The silence stretched out, thick with unspoken words and unresolved feelings. I could see the conflict etched on his face—one part regret, one part stubbornness, and perhaps a smidge of fear. I wanted to reach across the table, to bridge the gap between us, but the anger within me acted like a wall, fortified by betrayal.

"I thought we were building something here," I said, my voice quieter now, tinged with vulnerability. "But if this is how you treat me—if this is how you treat trust—I don't know if I can continue like this."

His expression shifted, the heat of anger dissipating to reveal something softer, something raw. "Evelyn, please don't say that. I care about you. I really do."

"Caring isn't enough if it comes with conditions, Nathaniel. If you care about me, then why would you ever think it was okay to involve my mother without telling me?"

His jaw clenched, and for a moment, the café faded into the background, the world outside becoming a blur of passersby and dimming sunlight. "I thought I could navigate this without dragging you into every detail. I thought I could shield you from the messiness of it all."

I scoffed, the sarcasm slicing through the air. "Shielding me? You've done the exact opposite. You've turned my life into a bigger mess."

His eyes narrowed slightly, and I could see the wheels turning in his mind as he struggled to find the right words. "What do you want from me, then?"

I leaned back, a harsh breath escaping my lips. "I want honesty, Nathaniel. I want to be part of this, but I can't do that if you're pulling strings behind my back."

The moment hung between us, heavy with realization. I saw the determination flicker in his gaze, a hint of understanding beginning to dawn. "Okay. I promise, no more secrets. But you have to trust me, too. We're in this together."

The words lingered in the air, a fragile thread of hope weaving through the chaos of my emotions. But trust, once shattered, was a difficult thing to reclaim. I stared at him, searching for the sincerity in his expression, hoping to find a glimmer of the man I had begun to fall for amidst the turmoil that threatened to consume us both.

The air between us was thick, almost electric, and the world around us faded to a distant hum as Nathaniel leaned in, his expression a potent mix of determination and vulnerability. The weight of his promise hung in the air like the rich aroma of coffee, a stark contrast to the bitterness I felt. My heart wanted to believe him, to hold on to the idea that we could work through this, but the shadows of doubt danced tantalizingly at the edges of my thoughts.

"What if I can't trust you anymore?" I asked, my voice barely above a whisper, but the gravity of the question loomed large. "What if this was just the tip of the iceberg?"

He met my gaze, his eyes steady and serious. "I get it, trust is hard to rebuild once it's broken. But we have something worth fighting for, don't we?"

The challenge in his tone ignited a spark of defiance within me. "You mean you think we have something worth fighting for? You've done a stellar job of proving the opposite."

Nathaniel sighed, a weary sound that tugged at my heartstrings despite the tension still crackling between us. "Look, I know I messed up. I should have told you the truth from the start. But that doesn't mean I don't want you in my life."

My fingers twitched against the cool surface of the table, a conflict of emotions wrestling for dominance within me. "So, what do you want? To just sweep this under the rug and pretend it didn't happen?"

He ran a hand through his tousled hair, frustration etching lines into his forehead. "No! I want to be honest, to be real with you. Can't we just take a step back and figure this out together?"

His plea hung in the air, both an invitation and a challenge, and as I studied him, I couldn't shake the feeling that we were at a crossroads. The café was abuzz with laughter and chatter, but we existed in our own bubble of uncertainty, a fragile ecosystem hanging by a thread.

"Fine," I said, my voice steadier than I felt. "But this isn't just about your choice to speak with my mother. It's about everything—communication, transparency, and respect. If you want me in your life, you have to understand what that means."

A flicker of relief crossed his face. "Okay, I can do that. Let's just start fresh. I won't involve your mother again without your knowledge. And if you have any concerns, I want you to voice them."

The sincerity in his eyes held a promise, a glimmer of hope that began to chip away at the walls I had built around my heart. "I appreciate that, but you have to understand my perspective. This business—my family—it's complicated. You're a part of it whether you want to be or not."

"Then let's figure out how to navigate that together," he said, his voice low and earnest.

The tension between us slowly began to dissolve, replaced by a tentative truce that felt both precarious and exhilarating. As we talked, I found myself laughing again, the easy banter we shared creeping back into our conversation. But beneath the surface, the unease lingered, a silent reminder of the precarious ground we stood on.

"I can't believe you thought talking to my mother was a good idea," I teased, a playful edge to my voice. "What's next? You'll be inviting her to our next date?"

"Only if you promise to wear your best dress," he shot back, a teasing glint in his eye.

"Ha! As if I'd wear anything less," I retorted, smirking as the tension began to feel lighter, almost manageable.

With each laugh, each quip, I could feel the barriers between us lowering, but a part of me remained wary. Nathaniel leaned closer, his voice dropping to a conspiratorial whisper. "So, what do you say we put this behind us and focus on what's really important?"

I raised an eyebrow, curiosity piqued. "And what's that?"

His smile turned sly, that charming grin that had once made my heart race. "How about we plan a little getaway? Just the two of us."

I hesitated, considering the idea. "A getaway? Now?"

"Why not? We could drive out to the lake, spend a weekend away from all this chaos. Just us, the stars, and a bottle of wine. I promise no family business talk."

The thought of escaping the current mess was tempting, a siren call to adventure that tugged at my heartstrings. But just as quickly as the idea sparked excitement, it also ignited doubts. "Nathaniel, we still have things to figure out. I can't just run away from my problems."

"I'm not asking you to run away," he replied softly, his gaze unwavering. "I'm suggesting we step away for a moment, breathe, and recalibrate. We can face everything when we get back, but first, let's make some good memories."

His sincerity washed over me like a gentle wave, and I found myself weighing the risks against the potential reward. Perhaps it was time to step away from the turmoil, even if just for a moment. The thought of being somewhere beautiful, where laughter could drown out the noise of our worries, sent a thrill through me.

"Okay," I finally said, a smile creeping onto my lips. "Let's do it. But if you mention my mother once, I'm packing my bags and heading home."

He chuckled, the tension between us easing as he reached across the table to take my hand. "Deal. Just us and a little adventure, no strings attached."

As we left the café, the sun dipped lower in the sky, casting a warm golden glow across the pavement. I felt lighter, like a weight had been lifted from my shoulders. With Nathaniel at my side, I was ready to step into this unexpected journey, even if the road ahead was still unclear.

But as we walked, hand in hand, a shadow flickered at the edge of my thoughts—a reminder that every adventure comes with its own challenges. And while I was determined to embrace the moments of joy, the chaos of the world I had tried to leave behind still loomed, waiting for its moment to strike.

The weekend unfolded like a freshly unwrapped present, each moment filled with the kind of anticipation usually reserved for birthday surprises. Nathaniel and I hit the road early, the sun stretching its golden arms across the horizon as we drove out of the city. The rhythmic hum of the tires against the asphalt set a steady pace for our journey, while the radio played a mix of soft tunes that seemed to echo the tentative hope blooming between us.

As we crossed the border into the countryside, the landscape transformed into a tapestry of lush greenery and wildflowers dancing in the breeze. I could feel the weight of the week beginning to lift off my shoulders, replaced by the promise of fresh air and freedom. Nathaniel's laughter filled the space between us, a sound that now felt like a balm to my frayed nerves.

"Did you ever think you'd be taking a spontaneous trip with a guy who has the charming ability to irritate you one minute and make you laugh the next?" he asked, a teasing glint in his eye.

I feigned a thoughtful expression, tapping my chin dramatically. "I don't know, Nathaniel. It's quite the gamble, really. But I figured the car ride would be the perfect place for an escape plan in case I needed to bail."

"Oh, please," he scoffed playfully. "As if you could resist my unparalleled charisma and devilishly good looks."

"Devilishly good looks? More like dangerously untrustworthy," I shot back, unable to keep the grin off my face.

With each mile that slipped by, the tension from our earlier confrontation seemed to dissipate, replaced by the easy rhythm of conversation and shared laughter. We navigated through winding roads, framed by trees that formed a protective canopy overhead, as if nature itself conspired to shield us from the world's chaos.

As we neared the lake, the sun dipped lower in the sky, casting a shimmering glow on the water that looked almost otherworldly. "This place is beautiful," I breathed, awestruck by the scene unfolding before us.

Nathaniel parked the car and we stepped out, inhaling the crisp, clean air that filled our lungs like a refreshing promise. The lake sparkled under the soft light, inviting us to explore its edges. We wandered along the shore, our fingers brushing against each other, igniting sparks of warmth that pulsed like a heartbeat.

"Let's find a spot for a picnic," Nathaniel suggested, his enthusiasm infectious.

"Great idea! Just no sandwiches that taste like cardboard, okay? If I wanted that, I would've stayed home," I replied, nudging him playfully.

"I'll do my best, but I make no promises," he said with mock seriousness. "You'll just have to trust me."

Trust. The word echoed in my mind, an elusive concept that seemed to dance just out of reach. As we spread out the blanket, I couldn't shake the remnants of our earlier conversation. It was easy to get lost in the moment, but I knew the underlying issues weren't resolved. Still, the laughter we shared, the way our eyes sparkled in the fading light, made it momentarily easier to forget.

After we settled down, we unpacked our meal—a carefully curated selection of artisan cheeses, fresh fruits, and the sweetest pastries I could have imagined. Each bite tasted like freedom, a delicious reminder that sometimes, life could be surprisingly delightful.

"Okay, we need to make a toast," Nathaniel said, raising a sparkling water bottle as if it were the finest champagne.

"To us," I said, clinking my bottle against his. "For giving each other a second chance. Or at least the illusion of one."

He chuckled, the sound light and airy. "I'll take that. And to navigating the messiness of life together. Cheers!"

As we enjoyed our makeshift feast, the conversation flowed effortlessly. We talked about everything and nothing—our favorite childhood memories, our most embarrassing moments, and the dreams we hadn't yet pursued. Laughter punctuated the air, weaving a tapestry of connection that wrapped around us like a warm blanket.

But as the sun began to sink lower, painting the sky in hues of pink and orange, a shadow flitted across my mind. "So, what about your mother?" I asked, my voice almost tentative. "What happens when we go back?"

Nathaniel's smile faded slightly, and for a moment, the air turned thick with unspoken tension. "I guess we'll just have to face it," he said, his tone shifting to something more serious. "We can't keep avoiding the conversation, can we?"

"No, we can't," I admitted, my heart racing at the thought of returning to reality. "But I need to know where you stand. Are you going to keep making decisions for me? Or will you include me from now on?"

He took a deep breath, his gaze locking onto mine with an intensity that sent shivers down my spine. "I promise, from now on, you're part of the conversation. No more secrets, no more surprises."

We held each other's gaze, the vulnerability in his eyes reflecting my own fears. I wanted to believe him, wanted to step into this new chapter with hope. But just as I began to feel a sense of relief, a commotion disrupted our peaceful moment.

From across the lake, I noticed a group of people gathered near a small wooden dock, their voices rising in a mixture of excitement and alarm. I stood up, squinting to see better, my stomach knotting as I recognized a familiar face among the crowd.

"Is that my mother?" I gasped, a mixture of disbelief and dread surging through me.

Nathaniel followed my gaze, his expression shifting from curiosity to concern. "What's she doing here?"

"I don't know," I muttered, panic clawing at my insides. "We need to find out."

We rushed toward the growing crowd, each step heavy with uncertainty. As we got closer, I could hear snippets of conversation, fragments that made my stomach twist.

"...found something in the water...looks serious..."

"What do you mean? Is someone hurt?"

My heart raced, each beat pounding in my ears like a warning bell. I pushed my way through the throng, Nathaniel at my side, the world narrowing to the singular focus of reaching my mother. The crowd parted slightly, revealing a small boat bobbing in the water, the reflection of the sinking sun dancing ominously on its surface.

As we reached the edge of the dock, my breath caught in my throat. My mother stood there, her face pale, eyes wide with shock. I caught her gaze, and in that moment, everything else faded away.

"Evelyn!" she shouted, her voice trembling as she pointed toward the water. "There's something down there!"

The world around me blurred, the gentle sound of the lake turning into a deafening roar as I followed her gaze. And then, just beneath the surface, I saw it—something dark and ominous that sent a chill racing down my spine, freezing the very blood in my veins.

"Get back!" Nathaniel shouted, pulling me closer as realization struck like lightning. My heart pounded against my ribcage, the promise of a carefree weekend shattered in an instant, leaving only questions and an unshakable sense of dread hanging in the air.

Chapter 16: The Price of Ambition

The hum of the sewing machines enveloped me as I stepped into the workshop, a symphony of creativity that mingled with the scent of fabric and fresh coffee. Sunlight streamed through the tall windows, illuminating the cluttered workspace where rolls of vibrant material sprawled across tables like colorful waves crashing onto a shore. The atmosphere buzzed with a frenetic energy, each designer lost in their own world, yet tethered by a shared dream of making their mark on the fashion landscape. I inhaled deeply, letting the familiar scents wrap around me like a well-loved blanket, reminding me of the reasons I had fled the quiet confines of my past.

I hadn't realized how much I had missed this feeling—the exhilaration of creation, the thrill of exploration, and the quiet camaraderie that flourished among those who understood the price of ambition. Each stitch sewn and fabric cut felt like a breath of fresh air, a momentary escape from the swirling chaos that occupied my heart. My hands tingled with anticipation as I selected a bolt of rich emerald satin, the texture smooth against my fingertips, inviting my imagination to run wild.

"Hey, are you going for a disco ball theme or just trying to catch the eye of someone special?" A voice broke through my reverie, teasing yet warm. I turned to find a woman with fiery red hair pulled into a messy bun, her hands covered in chalk dust and her shirt splattered with paint. She wore a playful grin that suggested mischief and familiarity, even though I had never met her.

"Neither, but I'm not opposed to drawing attention," I replied with a smirk, my pulse quickening slightly at the banter. "It's all about standing out in a sea of black, isn't it?"

"True enough. I'm Zara, by the way. Welcome to the chaos." She extended a paint-stained hand, and I took it, feeling a surge of warmth and energy pass between us.

"I'm Lila. Just trying to find my footing among these towering giants of fashion."

"Trust me, we're all just as lost as you are. This city has a way of making you feel like you're standing on a tightrope, doesn't it?" Her laugh was infectious, and I felt a smile spreading across my face as I nodded. "But that's what makes it exhilarating. The thrill of falling is just as exciting as the chance of flying."

As we worked side by side, the conversation flowed effortlessly, punctuated by sharp wit and laughter. Each designer shared snippets of their lives, revealing struggles with self-doubt, rejection, and the relentless pursuit of success. I felt an undeniable connection, a sense of belonging that had eluded me in my solitary endeavors.

Zara leaned closer, lowering her voice conspiratorially. "So, what's the real story behind those eyes? They look like they've seen a lot more than just fabric swatches and sewing needles."

I hesitated, the weight of Nathaniel's absence pressing against my chest. The thrill of this new space clashed violently with the turmoil brewing within me. "It's a long story," I began, my voice tinged with uncertainty. "One that involves a man who could charm the buttons off a designer jacket."

"Ah, the infamous 'him.' They always seem to know how to pull at the seams of our hearts, don't they?" Zara's expression shifted to one of empathy mixed with mischief. "Let me guess—dashing, ambitious, and possibly a little dangerous?"

"Something like that," I replied, a soft laugh escaping my lips despite the ache in my heart. "We had our moments, but the ambition that brought us together also drove us apart. I just don't know if I can move on."

"Maybe you're not meant to," she suggested, her eyes sparkling with curiosity. "Maybe it's about finding a way to weave him into your story without letting him dictate the pattern."

Her words resonated deeply, stirring something within me. Perhaps it wasn't about erasing Nathaniel from my narrative but rather integrating the lessons learned from our tumultuous relationship. The idea of blending the vibrant threads of my past with the vibrant fabric of my present felt liberating.

Just then, a commotion erupted across the room. A man burst through the door, his presence electrifying the air as he scanned the workshop with an intensity that demanded attention. He had dark hair tousled in a way that suggested both artistry and recklessness, dressed in a tailored jacket that hinted at his success. I felt my pulse quicken involuntarily as I recognized him—the designer whose work I had admired from afar, a name that reverberated through the industry like a striking chord.

"Alright, everyone! Gather around!" he called, his voice rich and smooth, capturing the room's full attention. "Today's workshop is all about breaking boundaries. Who's ready to push their creative limits?"

As the designers flocked to him, buzzing with excitement, I felt a strange mixture of admiration and trepidation. His gaze swept across the crowd, finally landing on me. For a brief moment, I was frozen, the world around me blurring as our eyes locked. There was something unspoken, a challenge hidden beneath the surface, igniting a spark I hadn't felt in ages.

"Lila," he said, stepping closer, the other designers fading into the background. "I hear you're not afraid to stand out. Let's see what you've got."

The words hung in the air, a tantalizing invitation laced with intrigue. As I returned to my fabric, I could feel the weight of ambition pressing against my chest, mingling with a renewed determination. Maybe the price of ambition was high, but in that moment, surrounded by the vibrant colors of hope and creativity, I was willing to pay it.

The workshop buzzed with excitement, a blend of ambition and creativity that made the air electric. As the charismatic designer stood before us, I could feel the pulse of inspiration thrumming through the room, echoing the rhythm of my racing heart. I glanced around, taking in the eager faces of my fellow designers, each one a tapestry of hope and talent. It was a stark reminder that we were all here, driven by a shared dream, yet tangled in our own personal battles.

"Alright, let's start with a little icebreaker," he announced, flashing a grin that could only be described as disarming. "Tell us your name and one wild idea you've been dying to try but haven't had the guts to attempt."

One by one, hands shot up, laughter bubbling through the crowd as each designer unveiled quirky concepts—dresses that doubled as sleeping bags, suits that changed color based on mood, and skirts that played music. Each idea was a glimpse into their creative souls, unfiltered and vibrant. I felt the knot of anxiety in my stomach loosen slightly, a sense of camaraderie weaving its way through the room.

When my turn arrived, I took a deep breath, fighting the urge to downplay my ambitions. "I'm Lila, and I've always wanted to design a collection that tells a story. Each piece would be inspired by a different emotion, a fabric diary of human experience." My voice was steady, and for a moment, I felt the weight of my dreams lifting, buoyed by the room's encouraging energy.

"Now that's what I'm talking about!" he exclaimed, his enthusiasm infectious. "Let's turn that idea into reality. We have a challenge ahead of us today that will push all your boundaries. Let's see what stories your fabrics can tell."

The afternoon unfolded like a vivid dream. We were divided into small teams, and I found myself paired with Zara and another designer named Marco, a tall man with an effortless swagger and a knack for bold designs. We brainstormed, feeding off one another's creativity like a well-oiled machine.

"So, if we're telling stories, we need a twist, something unexpected," Marco said, his brows furrowing in thought. "How about we incorporate recycled materials? A narrative of rebirth and sustainability, a phoenix rising from the ashes?"

I nodded, intrigued. "That's brilliant! It's not just about fashion; it's about making a statement. We could use denim scraps for a modern twist on a classic silhouette."

Zara's eyes sparkled as she added, "And let's not forget texture. Maybe some velvet to represent comfort and warmth, juxtaposed with the rawness of the denim. It'll be like a conversation between two worlds."

The ideas flowed freely, our energy crackling in the air, and for the first time in a long while, I felt a flicker of joy igniting within me. As the hours passed, laughter and shouts of excitement filled the workshop, drowning out the remnants of doubt that had lingered in my mind.

But as we began sketching our designs, a shadow slipped across my thoughts. Nathaniel's face flashed in my mind, his eyes bright with ambition and the weight of expectations. I shook my head, trying to dispel the memory. This was my moment, a chance to reclaim my identity amid the chaos that had engulfed my heart.

As the evening sun dipped low, casting a warm golden hue across the workshop, we gathered to present our concepts. My heart raced as I watched other teams share their visions, each presentation more impressive than the last. When it was finally our turn, I took a deep breath, stepping forward with my sketch in hand.

"This is our story," I began, gesturing toward the colorful array of drawings spread across the table. "It's about transformation and embracing imperfection. Each piece reflects the struggle we all face, yet embodies the beauty that emerges from it. We've chosen to use recycled materials to highlight sustainability and remind us that what's old can be reborn into something stunning."

The room erupted in applause, and I felt a rush of pride coursing through me. Zara and Marco beamed, their excitement palpable. It was a moment of triumph, a small victory that reminded me why I had fallen in love with fashion in the first place.

As the workshop wrapped up, the designer praised our efforts, and I felt a sense of belonging enveloping me. "This city can be brutal, but it's also a canvas," he said, looking directly at me. "Embrace every challenge, every heartbreak, and let it inspire your creations. That's what makes you unique."

As the crowd dispersed, I lingered, reluctant to leave this newfound sanctuary. Just then, Zara sidled up beside me, her expression contemplative. "So, what's next for you, Lila? More design workshops, or is there someone out there waiting to be swept off their feet?"

I chuckled, rolling my eyes playfully. "Honestly? I could use a break from the romantic entanglements. The last one almost had me tangled in knots."

Zara's laughter danced in the air. "Ah, but love is the best inspiration. You never know what kind of magic it can bring to your designs."

"Magic or mayhem," I replied, a hint of sarcasm creeping into my tone. "Let's just say I'm focusing on threads and fabrics rather than heartstrings for a while."

But as I spoke, a familiar figure caught my eye just outside the door. Nathaniel stood there, framed by the soft glow of the setting sun, an expression of determination etched across his features. My breath hitched, a surge of emotions colliding within me—frustration, longing, and a flicker of hope.

"Speaking of threads, it seems the past isn't quite ready to let go of me," I muttered, my heart racing as he stepped inside, his gaze locking onto mine with an intensity that made the room fade into the background.

"Lila," he said, his voice low and rich, "we need to talk."

The air thickened with tension, a palpable energy between us that crackled with unresolved feelings. I could feel the vibrant world of creativity around me shifting as the reality of our unfinished business loomed large. The workshop, once a sanctuary, now felt like the stage for a complicated play—a drama waiting to unfold.

The tension in the room crackled like static electricity as Nathaniel stepped inside, his presence demanding attention in a way that felt simultaneously thrilling and daunting. My heart raced, caught in a whirlwind of emotions that threatened to spill over. I forced myself to breathe, reminding myself that I was no longer the girl wrapped in his charm, lost in a whirlwind of his ambition. I was Lila, an emerging designer carving out my own identity in this chaotic city.

"What do we need to talk about?" I asked, trying to keep my voice steady. The workshop, with its vibrant fabrics and buzzing creativity, suddenly felt constricting, as if the walls were closing in around us.

"I came to apologize," he said, his tone serious, the playfulness gone. "I've been a fool, and I need you to understand why things went the way they did."

My mind raced. Apologies were easy words for someone who had wielded ambition like a weapon. "You mean the way you walked away when it got tough? That kind of fool?"

"I know how it sounds, and I don't expect you to just forgive me," he said, stepping closer, the intensity of his gaze disarming. "But I've had time to think. I've been chasing after a dream that doesn't feel right without you in it."

"Now you want me in your dream?" I couldn't keep the bite from my voice, the edge sharper than I intended. "After everything?"

"I wasn't ready before," he admitted, frustration lacing his tone. "But being here today, seeing you thrive—it made me realize how much I've lost. I need you to give me a chance to explain."

Zara and Marco had retreated to a corner, their conversation drifting into the background as I weighed Nathaniel's words. The noise of the workshop faded, and I felt suspended in a moment that could tip in either direction—back into the comfort of old feelings or forward into an uncertain future.

"Why now?" I pressed, crossing my arms, trying to maintain a facade of strength despite the vulnerability swirling inside me. "What changed?"

He hesitated, his brow furrowing in thought. "I saw a glimpse of you today, Lila. The way you lit up presenting your ideas, the passion in your voice. It made me realize that I wasn't just losing a partner; I was losing my muse."

A rush of conflicting emotions surged through me—anger, sadness, longing. I could feel the hurt of our past gnawing at the edges of my resolve. "So you want me to be your muse again? Just like that?"

"No, not just a muse. I want you by my side, as a collaborator. I know I was selfish, focused only on my ambitions. I've learned that success means little without someone to share it with," he said, sincerity etched across his face.

As I looked into his eyes, I recognized the sincerity there, mingled with a hint of desperation. It felt like a trap, one I had narrowly escaped before. But what if—what if this time was different? The thought teased my mind, dangerous and alluring.

"Do you think this is about just us?" I asked, narrowing my eyes, trying to push through the layers of past disappointments. "Because you're still the same man who left without a second thought. It's not that easy."

He sighed, frustration evident. "I know it's not easy, but I want to prove that I've changed. The city's pressure can make you forget what truly matters. And what matters to me is you."

The sincerity of his words hung in the air, heavy and intoxicating. But before I could respond, Zara sidled up beside me, a playful grin on her face. "Looks like we have ourselves a classic romance in the making! Careful, Lila. He's laying it on thick."

Nathaniel chuckled, the tension easing just a bit. "You know me too well, Zara. It's hard not to when I'm standing in front of the most talented designer I've ever met."

Zara raised an eyebrow, her smile widening. "Flattery will get you nowhere, buddy. Lila's made of stronger stuff. You'll need more than just words to win her back."

"Trust me, I'm prepared for whatever it takes," he replied, the determination returning to his voice.

Zara winked at me, her playful nature easing the weight of the moment. "You're going to need a game plan, Nathaniel. Women like Lila don't fall for the same tricks twice."

The humor felt like a lifeline, grounding me as I grappled with the whirlwind of emotions. But as I looked back at Nathaniel, the vulnerability in his eyes made me reconsider. Perhaps there was a glimmer of hope buried beneath the layers of past grievances.

"Okay," I said finally, my voice steady. "If you want to prove you've changed, then let's see it. I'll give you a chance to show me, but it's not just about you. I need to feel like my ambitions matter, too."

He nodded, a flicker of relief washing over his face. "I promise you'll have that. Let's start fresh."

Zara clapped her hands, her excitement infectious. "This is going to be the ultimate comeback story! Love, ambition, and a dash of drama. What's not to love?"

But just as I felt the tension start to ease, the door swung open again, and in walked a woman with an air of authority, her presence commanding the room. Dressed in an impeccably tailored suit, she carried an aura of confidence that made everyone stop and stare.

"Excuse me, but is this the workshop where dreams take flight?" she asked, her voice smooth yet sharp. "Because I'm looking for the next big thing in fashion, and I'm willing to invest."

All eyes turned to her, and I felt the weight of possibility hanging in the air. "Who are you?" I managed to ask, curiosity piquing my interest.

She smiled, a knowing glint in her eyes. "Let's just say I have a penchant for spotting talent. And right now, you're all on my radar."

Nathaniel shifted slightly, his expression betraying a mixture of intrigue and caution. "What do you want with us?"

"I want to see your work, and I'm looking for partnerships. The fashion world is changing, and I want to be ahead of the curve," she replied, locking her gaze on me. "You, especially, have something unique. I can see it in your eyes."

My heart raced. This was an opportunity, a door opening wide. Yet with Nathaniel standing beside me, the complexities of our relationship loomed large. Was I ready to intertwine my ambitions with his, or was this the moment to seize for myself?

Just then, the ground beneath my feet felt precarious, teetering between the allure of potential and the weight of unresolved feelings. The last threads of my past were threatening to unravel, and in that split second, I knew everything was about to change.

"Are you ready to make a decision?" the woman asked, her eyes sharp as daggers, poised to carve out the future in one swift motion.

Before I could respond, a loud crash resonated from the back of the workshop, drawing everyone's attention. An entire rack of fabric had toppled over, spilling vibrant colors across the floor like a chaotic canvas. The room erupted into startled gasps and laughter, but all I could focus on was the fleeting moment of clarity I had just experienced.

As I turned back to face Nathaniel and the enigmatic woman, the uncertainty swirled around me, heavy and suffocating. Choices lay before me like the fabrics scattered at our feet—each one a different path, each one with its own story to tell.

Chapter 17: Redemption and Resolve

The scent of rosemary and garlic wafted through the small apartment, mingling with the sound of bubbling marinara sauce on the stove. I stood in the kitchen, stirring the sauce with a wooden spoon, my heart racing in rhythm with the simmering pot. This dinner was more than just a meal; it was my lifeline, a chance to bridge the widening chasm that had formed between us. The clock on the wall ticked steadily, its sound somehow both reassuring and oppressive. With every passing second, the weight of unspoken words loomed larger, as if they were gathering like storm clouds just outside the window.

The table was set for four, its surface gleaming with the warmth of the candlelight flickering in soft, golden hues. I had chosen our best plates, the ones with delicate blue patterns that danced around the edges, a stark contrast to the mundane, practical life we often settled into. Ivy was on her way, and Nathaniel would follow shortly after, each of them unaware of the storm brewing beneath the surface of my meticulously planned evening. I hoped, with every fiber of my being, that this night would be different.

As I arranged the fresh bread into a basket, a knock on the door jolted me from my thoughts. My heart raced with both excitement and dread. I wiped my hands on a dish towel and opened the door to reveal Ivy, her curly hair bouncing in the chilly evening air. "Hey, you! It smells amazing in here!" she exclaimed, stepping over the threshold with a flourish, her cheerful demeanor like a warm ray of sunlight piercing through clouds.

"Thanks! I'm trying to impress," I replied, forcing a smile that felt more like a mask than genuine warmth. Ivy could always sense when something was amiss, and I needed to maintain this façade for just a little while longer. "Nathaniel should be here any minute. I hope you're hungry."

"Starving! What's on the menu?" she asked, making her way to the kitchen, where the aroma seemed to intensify. I watched her eyes widen as she took in the colorful array of dishes I had prepared, each one a reflection of my effort to mend our fractured bonds.

"Spaghetti and meatballs, of course," I said, shrugging as if it were the most casual thing in the world. "And a salad with that fancy dressing you taught me to make."

"Did you use the good olive oil?" she asked, her tone suddenly serious. "You know how I feel about cheap oil."

"Of course!" I laughed, the sound a little too bright, a little too forced. "No expense spared tonight."

Just as the words left my mouth, another knock sounded, this one deeper and more assured. I opened the door, revealing Nathaniel standing there, his frame tall and imposing, yet his expression softened as he caught sight of Ivy and me. "Hope I'm not late," he said, stepping inside and brushing off his coat. "Traffic was a nightmare."

"You're right on time. Dinner is almost ready!" I gestured toward the table, my heart pounding. The atmosphere in the room felt electric, charged with unspoken feelings and lingering tensions.

I tried to keep the conversation light as we settled around the table, but the words hung in the air like heavy fog, each laugh mingling with uncertainty. Ivy, bless her heart, made an effort to fill the silences with stories from her day, her enthusiasm a welcome distraction from the weight I felt pressing down on me. But every now and then, Nathaniel's eyes would catch mine, and in those fleeting moments, a world of emotions passed between us—frustration, longing, fear.

As we finished the meal, I gathered my courage, my hands trembling slightly as I pushed back my chair. "I want to share something," I said, my voice barely above a whisper. The laughter faded, and the room became still, the flickering candlelight casting shadows that danced along the walls. Ivy's eyes sparkled with curiosity, while Nathaniel's brow furrowed, a mix of concern and interest etched on his face.

"What's on your mind?" Ivy prompted, her tone inviting, encouraging.

Taking a deep breath, I locked eyes with Nathaniel. "I feel like I've lost my voice lately. Everything has been so chaotic, and I've kept my feelings bottled up. I thought hosting this dinner would be a way to reconnect, to remind us of the bonds we share."

Nathaniel's gaze softened, the tension in his shoulders easing. "I've felt that too. It's been hard to navigate everything that's happened," he admitted, his voice steady yet vulnerable. "I've been afraid of saying the wrong thing, of making it worse."

"Me too," I confessed, relief washing over me as I realized I wasn't alone in this. "I thought if we just stayed busy and distracted, it would go away. But it hasn't. We need to talk about what's really going on."

As the words flowed from my lips, I felt the air shift. The honesty hanging between us created a fragile connection, one that felt both frightening and exhilarating. The evening was transforming from a mere dinner into a pivotal moment of understanding, each revelation stripping away layers of miscommunication and hurt.

"I don't want to lose what we have," I added, my voice cracking slightly. "You both mean too much to me."

Ivy reached across the table, her hand warm and reassuring against mine. "We're in this together. Always," she said, her sincerity radiating like the candles glowing softly in the dim light.

Nathaniel's expression shifted, and for the first time that evening, I saw a flicker of hope in his eyes. "Let's not just talk about it tonight. Let's promise to keep this going, to check in with each other."

As the shadows receded and laughter once again filled the room, I couldn't shake the feeling that this was only the beginning. The road ahead might be fraught with challenges, but for the first time in a long time, I felt the weight of uncertainty lift just a little, allowing the light of understanding to shine through.

The flicker of candlelight danced across the walls, casting playful shadows that seemed to mimic the whirlwind of emotions swirling within me. Laughter still lingered in the air, a buoyant reminder that for a moment, we had pushed aside our doubts and hesitations. Ivy's stories of her latest escapades filled the room with a warmth that countered the coolness of the evening air, and Nathaniel, though more subdued, wore a smile that hinted at relief and something deeper.

"You know, I could really get used to these home-cooked meals," Nathaniel remarked, leaning back in his chair, his eyes sparkling like the stars peeking through the window. "If you keep this up, I might never leave."

Ivy snorted, her laughter a soft cascade. "Good luck with that! You're not ready for my cooking schedule."

"Please, I could survive off this for a year," he shot back, lifting his glass in mock toast to my culinary efforts. The moment was light, almost fragile, and I clung to it as if it were a lifebuoy thrown into turbulent waters.

"Just wait until I attempt dessert," I said, feigning confidence. "Then we'll see who's really ready for commitment."

The banter flowed easily, like the wine that filled our glasses, but beneath it all was an undercurrent of anticipation, a waiting tension that felt almost palpable. I knew we had cracked the surface, but how deep did the fissures run?

Once dinner settled, Ivy insisted we play a game—a classic diversion that would keep our minds occupied and our hearts light. "Let's do something ridiculous. How about charades? It'll be hilarious, and we need to lighten the mood!"

Nathaniel raised an eyebrow, a hint of mischief sparking in his expression. "You think we can lighten a mood that feels like it's been locked in a vault for years? Good luck with that."

"Oh, come on! It'll be fun! And who knows? Maybe you'll impress us all with your dramatic flair." Ivy winked at him, her playful spirit infectious.

"Fine, but if I end up embarrassing myself, I'm blaming you both," he replied, tossing his hands up in mock defeat.

As we shuffled to the living room, the air shifted, the lightness from dinner giving way to the familiar tension that had nestled in my chest. I could feel it again, that need to speak, to say what had been left unsaid, yet the game was a welcome distraction. I watched as Ivy acted out a wild creature, her exaggerated movements making us both laugh uncontrollably.

"Is it a bear? A drunken octopus?" Nathaniel guessed, feigning horror. .

"No, you idiot! It's a squirrel!" she shouted, collapsing into giggles.

In the midst of the laughter, a nagging voice in the back of my mind urged me to bring up the weight of our conversation from dinner. But as I watched Ivy's eyes sparkle with joy, I couldn't bear to shatter this fragile moment. Maybe this was what we needed—a reprieve, a chance to laugh before delving into the deeper waters of our relationships.

As the night progressed, the game revealed unexpected sides of us. Nathaniel, it turned out, had a flair for the dramatic that rivaled the best stage actors. His impersonation of a celebrity—complete with exaggerated facial expressions and a haughty accent—had us rolling on the floor. But just as the laughter peaked, I caught a glimpse of his eyes, darkened by something unspoken.

"You know, I didn't think we'd get this far tonight," he said, the lightness of his earlier demeanor dimming slightly. "I honestly expected us to sit in awkward silence, avoiding the elephant in the room."

Ivy's laughter faltered, and she looked between us, sensing the shift in the air. "Well, we didn't, so that's a win, right? We're still here, together."

"But are we really together?" I blurted out, the words escaping my lips before I could reconsider. The laughter faded, replaced by a heavy silence, and suddenly, I felt exposed, like I had stripped away the carefully placed layers of defense.

Nathaniel's brow furrowed, and he leaned forward, resting his elbows on his knees. "What do you mean?"

"I mean, we've all been dancing around each other, avoiding the tough conversations. I want us to be real—like we were before. I miss that."

Ivy shifted uncomfortably, her fingers fidgeting with the edge of her napkin. "It's scary to be real, though. What if it changes everything?"

I met her gaze, determination pooling in my chest. "What if it does? Maybe change isn't bad. Maybe it's what we need."

Nathaniel's expression softened, his shoulders relaxing as if I had lifted a burden off him. "I've felt lost. I've wanted to reach out, but I didn't know how."

"What's stopping you?" I asked, my voice steady, hoping to unearth the truths buried beneath our facade.

"Fear," he admitted, his honesty cutting through the air like a knife. "Fear of losing what we have, of breaking something that's already cracked."

"But it's cracked already, isn't it? We can't pretend it's not," I replied, my heart racing as I steered us toward a deeper truth. "We owe it to ourselves to try and fix it."

The silence that followed was thick, pregnant with possibility. I could almost hear the gears turning in Nathaniel's mind, the tension palpable as he contemplated the weight of my words. "Okay," he finally said, his voice barely above a whisper. "Let's do this."

With a shared look of resolve, we moved from the remnants of dinner to the couch, the three of us forming a circle that felt sacred, like we were about to unveil the core of our intertwined lives.

"Here's the deal," Ivy began, her voice steady but filled with a spark of courage. "No holding back. Let's share what's really been bothering us. I'll go first."

As she spoke, her words poured forth like a long-awaited flood, washing over the walls we had built. I could feel my own fears echoing in her sentiments, each confession drawing us closer to the heart of our shared struggles. The night unfolded like a delicate flower, each petal revealing another layer of ourselves—vulnerable, raw, and undeniably beautiful in its truth.

And for the first time in what felt like an eternity, I realized that the path toward redemption might just be illuminated by the courage to be vulnerable.

The atmosphere in the room crackled with an intensity that felt both exhilarating and unnerving. Ivy had just finished sharing her fears about feeling inadequate at work, her eyes shimmering with unshed tears. Nathaniel and I exchanged glances, an unspoken understanding passing between us as we realized the depth of Ivy's struggles mirrored our own.

"Thank you for being so open," I said, my voice steady despite the vulnerability swirling around us. "It's refreshing to finally share our truths. I've felt like I've been walking on eggshells for far too long."

"Right? Like we're all part of some bizarre charade where we pretend everything's fine when it's not," Ivy replied, brushing a loose curl from her face, her demeanor shifting from one of anxiety to determination. "But that's not what friends are for. We should be able to lean on each other without fear."

Nathaniel leaned forward, his elbows resting on his knees. "I've held back because I didn't want to burden either of you. But the truth is, I've been drowning in my own thoughts. There have been nights when I've questioned everything—my career, my relationships... us."

His admission hung in the air, heavy and poignant. I could see the weight of it pressing down on him, and my heart ached in empathy. "We've all felt that way," I replied gently, searching for words that could bring him comfort. "But we don't have to carry it alone. That's why we're here, right? To support each other?"

He nodded slowly, the tension in his shoulders easing just a fraction. "I want to believe that. I really do."

The room felt smaller, almost intimate, as we continued to share our fears and dreams, each revelation breaking down walls we had constructed over the years. I listened as Ivy spoke about her recent promotion and the pressure that came with it, and I found solace in the shared burdens of our lives. It was as if we were chiseling away at the granite of our individual experiences to reveal something beautiful beneath.

"Honestly, though," Ivy said, a mischievous glint returning to her eyes, "I think we all need to channel our inner Marie Kondo. There's a lot of emotional clutter that needs tossing out."

Nathaniel chuckled, the sound warm and rich. "Emotional clutter? I'm pretty sure mine includes a few exes and a mountain of regrets."

"Oh, come on! That's not even the worst of it," Ivy teased, rolling her eyes. "At least your emotional baggage comes with some funny stories. I just have a stack of unread emails and a collection of face masks that I keep forgetting to use."

I couldn't help but laugh, the sound bubbling up like champagne. "I think we should have a cleanse night! Who needs a spa day when you can vent your feelings while slathered in overpriced creams?"

"Count me in!" Ivy declared, her eyes bright with excitement. "But we might want to skip the face masks for Nathaniel. I don't think he can pull off that cucumber look."

"Just you wait," he shot back, a grin breaking through the remnants of tension. "I'll rock that mask, and you'll both be so jealous of my glowing skin."

In that moment, the atmosphere lightened, laughter filling the gaps left by our earlier confessions. It was a reminder of how friendship could be a balm for the soul, even amidst the shadows of vulnerability. Yet, despite the joy, a part of me remained acutely aware of the storm clouds still hovering in the background.

As the evening wore on, we decided to tackle a particularly ridiculous game of 'Never Have I Ever.' The laughter rang out like a bell, a joyful noise that felt almost sacred in its spontaneity. Ivy kicked things off with a scandalous confession, and soon the air was thick with stories that blended embarrassment with hilarity.

"Never have I ever tried to sneak a drink into a movie theater," Nathaniel declared, his expression mock serious.

"Oh please, like anyone hasn't done that!" I shot back, grinning widely. "I'm pretty sure my college experience was built on that foundation."

"What about you, Ivy?" Nathaniel asked, waggling his eyebrows playfully.

She feigned contemplation, putting a finger to her chin. "Never have I ever had a crush on a teacher. Oh, wait!" She laughed. "I definitely did! Mr. Collins was quite the catch. So dreamy!"

"Ew, Ivy! How old were you?" Nathaniel teased, his voice dripping with exaggerated disgust.

"Old enough to know better!" she replied, rolling her eyes dramatically.

With each confession, I felt the bonds between us strengthen, the remnants of doubt slowly dissolving like sugar in warm water. But just as I was beginning to feel a sense of lightness, the doorbell rang, slicing through our laughter like a knife.

"Who could that be?" Ivy asked, her brow furrowing with curiosity.

"I wasn't expecting anyone else," I replied, glancing between Nathaniel and Ivy. "Should we ignore it?"

"I say we take a peek," Nathaniel suggested, a note of adventure lacing his voice.

As I approached the door, a knot formed in my stomach. Who could it be? I opened the door, and there stood Marissa, an old acquaintance I hadn't seen in ages. Her presence was unexpected, like a gust of wind sweeping through the room, bringing with it a whirlwind of emotions I hadn't anticipated.

"Hey! Sorry to drop by unannounced," she said, her voice bright yet tinged with an edge of uncertainty. "I was in the neighborhood and thought I'd see how you're doing."

The shock froze me momentarily, but I quickly masked my surprise with a smile. "Marissa! It's... been a while. Come in!"

As she stepped over the threshold, I noticed the energy in the room shift, an undercurrent of tension rippling through the air. Ivy and Nathaniel exchanged glances, their playful demeanor fading into uncertainty.

"Sorry to interrupt your gathering," Marissa continued, her gaze sweeping across the living room. "I hope I'm not crashing anything."

"No, not at all," I replied, forcing cheer into my voice. "We were just catching up."

But I could feel the dynamic change, the lighthearted atmosphere now thick with unspoken words and expectations.

"Right, a friend reunion of sorts," Nathaniel said, his tone neutral, but the sharpness in his gaze was unmistakable.

As the conversation faltered, I sensed a tightening of my chest, a whirlwind of questions flooding my mind. What did Marissa want? Why had she chosen this moment to appear?

"Can we talk for a moment?" Marissa asked, her voice dropping to a conspiratorial whisper.

My heart raced, the unease swirling within me like a tempest. I nodded, gesturing for her to follow me to the kitchen, where the remnants of our earlier laughter still lingered.

"What's going on?" I asked, my voice low, almost tentative.

She hesitated, her eyes darting to the doorway as if expecting someone else to walk through it. "I didn't want to bring this up in front of them, but I've heard things. Things that could affect all of us."

My breath hitched, anticipation coiling tight in my stomach. "What do you mean?"

As Marissa leaned in, her voice barely above a whisper, the world outside fell silent, the shadows growing longer and darker as the truth threatened to emerge, ready to unravel everything we had just built.

Chapter 18: Heartstrings

The air was electric with the promise of change, the summer's sultry grip finally yielding to the crisp embrace of autumn. Hand in hand with Nathaniel, I found solace in the familiar paths of Central Park, where the leaves whispered secrets in shades of amber and scarlet. Each step felt like a dance, the crunch of fallen foliage beneath our feet echoing the rhythm of our hearts—tentative yet hopeful. We ambled past the iconic Bow Bridge, the sun casting a golden sheen across the tranquil waters of the lake. I felt a thrill at every glance he threw my way, his smile as warm as the late afternoon sun, igniting sparks that flickered between us like fireflies on a summer's night.

"This place feels like it's alive, doesn't it?" I mused, stopping to watch a cluster of children darting after each other, their laughter mingling with the rustle of the leaves. The park, in all its vibrant glory, seemed to pulse with an energy that seeped into my very bones, awakening feelings I had thought long buried.

"Absolutely," Nathaniel replied, his eyes glimmering with mischief. "But I think it's just a reflection of our radiant presence here. We're practically the stars of this show."

I chuckled, shaking my head. "Please, no need for ego boosts. The stars are busy twinkling in the sky. I'm just happy to be sharing this moment with you."

He pulled me closer, and for a fleeting moment, the world around us faded, leaving only the warmth of his arm wrapped around my shoulders. It was easy to forget the jagged edges of our past—the secrets and lies that had almost unraveled us—when the sun dipped low and painted the sky in fiery shades of orange and pink. I felt the weight of his presence, comforting yet unnerving, as though he were a puzzle piece I had nearly lost, now found but still slightly askew.

As we strolled deeper into the park, the cacophony of the city softened, replaced by the chirping of crickets and the distant sound of a saxophonist weaving a melancholic tune beneath the canopy of trees. I breathed in the earthy scent of damp soil and decay, a reminder that beauty often flourished in impermanence. With every shared smile and lingering gaze, I hoped for a future where trust could flourish once more, yet the specters of betrayal loomed large in my heart, whispering doubts that tugged at the seams of my optimism.

"What's on your mind?" Nathaniel asked, his tone a delicate balance of curiosity and concern, as if he could sense the storm brewing beneath my composed facade.

I hesitated, the truth hovering just out of reach. "Just thinking about how different everything feels now. Like, I've always loved the city in fall, but this year... it's different."

His brow furrowed, the playfulness of our earlier banter giving way to a deeper understanding. "You mean, because of us?"

"Something like that," I admitted, the weight of honesty pressing on my chest. "I guess I'm still trying to wrap my head around everything. It feels like we're stepping into this new chapter, but... what if it's just another false start?"

"False start?" He paused, tilting his head as if weighing my words. "Look, I get it. We've been through the wringer. But you have to know, I'm here. I want to make this work."

His sincerity hit me like a gust of wind, knocking the breath from my lungs. The warmth of his hand against mine was a grounding force, yet the shadows of my insecurities flickered at the edges of my mind, clawing to the forefront. Could we really rebuild something so delicate?

"Can we really?" I whispered, casting my gaze downward, where fallen leaves swirled in the breeze, creating a chaotic dance that echoed my inner turmoil. "I mean, can you trust me not to run when things get tough? And can I trust you not to... well, hurt me again?"

The pause that hung in the air felt heavy, laden with the weight of our shared history. "I don't want to hurt you," he finally said, his voice barely above a whisper. "Not now, not ever."

The raw vulnerability in his words sent a ripple of emotion coursing through me. We stood at the precipice of something extraordinary yet terrifying. "I want to believe that," I confessed, my heart racing at the thought of risking everything again. "But trust doesn't come easy for me anymore."

"I get that," he replied, his grip tightening around my fingers. "But we're not the same people we were. I want to show you that I've changed, that I'm not going anywhere."

Just as I opened my mouth to respond, a stray dog barreled toward us, a blur of fur and excitement. It leaped into Nathaniel, knocking him back a step and eliciting a startled laugh from me. "Well, I guess this dog believes in second chances!" I teased, unable to suppress my amusement.

"Yeah, clearly!" Nathaniel chuckled, trying to regain his balance as he scratched the dog's ears. The unexpected interlude lifted the tension, reminding me that laughter, even in the midst of uncertainty, was a powerful balm.

As the dog bounded away, its energy infectious, I felt the barriers around my heart begin to soften. Perhaps, just perhaps, there was hope for us yet. With every step we took, we were forging a new path, one that could lead us toward the kind of love that was fierce and unyielding, capable of withstanding the tempests of our past. The journey would be fraught with challenges, but standing beside Nathaniel, I felt a flicker of belief ignite within me—a belief that we could weave together a tapestry of forgiveness and growth, one thread at a time.

The sun dipped lower, casting long shadows across the park, creating a patchwork of light and dark that mirrored the tumult of my thoughts. We strolled toward the Bethesda Terrace, where the fountain bubbled cheerfully, surrounded by tourists snapping photos and couples stealing kisses. A small child pointed, eyes wide with wonder, as the water shimmered under the golden light, reminding me of the innocent joys that often felt so distant from my own heart.

"Should we join the chorus of lovebirds at the fountain?" Nathaniel suggested, his eyes sparkling with mischief.

"Only if you're ready to reenact a scene from The Notebook," I teased, arching an eyebrow at him. "I'd need to see some serious water splashing for that."

"Please, I'd make Ryan Gosling look like an amateur," he shot back, puffing out his chest in mock bravado.

I laughed, the sound ringing out clear and bright, a welcome relief from the weight of our earlier conversation. There was a lightness in the air, a mischievous undertone that began to thaw the edges of my uncertainty. It was moments like these—Nathaniel's charm, the shared laughter—that reminded me why I had fallen for him in the first place.

We perched on the edge of the fountain, letting our feet dangle above the water, where golden leaves danced along the surface. The world swirled around us, a blur of vibrant colors and laughter, yet in this little pocket of time, it felt as if we were encased in our own bubble, safe from the outside.

"Do you remember the first time we came here?" Nathaniel asked, his tone shifting to something softer, more introspective. "You wore that ridiculous hat, and I spent half the day trying to steal it from you."

I grinned at the memory. "That hat was iconic! I'll have you know it was the centerpiece of my entire outfit."

"Iconic? More like an eyesore. But you made it work. I admired your commitment to style."

"Flattery won't get you everywhere, you know," I shot back, but my heart swelled at the fondness in his gaze.

He leaned closer, the playful atmosphere morphing into something deeper. "I think I'm just trying to remind you how far we've come. If we could survive that ridiculous day, then surely we can tackle the complexities of our present."

As I met his eyes, a flicker of warmth sparked within me, a fragile hope taking root. "You might have a point," I admitted, but a nagging voice in the back of my mind whispered warnings, reminding me of the fragility of our situation.

"Hey, what if we made a pact?" he proposed, excitement lighting up his face. "No matter what happens, we commit to at least one adventure together each week. Just us, no distractions."

My heart fluttered at the idea, yet my rational mind interjected with caution. "What kind of adventures are we talking about? We can't just leap into the unknown without a plan, can we?"

"Why not? Life is all about the unexpected. I mean, look at us now—who would've thought we'd find ourselves here, reminiscing about old times, laughing over ridiculous hats?" He flashed me that charming smile, the one that always sent a thrill through my veins.

"Okay, fine," I relented, feeling a mix of excitement and trepidation. "But you have to promise not to push me into anything crazy, like bungee jumping or skydiving."

He feigned shock. "You wound me! I only suggest the most exhilarating experiences. I promise I'll keep the bungee cords at bay."

"Good, because I'm not ready to test the limits of my heart in that way."

We both chuckled, and for a moment, it felt as if the shadows of our past were receding, pushed aside by the light of our laughter and the warmth of our connection. As the fountain splashed behind us, I imagined all the adventures waiting just around the corner, each one a stepping stone toward healing.

Nathaniel turned his gaze toward the sky, where the first stars began to twinkle against the dusky canvas of twilight. "You know,

I've always found the city to be full of surprises," he said, his voice turning contemplative. "Every corner holds a new story, just waiting to unfold."

"Like us?" I ventured, intrigued.

"Exactly! Just like us. Every moment spent together feels like a new chapter."

His words hung in the air, stirring something deep within me. We were woven into this grand tapestry of life, each thread representing a moment shared, a smile exchanged, a challenge faced together.

As we sat there, wrapped in the warmth of each other's presence, the gentle breeze carried the laughter of children playing and the soft notes of a nearby musician strumming his guitar. I watched as a couple danced nearby, lost in their own world, oblivious to the bustling crowd. There was an undeniable magic in the air, a reminder that life was fleeting yet full of possibility.

"Let's make a list," I suggested suddenly, feeling bold. "We could write down all the adventures we want to have—big or small. Just so we have something to look forward to."

"Now you're talking! We could call it our 'Adventure Bucket List.' I'll even provide the artistic flair—my handwriting is practically a work of art."

"Art of questionable legibility, I'd argue," I shot back, laughing as he pretended to be offended.

"Touché! But it's the spirit that counts, right?"

With laughter still dancing between us, we leaned in closer, the air thick with the promise of new beginnings. In that moment, under the watchful gaze of the stars and the comforting glow of the city lights, I felt a flicker of something I hadn't dared to acknowledge before: hope.

The evening unfolded in a blur of light and laughter, each moment more vibrant than the last. We explored the narrow paths that wound through the park, the leaves whispering secrets of seasons past, while Nathaniel shared stories from his childhood—some endearing, others downright embarrassing.

As he animatedly recounted a particularly disastrous camping trip involving a raccoon and a misfired marshmallow, I couldn't help but marvel at how easy it felt to fall back into this rhythm with him. The laughter we shared was more than just a distraction; it was a reminder of the bond we had built, one that had weathered storms but now glimmered with the potential for renewal.

But as the night deepened, a sliver of doubt crept back in, an unwelcome reminder of the past. Would the laughter last? Could we truly embrace this new beginning, or was it just another fleeting moment in the vast landscape of our history? I pushed the thoughts away, focusing instead on the warmth of his hand in mine and the joy radiating from our shared laughter, hoping against hope that this time, we would not only embrace the adventure but also emerge stronger on the other side.

As the evening wore on, the gentle hum of the city enveloped us, blending with the distant strains of music floating through the air. Nathaniel and I made our way to a nearby food truck, the tantalizing aroma of grilled cheese and garlic fries wafting toward us. I was grateful for the distraction. Conversations about our pasts felt much heavier than the possibility of cheese oozing between two golden slices of bread.

"Do you remember the last time we had street food?" Nathaniel asked, his eyes sparkling with mischief. "You got that absurdly large pretzel and claimed it was a symbol of our love."

I feigned horror, a dramatic hand pressed to my chest. "How dare you bring up my culinary genius! I thought we were over that."

"Over? Never! It's a classic." He stepped closer to the truck, where a group of patrons laughed as they waited for their orders. "What's on the menu tonight? I vote we get something ridiculous—something that will make our future children roll their eyes."

"Children?" I blurted, the word tumbling from my lips before I could catch it. The weight of it hung in the air like a stray balloon, bright and deflating.

Nathaniel raised an eyebrow, a teasing smirk dancing on his lips. "What? Do you see me as a fatherly figure now? I assure you, I can rock the dad jokes."

"Whoa, easy there! We're still in the phase of rebranding this relationship. Let's not jump straight to family planning," I replied, my heart racing at the thought of futures intertwined. "Maybe we should stick to food for now."

His laughter rang out, infectious and bright. "Fine, I concede. We'll tackle parenthood later. For now, let's stick to our cheese and fries. The perfect fuel for adventures."

As we placed our orders, the vendor shot us a grin, clearly enjoying our banter. The scent of melting cheese and buttery bread filled the air, and I couldn't help but feel lighter, as if the evening had wrapped us in a warm embrace. We grabbed our food and found a bench overlooking a small pond, where the moonlight shimmered on the surface, creating a picture-perfect scene.

"This is much better than that pretzel," I said, taking a hearty bite of my grilled cheese. "I think I may have discovered the secret to happiness."

"Ah, yes. The elusive grilled cheese theory." Nathaniel nodded solemnly. "We must take this knowledge and share it with the world. Who knew the path to enlightenment was so delicious?"

"Exactly! Maybe we should start a blog about it," I replied, laughter bubbling in my throat. "'Gourmet Grilled Cheese and Life Lessons' could be a hit!"

He leaned closer, his eyes narrowing as if considering the idea seriously. "But what if we run out of cheese metaphors? We need a backup plan."

"I'm sure we can pivot. Something about finding joy in the little things—like cheese!" I said, and we both burst into laughter, our shared joy echoing into the night.

With our bellies full and the cool breeze brushing against our skin, the moment felt too perfect, too serene, for my comfort. I could feel the tension from earlier creeping back, the shadows lurking just beyond the light. My heart clenched as I contemplated the fragility of what we were building.

"Tell me about your dream adventure," I said, trying to steer the conversation away from my unease. "Something completely out of the ordinary."

Nathaniel paused, his expression turning thoughtful. "I've always wanted to go to a food festival in another country—somewhere vibrant and chaotic. I can picture it: the smells, the sounds, the people bustling around us as we taste everything. Maybe a local market in Italy."

"I can see that for you," I replied, envisioning him wandering through sun-drenched streets, arms laden with goodies. "You'd probably make friends with a local chef who'd insist on teaching you how to cook traditional dishes. It sounds like a rom-com waiting to happen."

"Or a disaster! Imagine my cooking skills—an explosion of flour and chaos!" He laughed, and I felt a warmth spread through me, the laughter a salve against the gnawing doubts.

"I'd pay good money to see that," I said, leaning into him, feeling the reassuring heat of his body against mine.

As the laughter faded, a stillness settled over us, an unspoken acknowledgment of the deeper questions lingering beneath our playful banter. I turned my gaze to the pond, the water reflecting a myriad of stars above. "What if we could make that happen?" I asked softly, my heart racing at the thought of actualizing dreams together.

He tilted his head, his expression shifting from playful to sincere. "What do you mean?"

"Maybe we could plan something—an adventure together. Just the two of us, somewhere new."

He smiled, the corners of his eyes crinkling with delight. "I would love that. We could make a list, start plotting our great escape."

Before I could respond, a sudden commotion nearby drew our attention. A group of people gathered around a man animatedly gesturing toward a poster board propped against a tree. Curiosity piqued, Nathaniel and I exchanged glances and wandered closer, the laughter forgotten as we approached the crowd.

As we neared, I caught snippets of conversation, a rising excitement that felt almost electric in the air. "You won't believe what they found!" a woman exclaimed, her eyes wide. "It's unbelievable!"

"What are they talking about?" I whispered to Nathaniel, my heart beginning to race, not from the thrill of adventure, but from an inexplicable sense of dread.

"Let's find out," he replied, a hint of trepidation in his voice.

We squeezed through the throng until we reached the front, where the man with the poster stood tall, a wild light in his eyes. "Ladies and gentlemen! Just this afternoon, a local hiker stumbled upon a mysterious cave on the outskirts of the city!"

Gasps erupted from the crowd, and Nathaniel turned to me, his expression a mix of intrigue and concern. "A cave? What's so special about that?"

"Apparently, it's rumored to be filled with artifacts from the past—lost treasures, they say! Some even claim it's haunted!"

I felt my stomach churn, a knot of anxiety tightening within me. The idea of exploring a dark cave seemed both thrilling and terrifying. "Haunted? That doesn't sound like our kind of adventure."

But the allure of the unknown tugged at me, a siren call that was hard to resist. "What if we check it out?" Nathaniel said, eyes sparkling with enthusiasm.

I hesitated, my heart racing. "What if it's dangerous? What if we get lost?"

His gaze softened, the concern for me evident. "We'll go together. And if it's too much, we'll turn back. Just like that." He snapped his fingers playfully, but the weight of the unknown loomed over us, a dense fog of uncertainty.

Just as I opened my mouth to respond, a piercing scream cut through the night, slicing the moment in half. The crowd gasped, turning as one to see a figure stumbling back from the edge of the gathering, their face pale and wild. "It's true!" they shouted, breathless. "It's really haunted!"

My heart raced as I met Nathaniel's eyes, a mix of fear and excitement swirling between us. The promise of adventure hung in the air, tantalizingly close yet fraught with unknown dangers.

"Are you ready for this?" he asked, his voice low, urging me to make a choice.

As I stood on the precipice of this decision, the thrill of adventure clashed with my instincts to flee. Could we venture into the darkness together? Would we emerge unscathed, or would the shadows claim us?

I took a deep breath, the night closing in around us, and just as I was about to speak, the ground trembled beneath our feet, sending ripples of panic through the crowd.

Chapter 19: The Edge of Forever

The gallery buzzed with the frenetic energy of artists and patrons alike, a symphony of clinking glasses and murmured admiration. A myriad of colors splashed across the walls, but the vibrancy of it all paled in comparison to the brilliant canvas of Ivy's work, which seemed to hold the very breath of life within its swirls and strokes. As I stood there, clutching a glass of something effervescent—most likely champagne, though it could have been sparkling water for all I cared—I marveled at how the world felt like a painted canvas itself, every moment layered with the complexity of shadows and light.

Ivy had always been a whirlwind of creativity, her spirit vibrant enough to illuminate even the darkest corners of our lives. Yet now, as I watched her smile radiate like the very sun, I felt a heaviness settle in my chest, anchoring me to the ground. Her hair, a cascade of auburn waves, danced with the music, just like the whimsical thoughts that often flitted through her mind. She stood at the center of a small crowd, her laughter ringing out, infectious and genuine, while the world took note of the budding artist who dared to dream beyond the confines of our quiet little town.

"Isn't it amazing?" I whispered to no one in particular, my gaze unwavering from her luminous figure. "I mean, look at her."

A soft voice interrupted my reverie. "She deserves every bit of it." It was Claire, the kind-hearted woman I had met during my college days, her presence a comforting reminder of the past. "You've always been her biggest cheerleader, haven't you?"

"Cheerleader? More like her unofficial biographer," I replied, a playful smirk dancing on my lips. "I've documented every late-night existential crisis and impromptu art show in the living room."

We both chuckled, but my heart felt heavier than before. Ivy's success was as intoxicating as it was terrifying. Every cheer she received made me feel like I was clinging to the edge of a cliff, watching her soar into the skies while I remained rooted to the ground, uncertain of my own wings.

"Have you thought about what happens when she leaves?" Claire probed gently, her gaze shifting to Ivy as she spun, animatedly discussing her inspirations with a few intrigued attendees. "You two have been inseparable."

"Yeah, well... it's just a gallery showing, right?" I tried to sound casual, but the quiver in my voice betrayed me. "She'll still be my best friend."

"Distance doesn't always treat friendships kindly," Claire noted, her eyes filled with understanding. "But you two have something special. Just make sure to communicate."

I nodded, but even my optimism was tested. As Ivy continued to charm the crowd, a sinking realization swept over me: this was more than just a gallery. It was a launching pad, a gateway to a world of possibilities. I had always known Ivy was destined for greatness, yet now that it was unfolding, the thought of her departing felt like the very air had been siphoned from my lungs.

A soft nudge at my side brought me back to the moment. I turned to see Nathaniel, his tousled hair giving him an effortless charm, though his eyes held a shadow of uncertainty. "I thought I might find you here," he said, his voice low, threaded with an intensity that sent shivers down my spine.

"You mean hiding in plain sight?" I quipped, trying to lighten the mood as I leaned against the wall, my heart racing. "Because you're doing a fantastic job of blending in."

His lips quirked into a half-smile, but the tension between us was palpable. "Actually, I wanted to talk to you about something." He paused, his gaze flickering toward Ivy, then back to me, a mixture of excitement and fear flickering behind his dark eyes. "I've been offered a job abroad."

The words hit me like a brick, my breath catching in my throat. "Abroad? Like, across the ocean abroad?" I could feel my heart constricting as I processed the weight of what he was saying.

"Yeah, it's an amazing opportunity, and I... I'm considering it." His words came out in a rush, as though he was afraid to let them linger too long.

"Wow, Nathaniel, that's incredible," I managed, forcing a smile that didn't quite reach my eyes. The very idea of him leaving, of him pursuing a life that didn't include me, tightened the knot in my stomach. "But... when?"

"Soon," he said, his voice dropping an octave, and I could sense the hesitation. "I have to give them an answer by the end of the week."

A whirlwind of emotions surged through me, a tempest I couldn't quite untangle. Ivy was on the brink of her own departure, soaring into a new realm of possibilities, and now Nathaniel was throwing his own dreams into the mix. The people I loved most were carving paths away from me, and the thought felt like shards of glass lodged in my heart.

"Are you... are you excited?" I managed, each word laden with a weight that made it hard to breathe. "I mean, it's what you've always wanted, right?"

"Yeah, it is." He stepped closer, the air between us charged with unspoken words. "But it's also scary. Leaving everything behind... and you."

The look in his eyes made my heart flutter, and for a moment, the world around us faded. "We could still keep in touch," I suggested, my voice barely above a whisper. "Like, you know, FaceTime and stuff. Maybe I could even come visit."

Nathaniel's smile dimmed slightly, a flicker of sadness passing across his face. "It wouldn't be the same, would it? I mean, this is a big change, and I don't want to just... float through it. I want to dive in."

"Then dive," I urged, my heart aching. "But what about us? What do we do about this?"

He sighed, his frustration palpable. "I don't want to lose what we have, but I don't know how to make it work if I'm thousands of miles away."

As the gallery lights twinkled like stars, illuminating the hopeful faces of those around us, I felt an overwhelming sense of being trapped in a moment that demanded I choose. Would I let Ivy chase her dreams, let Nathaniel pursue his, all while I remained suspended in a reality I wasn't sure I could bear? The realization sank deep, a hard truth that twisted in my gut: loving someone meant knowing when to let them go, but doing so felt like tearing my heart out, piece by piece.

Just then, Ivy approached us, her eyes sparkling with excitement, completely unaware of the storm brewing in the space around us. "You two look deep in conversation! What's going on?" she asked, her laughter ringing out like a joyful bell.

I exchanged a glance with Nathaniel, the unsaid words hanging in the air. In that moment, surrounded by the beauty of Ivy's success, I realized this wasn't just about her or Nathaniel. It was about me, too, and the painful, exhilarating journey of learning to love in a world that was constantly changing.

The night wore on, the gallery pulsating with life, yet I felt as if I were standing on the periphery of my own existence. Ivy, radiant in her element, was a force of nature, her energy an electric current that flowed through everyone she touched. The conversations swirled around me like paint on her canvases—bright, chaotic, and vibrant—but the laughter felt distant, muffled by the growing unease in my chest.

"Are you okay?" Nathaniel's voice pulled me from my thoughts, and I turned to find him watching me closely, his brow furrowed with concern. It was endearing and maddening all at once, like a well-meaning puppy trying to predict a thunderstorm.

"Just enjoying the view," I said, gesturing towards Ivy, who was now surrounded by admirers, her laughter cutting through the air like a clear bell. "Isn't she incredible? It's hard not to feel a little starstruck."

His gaze followed mine, but there was a shadow behind his eyes, something unsaid lingering in the air between us. "She is. But you're the one who should be in the spotlight too. You've always been her rock, supporting her from the sidelines."

"More like her loudest cheerleader," I replied, a wry smile pulling at my lips. "But honestly? I'm terrified of what happens next."

Nathaniel's expression shifted, understanding creeping into his features. "I know. But you'll be okay, right? You're not just Ivy's support system. You have your own dreams too."

I opened my mouth to respond, but the words tangled in my throat. Yes, I had dreams—somewhere in the back of my mind, they flickered like distant stars—but they felt overshadowed by the looming possibility of Ivy's departure and Nathaniel's potential journey abroad. Did I even know what I wanted anymore?

As Ivy's laughter filled the space, I realized how accustomed I had grown to her presence. The thought of losing her was a dull ache, but the prospect of Nathaniel leaving sent sharp pangs of anxiety racing through me. I glanced at him, a man whose dreams mirrored my own fears, standing there with a hopeful smile that belied the chaos unfolding beneath the surface.

"I guess we're both on the brink of something," he said, his voice soft, the gravity of the moment sinking in. "Just different directions."

"Right." My heart thudded, a harsh reminder of the fragile threads connecting us all. "And here I am, stuck in the middle of a painting that's about to become abstract."

He chuckled, the tension between us easing for a brief moment. "Well, you could always add a splash of color. Life's a canvas, after all."

"More like a Jackson Pollock piece," I countered, rolling my eyes playfully. "Beautiful chaos, but you can't quite tell what it is."

Just then, Ivy reappeared at our side, her cheeks flushed with excitement, the sparkle in her eyes hinting at the secrets of the universe. "You two look deep in conversation. What were you plotting? World domination? A secret art heist?"

"More like strategizing how to survive your departure," I said, unable to suppress the slight tremor in my voice.

She leaned in, concern clouding her features. "Hey, I'm not going anywhere just yet. This is only the beginning, right?"

"Right," I said, though the uncertainty in my heart weighed heavily. "But you're about to take on Los Angeles, Ivy. I mean, that's huge."

She waved a hand dismissively, the gesture more playful than anxious. "It's just a gallery showing! I mean, it's a big deal, but you've been my foundation through it all. I wouldn't have made it this far without you."

Her sincerity washed over me like a warm wave, and for a moment, I could forget the storm brewing in my chest. "Well, if you become famous and leave me behind, I'm going to start charging for all those late-night pep talks."

Ivy laughed, and the sound was pure, bright. "Deal. But you'd better come visit. I'll need my biggest fan in the front row when I have my first solo exhibition."

A sudden rush of joy swept through me, mingling with the underlying tension. "I'll be there, front and center, waving a gigantic foam finger."

As the night unfurled, the laughter and clinking glasses continued, a melodic backdrop to the unspoken feelings lingering in the air. The gallery was alive, a swirling mixture of talent and ambition, yet my heart felt like it was caught in a web of contradictions. Ivy was stepping into her destiny, while Nathaniel was contemplating his future thousands of miles away, leaving me with a gaping hole in my heart and a mind full of questions.

At some point, Ivy excused herself to mingle again, leaving Nathaniel and me standing at the edge of the crowd. His gaze shifted toward the paintings, a pensive look taking hold.

"Do you ever think about what you want?" he asked, his voice barely rising above the ambient noise.

I looked at him, surprise coloring my features. "You mean, besides cheering on Ivy? I guess I haven't given it much thought lately."

"Maybe you should. You deserve your own spotlight," he urged, stepping closer, his presence warm and comforting. "Don't let Ivy's success overshadow your own."

I chuckled, trying to lighten the mood. "Ah, yes, the classic 'find yourself while everyone else is winning awards' advice. Very sage."

"Not just advice—encouragement." His eyes bore into mine, earnest and deep. "You're talented, you know that. You could write, create, do something that makes your heart sing."

"Maybe," I replied, the wistfulness creeping into my tone. "But right now, I feel like I'm flailing. Ivy's flying, and I'm just trying to keep my feet on the ground."

His expression softened. "Sometimes, flailing can lead to flying. Just don't let fear hold you back."

I felt a warmth spread through me, a flicker of hope igniting in the pit of my stomach. "Okay, wise guy. But what about you? You're the one with the job offer in another country."

He sighed, running a hand through his hair, a gesture of vulnerability. "I know. And it terrifies me. But I have to chase this. It's what I've wanted for so long."

The sincerity in his voice struck a chord, stirring something deep within me. "Then go," I said, surprising myself with the strength in my words. "But don't forget about the people you leave behind."

"I won't," he promised, his gaze locking onto mine. "I'll take you with me, in a way. You'll always be a part of whatever I do."

I nodded, but a hint of sadness crept in. "And I'll always be here, cheering you on from afar. Just promise me we'll talk. You know, video calls and all that."

"Absolutely. No matter where I am, you're stuck with me."

Just as the conversation settled into a comforting rhythm, Ivy returned, a sparkle of mischief in her eyes. "You two are getting way too serious! What are we discussing? My imminent fame? Nathaniel's plans for world travel?"

"We were just plotting how to keep you grounded," Nathaniel teased, a playful smirk gracing his lips. "You know, just in case you get too big for your britches."

"Oh, please!" Ivy laughed, a bright sound that danced through the room. "If anything, I'll be sending you both care packages filled with 'I made it!' memorabilia."

As we stood together, the weight of the moment began to settle in. My heart felt heavy with anticipation, and uncertainty coiled tightly around my chest. As much as I wished for Ivy's success, I couldn't shake the feeling that our lives were about to change irrevocably, forcing me to confront a new reality where love, friendship, and ambition would intertwine in ways I couldn't yet imagine.

The night wore on, and the atmosphere shifted like the tide, rising and falling with the ebb of conversation and laughter. Ivy was caught in a whirlwind of admirers, her infectious enthusiasm drawing them in like moths to a flame. As I watched her interact, I felt a bittersweet cocktail of pride and dread swirl within me. She was stepping into her destiny, and I was being left behind, anchored in a reality that felt increasingly tenuous.

"Hey, we should get a group photo!" Ivy's voice rang out, slicing through the ambient noise, and a wave of excitement rippled through the crowd. "This is a moment worth capturing!"

I joined the throng as everyone gathered, trying to shake off the heaviness that clung to my thoughts. Nathaniel stood beside me, his arm brushing against mine, an electric spark in the air that distracted me, even if only for a moment. As Ivy orchestrated the scene, her energy electrifying, I caught Nathaniel's eye, and an unspoken understanding passed between us. The tension was still there, but the warmth of shared moments pulled at the edges of my uncertainty.

Ivy counted down, and we all squeezed together, our smiles stretched wide. "Cheese!" she shouted, the flash of cameras capturing us all in a single, vibrant moment—one I feared would become a distant memory sooner than I wanted.

"See? Isn't this fun?" Ivy beamed, looking at the photos being reviewed on various phones. "We're making memories!"

"Memories that may have an expiration date," I muttered under my breath, though I hoped my sardonic tone would go unnoticed.

Nathaniel caught my eye again, his brow slightly furrowed, and he leaned in closer, his voice low and conspiratorial. "We'll make new memories, you know. You're not getting rid of me that easily."

The sincerity in his tone sent warmth flooding through me, but I couldn't shake the feeling of impending loss. "You're the one who's leaving the country," I reminded him, my voice barely above a whisper. "Don't forget that."

Before he could respond, Ivy waved us over. "You two look too serious! Come on, we need more smiles!"

As the evening stretched on, the gallery buzzed with conversation and excitement, yet I felt increasingly isolated within the crowd. Ivy's laughter floated through the air, a buoyant sound that contrasted with the heaviness in my chest. With every passing moment, I was reminded of how close we were to a turning point, the kind that changes everything.

When the clinking of glasses quieted and Ivy gathered us once more, I braced myself for the inevitable. "I just want to say a huge thank you to everyone for coming tonight," she began, her eyes sparkling. "This is just the beginning for me, but I wouldn't be here without your support. You've all inspired me more than you know."

A wave of applause erupted, and I found myself caught in a swell of admiration for her. But then her gaze shifted, landing on me, a mixture of warmth and concern flashing across her face. "And a special shoutout to my best friend, who has always been my rock. Thank you for believing in me, even when I didn't believe in myself."

A knot tightened in my throat, and I forced a smile, the weight of her words settling in. "I'm just glad to help you find your way," I replied, though my voice was tinged with unsteady emotion.

Nathaniel stepped forward, his confidence growing as he took Ivy's hand. "You're not just an artist, Ivy. You're a force to be reckoned with. Los Angeles won't know what hit it."

With her usual flair, Ivy giggled and nudged Nathaniel playfully. "Look at you, acting all serious. Next, you'll be telling us how to properly critique art."

The laughter that followed felt like a lifeline in the swirling chaos, a momentary reprieve from the impending changes that loomed over us. But the reprieve was short-lived. As Ivy basked in the attention, I caught Nathaniel's eye again. He motioned for us to step aside, and I felt a rush of nerves.

"What is it?" I asked as we moved to a quieter corner of the gallery, away from the thrumming energy of the crowd.

He hesitated, his expression shifting from playful to contemplative. "I want to tell you something, but you have to promise to hear me out without getting mad."

"Okay..." My heart raced as I prepared for whatever bombshell was about to drop.

"I've been thinking a lot about this job offer," he started, his voice steady but tinged with an edge of uncertainty. "And while I want to take it, there's something I need you to understand."

I felt my heart race, an unsettling mix of fear and curiosity. "What do you mean?"

He took a deep breath, his gaze unwavering. "I've been offered a position that would require me to not just relocate, but to travel extensively. It's an amazing opportunity, but it could also mean I'm away for long periods. I need to know if you're okay with that. I don't want to drag you into something complicated."

The weight of his words settled like lead in my stomach. "You're already leaving. Why complicate it further?"

"I want you to be a part of this, but I also need to know you're on board. I don't want to hurt you," he said, his voice low and sincere.

As his words hung in the air, I struggled to breathe. The thought of him leaving without a trace, a shadow of what we could have been, felt like a jagged blade. "Nathaniel, it's not just about you. It's about us. You can't just drop this on me and expect me to be okay with it."

He stepped closer, urgency in his eyes. "I'm not asking for an answer now. I just want you to think about what this means for us. For you. I care about you too much to go into this without making sure you're okay."

Just then, Ivy appeared, her smile brightening the dimming mood. "There you two are! I was just about to send a search party. Are you plotting your escape?"

"Something like that," I replied, forcing a smile, though the conversation with Nathaniel had left my heart feeling frayed.

"Good, because I need both of you to help me celebrate!" she exclaimed, oblivious to the tension that lingered. "We're taking this party to the next level!"

The crowd began to cheer, and Ivy led us toward a makeshift stage where a local band had begun to set up. The buzz of the gallery transformed into something electric, an excitement that lifted my spirits momentarily.

"Let's dance!" Ivy declared, pulling me into the throng of people, her laughter weaving through the fabric of the night.

As the music swelled, I lost myself in the rhythm, trying to drown out the chaos swirling in my heart. But even amidst the joy, Nathaniel's words echoed in my mind, heavy and insistent. Would I really be able to let him go, to support his dreams while grappling with the uncertainty of my own?

The band played a lively tune, and Ivy twirled, her spirit a dazzling light that momentarily dispelled my worries. I caught Nathaniel's eye across the crowd, and he grinned, the weight of our earlier conversation replaced by the moment's infectious energy. But as the night wore on, I couldn't shake the feeling that time was slipping away, each passing moment bringing us closer to a cliff's edge I wasn't ready to face.

Just as I turned back to Ivy, my breath caught in my throat. A familiar figure stood at the entrance, shadowed by the bright lights of the gallery. It was a face I hadn't seen in years, a ghost from my past that threatened to unravel the delicate balance I'd fought so hard to maintain. My heart raced, and as the crowd continued to pulse around me, I could feel the ground shifting beneath my feet, pulling me toward a fate I couldn't quite comprehend.

"Who is that?" I whispered to Ivy, panic creeping into my voice.

Her gaze followed mine, and her laughter faded, replaced by a look of concern. "I have no idea, but it looks like someone's about to make a scene."

And just like that, the night spiraled into a new direction, the delicate threads of my life intertwining with an unknown force that threatened to change everything.

Chapter 20: Chasing Shadows

The evening light draped over our cramped apartment like a warm shawl, spilling gold onto the hardwood floors and illuminating the corners that were usually shadowed. I leaned against the kitchen counter, cradling a chipped mug of herbal tea—my nightly ritual that Ivy always teased me about. "You know, that stuff tastes like dirt," she'd say with a laugh, but tonight her laughter felt more like a distant echo than the joyous melody it had once been.

I watched her move around the living room, folding clothes with a precision that belied her carefree spirit. Each item she tucked into a box held a piece of her—t-shirts that had seen better days, a pair of shoes that had danced through countless nights, a framed photo of the two of us on the rooftop, the city skyline draped in twilight, our faces aglow with dreams and laughter. My heart clenched at the thought of each cherished fragment leaving our shared space, the very fabric of our friendship slowly unraveling as she packed her life into boxes.

"Are you really going to take that monstrosity with you?" I called out, eyeing a particularly gaudy lamp that had always seemed out of place in our eclectic home. Ivy turned, her dark hair falling into her eyes, and for a moment, her expression was indecipherable. Then she broke into a smile, that kind of infectious grin that made the world seem a little less daunting.

"Of course! This beauty deserves a chance in the sun. You can't stifle her brilliance just because you can't appreciate it," she quipped, striking a pose as she held the lamp above her head like a trophy. I rolled my eyes, the corners of my mouth twitching upward despite the weight in my chest.

The laughter faded as the reality of our impending separation loomed between us like an uninvited guest. "It's going to be weird without you," I confessed, my voice quieter now. I shifted my weight, suddenly feeling the urge to shrink into myself, to retreat into the safety of my thoughts. "You know, I always thought we'd figure out our lives together."

Ivy's expression softened, and she set the lamp down with exaggerated care, stepping closer to me. "What do you mean?" she asked, her eyes searching mine for the truth buried beneath layers of bravado.

"I just... I feel like I'm at a crossroads or something," I admitted, glancing away, unable to meet her gaze. "While you're off chasing your dreams in Los Angeles, I'm stuck here, holding onto the past like it's the only thing I have left."

"Stuck?" she echoed, tilting her head as though the word itself tasted strange. "You're not stuck, Emma. You're just... in a transition. You have to give yourself the same grace you'd give me."

"Grace," I scoffed, letting out a short laugh. "That sounds nice, but I'm not sure it applies to me right now. You're off to make movies and live the glamorous life, while I'm—"

"While you're exactly where you need to be," Ivy interrupted, her voice firm. "You've always had this talent, Em. You just have to decide to use it." Her words hung in the air, a challenge and a comfort all at once.

"Easy for you to say," I replied, a teasing lilt creeping into my tone. "You're leaving behind a collection of memories for a whole new adventure. Meanwhile, I'm over here planning my weekly grocery runs and wondering what brand of toothpaste is going to be my next existential crisis."

Ivy's laughter was a bright spark, illuminating the dimming room. "Maybe you should spice things up. Buy the fancy toothpaste. You deserve it," she replied, her eyes twinkling with mischief. "But seriously, you need to take a leap. Remember when we painted the mural in the alley? You had that wild idea, and look at the masterpiece we created! You're capable of so much more than just being the reliable friend holding my hand."

I felt a warmth bloom in my chest at the memory. The night we painted that mural had been chaotic and magical, the two of us covered in vibrant colors, our hands sticky with paint and our hearts free. But I was terrified of the leap she suggested, terrified of stepping outside the carefully constructed safety net I had built around myself.

"What if I fall?" I murmured, a whisper against the backdrop of our bustling neighborhood.

"What if you fly?" Ivy countered, the challenge clear in her tone. Her expression shifted from playful to serious, and the air between us thickened with the weight of her words. "Emma, you have to trust yourself. Don't let fear decide your future."

Her words sparked something deep within me, a flicker of a flame that had long been dormant. But still, the doubts crept in, gnawing at the edges of my resolve. I was afraid of the unknown, of leaving the comfortable patterns of my life behind.

"I just don't know what to do next," I admitted, my voice trembling slightly. "It's like I'm standing on the edge of a cliff, and I can't see what's below."

"Then don't look down," Ivy urged, her voice steady and reassuring. "Look ahead. Look at all the possibilities waiting for you. You're not just my best friend; you're an artist, a storyteller. You have a gift that's begging to be unleashed."

I felt my breath catch, a rush of emotions swirling inside me. Her unwavering belief in me felt like an anchor, a lifeline thrown into turbulent waters. But could I really leap? Could I really embrace the uncertainty and venture out into a world that had always seemed so vast and intimidating?

In that moment, the street below seemed to pulse with life. Cars honked in a cacophony of urban symphony, laughter floated up from the cafes, and the sun dipped lower, painting the sky in hues of orange and pink. And as I stood there, I realized that maybe—just maybe—I could find the courage to chase my own shadows, to paint my own story against the vibrant canvas of life that awaited me.

The morning after our heart-to-heart, I woke to the sunlight streaming through the window, painting golden stripes across the walls. For a moment, the world felt tranquil, like a quiet promise hanging in the air. I blinked away the remnants of sleep, letting the warmth wash over me, but as soon as my feet hit the floor, reality crashed back. The sight of boxes stacked precariously in the living room and Ivy's half-packed suitcase served as a stark reminder that time was slipping away.

I hurried through my morning routine, the smell of fresh coffee guiding me to the kitchen. The rhythmic drip-drip of the coffee maker felt like a ticking clock, each droplet echoing the seconds that led Ivy closer to her departure. I poured myself a cup and stared into the dark liquid, wondering if it would provide clarity or simply fuel my anxiety.

As I stood there, lost in thought, Ivy burst into the kitchen, her wild curls bouncing like springs of enthusiasm. "Good morning, sleepyhead!" she chirped, her voice bright enough to cut through my morning haze. She was wearing her favorite oversized sweater, the fabric hanging on her like a cozy blanket, and her eyes sparkled with a mixture of excitement and mischief.

"Are you sure you don't mean 'goodbye' instead?" I teased, feigning a dramatic sigh as I poured her a cup of coffee. "How many more mornings will we have like this?"

"Too many for you to be this gloomy," she replied, swiping a spoonful of sugar from the counter and adding it to her cup. "I refuse to let you wallow. We have adventures to plan."

"Adventures? Like what? Exploring the depths of my closet for more clothing I never wear?" I replied, a smirk tugging at my lips.

"Precisely," she said, pointing at me with her spoon like a wand. "But more importantly, we need to celebrate. Tonight, we're having a proper send-off. A last hurrah before I go off to the land of palm trees and sunshine."

I raised an eyebrow, the idea swirling in my mind like a fresh breeze. "A send-off? What exactly do you have in mind? A rooftop party with a view? Fancy cocktails? A drum circle?"

"Better," she grinned, her excitement palpable. "A scavenger hunt through the city. Think of it as a love letter to Manhattan, with all our favorite spots. I want to leave knowing we really soaked it all in."

I couldn't help but laugh, the idea already igniting a spark of enthusiasm within me. "You do realize we're going to look ridiculous, right? Two grown women running around like kids in a playground?"

"Exactly!" Ivy chirped, her eyes dancing. "We're going to make a spectacle of ourselves. Plus, who knows what kind of crazy adventures we might stumble into? This city has a way of surprising you when you least expect it."

As the day unfolded, Ivy and I transformed from two friends steeped in nostalgia to partners in a whimsical quest. We spent the afternoon drafting our list of stops: the art gallery where we had our first disagreement over which painting was the most pretentious, the tiny bakery with the best chocolate croissants, and, of course, the park where we'd once crafted our own "urban escape" with a picnic blanket and an assortment of snacks.

With our plan set, we found ourselves strolling down the vibrant streets of Manhattan, the autumn air crisp and inviting. The leaves were beginning to turn, painting the sidewalks in hues of amber and crimson. I could smell the rich aroma of roasting chestnuts from a vendor nearby, a scent that wrapped around us like an old friend.

"Alright," Ivy declared, tapping her phone to check our first destination. "First stop: the bakery. Who can resist chocolate croissants?"

I grinned, feigning a dramatic sigh. "Well, if you insist, I suppose I could be persuaded."

As we approached the bakery, the display cases gleamed like jewels, each pastry a work of art. The warm scent of freshly baked bread enveloped us, making it impossible to resist. We stepped inside, greeted by the cheerful bell above the door, and the counter was lined with mouthwatering treats.

"Two chocolate croissants, please!" Ivy announced, her voice ringing with enthusiasm. The baker, an elderly man with flour dusting his apron and a twinkle in his eye, nodded and handed over our pastries.

"Perfect! Now, let's find a place to enjoy these," I suggested, taking a bite of my croissant. The chocolate oozed delightfully, melting into the buttery layers, and I closed my eyes, savoring the moment.

As we stepped outside, Ivy's eyes sparkled with the thrill of adventure. "Okay, next on our list: the park! I want to relive our picnic experience, but with a twist. How about we grab a couple of iced coffees first?"

With pastries in hand and laughter spilling from our lips, we set off toward the park. The sun hung low in the sky, casting a warm glow over the city, and with each step, I felt my worries dissolve, replaced by the intoxicating feeling of freedom and spontaneity.

"Look!" Ivy pointed, her voice animated. "There's that street performer we always used to stop and watch. Let's go!"

As we approached the performer, a man juggling flaming torches with incredible precision, the crowd around him erupted into cheers. Ivy and I joined in, clapping and laughing, our hearts swelling with joy. For a moment, it felt as if the world had paused, and we were the only two people who mattered, lost in our own bubble of exhilaration.

"Do you remember when we thought we could juggle like that?" I asked, chuckling at the memory.

"Don't remind me! We nearly burned down your kitchen," she replied, her laughter ringing clear and bright. "But you know what? I think we should try again sometime. New city, new adventures. What do you say?"

"Maybe in your new apartment, so I don't risk my life again," I shot back, smirking.

As the sun dipped lower, casting a warm glow over the park, Ivy and I settled on a bench, our chocolate croissants and iced coffees in hand. We watched as children ran around, couples strolled hand in hand, and the city pulsed with life around us. In that moment, I felt a surge of gratitude for the memories we had crafted, the laughter we shared, and the unbreakable bond that connected us.

But just as the atmosphere shimmered with nostalgia, an unexpected shadow swept in. A figure emerged from the crowd—a tall man with dark hair and a determined stride, his eyes scanning the park as if searching for someone. My breath hitched as I recognized him; the last person I expected to see today, let alone in this moment.

The figure standing in the distance drew closer, and as the sun dipped lower, the light caught his face just right, revealing that unmistakable smirk. It was Jake, my ex-boyfriend, the one who had walked out of my life as abruptly as a scene cut from a movie. My heart raced—not from excitement but from a bewildering mix of emotions that had long since been buried. What was he doing here, of all places?

Ivy, oblivious to the whirlwind of thoughts crashing in my mind, chattered animatedly about the park's charm. "Can you believe this place? I used to think it was overrated, but now, I'm not so sure!

Look at the way the light hits the trees. It's like something out of a postcard!"

"Yeah, it's great," I managed, my gaze still fixated on Jake. He was now approaching with purpose, his dark hair tousled and that familiar glint in his eye—the one that always made my heart flip, even now. I cursed under my breath, desperately willing him to turn around and walk the other way.

"Emma!" he called out, his voice breaking through the laughter and chatter of the park. It felt like an electric shock, jolting me back to a time when everything felt simpler, yet infinitely more complicated.

"Please don't," I muttered, but Ivy's keen eyes had already caught sight of him, her excitement palpable.

"Wait, do you know him?" she asked, a grin spreading across her face as she leaned closer, clearly enjoying the drama unfolding before her.

"Oh, just someone from my past," I replied, hoping my nonchalance masked the sudden tension curling in my stomach.

"Someone who looks like he's come to apologize," Ivy teased, nudging me playfully. "What's the story? Should I be preparing for a heartfelt reunion?"

I barely had time to respond before Jake was upon us, his presence commanding the space around us. "Emma," he said, his tone a mix of surprise and something softer, almost vulnerable. "I didn't expect to see you here."

"Clearly," I replied, trying to keep my voice steady, though the sharpness in my words betrayed me. "What brings you to the park today?"

He rubbed the back of his neck, a gesture I remembered well. "I was just passing by and thought I'd stop. I didn't know you'd be here."

"No one does," I shot back, unable to suppress the edge of sarcasm. "I've been hiding in plain sight, you know."

Jake's expression shifted, the slight crinkle between his brows revealing a flicker of concern. "I didn't mean to... I mean, I didn't know you were with someone." His gaze darted to Ivy, and I could see the wheels turning in his head.

"Someone?" Ivy's eyes widened in delight. "Oh, we're not a couple! She's just being dramatic, which is a full-time job for her."

Jake chuckled softly, the tension easing slightly. "It's nice to meet you. I'm Jake."

"Nice to meet you, Jake," Ivy replied, her eyes dancing with curiosity. "So, what's the story? Why are you here now?"

I shot Ivy a warning look, my heart pounding as the air grew thick with unspoken words. This wasn't a conversation I wanted to have, especially not in front of Ivy, who was now sitting back with her popcorn—figuratively speaking, of course.

"Just came to... reconnect," Jake said, his gaze shifting back to me. "Things were left unresolved between us, and I thought I should at least try to clear the air."

"Reconnect? Really?" I felt a rush of indignation. "You vanished without a word. What's changed now? Did you just realize I exist again?"

"I didn't come here to argue," he said, his voice steady yet edged with frustration. "I came here to apologize—to you. I made mistakes, and I want to make them right."

Ivy's gaze darted between us like a tennis match, her curiosity palpable. "Apologizing? You mean you left her hanging without so much as a text? That sounds like a real charmer."

Jake ran a hand through his hair, exasperation flickering across his features. "I know I messed up. I was young and stupid. But Emma... I've thought about you. A lot."

"Is this the part where I'm supposed to be impressed?" I shot back, crossing my arms defiantly. "You think an apology is enough to just wipe the slate clean?"

"I'm not asking you to forgive me right now," he replied, his tone dropping into something softer. "But I hope we can talk. I miss our friendship."

The word 'friendship' felt like a slap. The memories surged forward—quiet evenings spent talking about everything and nothing, spontaneous adventures that had once filled our days with joy. But it all felt tainted now, each recollection weighed down by the bitter taste of betrayal.

"Why now, Jake? Why here?" I asked, my voice trembling slightly, as if I were standing on the edge of a precipice. "Why would you want to dredge up the past just as I'm trying to move on?"

"I don't know," he admitted, his gaze earnest. "Maybe it's selfish, but I want to see if there's still something left between us. I thought coming here, to this place, might help."

I glanced at Ivy, who wore a mixture of encouragement and concern on her face. "You can't expect her to just accept that you're back and everything's fine now," she interjected, her protective instincts kicking in. "You hurt her, Jake."

"I know," he replied, looking genuinely remorseful. "And I deserve that. But if I could just have a chance to explain—"

"I don't need explanations," I cut him off, my frustration bubbling over. "What I need is closure, something you didn't give me when you walked away. I'm not looking to pick up where we left off. I'm trying to create something new for myself."

Jake opened his mouth, his expression shifting from hurt to determination, and for a fleeting moment, I thought he might finally understand. But before he could respond, a loud commotion erupted nearby, drawing the attention of everyone in the park.

I turned instinctively, the sound of raised voices and shouts slicing through the moment. A small crowd had gathered, a woman gesturing wildly, her face contorted with anger. The atmosphere shifted instantly, tension thickening as people began to murmur and point.

"Let's go see what's happening," Ivy suggested, the excitement bubbling in her voice, but I felt rooted in place, my heart racing for reasons I couldn't quite decipher.

"Emma, wait," Jake said, reaching out, but I stepped back, the distance between us suddenly feeling insurmountable.

With a glance back at Ivy, who seemed equally torn between curiosity and concern, I felt the ground beneath me shift. "I can't deal with this right now," I muttered, turning away from Jake, feeling the weight of unfinished business hanging in the air.

But as I took a step forward, I caught sight of a figure in the crowd—a flash of a familiar jacket, unmistakable even in the chaos. My breath hitched, the world around me fading as recognition crashed over me like a wave. It was him, standing there with a fierce expression, an urgency in his eyes that set off alarms in my heart.

And just like that, my life spiraled into uncertainty, the shadows of my past threatening to envelop me as I faced an unexpected truth: I was about to confront something I thought was long buried.

Chapter 21: A Heart Divided

The faint hum of the city vibrated through my bones as I stepped onto the bustling streets of SoHo, my heart a mix of hope and apprehension. Each block was alive with the scent of fresh coffee mingling with the sweet notes of baked goods from the corner café. I took a deep breath, inhaling the intoxicating aroma, yet it did little to quell the flutter of uncertainty in my chest. Ivy's departure left behind a chasm in our apartment, one that I filled with fabric swatches, sketchbooks, and the faint echoes of laughter that now felt like distant memories. It was as if a ghost had taken residence in my mind, whispering doubts that ricocheted off the walls of my ambition.

Nathaniel walked beside me, his presence a sturdy anchor against the turbulent sea of my thoughts. He was everything I admired: intelligent, witty, and unyieldingly supportive. The way he tilted his head slightly while listening made me feel as though I were the center of a universe solely designed for our conversations. But even the warmth of his hand brushing against mine couldn't chase away the chill of my divided heart. I glanced at him, catching the glimmer of streetlights reflecting in his deep-set eyes, and wondered if he could sense the storm brewing inside me.

"Is it just me, or is this the perfect night for some gelato?" he asked, breaking the tension that hung between us like a fragile spiderweb.

I couldn't help but smile, the corners of my lips lifting despite the weight on my heart. "You always know how to distract me."

"Distraction is my specialty," he quipped, feigning a mock-serious tone. "I'd even add it to my résumé if I could."

As we meandered toward our favorite gelato shop, I was struck by how much I relished our banter. It was like a well-rehearsed play, each line delivered with just the right amount of flair. Yet, beneath the laughter, I felt the weight of my own hesitations. The dreams I had fought so hard to bring to life were now entangled in the delicate threads of our growing relationship. Nathaniel's support felt like a lifeline, but it also left me with a nagging fear of losing my independence.

"What flavors are calling your name tonight?" he asked, his hand brushing against mine as we approached the colorful display of gelato.

"Maybe pistachio? Or dark chocolate?" I mused, pretending to contemplate the decision as if it were the weighty matters of life.

"Ah, a woman of taste!" he exclaimed, gesturing dramatically. "But why choose? Why not get both?"

I laughed, the sound a little too bright, a little too forced, but it felt good to engage in this simple moment of joy. "I suppose you're right. When in doubt, always opt for excess."

We stepped inside the quaint shop, where the air was thick with sweetness, and the vibrant colors of gelato seemed to dance in the soft lighting. I watched as Nathaniel leaned toward the counter, engaged in a spirited conversation with the barista about the merits of coconut milk-based gelato. There was something so infectious about his enthusiasm; it made my heart swell. Yet, even as I savored the rich texture of my chosen flavors, an underlying tension gnawed at me.

With each bite, I could feel my thoughts spiraling back to Ivy. She had always been the dreamer, the wild spirit who dared to chase the impossible. Losing her felt like a betrayal of my own aspirations. "You know," I started, my voice softer than I intended, "sometimes I wonder if I'm good enough to make it in this industry. There's so much competition, so many voices that drown out my own."

Nathaniel's brow furrowed, his gelato momentarily forgotten. "That's absurd. You're brilliant, and your designs are unique. The world needs what you create."

"But what if it isn't enough?" I replied, a hint of frustration coloring my words. "What if I'm just chasing a dream that isn't meant for me?"

He took a step closer, his eyes searching mine, as if attempting to peel back the layers of my doubts. "Do you really believe that? You're not just chasing a dream; you're creating one every day. You have a gift, and the world is ready for it."

"Then why does it feel like I'm standing at the edge of a cliff, afraid to leap?" I asked, my voice barely above a whisper.

"Because sometimes the hardest leap is believing in yourself," he said, his tone a blend of encouragement and empathy. "But you don't have to do it alone. I'm here, every step of the way."

His words wrapped around me like a warm embrace, yet beneath the surface, an unsettling truth simmered. His unwavering belief in me sparked a flicker of desire for something deeper, something more. But the very idea of commitment sent tremors of fear coursing through me. I didn't want to become someone else's shadow or relinquish the fierce independence I had fought so hard to cultivate.

With our gelato half-eaten, we strolled toward the nearby park, where the trees rustled gently in the evening breeze. The air was electric with the promise of autumn, the leaves hinting at the fiery colors soon to blanket the city. I paused beneath a particularly large oak, its gnarled branches stretching overhead like a protective canopy.

"Sometimes I feel like I'm lost in this maze of expectations," I confessed, my voice breaking slightly as I stared at the ground, unwilling to meet his gaze. "I want to soar, but I also want someone to share it with. I just don't know how to balance it all."

"Life's not about balancing; it's about finding a rhythm," he said softly, stepping closer. "And if anyone can dance through it all, it's you."

His words sent a jolt through me, igniting a flicker of hope alongside the anxiety. I wanted to believe him, to embrace the possibilities he envisioned. But as I looked into his earnest eyes, I felt the familiar flicker of doubt creep back in. What if I let him down? What if I let myself down?

The night air grew crisp, teasing the edges of my thoughts as Nathaniel and I walked side by side, our gelato cups long discarded on a nearby bench. The world around us pulsed with life, the sounds of laughter and clinking glasses drifting from the bars lining the street, yet I felt encased in a bubble of uncertainty. Each step echoed the tumult within me, a rhythm of conflicting desires that threatened to drown out the laughter of the city.

"Do you want to grab a drink somewhere? I hear that new speakeasy just opened up," Nathaniel suggested, his enthusiasm palpable. The way his eyes sparkled with excitement always drew me in, but tonight, the idea felt heavy.

"I don't know," I hesitated, glancing down the street where the neon lights flickered like beacons of promise. "I'm just not in the mood to be around people."

He studied me for a moment, the corner of his mouth quirking up in that familiar half-smile that promised understanding. "We could always just sit on a stoop and contemplate the universe. Or, you know, how I'm definitely the superior gelato connoisseur."

I chuckled, the sound a fleeting respite from my swirling thoughts. "You're really leaning into this whole distraction thing, aren't you?"

"Hey, it's a gift. Not everyone can excel at avoiding serious discussions," he quipped, lightly bumping my shoulder with his. "But seriously, I get it. You've got a lot on your mind, and if I'm going to keep you around, I should probably be a good listener."

I sighed, the weight of my thoughts pressing down harder than the cool breeze. "It's just... Ivy's absence is still so fresh. I thought I could dive into my work and make it all go away, but instead, it's like every sketch I create is a reminder of what's missing."

Nathaniel's expression shifted, a hint of concern replacing his playful demeanor. "Have you talked to her? Maybe she could help."

"Talking to Ivy would mean facing the fact that I'm no longer the person she knew. She believed in a version of me that I'm still trying to find," I admitted, my heart racing at the thought.

He reached for my hand, the warmth of his grip grounding me. "You're not defined by your past. You're creating your own path. But you've got to be honest with yourself, too."

His words hung in the air, heavy with unspoken implications. I could feel the longing in his gaze, the silent wish for me to share the tangled thoughts in my heart. But vulnerability felt like an open wound, and I wasn't sure I was ready to expose it. "What if I'm not ready to face that truth?"

"Then let's just sit here, with the stars and the city, and not worry about tomorrow," he suggested, settling onto a stoop nearby and pulling me down beside him. "I'll make sure you don't have to talk if you don't want to."

With the sounds of the city bustling around us, I leaned back, allowing the cool surface beneath me to absorb some of my tension. We sat in silence for a few moments, the night wrapping around us like a comforting blanket.

"You know, when I first moved to the city, I thought it would be a lot more glamorous," I finally confessed, breaking the comfortable quiet. "I imagined rooftop parties and meaningful connections, but mostly, it's just been... a lot of this."

"A lot of sitting on stoops, contemplating life?" Nathaniel asked, feigning a dramatic gasp. "What a disappointment! I guess you'll just have to suffer through my company instead."

I laughed, a genuine burst of sound that felt like a small victory against the tide of doubt. "It's not so bad. Honestly, I like these moments with you. They're refreshing, like an unexpected rain on a summer day."

"Ah, I'll take that as a compliment," he said, feigning mock pride. "I'm practically a human shower of joy."

As the laughter faded, I found myself looking at him differently, taking in the way his hair curled slightly at the edges, the way his smile lit up his face, and the warmth radiating from his eyes. A wave of affection washed over me, mingling with that ever-present fear of commitment. Was it possible to want more and still feel like I was losing myself?

"Do you ever think about where we're headed?" I asked, the question slipping from my lips before I could reel it back in.

His brow furrowed slightly, and he seemed to weigh his response. "I think about it all the time. I mean, look at us. We're both so invested in our passions. It's like we're two pieces of a puzzle that don't quite fit yet."

"Or maybe we're just two pieces trying to find our way in a world that doesn't have clear edges," I offered, my heart racing as I spoke.

"That sounds a lot like life," he mused, his gaze distant as if he were peering into the future. "But sometimes, it's those jagged edges that create the most beautiful art."

A silence enveloped us, thick with possibilities. I watched as he absently played with a loose thread on his jeans, lost in thought. His vulnerability, the way he opened himself up to the world, ignited something within me. Maybe it was time to confront my fears, to lean into the unpredictable dance of life instead of shying away from it.

"You know, I've been thinking," I began, the words tumbling out in a rush, "what if I put everything on the line? What if I took that leap and really committed to my designs, to us?"

Nathaniel's head snapped up, his surprise evident. "Wait, are you saying you're considering actually jumping into the deep end?"

"I'm saying I want to explore what this could be," I clarified, my pulse quickening. "But I need you to promise me something first."

"Anything," he said, leaning in closer, the intensity in his gaze making my heart race even faster.

"Promise me that you'll help me navigate the chaos that comes with pursuing my dreams. That we'll find a way to balance it all without losing who we are."

He nodded slowly, a soft smile spreading across his lips. "I promise. But you need to promise me something in return."

"Deal," I said, intrigued.

"You need to promise to trust yourself as much as I trust you. No more holding back."

A spark ignited between us, a flicker of hope that pushed against the doubts I had clung to for far too long. For the first time in what felt like ages, the world seemed a little brighter, a little less daunting. It was a small step, but it was ours, and maybe, just maybe, it was the beginning of something incredible.

The city pulsed around us, a vibrant backdrop to the quiet awakening of my heart. Nathaniel's promise hung in the air like the first notes of a beloved song, and I could feel the tremors of possibility rippling through me. "Trust yourself as much as I trust you." Those words danced in my mind, igniting a flame of determination.

"Alright," I said, breaking the silence that had enveloped us after our promises. "I'll do it. I'll put myself out there, but it doesn't mean I'm not terrified."

Nathaniel grinned, his eyes sparkling with excitement. "Fear is just excitement in disguise. Think of it as your personal pep rally—minus the cheerleaders and pom-poms."

"Great, now I have to imagine myself in a tutu," I quipped, but his enthusiasm was infectious, and a reluctant smile tugged at my lips. "What does this leap look like, exactly? Am I supposed to hold an impromptu runway show in the middle of the street?"

"Maybe not quite that dramatic," he chuckled, his laughter rich and warm. "But I do think you should reach out to a few boutiques. Your designs deserve a spotlight, and you might be surprised at how many people are eager to collaborate."

The thought sent butterflies fluttering in my stomach, a mix of anticipation and apprehension. "You really think they'd want to see what I've been working on?"

"Absolutely. You've got talent. Besides, if anyone can sell a vision, it's you. Just imagine it: a stunning display of your designs, elegant models, and people marveling at your creations."

I could almost picture it—the lights, the fabric flowing like waves, the hum of excitement in the air. Yet, shadows of doubt crept in, whispering insidious thoughts that made me hesitate. "And what if they don't like it? What if it falls flat? Then what?"

He turned to me, his expression serious for a moment. "What if it doesn't? What if it opens doors you never even thought possible? Every great success has a dozen failures behind it. You can't let the fear of falling stop you from flying."

I nodded, absorbing his words. "You're right, I can't let fear stifle my dreams. But it's easy for you to say; you're not the one standing on that ledge."

"Then let me help you," he said, his voice steady, reassuring. "I'll be right there with you, cheering you on."

As we continued walking, the vibrant energy of SoHo wrapped around us, lighting up the night. Street musicians played nearby, their notes floating on the breeze, harmonizing with the rhythm of the city. We wandered past art galleries and boutiques, their windows aglow with enticing displays. Inspiration surged within me like a rising tide, and for the first time in a long while, I felt hope unfurling inside my chest.

"Okay," I breathed, determination coursing through me. "I'll reach out to the boutiques. I'll put together a lookbook and get my designs out there."

Nathaniel squeezed my hand, his smile radiating pride. "That's the spirit! Just remember, whatever happens, it's about the journey, not just the destination."

With newfound resolve, I headed home, my heart lighter than it had been in weeks. As I walked through our apartment door, the familiar silence wrapped around me, but instead of feeling empty, it felt like a blank canvas waiting for vibrant strokes of creativity. I could almost see Ivy's smile, hear her voice cheering me on.

In the days that followed, I poured myself into my work, sketching designs late into the night while Nathaniel's words echoed in my mind. I transformed our living space into a mini studio, fabric swatches strewn about like confetti from a celebration. The air was charged with the electric thrill of possibility, and each stitch felt like an affirmation of my ambition.

One afternoon, while hunched over my sewing machine, I received an email from a local boutique, inviting me to showcase a few pieces during their upcoming open house. My heart raced; this was it. My moment to leap into the unknown.

"See?" Nathaniel said, looking over my shoulder, excitement palpable in his voice. "This is just the beginning! You're going to be a sensation!"

I let out a breath I didn't know I was holding, a mixture of disbelief and elation coursing through me. "What do I do now? I only have a week to prepare!"

"Focus on what you want to showcase. Keep it simple, highlight your best work," he advised, and we both dove headfirst into the chaos of planning.

The next few days became a blur of fabric, sketches, and late-night brainstorming sessions fueled by coffee and adrenaline.

Nathaniel transformed from my boyfriend into my unofficial hype man, assisting me in every way possible. We sourced materials, set up a makeshift runway in the apartment, and even practiced my pitch in front of the bathroom mirror.

"Imagine the crowd, the lights," he said, waving his arms as if conducting an orchestra. "You're not just presenting your designs; you're telling a story. So give it the flair it deserves!"

But beneath the surface of my growing excitement, a knot of anxiety tightened. What if the story I told fell flat? What if they saw through my façade, exposed my insecurities? As the day of the showcase loomed closer, those doubts wormed their way back into my mind.

On the eve of the event, I found myself sitting on the edge of our bed, fabric scattered around me like fallen leaves. Nathaniel joined me, his expression thoughtful. "What's on your mind?"

"Everything," I admitted, my voice barely a whisper. "What if they don't see what I see? What if my vision doesn't resonate with anyone?"

He placed a reassuring hand on my knee, grounding me. "You have to trust your vision, trust that your art speaks for itself. And remember, you're not alone in this."

His words were a balm, but the truth was, I felt the weight of the world on my shoulders. Just as I opened my mouth to voice my fears, a loud knock on the door broke the moment, startling us both.

"Who could that be?" I muttered, glancing at the clock. It was late, and our apartment was usually a sanctuary of peace.

Nathaniel stood, his expression shifting to curiosity. "Let me check."

He opened the door, revealing a figure silhouetted against the hallway light. I could only see the outline at first, but a chill ran down my spine when I recognized the voice that followed. "Hello there. Mind if I come in?"

Ivy.

Her voice, once a familiar comfort, now struck a dissonant chord within me. Conflicting emotions surged—joy, anger, relief. All at once, I felt unmoored, the very foundation I'd started to rebuild beneath me shifting like sand.

"Uh, this is a surprise," Nathaniel said cautiously, stepping aside to let her in.

As Ivy crossed the threshold, her presence flooded the room, a whirlwind of energy and unresolved tension. She glanced around, her eyes landing on me with an intensity that made my heart race. "I heard you're doing something big, and I couldn't miss it. Can we talk?"

A thousand questions swirled in my mind, but the strongest was this: Was I ready to confront the past, especially when the future felt so precarious?

Chapter 22: The Ties That Unravel

The sky hung low and gray over New York City, the sort of dreary day that made you want to curl up under a pile of blankets with a hot cup of cocoa and forget about the world outside. I stood at my kitchen counter, the smell of freshly brewed coffee mingling with the scent of the cinnamon-swirled muffins I had hastily thrown together. I had hoped they might somehow make everything feel lighter, but the weight of my phone buzzing on the counter cut through the cozy atmosphere like a foghorn.

My mother's name flashed on the screen, and a tingle of dread wrapped around my spine. I had left Meadowbrook for a reason. The sprawling family estate, its white pillars rising like a proud sentinel against the backdrop of the distant hills, felt stifling after a few days in the city. I swiped to answer, bracing myself for the inevitable wave of familial expectations crashing over me.

"Darling! I hope I'm not interrupting anything important," my mother chirped, her voice a concoction of sweetness and urgency. I could picture her, all pearls and pastel silk, standing in the grand foyer of our home, ready to orchestrate the next family gathering like it was the production of a Broadway show.

"Just making some muffins," I replied, forcing a lightness into my tone, the kind that never quite reached my heart. "What's going on?"

"Your father and I have been discussing the future of Hart & Co. You really must come home this weekend. We need to talk about your role." Her voice took on that familiar note of pressure, as if it were my duty to set aside my dreams in favor of the family business.

I glanced out the window, where raindrops began to streak down the glass, mirroring my growing sense of panic. "Mom, I—"

"Please, Isabelle. It's important. Your father is worried. He thinks the company needs a fresh perspective, and who better than you?"

A fresh perspective. My heart clenched at the words. I had worked hard to carve out a life for myself here, far from the sprawling fields of my childhood, where the cloying scent of lavender filled the air and every corner of the house whispered memories of expectations.

"I'll think about it," I finally said, feeling like a traitor to both my aspirations and my family. We ended the call, and I took a deep breath, wishing I could pluck the worries from my mind like petals from a daisy.

Nathaniel wandered into the kitchen, his tall frame filling the space with an easy confidence that usually made me feel grounded. Today, however, I sensed a storm brewing behind his stormy blue eyes. "What did she want?" he asked, leaning against the counter, arms crossed, casual yet somehow demanding.

"Just the usual family business stuff," I replied, trying to keep my tone light as I poured him a cup of coffee. "You know how they are."

He took the cup but didn't drink. Instead, he set it down, the clink of porcelain echoing in the silence that followed. "Isabelle, you've been 'thinking about it' for weeks now. You can't keep putting off your family obligations for this... this life you're trying to build here."

I bristled at his tone, a tension crackling in the air between us. "It's not just about me anymore, Nathaniel. It's about my family, our legacy."

"And what about your dreams?" His voice rose slightly, frustration threading through his words. "You think I want to be the guy holding you back? I want to support you, but you keep putting them ahead of everything else."

I could feel the anger and hurt simmering just beneath the surface, each of us clutching our own convictions like shields. "You don't understand. You never lived in the shadow of expectations!

They built that business from the ground up. It's not just some 'legacy' to toss aside."

"Maybe it's time to toss it!" Nathaniel shot back, and I flinched as the words hung heavy between us, sharp as glass. "You're an incredible woman, Isabelle. You deserve to follow your own path, not just the one they've laid out for you."

I wanted to argue, to point out the countless times I had tried to walk my own path while balancing the weight of my family's aspirations. Instead, I found myself quiet, my heart pounding in my chest, battling the desire to scream and the urge to break down in tears.

Just then, my phone buzzed again, another urgent message from my mother, and I sighed, feeling the walls close in. I grabbed my bag, the clattering of my keys echoing like a countdown to some inevitable fate. "I need to go," I said, the words slipping out before I could think better of them.

"Isabelle," Nathaniel began, but I cut him off, the frustration bubbling over.

"I have to figure this out, Nathaniel! I can't keep waiting for the right moment when my family is calling me back home." I felt a rush of heat in my cheeks, a mixture of anger and desperation that threatened to spill over. "You just don't get it, do you?"

"I thought we were a team," he replied, his voice strained but firm, like a taut wire ready to snap.

"Maybe you should reconsider your definition of 'team,'" I shot back, storming out of the kitchen and slamming the door behind me.

The rain had picked up, drenching the streets, blurring the lines of reality as I stepped out into the chaos of the city. My heart raced, a riot of conflicting emotions swirling within me as I tried to make sense of my choices. The blare of car horns and the chatter of pedestrians faded into white noise as I walked, each step feeling heavier than the last.

In that moment, I felt as if I were being pulled in two directions, my heart anchored in the warmth of Nathaniel's arms but tethered to the roots of my family's legacy. I paused under the awning of a café, rain pouring down like a waterfall, and closed my eyes, letting the cool droplets wash over me. I didn't know which way to turn, but the tug of duty was growing stronger, entwining itself around my heart like ivy, suffocating yet familiar.

The rain had become a relentless curtain, blurring the cityscape into a watercolor of muted grays and blues. As I navigated the puddles that formed along the sidewalk, my mind whirled like the eddies swirling in the storm drains. Every raindrop seemed to echo my turmoil, the thundering of the sky matching the pounding of my heart. I ducked into a nearby café, the bell above the door chiming like a belligerent reminder that life continued, oblivious to my internal struggle.

The air inside was warm and rich with the aroma of espresso and fresh pastries, a welcome embrace from the biting chill outside. I found a corner table and sank into a chair, desperate for a moment of quiet reflection. My fingers tapped nervously against the smooth surface of the wooden table, each tap mimicking the rhythm of my racing thoughts. As I stared out the window, the droplets raced down the glass like my fleeting moments of clarity, each one slipping away before I could grasp it.

"Isabelle? You look like you've just faced down a herd of stampeding buffalo," a familiar voice called from across the room, breaking through the fog of my thoughts. It was Clara, my best friend and confidante, the kind of person who could unearth a smile even in the darkest of moments. She wove her way through the tables, her curly hair bouncing in sync with her lively energy, until she settled across from me, her eyes sparkling with concern.

"Buffalo, huh? That's quite the image," I replied, managing a weak grin. "More like I've been trampled by my own expectations."

She reached for my hand, her grip warm and grounding. "Talk to me. What's going on? You look like you've seen a ghost."

I took a deep breath, feeling the tension begin to unravel just a bit under her gentle inquiry. "It's my family. They want me to come home this weekend to discuss the future of the business."

Clara raised an eyebrow, a playful smirk dancing on her lips. "And let me guess, you want to run screaming into the nearest exit?"

"Something like that," I admitted, the weight of my thoughts spilling out into the open. "It's just... I left for a reason. I thought I could build something for myself here, and now it feels like I'm being pulled back into that world, like a marionette with strings attached."

"Hey, you're no puppet," Clara said, her tone fierce and protective. "You're a strong, independent woman who can choose her own path. You just have to decide which direction that path leads you."

I nodded, grateful for her unwavering support, yet the uncertainty lingered like a shadow in the back of my mind. "It's not that simple. There are expectations—my parents built that business from the ground up. They need me, and part of me feels guilty for wanting to say no."

"Guilt can be a slippery slope," Clara replied, her eyes narrowing as if weighing my words carefully. "You have to remember that while they may need you, you need to put yourself first, too. What do you really want?"

The question hung in the air, heavy yet inviting. I opened my mouth to answer, but the words caught in my throat. What did I want? The truth was buried under layers of familial duty and societal expectations, waiting for the right moment to rise to the surface.

"I want... I want to be happy," I finally said, each syllable heavy with longing. "But it feels like I'm being asked to choose between my happiness and my family. And the last thing I want is to let them down."

"Is it really letting them down if you pursue your dreams?" Clara challenged gently, leaning in closer. "You've worked so hard to create a life that's true to you. You deserve that freedom."

Before I could respond, the café door swung open with a dramatic flourish, and in walked Nathaniel, his coat drenched from the downpour. He scanned the room, and when his gaze met mine, the tension that had simmered between us earlier ignited all over again.

"Fancy running into you here," he said, his voice carrying a mix of surprise and annoyance, as he made his way toward our table.

"Clara was just giving me a pep talk," I said, trying to keep my tone light, but the words felt heavy in my mouth.

"Glad to hear it," he replied coolly, wiping rain from his brow. "I didn't realize you were such a fan of advice. Perhaps you should take it."

The air thickened, and I could feel Clara's eyes darting between us, the tension thick enough to slice with a knife. "I think I need another coffee," she said, rising from the table with remarkable speed. "And I'll let you two... catch up."

As she slipped away, the silence between Nathaniel and me felt like an unbridgeable chasm. "Why are you here?" I asked, my words sharper than intended.

"Because I wanted to see you. I thought we could talk."

"Talk about what? My impending return to Meadowbrook and the family business?"

"Is that what this is about?" he replied, his voice tight, the frustration clear in his eyes. "Isn't it obvious that your family is calling you back? You can't ignore that."

"And what if I want to ignore it?" I shot back, feeling my pulse quicken. "What if I want to stay here and continue building a life with you?"

"Then you need to make that choice, Isabelle. But it feels like you're caught between two worlds, and I'm not sure I'm on the list of priorities." His words cut deep, and I felt a swell of anger rise within me.

"You think I don't want you in my life? That I'm trying to choose my family over you?"

"I don't know what to think," he replied, exasperation lacing his tone. "You keep saying you want to build a future, but every time they call, it's like you drop everything to run back home."

"And what do you want me to do? Cut ties with my family? Throw away the life they've built?" I leaned closer, desperate to bridge the distance growing between us. "I'm trying to navigate this, Nathaniel, but I can't do it alone."

His expression softened, just a fraction, as he took a step closer. "I want you to find your voice in all of this. I want you to choose your path, whatever that looks like, and I want to be part of it."

The sincerity in his voice hit me like a tidal wave, washing away some of the anger and frustration. "You really mean that?" I asked, my heart pounding with the weight of vulnerability.

"I do. But you have to be honest with yourself first."

The world outside faded as I looked into his eyes, the storm both outside and within me raging on. I had a choice to make, one that could redefine everything I thought I wanted. As the rain continued to drum against the window, I felt the first stirrings of clarity breaking through the chaos, like sunlight piercing through the storm clouds. But would I have the courage to seize it?

The warmth of Nathaniel's gaze lingered like sunlight spilling through a window, but the storm brewing between us felt far more daunting. The café's comforting ambiance became a battleground as I grappled with the enormity of my choices. I felt the walls closing in, and my thoughts ricocheted around my mind like loose change, desperate to settle but unable to find a resting place.

"I'm trying to figure this out," I said, my voice a fragile whisper, barely rising above the din of clinking cups and casual conversations. "But it feels like the more I try to balance everything, the more everything falls apart."

Nathaniel sighed, his frustration palpable, but beneath that lay a current of compassion that tugged at my heart. "Maybe it's time to let go of the idea that you have to balance everything perfectly. Life isn't a tightrope walk. It's a messy, unpredictable journey, and sometimes you have to make a leap."

"Easier said than done," I countered, a hint of bitterness creeping into my tone. "It's not just my happiness at stake. My family has built something incredible, and walking away feels like turning my back on their sacrifices."

"Or maybe it's about not sacrificing your own happiness," he replied, his eyes locking onto mine with an intensity that made my heart race. "You're not responsible for their choices, only your own."

His words struck a chord within me, resonating like a note from a well-tuned piano, and I felt the weight of guilt I had carried for so long begin to waver. Just as I opened my mouth to respond, my phone buzzed violently against the table, cutting through our moment like a knife.

I glanced at the screen. It was another message from my mother, a quick succession of texts that sent a jolt of anxiety racing through me. "We need to discuss your future," the latest one read, and I could almost hear her voice, sweet yet tinged with urgency. "It's crucial. Please call."

Nathaniel observed my shifting expressions, his brow furrowing with concern. "What did she say?"

I hesitated, torn between the urge to share everything and the instinct to shield him from the weight of my family drama. "It's just my mother being... insistent."

"Insistent?" His skepticism was palpable. "Doesn't sound like just another family chat to me."

I chewed on my lip, wrestling with the truth that felt too raw to articulate. "She wants me to come home to talk about my role in the business," I admitted, my voice barely above a murmur. "And she's making it sound like an ultimatum."

Nathaniel's expression shifted, the storm in his eyes darkening as he leaned back, crossing his arms. "An ultimatum? Isabelle, that's not fair to you. You shouldn't feel pressured to abandon your life here for something you're not even sure you want."

"I know that! But what if they genuinely need me?" The frustration bubbled within me, threatening to overflow. "What if I'm the only one who can help?"

"Or what if they're just manipulating you to get what they want?" His voice cut through the tension, sharp yet unwavering.

The words landed like ice in my veins, and I recoiled at the truth nestled within them. My parents had always had a way of making me feel responsible for their dreams, and I had allowed that sense of obligation to cloud my judgment.

"Maybe you're right," I conceded quietly, feeling the weight of the decision begin to shift. "But I just wish it were easier. I want to honor them, but I also want to honor myself."

"That's the crux of it, isn't it?" he said, his voice softening. "Finding the balance between loyalty and love. But you can't lose sight of who you are in the process."

As his words settled, I felt a flicker of resolve ignite within me. I could be loyal to my family without losing myself, but it would take strength—strength I wasn't sure I possessed. The thought sent a shiver through me, and I leaned back, gathering my thoughts as I watched the raindrops race each other down the glass.

The café door opened again, this time admitting a gust of wind that sent a chill through the room. I turned, distracted by the sudden commotion, only to see a figure silhouetted against the gray light outside. My heart dropped as I recognized him.

"Julian," I whispered, the name slipping past my lips like a curse.

He stepped inside, shaking off rain like a dog, his gaze scanning the room until it landed on me. A tight knot formed in my stomach. Nathaniel had gone rigid, his expression a mask of tension as Julian made his way over.

"Isabelle, fancy seeing you here," Julian said, a smirk dancing on his lips, his voice smooth like silk. He was dressed impeccably, as always, with an air of confidence that could be disarming.

"What do you want?" I shot back, my tone sharper than intended, the underlying resentment bubbling to the surface.

"I came to see how my favorite cousin is doing. You know, since we haven't caught up in a while." His gaze flicked to Nathaniel, the tension between them palpable.

"Julian, we're in the middle of something," Nathaniel interjected, his voice low, protective.

"Oh, I can see that," Julian replied, feigning innocence. "But this is important. Isabelle, your family is in quite the pickle, and I think you should know about it."

"What do you mean?" I asked, my heart racing, dread curling in my stomach like a snake preparing to strike.

Julian leaned closer, lowering his voice as if sharing a secret. "There are changes happening at Hart & Co. Changes that could affect everything, including your place in the family business."

The words hung in the air, a heavy fog of uncertainty. "What kind of changes?"

"Let's just say some people aren't as loyal as they appear. If you don't act soon, you might find yourself on the outside looking in."

Nathaniel shifted next to me, the heat radiating off him making me acutely aware of how fragile this moment felt. I could see the flicker of concern in his eyes, matching the tempest within me. "What are you saying?" I pressed, desperation clawing at my throat.

"I'm saying your family may not be what they seem, Isabelle. And you're running out of time to figure out where you really belong."

With that, Julian turned, a knowing smirk on his face as he strode away, leaving a trail of tension and uncertainty in his wake. The café felt stifling, the air thick with implications and unspoken fears. I felt like a marionette caught in the strings of my family, each move dictated by their desires while my own yearned for freedom.

"I can't believe this," I whispered, my heart pounding. "I have to go back, don't I?"

Nathaniel's expression darkened, and the storm that had calmed moments before swirled back to life. "You can't make a decision based on his words. Not without knowing the truth."

"I don't have the luxury of time," I replied, the reality crashing down like the storm outside. "If there's something going on with my family, I need to confront it head-on."

As I stood up, the weight of uncertainty hung heavy around me. I was at the precipice of change, and I could feel the winds of fate gathering around me.

"Isabelle, wait—" Nathaniel began, reaching for my arm, but I pulled away, determination fueling my steps. I couldn't afford to falter, not now.

As I stepped out into the rain, the cold air wrapping around me like a shroud, I felt an electric charge in the air, a sense of impending confrontation looming on the horizon. Every instinct screamed at me to run back to the safety of Nathaniel's arms, but I pressed forward, knowing that the answers lay somewhere in the storm.

With each step, the chaos of my life echoed in my mind, a cacophony of unresolved feelings and looming decisions, and as I navigated the slick pavement, a dark figure appeared in the distance—someone waiting for me, someone whose presence sent a shiver down my spine.

The rain fell harder, mingling with the uncertainty of my choices, and as I drew closer, the air crackled with tension, my heart racing in anticipation. Would I find clarity or face the unraveling of everything I held dear? The question loomed, hanging in the stormy air like a storm cloud pregnant with rain, ready to burst.

Chapter 23: A Glimmer of Hope

The fabric swatches lay scattered across my dining table, a riot of colors and textures clamoring for my attention. Silk and cotton, chiffon and velvet, each whispering promises of elegance and comfort, urging me to create something that was distinctly, undeniably mine. My fingers brushed over a deep emerald green, a shade reminiscent of the first leaves unfurling in spring, and a thrill pulsed through me. This was my antidote to the chaos swirling around my heart. Each thread I selected felt like a thread I could weave into the tapestry of my own narrative, crafting a collection that wasn't just a reflection of my aesthetic but a celebration of resilience and transformation.

The city outside my window throbbed with life, a symphony of sounds that danced in rhythm with my thoughts. Car horns blared in the distance, accompanied by the occasional laughter of strangers mingling on the sidewalks below. I had always found inspiration in the streets of New York—its energy a constant reminder that beauty could be born from even the most frenetic moments. Today, as I poured over my sketches, the skyline loomed majestically against the pale blue sky, each building a beacon of ambition and dreams. I wanted to encapsulate that spirit in my designs, to bottle the essence of hope and heartache into garments that would flutter gracefully around their wearers.

Nathaniel leaned against the doorframe, a lazy smile curving his lips as he watched me work. His dark hair fell into his eyes, the sunlight catching the warmth of his skin, turning him into a living portrait of relaxed confidence. "You know," he said, crossing his arms over his chest, "if you keep biting your lip like that, you're going to chew it right off. What's got you so wound up?"

I glanced up, the corners of my mouth lifting slightly at his playful tone. "It's just—" I paused, my heart flipping as I weighed my words. "I'm pitching a new collection to a group of industry professionals next week, and I want it to mean something. I want them to feel what I feel when I look at these fabrics."

His brow furrowed in that way that always made my insides flutter. "What do you feel?"

I hesitated, my fingers stilling over a sketch of a flowing gown, its silhouette inspired by the wild freedom of the sea. "I feel like I'm reclaiming myself," I admitted. "After everything that's happened, I want to show that I'm not just a designer—I'm a survivor. And if I can do that through fashion, then maybe... maybe I can find a way to navigate my life too."

His expression softened, the playful glint replaced by something deeper, more sincere. "You're going to knock their socks off, you know that? You have this incredible way of capturing emotions and turning them into art."

The warmth in his gaze wrapped around me like a blanket, and I couldn't help but smile at the compliment. Nathaniel had been my steadfast anchor through the recent storms, always encouraging me to dive deeper, to explore the vulnerable corners of my creativity. Yet, despite the encouragement, a nagging fear festered in the back of my mind. What if my designs weren't enough? What if I failed to convey the complexity of my emotions?

As the days slipped by, I found myself submerged in my work, the sketches piling up like a waterfall of ideas that I was desperate to share with the world. I draped fabrics over mannequins in my tiny studio, standing back to evaluate how they danced in the light. Each piece was an exploration—a journey through the landscapes of my heart. I poured over my inspirations: the sharp lines of the city's architecture, the soft curves of the surrounding parks, the laughter and tears of everyday life.

By the time the day of the pitch arrived, I was a bundle of nerves wrapped in layers of silk and tulle. My collection shimmered like a dream come to life, each piece a testament to my journey of self-discovery. Nathaniel stood by my side, his presence a calming balm against the impending storm of anxiety swirling in my chest. "Just breathe," he murmured, brushing his fingers over my arm, igniting a spark of courage within me. "You've put your heart into this. They'll see that."

As we stepped into the sleek, modern gallery that housed the event, my senses heightened, the atmosphere alive with chatter and excitement. Industry leaders, influencers, and fellow designers buzzed around, their eyes sparkling with anticipation. I could feel the weight of their expectations pressing down on me, and yet, amidst the chatter, my heart swelled with hope. I was ready to unveil my vision, to share the narrative that had been stirring within me like a gentle tide.

When my turn arrived, I stood before the crowd, the lights dimming as I cleared my throat, the fabric swatches shimmering under the spotlight. I introduced my collection, my voice steady yet infused with the passion that surged through my veins. "Fashion is not just about clothing; it's a language of emotion," I began, my gaze sweeping across the room, catching the attention of those I hoped to impress. "These pieces tell a story—a story of rebirth, of resilience, and of embracing every facet of who we are."

As I unveiled each design, the audience shifted in their seats, intrigue etched across their faces. I described the inspiration behind the flowing lines of the dresses, the bold colors reflecting the depths of human experience, the textures mimicking the complexities of love and loss. With every word, I wove my heart into the fabric of the presentation, revealing layers of my journey as I showcased each piece.

When the final gown, a breathtaking creation that billowed like clouds at sunset, took its place on the pedestal, the room erupted in applause. My heart raced as I stood there, absorbing the validation of my effort. Hope flickered in my chest, its light brightening the shadows that had lingered for far too long. In that moment, I felt a profound connection to the art I had created, a promise that perhaps I could indeed balance my ambitions with the love I held for Nathaniel and for myself.

The applause resonated in my chest, a rhythmic thrum that matched the pulse of my excitement. As the last notes of appreciation faded, I stepped back, a whirlwind of emotions crashing over me like waves against the shore. I had poured my soul into that collection, each piece an echo of my journey, a stitched testament to the resilience I had fought to reclaim. And now, standing before a sea of faces, their expressions alight with admiration, I felt the first real stirrings of belief creeping into my heart.

Nathaniel, leaning against a nearby wall, his hands tucked casually into his pockets, caught my eye. His smile was broad, his pride palpable. "See? I told you they'd love it," he said, his voice rich with warmth and encouragement. "You're a force, and they were just waiting for someone to show them what real passion looks like."

The buoyancy of his words filled me with a spark I hadn't felt in ages. I glanced around the room, catching snippets of conversations buzzing through the air. "Did you see the cut on that last gown? Pure genius!" One woman exclaimed, her voice an excited whisper.

"Absolutely! And the colors—breathtaking!" another chimed in, her enthusiasm contagious.

A new wave of confidence surged within me, and for the first time, I felt more than just relief; I felt exhilaration, the kind that sent shivers down my spine. As industry professionals began to approach, eager to discuss collaborations and offers, I couldn't help but let out a laugh, a sound bursting forth unrestrained. It was as if the weight of expectation had evaporated, leaving me buoyant and free.

Yet, just as I began to bask in the warmth of success, a familiar face caught my eye, one that sent a chill spiraling through me.

Veronica, my former mentor, stood at the edge of the crowd, arms crossed tightly over her chest. She had always been the epitome of polished elegance—sharp, uncompromising, and entirely intimidating. I had admired her tenacity once, but now, that admiration felt like a distant memory, overshadowed by a gnawing anxiety.

Nathaniel noticed my stiffening posture. "You okay?" he asked, his voice low, laced with concern.

"Yeah, just... Veronica," I replied, my tone barely concealing my unease. "She's probably here to critique everything."

He stepped closer, his presence a reassuring anchor. "Let's handle this together. You're in charge now, remember?"

With a deep breath, I nodded. I was done cowering in the shadows. I had come too far to let someone else dictate my narrative. The more I thought about it, the more I realized that this was my moment. And I wasn't about to let it slip through my fingers.

"Excuse me, can we take a picture?" A young woman approached, her eyes sparkling with admiration. "I've followed your work for so long! You're such an inspiration!"

I flashed her a genuine smile, the kind that illuminated my face and chased away lingering shadows. "Of course! I'd love that."

As we posed, I felt a warmth blooming within me—a sense of belonging, of purpose. The picture snapped, I felt my energy shift, the earlier tension dissolving into the atmosphere around us. Veronica remained a constant specter at the edge of my vision, but I could almost ignore her now.

However, as fate would have it, she chose that moment to step forward, her heels clicking sharply against the polished floor. "I see you've been busy," she remarked, her voice smooth like silk, yet carrying an undertone that suggested ice beneath. "Impressive presentation, though I do wonder if it truly reflects your abilities."

The crowd around us fell silent, the air thickening with anticipation. I could feel Nathaniel's presence beside me, a reassuring force ready to buffer the impending storm. "Thank you, Veronica," I said, forcing my voice to remain steady. "I've poured everything into this collection, and I think it speaks for itself."

"Ah, but does it? Or is it simply a reflection of your current emotional state?" Her words dripped with condescension, but I wasn't about to let her undermine my hard work. "Fashion is a business, not just a canvas for your feelings."

I took a step closer, matching her intensity with unwavering resolve. "And I've learned that business thrives on authenticity. If my feelings can inspire a piece of art that resonates with others, then I'm doing something right."

A flicker of surprise crossed her face, quickly masked by the practiced neutrality she wielded like armor. "We'll see how long that authenticity lasts when the pressure mounts," she shot back, her voice barely containing its disdain.

Just as I opened my mouth to retort, Nathaniel spoke up, his tone light yet firm. "You know, Veronica, it's refreshing to see someone use their experiences as fuel for their creativity. Maybe instead of casting doubt, you could offer support?"

Her gaze flickered to him, the surprise in her eyes momentarily disarming her. "And you are?"

"I'm her partner, in both life and fashion," he replied, a hint of pride coloring his words. "I'm all about building each other up, unlike some."

The crowd around us buzzed with murmurs, the atmosphere thick with tension and anticipation. A wry smile played on my lips as I caught the glimmer of surprise in Veronica's expression. It felt empowering, standing here with Nathaniel, my heart steady despite the storm brewing.

"Consider this a reminder," I said, my voice cutting through the tension like a knife. "Creativity thrives in a nurturing environment, not a critical one. I hope you'll find a way to embrace that."

With that, I turned away, allowing the crowd to swell around us. The remnants of my earlier anxiety began to fade as I immersed myself in the conversations, each exchange a step further away from the doubt Veronica had tried to sow. The laughter and enthusiasm of those who admired my work wrapped around me like a warm embrace, bolstering my spirit.

As the evening wore on, I reveled in the unexpected connections forming around me. Each compliment, each shared enthusiasm, was a piece of the mosaic I was creating, not just in fabric but in my life. And standing beside Nathaniel, the tension from my encounter with Veronica melted away, replaced by a sense of belonging that I hadn't felt in ages.

As the night drew to a close and people began to filter out of the gallery, Nathaniel turned to me, his eyes dancing with mischief. "So, are you ready to celebrate your glorious victory? Maybe we should find somewhere with terrible karaoke and overly sweet cocktails."

I laughed, the sound bright and genuine. "Only if you promise to sing a power ballad and make a complete fool of yourself."

"Deal," he replied, a roguish grin lighting up his face.

And just like that, the shadows of doubt faded into the background, overshadowed by the bright promise of new beginnings, laughter, and love. With Nathaniel by my side, I was ready to embrace whatever came next, the world opening up before me like a canvas waiting for its next masterpiece.

The vibrant lights of the city blurred into a constellation of colors as Nathaniel and I made our way down the bustling streets. The celebratory spirit lingered in the air, crackling like static electricity, invigorating me as we ambled toward a cozy bar known for its questionable karaoke performances and an endless supply of cocktails that were more sugar than spirit. My heart swelled with a delicious blend of triumph and relief; the tension from earlier had melted away, replaced by a buoyancy that seemed to defy gravity.

As we entered the bar, the faint strains of a pop ballad floated through the air, setting the tone for an evening filled with laughter and perhaps a few embarrassing moments. I scanned the room, my gaze landing on the well-worn stage adorned with a frayed microphone, and I couldn't help but chuckle. "This place is a gem," I said, shaking my head in mock disbelief. "I can't wait to see how bad the singing really is."

Nathaniel leaned close, his breath warm against my ear. "I think you underestimate the local talent. I've heard some unforgettable performances here—mostly for their sheer audacity." His eyes sparkled with mischief, igniting a playful challenge that danced between us.

"Let's grab a drink first," I suggested, nudging him toward the bar. "I need a little liquid courage before I let you serenade me with your dulcet tones."

He laughed, a deep, infectious sound that sent a thrill through me. As we ordered our drinks, I felt the weight of the day lift further, the chatter of patrons blending into a comforting hum that wrapped around us like a soft blanket.

With drinks in hand, we settled into a booth, the leather cracked and worn but inviting. I sipped my cocktail, the sweetness bursting on my tongue, and leaned back, soaking in the moment. "So, tell me about your grand plans for tonight. Are you going to bring down the house, or should I be prepared to save you from embarrassment?"

Nathaniel leaned forward, his expression feigning seriousness. "Oh, I have a plan. I'm going to sing my heart out to you, and then you're going to feel compelled to join in, proving you're just as bad as I am."

"Is that how this works? What a lovely scheme," I quipped, rolling my eyes with a smile. "I'm not falling for it."

"Too late! You're already on the hook," he said, grinning broadly. "Besides, you owe it to your adoring fans after that stunning fashion show."

Just then, the host stepped onto the stage, an exuberant figure with a glittery jacket and an infectious energy that drew everyone's attention. "Welcome to our karaoke night!" he boomed, the microphone crackling with enthusiasm. "Tonight, we celebrate the brave souls who will sing their hearts out and maybe even make fools of themselves! Who's ready for a night of unforgettable performances?"

The crowd erupted in cheers, and as the first singer took the stage, I felt a rush of excitement coursing through me. "This is going to be ridiculous," I said, shaking my head in disbelief as the woman launched into a dramatic rendition of a classic love song. "And I love every second of it."

As the night unfolded, the performers varied wildly in talent, each one brimming with the courage to bare their souls under the unforgiving glow of stage lights. Nathaniel and I traded witty commentary, the banter flowing as smoothly as the drinks.

"Okay, I've got to admit, I'm starting to feel inspired," I said, glancing at the stage where a man was belting out a particularly cringeworthy pop song. "If they can do this, surely we can't let ourselves be outdone. You ready to make some memories?"

"Oh, I'm more than ready," he replied, his expression shifting from playful to determined. "But you first."

I hesitated, the thought of stepping onto that stage stirring a mix of excitement and dread. "What if I bomb?"

"Then you'll join the ranks of karaoke legends," he said, raising his glass in a mock toast. "To epic failures and unforgettable moments!"

With a deep breath, I relented, buoyed by his infectious enthusiasm. "Alright, but if I end up on the floor in embarrassment, it's your fault."

I rose from the booth, the lights bathing me in a warm glow as I approached the stage. A sense of exhilaration coursed through me, a reminder of the power of stepping outside my comfort zone. Grabbing the microphone, I took a moment to survey the crowd, a sea of smiling faces eager for entertainment.

"Okay, folks," I said, trying to mask the tremor in my voice with humor. "I'm about to prove that fashion isn't the only thing I'm passionate about."

The crowd erupted in cheers, the warmth of their encouragement washing over me. With my heart racing, I launched into a lively pop song, my nerves transforming into exhilaration as I surrendered to the rhythm. The energy of the room surged, and I found myself lost in the moment, the laughter and cheers of the audience driving me forward.

As I belted out the chorus, I spotted Nathaniel in the crowd, his eyes gleaming with pride. He mouthed the words "You're amazing!" and my heart soared. I was in this moment, fully alive, and the worries that had plagued me earlier began to dissipate.

When I finished, the crowd erupted in applause, and I returned to our booth, breathless and giddy. "That was exhilarating!" I laughed, sinking back into the seat. "I didn't even care if I sounded terrible!"

"Exhilarating doesn't even begin to cover it. You were phenomenal!" Nathaniel replied, his gaze unwavering. "You're a natural up there. The crowd loved you!"

"I think I just need to embrace my inner diva more often," I said, grinning. "You'd better watch out; I might just take over the karaoke circuit."

"Please do," he said with a laugh. "It'll be the best thing to hit this town since sliced bread."

As the evening continued, we reveled in the camaraderie, the laughter echoing into the night. But just when I thought the fun could last forever, the energy in the bar shifted. The door swung open, and a chill swept through the room, drawing my attention to the figure standing in the entrance.

It was Veronica, her expression a blend of surprise and something darker as she scanned the room, finally locking eyes with me. My breath hitched, a sense of foreboding creeping into the air. The room buzzed around us, but time seemed to slow as she strode toward our table, her heels clicking ominously on the floor.

"Looks like you're having quite the evening," she said, her voice smooth but laced with an edge that sent shivers down my spine.

Nathaniel stiffened beside me, his earlier warmth replaced by an alert tension. "Can we help you with something?" he asked, the protectiveness evident in his tone.

"Actually, I was hoping to have a word with you," she said, her gaze fixed on me, the challenge in her eyes unmistakable.

I felt the room's atmosphere shift, the playful energy draining as a thick tension filled the air. "About what?" I managed to ask, my heart racing.

Her smile didn't reach her eyes. "Oh, I think it's time we discussed your future. I have some interesting information that could change everything."

The weight of her words hung heavily between us, and as I met Nathaniel's concerned gaze, a knot formed in my stomach. This was not the conversation I had anticipated as I had stepped onto that stage, and the spark of hope I had been cherishing suddenly felt dangerously fragile.

Chapter 24: The Call of Home

The air in Meadowbrook hung thick with nostalgia as I parked my car on the gravel drive, the crunch beneath the tires a familiar sound that echoed through my childhood. The quaint little town, with its charming storefronts and flower-laden window boxes, welcomed me back like an old friend—one I hadn't seen in far too long. The scent of baked goods wafted from the bakery around the corner, mingling with the earthy aroma of the fallen leaves that crunched underfoot. Yet, beneath that comforting layer of familiarity lurked an oppressive sense of expectation, a shadow that danced just beyond my peripheral vision.

I stepped out, letting the cool autumn breeze tousle my hair. The sky overhead was a slate gray, the kind that promised rain but never quite delivered. It felt as if the clouds were holding their breath, waiting for me to make my move. As I walked up the path to my parents' house, the rickety wooden porch creaked beneath my weight. I hesitated, my hand lingering on the doorknob. What awaited me inside? Would it be the warmth of home or the chill of confrontation?

I pushed the door open, and the familiar scent of my mother's lavender oil enveloped me. It was a perfume of my childhood, mingling with the unmistakable aroma of a home-cooked meal—tonight, it was her famous chicken pot pie, bubbling with promises of warmth and comfort. I could hear my mother humming softly in the kitchen, a tune that always made the corners of my heart soften. But there was a heaviness that hung between us, a gap created by unspoken words and unfulfilled dreams.

"Mom?" I called out, stepping into the living room. The walls were adorned with family portraits, each one a snapshot of a different time in our lives, filled with laughter and love. Yet now, they felt like silent witnesses to the discord simmering beneath the surface.

She appeared in the doorway, flour dusting her apron and a smile that faltered as our eyes met. "Honey, you're here!" Her voice was filled with warmth, but I detected a trace of something else—an apprehension that mirrored my own.

"Hey, Mom." I embraced her tightly, inhaling the familiar scents of home and comfort. But the embrace was quick, and the weight of our reality pulled us back to our respective corners. "I thought I'd stop by for the weekend."

She nodded, wiping her hands on the apron. "That would be lovely. Your father is out in the garden, probably trying to coax life out of the roses again." There was a hint of humor in her tone, but the laughter didn't quite reach her eyes.

I wandered into the kitchen, the heart of our home. As she stirred the bubbling pot on the stove, I watched her, taking in the small details: the way her silver hair caught the light, the way her hands moved with a practiced grace. It struck me then, like a bolt from the blue, that this was the woman who had once been a vibrant dreamer, her own aspirations quietly tucked away behind the daily grind of life and family.

"Mom, can we talk?" The words slipped out before I could stop them, urgent and desperate. I had come here to mend the cracks, but I needed to understand what lay beneath them.

She turned, her expression shifting from surprise to something more serious. "Of course. Is it about the job? Or...?"

I could see the worry etched in her features, a mirror of my own fears. "It's everything, really. I feel like I'm being pulled in different directions, and I'm not sure where I belong anymore."

The silence that followed was thick, almost tangible, as if the air itself was waiting for her response. Finally, she spoke, her voice quiet yet resolute. "You know, I had dreams once too. I wanted to open a little boutique, to create something beautiful that was all my own."

The revelation struck me like a tidal wave. My mother, the woman who had always been my anchor, had once yearned for something beyond the confines of our family's expectations. "Why didn't you?" I asked, unable to mask my surprise.

She sighed, the sound a mix of regret and acceptance. "Life happened. I married your father, and suddenly, the dreams felt selfish. There were bills to pay, children to raise. I pushed those desires aside, convinced that nurturing a family was the only thing I could do."

The admission hung between us, heavy and fragile. I searched her face, looking for traces of the woman she once aspired to be. "But it doesn't have to be that way for me, right? I don't have to give up on my dreams to honor our family."

Her eyes glistened with unshed tears. "You're right. I didn't realize it until now. I pushed my dreams away, but I've always wanted you to chase yours. I thought if I held on tight, you wouldn't make the same sacrifices I did."

The truth settled over us, a comforting blanket woven from shared struggles and unspoken desires. "Then let's figure this out together," I urged, emboldened by her honesty. "I don't want to feel like I'm trapped in a legacy that doesn't fit me. I want to honor our family without losing myself in it."

Her smile, once strained, blossomed with warmth. "You have to follow your own path, darling. Just promise me you'll visit more often. I miss you when you're away."

"I promise," I whispered, the weight on my chest easing, replaced by the thrill of newfound understanding. In that moment, the pull of home shifted. It was no longer just a tether to the past but a launchpad to the future, one that honored both my roots and my aspirations.

As we shared stories over dinner, the conversation flowed more freely than it had in years. My father's laughter echoed through the house, filling the spaces where silence had once reigned. It felt like a reunion, not just with my family but with parts of myself I had buried beneath ambition and uncertainty. In that laughter, I heard the call of home, a melody that sang of love, resilience, and the freedom to chase my own dreams.

Dinner at the kitchen table felt like a scene plucked from a play, the familiar rhythm of our family's banter swirling around like the steam rising from the chicken pot pie. My father, ever the jokester, launched into an animated tale of his latest gardening escapade. His words danced with the colorful imagery of overly ambitious tomato plants and a neighborhood rivalry that would put any soap opera to shame. Laughter bubbled over the edges of the table, warm and welcoming, yet I couldn't shake the feeling that something deeper was at play, lurking just beneath the surface.

"Dad, how's your tomato war with Mr. Finch going?" I asked, trying to join in while still keeping an ear tuned to my mother, who was focused on plating the meal.

"Oh, you mean the war where I'm clearly winning?" he shot back, his grin infectious. "I believe I have a few prize-winning heirlooms coming in. Did I mention I named them after you?"

"Great, my legacy will be immortalized in vegetables," I quipped, leaning back and trying to relax. The conversation flowed seamlessly, yet an undercurrent of tension rippled through the joy. The soft clinking of forks and knives filled the spaces between the laughter, but the weight of unaddressed issues loomed large.

"Speaking of legacies," my mother interjected, setting down the last plate with an air of gravity that drew all eyes to her. "We should talk about the store, sweetie."

The store. My family's pride and joy, a charming little shop filled with handcrafted goods that had been in our family for generations.

But for me, it was more than that; it represented everything I felt obligated to uphold. "Right," I said, bracing myself. "What's the plan this time?"

Her eyes sparkled with a mix of hope and worry. "I know you've been busy with your job, but we could really use your help. It's the busy season, and sales are down a bit. With your experience—"

"Mom," I interrupted gently, "I appreciate that, but I've got my own projects and dreams to chase. I don't want to feel like I'm stepping into shoes that were never meant for me."

"Of course, but you're part of this family, and we want you to be involved," she replied, her tone softening. "You could bring in new ideas, fresh energy. Just think about it."

My father nodded, adding, "Besides, what's the harm in helping out a bit? You know how much it means to your mother. And who knows, it might rekindle something for you."

"Or it might trap me," I countered, my voice firmer than I intended. I could feel the walls closing in, the expectations constricting like a noose. "I've spent too long trying to live up to everyone else's dreams. I don't want to lose sight of what I truly want."

Silence fell like a heavy blanket over the table, the jovial atmosphere now tinged with unease. My mother looked down, her fingers tracing the rim of her plate as if it held the secrets of the universe. I could sense my father's discomfort, the way he shifted in his chair, uncertain of how to navigate the rising tension.

"Okay," my mother said finally, her voice barely above a whisper. "We just want you to be happy, you know that. You've been so far away, pursuing your career. We're proud of you, truly."

"Then let me be proud of myself," I replied, my heart racing. "I don't want to be the family member who comes home to save the day. I want to be me, whoever that is."

The air crackled with unspoken words, and my heart ached as I watched my mother's shoulders droop slightly. I understood her intentions, but the road to hell was paved with good intentions, and right now, I was a little hellbound.

Dinner resumed, but the laughter was muted, the chatter punctuated by occasional glances filled with unsaid sentiments. I pushed my food around on my plate, the chicken pie now cold and uninviting, my stomach twisting in knots. Eventually, I excused myself, retreating to the sanctuary of my childhood room.

The walls were still painted a soft lavender, adorned with posters from my teenage years, a jumbled array of dreams and aspirations that seemed to taunt me now. I sat on the edge of the bed, the familiar quilt beneath me a comforting weight, yet my heart felt anything but settled. My thoughts were a whirlwind, and for the first time in ages, I felt completely lost.

I glanced at my phone, the screen illuminating with a message from Ava, my best friend from college. "Miss you! Let's catch up this week? We need our wine night." Her words pulled me momentarily from the spiral of doubt.

Just as I was about to respond, I heard a soft knock at the door. "Can I come in?" My mother's voice, hesitant yet filled with that maternal warmth I had missed.

"Yeah, of course," I replied, trying to gather my scattered emotions.

She entered slowly, as if stepping onto hallowed ground, and sat beside me. "I didn't mean to push. I know you've worked hard to carve your own path."

"It's okay, Mom," I assured her, feeling the tension begin to dissipate. "I just... I don't want to feel like I'm a pawn in the family business. I want to forge my own path without feeling guilty about it."

"I understand," she said, her voice steadying. "But maybe it doesn't have to be one or the other. You can support us and still follow your dreams."

"But what if I fail? What if I can't balance both?" The words tumbled out, raw and unfiltered. "I don't want to let anyone down."

"Sweetheart, failure is a part of life. I've learned that the hard way," she said, her gaze unwavering. "But you have to learn to take the risk. I didn't, and it's something I regret deeply. If you need to spread your wings, then do it. Just remember that this family will always be your safety net."

Her honesty washed over me like a gentle tide, reassuring and warm. The pressure began to ease, and I could finally breathe again. Maybe it was time to stop thinking of my family as a weight holding me back, but rather as the solid ground from which I could leap.

"Thanks, Mom," I said, my voice thick with emotion. "I want to make you proud, but I also want to make myself proud. It's a balancing act I'm still trying to master."

"We're proud of you already, no matter what path you choose," she reassured, pulling me into a tight hug. "Just promise you'll keep talking to me. No matter where life takes you."

In that moment, surrounded by the love of the woman who had once sacrificed her dreams for mine, I felt the first flickers of determination ignite within me. The road ahead would be a winding one, filled with its own challenges, but maybe—just maybe—I could find a way to navigate it that honored both my roots and my aspirations.

The next morning, the sunlight spilled into my childhood room, draping everything in a warm golden hue. I lay awake, surrounded by the gentle whispers of the past. Each dust motes dancing in the air seemed to echo the voices of my childhood, a time when my biggest worry was which friends could play outside after school. Now, that innocence felt like a distant memory, overshadowed by the weight of expectation and the fear of becoming someone I wasn't.

The enticing aroma of freshly brewed coffee wafted through the house, pulling me from my reverie. I slipped into an oversized sweater, one that felt like a hug, and padded my way to the kitchen. My mother was already bustling about, the sound of her movements as comforting as the familiar scent of lavender wafting from her hair.

"Good morning, sleepyhead," she called over her shoulder, pouring steaming coffee into a vibrant mug adorned with a cartoon cat. "I made your favorite pancakes. You know, the ones I can never replicate outside of this kitchen."

I chuckled, my heart warming at the sight of her. "Only because you put love into them. I don't think any chef can replicate that secret ingredient."

"Flattery will get you everywhere," she quipped back, a playful glint in her eye. We settled into an easy rhythm as we shared breakfast, the conversation flowing freely. "So, what's the plan for today?" she asked, glancing at me with that motherly concern that said she hoped I'd consider lending a hand at the store.

"I thought I might take a walk around town," I replied, savoring the fluffy pancakes. "I want to reacquaint myself with Meadowbrook, see what's changed since I've been gone."

"Just remember to visit the old bookstore. I heard they have a new shipment of novels that you might like," she said, her tone softening. "And who knows, you might even bump into someone you know."

"Or someone I'd prefer not to," I teased, my mind flitting back to memories of high school. The inevitable encounters with ex-classmates could be charming or cringe-worthy, depending on the circumstances.

With a smile still lingering on my lips, I decided it was time to embrace the day, pulling on a pair of worn sneakers and stepping outside. The crisp morning air brushed against my skin, awakening my senses. I strolled through the streets, each step a reminder of all the dreams and aspirations I had left behind. The town felt both foreign and familiar, as if it had been holding its breath in anticipation of my return.

As I passed by familiar landmarks—a cozy café, a flower shop bursting with color, the park where I'd spent countless afternoons—nostalgia washed over me. I noticed a new mural on the side of the café, vibrant and alive with swirling colors and abstract shapes. It spoke of change, of evolution, and I found myself smiling at the thought that maybe I could embrace the same.

When I reached the bookstore, the door jingled cheerfully as I stepped inside. The smell of old paper and ink wrapped around me like a well-loved blanket. Rows of shelves groaned under the weight of stories waiting to be told, and I could feel my heart swell with excitement. I meandered through the aisles, running my fingers along the spines of the books, as if they were old friends.

"Looking for something specific?" a voice broke my reverie, pulling me from my thoughts.

I turned to find a familiar face. Ryan, my high school crush, now a dapper man with an air of confidence that caught me off guard. He wore a flannel shirt rolled up to the elbows, revealing toned arms and a smile that could light up the room.

"Just browsing," I replied, trying to sound nonchalant. "What about you?"

"Same here. I've been trying to catch up on all the local authors. There's some talent brewing in this town," he said, his eyes sparkling with enthusiasm.

"Didn't know you were a literary connoisseur," I teased, leaning casually against a shelf.

He chuckled, and I felt that old spark, the thrill of connection I thought had long faded. "I like to think of myself as a man of many interests. Besides, someone has to keep the local book club in check."

"Ah, the local book club! I remember those gatherings—where everyone pretended to read the same book while really just gossiping about their neighbors."

He laughed, a warm sound that resonated deep within me. "Exactly! But they've evolved into something more. You should come sometime. We could use someone with your... expertise."

"Flattery again, Ryan?" I raised an eyebrow, my playful nature bubbling to the surface.

"Only speaking the truth," he replied smoothly, his eyes locking onto mine with an intensity that sent a shiver down my spine. "So, when are you moving back to be our resident expert?"

I hesitated, feeling the weight of my choices pressing down on me. "I'm not sure moving back is on the agenda just yet."

"Pity. We could use a little more excitement around here. Things have been a bit... stagnant."

"Stagnant? But look at this place! The mural outside, the new shops popping up—it's alive!" I gestured animatedly, but he merely shrugged.

"True, but it's different without you. I mean, we had a good thing going in high school."

Before I could respond, the door opened, and an older woman rushed in, her expression frantic. "Ryan! Have you heard? Something's happened at the old mill!"

We both turned, curiosity piqued. The old mill had long been abandoned, a relic of a bygone era. It had been the source of countless ghost stories during our teenage years, the place where we dared each other to venture after dark.

"What do you mean?" Ryan asked, stepping toward her, concern knitting his brow.

"They say there's been a fire! The fire department is on their way, but it's bad. They think it might have been arson."

My heart raced. A fire? Arson? My mind swirled with the implications. The mill was more than just a structure; it was a part of the town's history, a piece of my childhood.

Without thinking, I grabbed Ryan's arm. "We should go see."

"Are you sure? It could be dangerous," he cautioned, but his eyes sparkled with the thrill of adventure.

"Dangerous is my middle name," I shot back, adrenaline coursing through my veins.

With a determined nod, we dashed out of the bookstore, the sounds of the town fading into a blur as we raced toward the mill. Each step felt like a leap into the unknown, the air thick with uncertainty. The thrill of potential danger mixed with the echoes of memories long buried, igniting a fire of its own within me.

As we approached the old mill, the sirens wailed in the distance, the acrid scent of smoke tangling with the crisp autumn air. In the distance, flames flickered and danced, licking the edges of the weathered wood, illuminating the darkening sky. My breath caught in my throat.

"What are we walking into?" I whispered, my heart pounding with a mix of fear and exhilaration.

Ryan squeezed my hand, a silent promise that we would face whatever lay ahead together. The shadows of our past loomed large, but the uncertainty of the future crackled with potential. Just as we reached the edge of the crowd gathering at the mill, a loud explosion rattled the ground beneath us, sending a spray of embers into the air.

"What was that?" I gasped, eyes wide as I took a step back.

Before Ryan could respond, a figure darted out from the smoke, clutching something tightly in their hands. My heart raced as I recognized the face emerging from the chaos—someone I had never expected to see again.

"Lucy?"

The name tumbled from my lips in disbelief, but the answers I sought were just beyond the smoke, hovering on the brink of revelation and danger.

Chapter 25: The Fork in the Road

Returning to New York, I was greeted by the chaos that seemed to swirl around the city like a fresh storm, palpable and electric. The cacophony of honking taxis, the chatter of hurried pedestrians, and the distant wail of sirens created a familiar, disorienting symphony. I stepped off the subway, my heart racing not just from the thrill of the bustling metropolis but also from the bittersweet weight of what awaited me. Nathaniel stood at the station, his smile as wide as the horizon, eyes sparkling with a fervor that both captivated and unnerved me.

He was full of dreams—ambitious dreams, the kind that made you believe in possibility, the kind that fluttered in your chest like a caged bird. I couldn't help but smile back, but underneath the warmth of that grin lurked a shadow of anxiety. "Can you believe it?" he exclaimed, nearly bouncing on his heels. "I got the position! The international team is amazing, and I'll be working in Paris for at least a year."

"Paris," I echoed, as if tasting the word would somehow ground me. The city of lights, of romance, a dream I had held dear. But my dream seemed to conflict with his. "That's incredible, Nathaniel. I'm so proud of you." The words slipped out with practiced ease, a familiar mantra. Yet, beneath my gratitude lurked a torrent of doubt. What would this mean for us? For our relationship?

As we walked hand in hand through the vibrant streets, the evening air cool against my skin, I couldn't help but steal glances at him. He was a whirlwind of enthusiasm, animatedly recounting every detail of his new role, painting visions of croissants at dawn and evening strolls along the Seine. His laughter rang out, drawing smiles from passersby, and I found myself both enchanted and terrified.

The joy in his voice was a song I longed to sing along with, but an unsettling harmony played beneath it—a reminder that his journey would lead him farther away from me. The city seemed to pulse around us, alive with potential, yet I felt the distance growing.

Later that night, with the soft glow of candlelight flickering between us, I laid out the issue like a fine tapestry—delicate, yet threatening to unravel with the slightest tug. "What are we going to do?" My voice was barely a whisper, but it pierced the intimate silence that enveloped us.

His expression shifted, joy retreating like a receding tide. "What do you mean?" he asked, his brow furrowing as he leaned closer, a flicker of confusion in his gaze.

"We're at a crossroads, Nathaniel. You're chasing your dreams in Paris, and I'm here—what does that mean for us?" The question hung between us like the fragrant steam rising from our dinner plates, heady and thick, making it hard to breathe.

His laughter faltered, and the moment felt like glass shattering in slow motion. "You're really worried about this?" The surprise in his tone stung. "You should be happy for me, not—"

"Happy?" I interrupted, feeling the heat rise in my cheeks. "Of course, I want you to be happy. I just... I need to know what this means for us." My heart raced, a wild beast clawing at my ribcage, desperate to escape.

"It means I'll be working on amazing projects, in a city I've always dreamed of," he replied, frustration tinged with disbelief. "You should want to be part of that, not fight against it."

"Part of it?" I huffed, my own frustration bubbling to the surface. "What am I supposed to do? Sit back and watch your life unfold from a distance? It's like watching a movie where I'm not even a supporting character."

He ran a hand through his hair, a gesture I knew meant he was struggling to keep his composure. "You make it sound like I'm leaving you behind. I'm not. I want you to come with me."

The words were a lifeline thrown into turbulent waters, yet they felt heavy with implication. "You really think it's that easy?" I countered, trying to anchor myself amidst the tempest of emotions. "Pack my bags and follow you halfway across the world? I have a job here, a life here."

"I want you to be part of my life," he insisted, eyes searching mine for an answer I wasn't sure I could provide. "We can make this work. Love can bridge any distance."

Love. The word hung between us, shimmering with possibility yet laced with tension. My heart tugged in one direction, while my mind waged a silent war. "But what if it doesn't?" I shot back, my voice breaking slightly. "What if the distance makes us drift apart?"

Nathaniel's expression softened, the fire in his eyes dimming to a flicker. "We've been through so much together. Don't you believe we can survive this?"

In that moment, I felt the weight of our history—the shared laughter, the late-night talks, the dreams woven together like a fine tapestry. But I also felt the tug of the future, a vast, uncertain expanse stretching before us. "I want to believe that," I admitted, my voice trembling. "But can we really be sure?"

Silence settled between us, thick and suffocating. The candles flickered as if mirroring the uncertainty of our path. I wanted to reach out, to take his hand and forge a connection that would withstand the distance, but fear held me back. Would I be strong enough to weather the storm that lay ahead?

The truth was, as much as I wanted to celebrate his success, I couldn't help but feel a sense of impending loss. The idea of watching him pursue his dreams without me felt like standing on the edge of a cliff, the wind whipping through my hair, daring me to take the leap. Would I plunge into the depths of uncertainty, or would I retreat to the safety of the familiar? The fork in the road loomed before me, each path promising a different future, and I found myself torn between love and fear, ambition and the yearning for connection.

In the aftermath of our tumultuous dinner, the air between us was thick with unspoken words. I retreated to the sanctuary of my apartment, seeking solace in the familiarity of my surroundings. The walls, adorned with photographs of laughter and fleeting moments, felt like a gallery of our shared history, each image a reminder of the warmth we'd created together. Yet now, the snapshots seemed to mock me, gleaming with nostalgia while casting shadows of uncertainty.

I poured myself a glass of wine, the rich crimson liquid swirling like the confusion in my mind. With every sip, the bitterness of our conversation lingered on my tongue, mingling with the sweetness of memories that seemed ever more distant. How had we gotten here? I could still hear Nathaniel's voice echoing in my mind, a beautiful melody now laced with a discordant note. "We can make this work." The words were both a promise and a challenge, dangling between us like a tightrope strung over a chasm.

A gentle knock at the door pulled me from my reverie, and my heart leapt unexpectedly. I opened it to find Nathaniel standing there, his hair tousled and eyes slightly red, a look of determination etched across his features. "Can we talk?" he asked, his voice steady but laced with uncertainty.

I stepped aside, allowing him entry, the weight of the moment heavy upon us. The silence that settled was thick, laden with the aroma of my half-finished dinner and the lingering scent of the candles. It was as if the very walls were holding their breath, waiting for the storm to break.

"Look," he began, taking a deep breath as if steeling himself against a wave. "I didn't mean to push you away. I know this is big for both of us, and I thought—" he paused, searching for the right words, "I thought we could find a way through it together."

"Together," I echoed, feeling the word slip through my fingers like grains of sand. "But what does that really mean? You'll be in another country, Nathaniel. What if you get swept away by the Parisian charm, the job, the excitement? What if I become a mere memory, a character in your story rather than a part of your life?"

His eyes widened, the flicker of hurt cutting through the air. "You think I'll forget you? That I'll leave you behind?"

"I think it's a possibility," I countered, my tone sharper than intended. "I've seen it happen before. It's so easy to get lost in new beginnings, especially when they're as dazzling as yours."

A shadow crossed his face, and he stepped closer, reducing the space between us, and suddenly the air felt electrified, charged with tension. "You don't trust me," he said softly, disappointment evident in his voice. "You think I'd let something come between us so easily?"

"Trust isn't the issue," I replied, my heart racing. "It's reality. We both have dreams. Yours just happens to be across an ocean."

"Then let's find a way to make it work." His gaze was intense, earnest, as if his very soul was on display. "What if we tried something different? What if I came back every few weeks, and we made those moments count? Or—better yet—what if you visited me in Paris?"

The suggestion hung between us, tantalizing yet daunting, a shimmering thread that could either bind us closer or fray under the pressure. "Visiting you in Paris sounds amazing in theory," I said, a hint of sarcasm lacing my tone. "But what about my job? My life? I can't just pick up and go whenever you feel like it."

"Why not?" he challenged, his voice rising with passion. "You're talented, intelligent, and you deserve to chase your dreams too. What's stopping you?"

I opened my mouth to respond, but no words came out. What indeed was stopping me? The very notion that my life could intertwine with his in that way was both exhilarating and terrifying.

"It's not that simple," I finally managed, my heart pounding in my chest. "I have responsibilities here, a routine, and—"

"And what? You're afraid of change?" He crossed his arms, his brow furrowing as he studied me. "Is that it? Or is it that you're afraid of what it means if you say yes?"

The question landed with the weight of a sledgehammer, and I felt the room tilt precariously. "Maybe I am," I confessed, lowering my gaze. "Maybe I'm scared of uprooting everything for a dream that might not be mine."

"Then let's figure out what that dream looks like," he urged, stepping closer still, his voice a soothing balm against the sharp edges of my doubt. "Let's map it out together. You can explore your own opportunities in Paris while I pursue mine."

The prospect was tantalizing, yet it felt like a precarious gamble. "And what if we get there, and it doesn't work? What if our relationship can't survive the distance? What if we lose what we have?"

His frustration was palpable as he ran a hand through his hair, exhaling sharply. "Isn't it worth the risk to find out? Isn't what we have worth fighting for?"

His intensity wrapped around me like a comforting blanket, and for a brief moment, I could envision a life painted in shades of possibility, each stroke a reminder of our connection. Yet, just as quickly, shadows danced at the edges of my imagination, dark and whispering doubts.

"What if I can't keep up?" I murmured, the vulnerability leaking into my voice. "What if I can't handle the pressure?"

He reached out, cupping my face gently, his touch warm and grounding. "Then we figure it out. We tackle each challenge as it comes. I want to do this with you—wherever it leads. Just say you'll think about it."

The sincerity in his eyes ignited something deep within me, a flicker of hope battling against the fierce winds of fear. I wanted to believe him, to leap into the unknown without reservations, but the ground felt shaky beneath my feet.

"I'll think about it," I said slowly, a tremor of uncertainty threading through my words.

"Good." Nathaniel smiled, the tension between us beginning to ease. "I'll hold you to that."

The air shifted, lighter now, though the weight of our discussion still lingered like the scent of lingering smoke after a candle burns low. As we stood there, the world outside carried on—cars honking, people chatting, the city a relentless pulse—but in that moment, it felt as though everything had narrowed to just us.

"Let's make a deal," he said, a playful glint returning to his eyes. "For every week we're apart, I'll send you a postcard. But it has to be ridiculous—like me trying to master French cuisine or attempting to ride a bike along the Seine. You'll have to keep a scrapbook of my failed adventures."

"Are you saying you'll send me a postcard of you covered in flour?" I laughed, feeling a warmth spread through my chest, lifting the remaining weight of our earlier conversation.

"Absolutely. Just you wait. It'll be a culinary catastrophe worthy of the Louvre."

As we exchanged laughter, the night felt a little less daunting, the future slightly more vibrant. Perhaps this was how we would navigate the complexities of love and ambition—through laughter, through postcards filled with promises of adventure, and through the unwavering belief that we could find our way back to each other, no matter how far apart we might wander.

The weeks that followed our heartfelt conversation felt like a peculiar blend of anticipation and dread, each day blurring into the next, marked only by Nathaniel's enthusiastic texts and the distant hum of the city that seemed to echo my own internal chaos. I buried myself in work, tackling projects that felt increasingly trivial against the backdrop of his impending adventure. It was a deliberate distraction, a way to fill the hollow space that his absence began to carve out in my life, yet I knew the attempt was futile.

I found myself daydreaming during meetings, staring blankly at spreadsheets, and sighing over cold coffee. My mind wandered to Paris—its cobblestone streets, vibrant cafés, and the artistry that infused the very air. I envisioned Nathaniel under the Eiffel Tower, his laughter ringing out over the Seine, while I was here, tethered to the routine of office life. My heart twisted at the thought, longing to share in the excitement of his new adventure while grappling with the unsettling reality of distance.

One rainy afternoon, I sat at my favorite café, the warm aroma of espresso wrapping around me like a comforting blanket. The sound of raindrops tapping against the window created a rhythmic backdrop to my swirling thoughts. I had decided to indulge in a moment of introspection, scribbling my hopes and fears in my weathered notebook, the pages filled with half-formed ideas and dreams that often felt out of reach.

As I lost myself in contemplation, the bell above the café door chimed, drawing my gaze. Nathaniel walked in, shaking off the rain like a wet dog, his hair tousled and his cheeks flushed from the cold. My heart did a little leap in my chest. He scanned the room, his eyes lighting up when they found me, and I couldn't help but smile, that familiar warmth flooding back.

"Fancy seeing you here," he teased, sliding into the seat across from me. "I was starting to think you'd taken up a hermit lifestyle. No postcards yet?"

I laughed, the sound spilling into the air like bubbles in champagne. "I was just getting lost in my thoughts. You know, the typical 'what's my life become' musings."

He leaned closer, his expression shifting to one of concern. "Are you okay? You seem a bit... off lately."

"It's just a lot to process," I admitted, feeling a blush creep up my cheeks. "Your new job, the thought of you being in Paris, and me—well, me trying to figure out my own dreams in the shadow of yours."

Nathaniel reached for my hand, the warmth of his skin sending a comforting jolt through me. "We're in this together, remember? My dreams don't diminish yours. In fact, I think they could amplify them. You've got to believe that."

"I do," I replied, searching his gaze for reassurance. "But what if you fall in love with this new life and forget about the old one?"

"Forget about you?" He scoffed, a playful grin tugging at his lips. "That's like forgetting about my morning coffee—impossible and downright absurd."

"Glad to know I'm as essential as caffeine," I quipped, rolling my eyes. Yet, despite the jest, a flicker of unease remained, gnawing at my insides.

"I'll be back for weekends, and we can plan visits. It'll be an adventure," he said, enthusiasm shining in his eyes. "Think of the stories we'll have. You'll be my number one fan, and I'll send you photos of all my culinary disasters."

"Please tell me you won't send a picture of you covered in flour while attempting to make macarons," I joked, and we both laughed, the tension easing slightly.

But as I watched him, a thought began to worm its way into my mind—an unsettling notion that perhaps our lives were about to diverge in ways I couldn't predict. With the promise of Paris looming over us, everything felt like a beautiful yet precarious balance, teetering on the edge of something monumental.

Later that evening, after parting ways, I walked home under a sky thick with clouds, the air buzzing with impending rain. The city lights sparkled like tiny stars, illuminating the familiar streets that suddenly felt foreign. My heart raced as I considered the possibility of a future that didn't include Nathaniel, a scenario I hadn't fully prepared for. Would we really be able to navigate this divide? Would my heart remain steadfast in his absence?

Arriving at my apartment, I was greeted by silence, the kind that echoed in the corners and settled over me like a heavy shroud. I dropped my bag by the door and took a moment to gather my thoughts, pacing the room as if it could help me find clarity. My phone buzzed, and I jumped at the sound, heart racing once more.

It was a text from Nathaniel, a picture of him in front of a French restaurant, a goofy grin plastered across his face, with a caption that read, "Just checking out the competition. You know, in case I need a back-up plan."

I chuckled softly, but the laughter quickly faded, replaced by a knot of anxiety. I typed a response, my fingers hovering over the keys. "You'll always have a back-up plan," I wrote back, "just don't forget your original one."

Just as I hit send, a sharp knock echoed through the stillness of my apartment. I froze, heart pounding. I wasn't expecting anyone. I cautiously approached the door, my mind racing with possibilities. Could it be Nathaniel, surprising me? Or maybe it was a neighbor in need?

I opened the door, revealing a figure cloaked in shadows, the hallway light illuminating a familiar face. It was Lily, my best friend, her expression a mix of excitement and urgency. "You won't believe what just happened," she gasped, breathless and wide-eyed.

"What is it?" I asked, the sudden adrenaline spiking through my veins.

"I just heard from Ryan! He's back in town!"

The name hit me like a bolt of lightning, sending a rush of memories flooding back—flashes of summer nights and whispered secrets, laughter shared over ice cream, the heartbreak of saying goodbye. Ryan, my first love, had left the city years ago, his departure echoing through my heart long after he'd walked out of my life.

"What do you mean back in town?"

"He's here for a few weeks and wants to catch up. He texted me just now! I thought you should know."

My breath hitched, the weight of that name sending ripples of confusion and nostalgia through me. What did this mean for my world? For Nathaniel and me?

Just then, my phone buzzed again, a notification lighting up the screen. My heart dropped as I saw Nathaniel's name flash across it. "Can't wait for you to visit. Paris is beautiful, but it'll be even better with you here. Just think about it."

I glanced back at Lily, her eyes sparkling with excitement, unaware of the storm brewing within me. Would the arrival of Ryan change everything? Would my heart, already wrestling with the complexities of distance, now face another dilemma?

As I opened my mouth to respond to Lily, my phone vibrated in my hand. Another text. This one was from Nathaniel, but it wasn't a message I expected. "I think we need to talk."

The words sent a chill down my spine, and just like that, the fragile balance of my world threatened to shatter, leaving me at the precipice of uncertainty, wondering how everything would unfold.

Chapter 26: Love in the Balance

The sun dipped low, painting the sky in hues of gold and lavender as I ambled through the streets of Manhattan, each footstep echoing against the pavement, punctuating my thoughts. The rhythmic pulse of the city vibrated around me, a chaotic symphony that filled the void left by our heated discussion. I had wanted to scream, to shout until the words tumbled out of me like confetti, but instead, I had retreated into myself, feeling the weight of silence pressing down like the heavy coats of winter. Nathaniel's face loomed in my mind, his eyes fierce with frustration, and for a moment, I wondered if the city itself could provide a balm for my turbulent heart.

As I turned the corner onto a bustling street, the aroma of freshly brewed coffee wafted through the air, mingling with the sweet scent of pastries from a nearby café. I stepped inside, the bell above the door jingling softly, as if welcoming me back into a world of warmth and familiarity. The interior was a riot of colors, with splashes of vibrant artwork lining the walls, the canvas whispering stories of love and loss, joy and sorrow. I settled into a cozy corner, a small table adorned with a wildflower vase that tilted slightly, reminiscent of my own uneven journey.

With each sip of my cappuccino, the froth delicately dusted with cocoa, I felt the tension in my shoulders ease just a bit. I reached for my sketchbook, a faithful companion that had accompanied me through the ebbs and flows of life. The blank pages beckoned, a canvas for my swirling thoughts and unformed dreams. But as I sat there, pencil in hand, ready to breathe life into my scattered ideas, I found my mind drifting. I couldn't shake the image of Nathaniel's furrowed brow, the way his words had sliced through the air, sharp and unyielding.

"Dreams shouldn't be sacrificed for someone else," I muttered to myself, stirring my drink as if I could stir my thoughts into clarity.

"But what if those dreams also involve that someone else?" The question hung in the air, heavy and unwelcome. I glanced around the café, searching for inspiration, for something—anything—that could pull me from this introspection.

That's when I spotted her. A woman in her mid-thirties sat at the next table, her laughter a bubbling brook, infectious and bright. The sunlight caught her hair, illuminating the golden strands that danced with each movement. She was animatedly conversing with a group of friends, her hands weaving through the air as she recounted a story that seemed to pull them into her world. I felt a flicker of recognition; we had once shared laughter in the halls of our high school, swapping dreams like trading cards.

"Lila?" I called, an instinctive spark of nostalgia igniting within me.

She turned, her eyes widening with surprise. "Oh my gosh! Emily? Is that really you?" She leapt up, and in an instant, we were enveloped in a warm embrace that felt like slipping into a favorite sweater after a long, cold day.

After a few moments of excited chatter, we settled back into our seats, the café enveloping us in its cozy embrace. Lila's spirit was as vibrant as I remembered, and she was quick to pull me into her whirlwind of updates. "I've been working on a project that aims to bring art into underserved communities," she explained, her eyes sparkling with enthusiasm. "It's challenging but so rewarding! What about you? What have you been up to?"

As I shared snippets of my journey—my creative aspirations, the gallery shows I dreamed of participating in, and, of course, my tumultuous relationship with Nathaniel—Lila listened intently, her expressions mirroring the highs and lows of my narrative. It felt good to speak, to let the words flow unfiltered, as if shedding the weight I had carried alone for so long.

"I always admired your passion for art, Em. You were born to create," she said, her voice steady and encouraging. "Don't let anyone dim that light."

Her words hung in the air, luminous and penetrating, and I realized that I had let fear stifle my creative spirit, as if Nathaniel's expectations had woven themselves into a tight cocoon around me. In that moment, my heart began to thaw, and with it, a surge of clarity washed over me. I could chase my dreams without compromising my relationship, couldn't I? The balance didn't have to be so stark; it could be a dance, a rhythm that intertwined love and aspiration in beautiful harmony.

"Thanks, Lila. You've reminded me of something important," I replied, a genuine smile breaking through the fog. "I need to stop thinking in absolutes. Love shouldn't mean surrendering who I am."

With renewed resolve, I finished my drink and promised to stay in touch, Lila's presence a bright spark that rekindled the fire in my heart. As I walked out of the café, the city felt different, vibrant and alive, and I could almost hear the brush of my paint against canvas, the melody of creation whispering sweetly in my ear.

The sun dipped lower, casting long shadows as I wandered through the park, the gentle rustle of leaves creating a soft symphony above me. Children laughed nearby, their joy ringing out like music, and couples strolled hand in hand, each moment a reminder of love's tender embrace. But more than that, I felt a stirring within me, a sense of purpose that had lain dormant for too long. I could have both: love and my art, my dreams and Nathaniel.

With each step, I felt the weight of expectation begin to lift, replaced by the exhilaration of possibility. It was time to return, to confront Nathaniel with honesty and openness, to reveal not just my heart but the dreams that danced just beyond reach. I wouldn't compromise who I was; instead, I would invite him to see the beauty in the balance we could create together.

The evening air was tinged with the sweet scent of blooming lilacs, their fragrance weaving through the branches of trees as I made my way back to our apartment. Each step felt lighter, as though the very ground beneath me had shed the weight of yesterday's uncertainties. The city, with its cacophony of sounds, pulsed like a heartbeat, vibrant and alive. I navigated through the throngs of people, their laughter and chatter a soundtrack to my reawakened spirit.

Nathaniel had always been my anchor, but lately, it felt as if I had been tethered too tightly, my own desires threatened by the ropes of his expectations. The memory of my conversation with Lila still echoed in my mind, a gentle reminder that dreams and love didn't have to exist in separate realms. No longer would I let fear or complacency extinguish my ambitions.

As I approached our building, I paused for a moment, letting the cool evening breeze ruffle my hair. A flicker of apprehension danced in my chest—what if Nathaniel didn't understand? What if he dismissed my newfound resolve as just a fleeting spark? I shook my head, banishing those thoughts. Confidence was key. I had to be the artist I once dreamed of being, and that included reclaiming the vibrancy of my passion, regardless of how it might shift the landscape of our relationship.

The door creaked open, and the familiar scent of cedar wood and vanilla wafted toward me, a comforting embrace that felt like home. Nathaniel was at the kitchen island, his broad shoulders hunched over a canvas as he meticulously mixed colors, his brow furrowed in concentration. The sight stirred something within me, a blend of affection and an unsettling sense of loss for the vibrant lives we had once led.

"Hey, you," he said, glancing up with a smile that momentarily lit up his face. "You're back early. How was your day?"

"Revelatory," I replied, my voice laced with a teasing lilt. "I've decided I need to take more spontaneous adventures. You know, like climbing Everest or befriending a pack of wolves."

His laughter rang out, warm and inviting. "I'd pay to see you try that. You'd probably end up inviting them to tea instead of tackling a mountain."

"Exactly! But I'm thinking more along the lines of art shows and street performances." I leaned against the counter, watching him as he continued to mix paints. "I ran into Lila today."

"Lila? The one from high school?" He set down his brush and looked at me with genuine curiosity. "What's she up to?"

"She's working on an amazing project, bringing art to underserved communities. It made me realize how much I've lost sight of my own dreams." I paused, gauging his reaction. "I need to focus on my art again, Nathaniel. It's important for me to express myself."

His expression shifted, the warmth in his eyes replaced with a hint of concern. "I get that, but we've talked about this. You've been so focused on us—on building a life together. Are you sure you want to pull away from that?"

"Building a life together doesn't mean sacrificing my aspirations," I countered, my tone more assertive than I intended. "I want to include you in my world, but I can't do that if I feel like I have to put my passions aside. It's suffocating."

Nathaniel stepped back, crossing his arms, his jaw tightening. "I never meant to suffocate you, Emily. But what about my dreams? The gallery? Our plans? You know how important those are to me."

I felt the room shrink around us, the air thick with tension. "Your dreams matter, Nathaniel. But so do mine. We can find a way to merge them. I want to paint again, to explore the city's art scene, to create without the constant worry of disappointing you."

For a moment, we stood in silence, the weight of our words hanging heavy in the air. I could see the conflict in his eyes, a tempest brewing beneath his calm demeanor. "I just thought we were on the same path," he finally said, his voice softer, almost vulnerable. "This feels like you're trying to pull away from what we have."

"No! I'm trying to strengthen what we have," I said, desperation creeping into my tone. "If I lose myself, how can I love you fully? It's not about choosing one over the other; it's about finding a balance."

His shoulders relaxed slightly, but I could tell he was still struggling to grasp the notion. "How do we do that?" he asked, his expression a mixture of hope and uncertainty.

"Let's explore together," I suggested, a flicker of inspiration igniting within me. "We can attend galleries, find art festivals, and maybe even collaborate. I want you to see my world, and I want to understand yours. We can be partners in both our dreams."

Nathaniel considered my words, his eyes narrowing slightly as if he were mentally rearranging the pieces of our relationship puzzle. "You'd be okay with me pushing you out of your comfort zone? Because I won't just sit by and watch you waste your talent."

"I'd welcome it," I replied, feeling a surge of excitement at the idea of combining our passions. "Imagine the projects we could create. We could host workshops or even a joint exhibition. We'd be unstoppable."

A slow smile broke through the remnants of his hesitation. "I do like the sound of that. Maybe I've been a bit too rigid in my expectations. I just want to protect what we've built."

"And I want to help it flourish," I added, stepping closer, the space between us dissolving like the tension that had hung in the air. "Let's learn from each other instead of feeling like we're competing."

With a nod, Nathaniel reached for my hand, pulling me gently toward him. "Okay, let's make this work. I can't promise it'll be easy, but I'm willing to try if you are."

"Deal," I said, feeling a wave of relief wash over me. "I'll even let you decorate my studio. Just promise me no neon colors."

He chuckled, the warmth of his laughter flooding the room. "No promises. But I'll make sure to include a lot of 'serious artist' black."

"Fine," I laughed, a giddy sensation swirling in my stomach. "But only if you promise to keep your paint splatters to a minimum. Last time, it took me weeks to scrub my walls."

As we stood together, surrounded by the promise of new beginnings and shared aspirations, the shadows that had loomed over us began to recede. In that moment, we were no longer just two people navigating their paths. We were collaborators, dreamers, and above all, partners—ready to explore the boundless canvas of our lives together.

The next few days unfolded like an intricate tapestry, woven with moments of laughter, artistic collaboration, and a refreshing sense of purpose. Nathaniel and I transformed our apartment into a vibrant workspace, the walls gradually becoming a canvas for our shared dreams. We hung sketches and paintings, their colors splashed vibrantly against the muted beige of our home, creating a gallery that spoke to our journey.

Amidst the chaos of paint tubes and scattered brushes, our evenings were filled with impromptu brainstorming sessions that often devolved into playful banter. I remember one night in particular, the aroma of takeout lingering in the air as we spread our notes across the kitchen table.

"Okay, picture this," Nathaniel said, his eyes lighting up with enthusiasm. "An art show where we not only display our work but also invite local artists to showcase their talent. A community event, maybe even with a live band. It would be like a festival, not just a gallery opening."

VIBRANT ALLURE

I raised an eyebrow, a smirk playing on my lips. "A festival? And here I thought we were just going for the intimate gallery vibe. Next, you'll want to include food trucks and a petting zoo."

"Why not? Who doesn't love a good petting zoo?" he retorted, feigning seriousness. "Plus, everyone knows that cute animals draw a crowd."

"True," I admitted, laughing. "I'd attend anything if there were baby goats involved. But let's keep the theme focused on art—perhaps a gallery stroll with music and poetry readings."

"Poetry readings?" He wrinkled his nose, a mock disgust in his expression. "I thought we were trying to attract a lively crowd, not put them to sleep."

"Don't knock poetry! You'd be surprised how exhilarating it can be," I shot back, our friendly jabs fueling the creative spark between us.

Our planning sessions turned into something more, a dance of shared aspirations that felt like we were piecing together a puzzle we didn't know we had been searching for. Yet, amid the exhilaration, I couldn't shake the feeling that something lurked beneath the surface, a tension I couldn't quite articulate. It was as if our creative energy had brought us closer, but with it came the shadows of unspoken fears and lingering doubts.

As the date of our event approached, the days blurred into a flurry of preparations. Our apartment was often filled with the sounds of music and laughter, but underneath, a current of anxiety simmered. We bounced ideas off each other, the thrill of collaboration making my heart race, yet with each new sketch and each passing day, I sensed Nathaniel growing increasingly distant, his focus shifting from our project to the looming deadline of his gallery showing.

One evening, while I meticulously touched up the last of my paintings, I glanced up to find him standing in the doorway, a furrow creasing his brow. "You know, this might be a great opportunity to showcase my work too. I was thinking maybe I should just hang my pieces at your show. The more the merrier, right?"

I set down my brush, puzzled. "Isn't that a bit... presumptuous? We talked about this being a community event, about featuring emerging artists. Your work deserves its own spotlight, Nathaniel."

"It's just a thought," he replied curtly, and I caught the hint of defensiveness in his tone. "Maybe I want to be part of your world, you know?"

"Part of my world?" I echoed, confusion creeping into my voice. "But this is our world. I don't want you to feel like you have to merge our identities. This is about celebrating both of us."

His gaze hardened, the weight of our discussions from days before creeping back into the room like an unwelcome guest. "I just want to make sure I'm not overshadowing you. It's hard to tell what's too much and what's not when you're busy fighting for your place."

The air crackled between us, the playful banter dissipating into something heavier, more volatile. "I'm not fighting you, Nathaniel. I'm trying to build something together," I retorted, my frustration mounting. "You're not in competition with me; we're supposed to be allies in this journey."

His shoulders stiffened, and for a moment, I thought I saw a flicker of vulnerability in his eyes, but it quickly vanished behind a mask of resolve. "I don't know if I can handle the pressure of being part of your dreams. It feels like I'm being pulled into a world that isn't mine."

"Why does it have to be a world that isn't yours?" I asked, my voice softening. "This is our chance to create something together. You can't keep pulling away every time I make a move."

"Maybe you should ask yourself if I'm pulling away or if I'm simply realizing that I have my own dreams to chase," he shot back, the sting of his words hanging heavy in the air.

I stood there, heart racing, caught in the whirlwind of his sudden shift. "What do you mean by that?"

His eyes narrowed, the resolve returning. "Maybe I need to think about what this really means for me. This could be more than just art, you know?"

Before I could respond, the doorbell rang, cutting through the tension like a knife. Nathaniel's expression changed, a flash of relief darting across his face. He turned away from me, moving toward the door, and I felt a sudden chill as uncertainty slithered into my heart.

I followed him, curiosity piqued. Who could it be at this hour? As Nathaniel opened the door, a figure stood silhouetted against the hallway lights, a familiar shape that sent a jolt through me. It was Lila, her vibrant smile a stark contrast to the storm brewing inside our apartment.

"Hey! I came to drop off some flyers for the event," she said, her voice bright and cheerful. But as she stepped inside and her eyes landed on Nathaniel and me, the atmosphere shifted. She sensed it instantly, the tension lingering like smoke after a fire.

"Am I interrupting?" Lila asked, glancing between us, a hint of concern creeping into her expression.

"No, not at all," Nathaniel replied too quickly, brushing off the unease. "We were just discussing some last-minute details."

Lila's gaze lingered on me, her intuition sharp as ever. "Right. Well, I thought it would be fun to go over the plans together. Maybe even brainstorm some promotional ideas? Get everyone excited about the event."

As she spoke, I couldn't shake the feeling that this unexpected visit was more than just a friendly gesture; it was a lifeline thrown into turbulent waters, an invitation to escape the storm that had been brewing between Nathaniel and me.

But as I looked at Nathaniel, I could see the tension still lurking behind his eyes, a storm of unspoken words waiting to be unleashed.

Just then, I noticed something flicker behind him—a shadow lurking in the hallway, something dark and foreboding that sent a shiver down my spine.

Before I could process it, the lights flickered ominously, and the atmosphere shifted again. The door creaked wider, and just as I was about to voice my concern, I felt a presence, a looming figure I couldn't yet see. The air turned electric, a crackle of uncertainty swirling around us, and the words I had been meaning to say became tangled in a web of anxiety.

"Let's talk about what we really want," I began, only to be interrupted by a sudden, sharp knock that echoed through the room, sending a chill down my spine.

Chapter 27: The Weight of Choices

Standing before the mirror, I couldn't help but examine every detail of my reflection as if it were a stranger. My fingers brushed against the delicate fabric of the dress I had chosen for the showcase—a vibrant hue of cerulean, reminiscent of the ocean just after a storm, draping elegantly over curves that I had only recently learned to embrace. It shimmered under the soft light of my apartment, a glimmering promise of the creativity and hard work that had gone into its making. Yet, beneath the surface of that shimmering fabric, a tempest brewed within me.

Each stitch I had sewn into this collection was not merely a thread of fabric but a thread of my soul, woven with aspirations, fears, and a relentless pursuit of a dream that felt both intoxicating and terrifying. The weight of my choices pressed heavily against my chest, an anchor tethering me to the floor, while my heart raced with the thrill of the unknown. I could almost hear the whispers of my hopes, urging me to take the leap, while the echoes of doubt lurked in the corners of my mind, reminding me of the risks that came with every choice.

"Why do you look like you're about to jump off a cliff?" Nathaniel's voice broke through my reverie, warm and teasing, a soothing balm against my turmoil. He leaned against the doorframe, arms crossed, his hair tousled in a way that suggested he had been raking his fingers through it—a habit of his when he was deep in thought. The sunlight filtering through the window painted him in soft hues, highlighting the contours of his jaw and the playful glint in his hazel eyes. It made my heart flutter, a strange contradiction to the heavy weight I felt.

"I'm just... contemplating the abyss," I replied, forcing a lightness into my tone, though the words carried more gravity than I intended. "You know, the whole 'what if I fail and ruin everything' situation?"

"Ah, the classic artist dilemma," he said, stepping further into the room, the scent of sandalwood and fresh coffee trailing behind him. "I think that comes with the territory. But look at you! You're practically glowing with talent. Plus, I hear the abyss is a pretty overrated destination."

I turned to face him, allowing a smile to break through the tension. "You always know how to make me feel better, don't you?"

"It's a gift," he replied, a hint of mischief dancing in his eyes. "But seriously, do you really think you'll fail? After everything you've poured into this? You're a force to be reckoned with, not just some artist tossing a paintbrush at a canvas."

His unwavering belief in me ignited a flicker of hope amidst my fears. Nathaniel had been my anchor, my unwavering support as I dove deeper into the world of fashion design. He had a way of infusing ordinary moments with magic, making every mundane task feel monumental. Yet, beneath his charming exterior, I sensed an undercurrent of restlessness, an unspoken tension that simmered between us, brewing like a pot on the verge of boiling over.

"Maybe I just don't want to disappoint you," I confessed, my voice barely above a whisper, laden with the weight of vulnerability. "You've invested so much in me. What if I mess this up?"

"Disappoint me?" He shook his head, laughter dancing on his lips. "You're already way past that point, sweetheart. If you mess this up, it'll be the best 'mess up' anyone has ever seen. I'll be there, front row, cheering like a lunatic."

The image of him, exuberantly supportive amidst a sea of critical faces, sparked warmth in my chest. Yet, another wave of unease crashed over me. What would happen after the show? Would my success eclipse our budding relationship? I had never wanted to be one of those artists whose dreams overshadowed everything else.

As I prepped for the evening, I could feel the universe shift around me, the air thick with possibilities and fears. The night ahead held a promise of potential, yet a nagging doubt clung to my thoughts. I turned back to my reflection, reminding myself that this showcase was not just a culmination of my hard work; it was a new beginning, a chance to declare who I was in a world that often felt indifferent.

"Let's grab some food before the madness, shall we?" Nathaniel suggested, breaking my train of thought. "You need fuel for the fire."

I raised an eyebrow, a playful challenge in my eyes. "What if I told you I was too nervous to eat?"

"Then I'd suggest you get your priorities straight," he replied, mock seriousness etched on his face. "Food before fashion, darling. That's the secret to success."

A laugh escaped my lips, a genuine release of the tension that had wound itself so tightly within me. "Alright, fine. But only if you promise not to mock me when I can't choose between the truffle fries and the nachos."

"Deal," he said, a triumphant grin spreading across his face. "But I can't make any promises about mocking you for your choice of drink. I mean, come on, a 'virgin' anything? You're way too talented for that."

With a playful shove, I headed toward the door, my heart a little lighter, but still wrestling with the weight of uncertainty. As we stepped out into the cool evening air, I couldn't shake the feeling that tonight would not only test my designs but also the delicate threads of the bond we had woven. Choices lay ahead, and each one would come with its own weight, but for now, I would breathe in the moment and let the night unfold as it wished.

As we strolled through the bustling streets, the warm glow of streetlights illuminated our path, creating an ambiance that felt both intimate and electric. I inhaled deeply, the scents of grilled vegetables and sweet pastries wafting from nearby food stalls, mingling with the faint aroma of rain-soaked pavement. The world around us buzzed with life, laughter spilling into the night as couples and friends gathered, a vibrant tapestry of stories unfolding in every direction.

"Is it too cliché to say this feels like a scene from a rom-com?" Nathaniel mused, his eyes sparkling with mischief. He stopped abruptly, feigning an exaggerated pose, one hand on his hip, the other pointing dramatically toward the moonlit sky. "You know, the kind where the characters realize their love amidst a backdrop of street food and twinkling lights?"

I couldn't help but laugh, shaking my head at his theatrics. "Oh please, we're hardly in a movie. This is real life, filled with greasy fries and questionable choices. Though I must admit, your moon pose is award-worthy."

He dropped the pose with a flourish, a mock pout forming on his lips. "You wound me, dear artist. I'll have you know I was born for the spotlight. But let's not pretend that this night isn't ripe with potential for dramatic revelations."

A shiver of excitement coursed through me, tinged with the ever-present anxiety that came with uncharted territory. We rounded a corner and approached a small food truck, the vibrant red exterior promising delicious offerings. The chef, a jovial man with an impressive beard, greeted us with a booming voice.

"Welcome! You've stumbled upon the best-kept secret in the city! What can I get for you? Our truffle fries are legendary!"

"See?" Nathaniel said, nudging me playfully. "Legendary. How can you resist?"

With a playful roll of my eyes, I stepped forward, scanning the menu. "Okay, truffle fries it is. But if they don't live up to the hype, I'm blaming you for my dinner disappointment."

"Don't worry," he reassured me, leaning close as he ordered. "If they're not good, we can always drown our sorrows in nachos. You know I'm always prepared for a backup plan."

As we waited for our food, I studied him, the way he effortlessly engaged with the world, drawing laughter and light from everyone around him. He was a natural, a beacon of warmth and humor that made everything feel more vibrant. Yet, as I admired him, a flicker of uncertainty crept back in. Was I ready to embrace the potential of our relationship, or would my ambition swallow me whole?

Our fries arrived, golden and crispy, the tantalizing scent wrapping around us like a warm embrace. I took a bite, and the explosion of flavor was every bit as magical as promised. "Okay, I'll concede. These are incredible. But what's next on your legendary list?"

"Ah, the night is still young. We could go to that new gallery opening down the block. I hear the artist has a unique twist on traditional themes," Nathaniel suggested, his enthusiasm palpable. "Or we could find a cozy corner and engage in philosophical debates over whether or not the nachos count as a legitimate dinner."

"Philosophical debates, you say?" I feigned deep thought, placing my hand on my chin. "I believe the nachos could be a gateway to a whole new culinary experience, but only if paired with the right drink. A margarita, perhaps?"

"Clearly, your culinary skills extend beyond just fabric design," he chuckled, his gaze meeting mine, that familiar spark igniting between us. But in that fleeting moment of connection, I couldn't help but wonder if this was the calm before a storm.

With our fries devoured and laughter echoing in the air, we made our way to the gallery, the atmosphere shifting to one of hushed reverence as we entered. The soft hum of conversation mixed with the gentle melodies of a live pianist tucked into a corner. The walls were adorned with vibrant canvases, each one a world unto itself, brimming with emotions that resonated deeply.

"Look at that one," Nathaniel said, pointing to a swirling mass of colors, a tumultuous ocean that captured the essence of chaos and beauty. "It reminds me of you."

"Me?" I asked, taken aback. "That's a bit much, don't you think?"

"No, really. It's dynamic, full of passion and intricacy, but there's also a calmness in the chaos. Just like you." His words wrapped around me, warm and intoxicating, but they also set off alarm bells in my mind.

"I appreciate the compliment, but I'm not sure I'm as impressive as that painting," I said, a hint of doubt creeping in. "What if I don't live up to the expectations?"

He stepped closer, the warmth of his presence grounding me amid the swirling colors and emotions. "You're already living up to so much more than you realize. You have this incredible talent that draws people in, and I think you're just beginning to understand how remarkable that is."

Before I could respond, a voice pierced the atmosphere, a familiar yet unwelcome sound that sent a shiver down my spine. "Well, well, if it isn't the golden girl and her shadow."

I turned to see Veronica, my former mentor, striding toward us, her heels clicking against the polished floor with a confidence that dripped with disdain. Her perfectly coiffed hair framed her face like a halo, but the sharpness of her gaze held a different kind of light—one that spoke of rivalry and unresolved tension.

"Veronica," I said, forcing a smile that felt more like a grimace. "What a surprise."

"Oh, I'm sure it is," she replied, her voice dripping with sarcasm. "I didn't expect to find you here, so close to your big night. I'd have thought you'd be too busy panicking about the inevitable disappointment."

"Or perhaps I'd be too busy enjoying the company of someone who genuinely appreciates art," I shot back, trying to maintain my composure.

Nathaniel placed a reassuring hand on my back, a subtle reminder that I wasn't alone. "We were just discussing how important it is to embrace creativity in all its forms," he said smoothly, attempting to diffuse the tension.

"Creativity, yes, but darling," Veronica leaned in closer, her smile sweet but her words sharp, "what's art without a little controversy? You know that all eyes will be on you, waiting for you to slip up. Just a little hiccup, and all of your dreams could go up in smoke."

The air around us thickened, and I could feel my heart racing, caught in a web of anxiety and determination. This was the moment I had been dreading—a confrontation with my past that could very well define my future. But rather than crumbling under her gaze, I straightened my shoulders, fueled by the very fears she had so artfully invoked.

I took a deep breath, the tension crackling in the air like a charged storm. Veronica's gaze bore into me, sharp as a knife and just as cutting. "You must be so proud," she continued, a smirk playing at the corners of her mouth. "You've managed to snag a spot in this showcase with your little passion project. But tell me, how does it feel to know you're merely the latest trend, soon to be forgotten when the next hot designer comes along?"

"Actually," I said, forcing my voice to remain steady despite the churning in my stomach, "I'm quite excited about what I've created. It's not about being trendy; it's about authenticity. Something you might want to consider."

Nathaniel's presence beside me was a comfort, his fingers brushing against mine in a subtle gesture of support. I could feel the warmth radiating from him, grounding me against Veronica's biting remarks. "Look," he interjected, his tone calm yet firm, "everyone here is celebrating creativity and passion. It's a positive environment, and I'm sure that even you can appreciate that."

Veronica laughed, a sound that rang hollow, echoing through the gallery. "Oh, sweetheart, I thrive on the chaos of competition. It's what keeps this industry alive. Without it, we'd all be stagnant, lost in our own little worlds."

"Or perhaps," I countered, emboldened by Nathaniel's support, "it's about lifting each other up. We all started somewhere, didn't we? You weren't always at the top."

Her expression shifted, the facade of confidence faltering for just a moment. "Touché," she said, but the sharpness returned as quickly as it had dissipated. "Just don't get too comfortable, darling. The spotlight can burn hotter than you think."

With that, she turned on her heel and sauntered away, leaving behind an icy chill that lingered in the air. I exhaled slowly, releasing the tension that had coiled tightly within me. "Wow," I said, shaking my head. "I'd forgotten how delightful she is."

"Delightful, indeed," Nathaniel replied, a grin tugging at his lips. "But she's just a footnote in your story. Remember, it's your night. Don't let anyone dim your light."

As the evening progressed, the atmosphere buzzed with excitement, art and music weaving a tapestry of creativity that seemed to pulse with life. Yet, despite the vibrant surroundings, I couldn't shake the unease that had settled in the pit of my stomach. I was about to step onto a stage that felt both exhilarating and terrifying, and the stakes seemed to rise with each passing moment.

"Let's find a quieter place," I suggested, feeling the need to escape the throng of guests, the cacophony of chatter mingling with my swirling thoughts. Nathaniel nodded, guiding me to a small alcove adorned with abstract sculptures that danced in the dim light, their forms shifting with the flicker of candles.

"I'm glad we're here," I said, leaning against a cool marble surface, grateful for the momentary reprieve. "It feels like the world just shrank a little."

"Just us and art," he said softly, his eyes searching mine. "What are you really feeling?"

The vulnerability in his gaze mirrored the chaos in my heart. "I'm scared," I admitted, the truth tumbling out in a rush. "What if I fail? What if I stand there and nothing happens? What if everything I've worked for just... vanishes?"

"Failure is part of the process," he reassured me, stepping closer. "But what you're creating is more than just a collection. It's a piece of you. It can't vanish unless you let it. Just look at everything you've accomplished, all the risks you've taken."

His words wrapped around me like a warm embrace, yet the fear still clung to me like a shadow. "I know, but—"

"No 'buts.' Just embrace the moment," he interrupted, a spark of determination igniting in his eyes. "And if anyone can appreciate what you've poured into this, it's the audience that's coming to see you. They want to see your vision."

With a nod, I took a breath, trying to harness his conviction. Just then, a buzz filled the air, the sound of anticipation rising around us as the showcase began to unfold. The spotlight beckoned, a siren call that both thrilled and terrified me. "I guess it's time," I said, my voice barely above a whisper.

"Hey," Nathaniel said, tilting my chin up with a gentle touch. "No matter what happens out there, remember I'm right here. You've got this."

With his words echoing in my mind, I stepped back into the bustling crowd, each heartbeat synchronized with the rhythm of the night. The lights dimmed, and a hush fell over the audience as the first model stepped onto the runway, showcasing a piece that mirrored the colors of a sunset—a breathtaking array of oranges and pinks that shimmered like a dream.

As the models glided past, showcasing the collection I had poured my heart into, the energy in the room shifted, igniting a flame of excitement within me. The applause surged, rippling through the crowd like a wave of enthusiasm, and I felt my spirits lift with each passing look. I watched, captivated, as my designs came to life, each piece telling a story that resonated with the audience.

But as the final model approached, a figure caught my eye, standing at the back of the room—a tall silhouette, unmistakable yet out of place. My breath caught in my throat, confusion gripping me. It was Michael, the industry titan who had turned me away years ago, a man whose opinion had once sent me spiraling into doubt.

I felt my pulse quicken, the weight of his gaze heavy on me. The cheers faded into a low hum as I focused on him, the thrill of the moment overshadowed by a sudden fear. Why was he here? Had he come to critique, to see if I had truly grown, or to gloat over my struggles?

With the final model's walk coming to an end, the applause erupted, echoing like a heartbeat through the gallery. I stood there, caught in a whirlwind of emotions, exhilaration mingling with dread. Nathaniel, ever perceptive, caught the shift in my demeanor. "What's wrong?" he asked, concern lacing his voice.

I gestured toward Michael, whose expression was inscrutable. "He's here. After everything... I didn't expect to see him tonight."

"Is that a bad thing?" Nathaniel's brow furrowed, and I could feel the tension building like a brewing storm.

"I don't know," I admitted, feeling the weight of uncertainty crash over me again. "He represents everything I've fought against, every doubt I've tried to silence."

"Then let this be your moment," Nathaniel urged, his voice a calming anchor amidst the chaos. "You've overcome so much. Don't let his presence take away from your triumph tonight."

But as I prepared to take the stage, the room shifted once more. The lights dimmed further, casting shadows across the crowd, and the excitement morphed into an undercurrent of something darker. I could feel the anticipation in the air, electric and fraught with tension. Just then, the power flickered, a brief stutter that sent murmurs racing through the audience.

I steadied myself, forcing my breathing to remain even as the lights flickered back on, revealing Michael standing, arms crossed, an expression I couldn't quite decipher etched across his face. The atmosphere hung thick with uncertainty, the crowd now expectant, teetering on the edge of something monumental.

In that moment, as the applause continued to thunder around me, a chill ran down my spine. This was not just about my showcase anymore; it was about to become a confrontation—a clash between my past and the future I had fought so hard to build.

And as I stepped forward into the spotlight, I realized that the weight of choices was heavier than I had anticipated, and I was about to find out just how far I was willing to go to seize my moment.

Chapter 28: The Grand Reveal

The lights flickered to life, casting a golden hue over the sleek runway, and my heart drummed a wild rhythm in my chest. The intoxicating scent of fresh paint mingled with the subtle notes of perfume drifting from the guests, creating an atmosphere thick with anticipation. I stood backstage, the cacophony of voices rising and falling like a tide around me, each laugh, each whisper, pushing me closer to the precipice of my dreams. My fingers danced nervously over the hem of the gown I had crafted with painstaking care—each stitch a testament to late nights spent hunched over fabric swatches, the hum of my sewing machine serenading my ambitions into the wee hours.

With a deep breath, I caught sight of Nathaniel in the front row, his dark hair tousled, as if he'd just stepped out of an artful magazine shoot. He exuded an effortless charm that drew me in like a moth to a flame, and for a moment, the chaos around me faded. His gaze held mine with a warmth that ignited a spark of hope in my chest. My heart, usually steady in its quietude, suddenly threatened to escape its cage. The way he looked at me felt like a blessing, a secret promise nestled beneath the surface of the crowd's exuberance.

When my name echoed through the speakers, I stepped forward, the spotlight engulfing me like a lover's embrace. The music swelled, each note resonating with my heartbeat. I wore the gown—a symphony of soft lavender and shimmering silver, its flowing fabric whispering around my legs like a gentle breeze. I felt the power of the moment settle over me like a delicate veil. I was no longer just a girl from a small town; I was an artist, a creator, and tonight was my canvas.

The audience's murmurs crescendoed into applause, waves of sound crashing over me as I glided down the runway. Each step felt lighter, buoyed by the energy radiating from the crowd. I caught snippets of conversation—genuine admiration, critiques that danced on the edges of envy, and whispers of future collaborations. This was what I had worked for, what I had yearned for through countless rejections and sleepless nights. And yet, as the applause washed over me, an unexpected shadow flickered at the edges of my joy. The realization came slowly, threading its way through my triumphant haze: I stood alone, and the triumph felt tinged with a bittersweet edge.

As I reached the end of the runway, I paused, striking a pose that felt both powerful and vulnerable, embodying the culmination of my journey. The applause thundered, a standing ovation that felt both exhilarating and isolating. I turned to see Nathaniel, his eyes glimmering with pride. He met my gaze, and the way his lips curled into that infectious smile made my heart stutter. I longed for him to join me in this moment, to share the victory, yet he remained seated, a spectator to my triumph.

With the final pose held, I took a deep breath, savoring the rush of accomplishment. The moment stretched on, a delicious eternity where everything felt perfect, even as the world shifted beneath my feet. I glanced back down the runway, where my team awaited, faces aglow with excitement. Each of them had poured their heart and soul into the pieces that were now strutting before the audience, and I wanted nothing more than to celebrate with them. But that longing for connection, for shared joy, sat uneasily beside the gaping hole of loneliness that clawed at me.

As I made my way backstage, the applause faded, replaced by a flurry of activity. Designers and models mingled, laughter punctuating the air like the sharp snap of a camera shutter. I caught sight of Sophie, my friend and fellow designer, her cheeks flushed with exhilaration. She rushed over, throwing her arms around me in an exuberant embrace. "You were amazing! The crowd loved you! Did you see how they reacted to the last piece? You're a star!" Her enthusiasm was infectious, yet my heart remained heavy, a tight knot of conflicting emotions.

"Thanks, Sophie. I just... I thought it would feel different, you know?" I glanced at the swirling sea of faces, the glimmer of success refracting in the lights like diamonds scattered across velvet. "I thought I'd feel more whole."

She stepped back, tilting her head as she studied me. "You need Nathaniel here with you. He's been watching you like a hawk. Did you see how proud he looked?"

I nodded, remembering the way his eyes had sparkled with admiration, the way his focus had never wavered. "Yeah, but I'm not sure it's enough. What if I'm just this fleeting moment for him?" The thought cut deep, sharper than any pair of scissors I wielded in the studio.

"Stop it!" Sophie shook her head, her golden curls bouncing wildly. "You're more than just a moment. You're a force. Besides, you deserve to be celebrated. If he can't see that, then maybe he's not the right guy for you."

Her words sparked a fire within me, the kind that ignites when you're on the verge of something new and daring. But the flicker of doubt still lingered, gnawing at the edges of my heart. As I scanned the crowd beyond the backstage curtain, I saw Nathaniel still seated, his gaze glued to the runway, lost in thought. That image of him—captivated yet distant—etched itself into my mind, and I knew that the heartache I felt wasn't just for my dreams but for a love that seemed to teeter on the edge of uncertainty.

Backstage, the air hummed with frenetic energy, alive with the chatter of designers dissecting the show, models exchanging laughter, and the hum of stylists frantically touching up hair and makeup. I felt as though I'd just stepped off a cliff into a world of wonder, but with each heartbeat, the exhilaration began to fade, replaced by the gnawing sensation of emptiness that hung over me like a heavy fog.

Sophie, still buzzing from the excitement, looped her arm through mine and pulled me toward a small cluster of my friends who had come to support me. "You need to celebrate!" she insisted, her enthusiasm radiating like sunlight. "It's not every day you pour your soul into something and it's met with such acclaim. We should go out, paint the town red! Or at least a nice shade of lavender, considering your latest collection."

Her light-heartedness was contagious, yet the moment I caught Nathaniel's eye again, standing alone, his brow slightly furrowed in thought, the weight returned. I wasn't ready to celebrate without addressing the quiet tension simmering beneath the surface of my triumph. "What if he's just here for the show?" I murmured, half to myself.

"Are you kidding?" Sophie raised an eyebrow, her expression a mixture of disbelief and annoyance. "He practically glows when he looks at you. That's not just 'here for the show' energy; that's 'I-want-to-know-everything-about-you' energy. If I didn't know better, I'd say he's smitten."

Her words danced around my head like confetti, yet they didn't settle into any comforting patterns. Instead, they drifted, elusive as shadows in the corner of my mind. I was an artist, sure, but I was also a woman caught between ambition and affection, and the clarity I sought seemed just out of reach.

"Alright, but what if I'm just imagining things?" I took a deep breath, trying to tame the flurry of thoughts spiraling around my heart. "What if this is just a fleeting spark for him, and I'm the one who's reading into it?"

Sophie threw her head back, laughing, the sound bright and carefree. "Sweetheart, if that man is just playing games, then I'll wear a clown wig for the next month. You deserve more than to be a passing thought in anyone's mind. If you want him, go after him. What do you have to lose?"

Her resolve ignited a fire in me, a quiet determination that sparked with the flicker of hope. I watched as Nathaniel drifted closer to the backstage entrance, a lone figure against the riotous backdrop of celebration. It was now or never. I couldn't let the noise of the crowd drown out the possibilities that lay within reach.

With a nod to Sophie, I moved toward Nathaniel, weaving through the throng of admirers. Each step felt heavier, my heart racing not from fear but from anticipation. As I approached, his eyes flickered to me, an instant recognition sparking in the air between us.

"You were incredible," he said, his voice low and sincere, brushing away the surrounding chaos. The way he said it made my knees weak, as though the truth of his words wrapped around me like a warm embrace.

"Thanks, it felt... different. I expected this rush of joy, but it's complicated." I bit my lip, the words spilling out before I could rein them in. "There's so much noise around, but inside, I feel this pull toward something deeper."

He regarded me thoughtfully, and for a moment, the world around us dissolved into a soft haze. "You know," he began slowly, "you're not just an artist. You're a storyteller. Each piece you create holds a piece of you, a piece of your journey. That's what makes it so powerful."

A flutter of warmth spread through me, and I realized he understood me in ways I hadn't yet fully grasped myself. "And what if the story I'm telling isn't the one I thought I was?"

Nathaniel stepped closer, his expression earnest. "Maybe it's time to write a new chapter, one where you let someone in, someone who sees you for all you are."

His gaze held mine, and the warmth in his eyes began to thaw the walls I'd built around my heart. The doubts, the fears—all of it felt manageable in that moment, like the fading echoes of the show that had just concluded.

"But I'm scared," I confessed, the vulnerability slipping out like a secret I hadn't meant to share. "What if I'm not enough? What if I let you in and it all falls apart?"

"Then we'll rebuild it together." He reached out, taking my hand in his, his touch gentle yet grounding. "Nothing worth having comes without risk. You taught me that much."

Just then, the raucous laughter of our friends erupted behind us, snapping the moment like a fragile string. I glanced back to see Sophie grinning, an impish glint in her eye, clearly eavesdropping.

"Hey, lovebirds! Can we join the party or are you two planning a secret rendezvous right here?" she teased, the words light yet laced with the genuine affection of a true friend.

The tension in my shoulders eased, and I couldn't help but chuckle. "Just sharing a moment of profound wisdom," I shot back, glancing at Nathaniel, who raised an amused eyebrow.

"I thought it was more like a high-stakes game of emotional chicken," he quipped, his lips curling into that crooked smile that always sent my heart racing.

"Touché," I said, appreciating how effortlessly he turned the moment into something playful. "But seriously, what are we doing? Are we ready to dive into this or just skimming the surface?"

With a determined nod, Nathaniel replied, "I'm all in. I want to know you, not just the artist, but the woman behind the creations. And I think you're worth every risk."

The sincerity in his voice ignited a flicker of courage within me, illuminating the shadows of uncertainty that had loomed for far too long. Maybe I could be brave enough to let someone in. I could create a new story, one filled with not just fashion but connection, laughter, and—dare I say—love.

As our friends swarmed us, laughter and joy intertwining in a beautiful chaos, I felt the weight of fear begin to lift. For the first time, I could see the potential in the darkness, a pathway illuminated by the possibility of something genuine and beautiful. The night was young, and with Nathaniel beside me, ready to explore whatever lay ahead, I felt a sense of belonging I hadn't realized I'd been craving.

Laughter bubbled around me like a sparkling brook as my friends and I spilled out of the showcase venue and into the crisp night air. The streetlights flickered overhead, casting a warm glow on the asphalt as we ambled down the street, the sound of our heels clattering a joyful rhythm beneath the star-studded sky. The energy was infectious, a heady mix of triumph and camaraderie. I felt buoyant, the worries of the past few weeks dissipating like steam from a cup of freshly brewed tea.

Sophie, ever the instigator of fun, declared, "Let's find the nearest bar that serves ridiculously overpriced cocktails!" She danced ahead, twirling like a sunbeam, her curls bouncing around her face. "I demand something with a ridiculous name, preferably involving fruit I can't pronounce!"

"Count me in for the fruit extravaganza!" I laughed, exhilarated by the sheer delight of the moment. Around us, the city buzzed with life, a vivid tapestry of lights, laughter, and fleeting glimpses of people living their own stories. It was the kind of night that felt alive, filled with possibility, and I was determined to embrace it.

As we turned the corner, I caught Nathaniel's eye, and the world narrowed to just the two of us amid the crowd. He walked beside me, a comforting presence, the air between us crackling with unspoken words and lingering glances. "You really rocked that show," he said, his voice low, laced with sincerity that made my heart race.

"Thanks! But the real showstopper was you in the audience," I replied, feeling bold. "You made me feel like I was walking on clouds."

His smile deepened, and for a heartbeat, we shared a look that felt electric. I couldn't help but wonder what would happen if I leaned in closer, if I let myself fall into the warmth of his gaze. But just then, Sophie's voice broke through the moment, reminding me of the vibrant world surrounding us.

"Come on, lovebirds! We're not getting cocktails for the sake of staring at each other! Let's celebrate!" She grabbed my hand and tugged me toward a cozy little bar nestled between two towering buildings, its exterior adorned with twinkling lights that beckoned us closer.

Inside, the atmosphere was alive with laughter and the clinking of glasses. The scent of citrus mingled with something sweet and fragrant, wrapping around me like a warm hug. We found a table in the corner, a perfect spot to absorb the vibrant chaos around us. As we settled in, I leaned back, a contented sigh escaping my lips.

"So, who's trying the 'Mango Madness' first?" Sophie grinned, her eyes gleaming with mischief. "I hear it's practically a party in a glass."

As we placed our orders, the conversation flowed easily, the kind of banter that felt like an extension of our friendship. Laughter echoed around us, and for a moment, I forgot about the weight of expectations and the uncertainty of my budding relationship with Nathaniel.

But as the cocktails arrived, each a vibrant swirl of colors and garnished with exotic fruits, I noticed Nathaniel's gaze had shifted. He seemed distracted, his eyes scanning the bar, landing on a figure a few tables away. My heart sank as I followed his gaze and found a woman seated there, her laughter bright and clear, a striking contrast to the dark waves of her hair and the bold lines of her designer outfit.

"Do you know her?" I asked, my voice barely above a whisper, though the question felt heavy in the air between us.

Nathaniel shifted in his seat, an unreadable expression crossing his face. "Not really. Just someone from the industry," he replied, though the way he said it felt vague, like a half-spoken secret.

"Right. Just someone," I echoed, trying to mask the knot of anxiety tightening in my chest. There was something in the way he looked at her, a flicker of recognition that sparked my insecurities. Was she a reminder of a world I couldn't quite penetrate?

Sophie, sensing the tension, chimed in, "Hey, let's play a game! What's your ideal cocktail name?"

"What? Is that even a game?" I laughed, grateful for the distraction.

"Absolutely! I'll start!" Sophie declared. "Mine would be called 'Sassy Citrus Delight,' complete with a twist of lime and a splash of sass!"

As my friends bantered back and forth, I forced myself to join in, each laugh chipping away at the heaviness. But my gaze kept wandering back to Nathaniel and the woman. She leaned in closer, and I felt the familiar pang of jealousy rise within me, each moment amplifying my insecurities like an echo in an empty room.

Finally, unable to resist any longer, I turned to Nathaniel. "So, what's your cocktail name? Is it 'The Enigmatic Stranger'?" I tried to inject humor into my voice, but the undertone of unease seeped through.

He chuckled softly, his gaze finally returning to me. "I'd say it's more like 'The Confused Artist,' trying to figure out which path to take."

His honesty was disarming, yet my heart wavered. "Well, you're not confused about me, are you?"

A flicker of uncertainty crossed his face, and just as I braced myself for his answer, a loud crash shattered the moment. Glass shattered against the floor, and the room fell silent, the laughter replaced by gasps and hushed murmurs. I turned to see the woman from the other table standing, her chair toppled over, and an icy chill swept through the crowd.

"Someone needs to get security!" she shouted, her voice dripping with agitation.

Nathaniel shot to his feet, his expression shifting into one of concern. "I'll check it out," he said, glancing back at me. "Stay here."

"Wait—" I began, but he was already moving through the crowd, the throng of people parting for him like waves retreating from the shore. My heart raced, confusion churning in my stomach as I struggled to make sense of the chaos unfolding before me.

Sophie leaned closer, her voice low. "What just happened? Is it me, or did that feel dramatic even for this crowd?"

"I don't know," I replied, anxiety twisting inside me like a knotted string. "But I think it's something more than just spilled drinks."

As Nathaniel reached the woman, the tension crackled in the air, thick with unspoken words and escalating emotions. My pulse quickened as I strained to catch snippets of their conversation. She gestured wildly, her hands slicing through the air as she spoke, her tone sharp and accusatory.

"What is going on?" I whispered, feeling a prickle of unease creep up my spine.

Just then, Nathaniel turned back toward me, his face set with an intensity I hadn't seen before. "You need to come here," he called out, urgency lacing his tone.

With a sudden surge of apprehension, I stood, my heart thundering in my chest as I stepped forward. This wasn't just a spilled drink; something deeper was at play. As I moved closer, the gravity of the situation settled over me like a heavy fog, each step carrying me toward an unknown that threatened to unravel the night entirely.

And just as I reached Nathaniel, the woman turned, her expression twisting into one of anger. "You think this is over?" she spat, her eyes blazing with something I couldn't quite decipher.

Nathaniel's face paled, and he looked between us, uncertainty flickering like a candle in the wind. "Wait, what's going on?"

"Nothing you need to worry about," she snapped, her tone icy. "But you will when the truth comes out."

The words hung in the air, heavy with implications, and as I stood there, the room spinning around me, I couldn't shake the feeling that this was just the beginning of something I had no idea how to navigate. The realization struck me: the night, which had begun with such promise, was about to change everything I thought I knew.

Chapter 29: Embracing Tomorrow

The park is alive with the crisp scent of autumn, the air tinged with a coolness that wraps around me like a cherished sweater. Leaves cascade in hues of burnt orange and golden yellow, twirling through the air before settling softly on the ground. I lean back against the cool metal of the bench, its surface a contrast to the warmth of Nathaniel's presence beside me. He is lost in thought, his brow furrowed slightly as he gazes at the winding path ahead, where couples stroll hand in hand, their laughter punctuating the quiet afternoon.

I can't help but study him—the way the afternoon light dances in his hair, highlighting the subtle curls that seem to have a mind of their own. He turns to me, his expression shifting as if he can feel my gaze. "What's going on in that mind of yours?" he asks, a teasing smile playing at the corners of his lips.

"Just wondering how we ended up here," I reply, my voice barely above a whisper. "You know, in a park on a Friday afternoon, discussing our futures like we're old souls sharing secrets over tea."

He chuckles, a rich sound that warms me from within. "Old souls? You're barely twenty-five. But I'll take that as a compliment."

I roll my eyes, but I can't suppress my smile. "Fair point. I suppose I've always been more of a 'let's plan our lives' type rather than 'let's see where the wind takes us.'"

Nathaniel's expression sobers, and he turns to face me fully. "Maybe we need to find a balance, then. You can't plan everything, you know. Sometimes, the unexpected is what leads to the best adventures."

Adventure. The word hangs in the air between us, heavy with implications. I think of all the risks I've taken to carve out a space in the fashion world—late nights stitching, networking in crowded rooms, the lingering doubt that dances at the edges of my confidence. "And what about you?" I ask, my heart racing. "You're off to Europe in a few months. That's a massive leap."

"Yeah," he says, his gaze drifting back to the path. "I keep thinking about all the places I'll go, the people I'll meet. But what if—what if it's not what I imagined? What if it changes me in ways I can't control?"

"Maybe it will change you, but that doesn't mean it's bad," I argue, feeling the familiar spark of determination surge within me. "We're both stepping into the unknown, but that's where growth happens."

Nathaniel nods, the weight of my words settling between us like a comfortable silence. "You're right. I guess it's just... scary."

"Scary is a good thing," I say, leaning closer. "It means we're on the brink of something incredible. Just think of the stories we'll have."

He laughs softly, but there's a flicker of uncertainty in his eyes. "Stories. Right. Like the one about how we both tried to live our dreams but ended up just—"

"Just what?" I interject, my heart pounding as I realize we're dancing around something deeper, something that could fracture the tenuous connection we've built.

"Just... apart," he finishes, his voice low. The truth hangs between us like a tightrope, the possibility of falling off into a chasm of unspoken feelings and unresolved fears.

"No, I refuse to accept that." I lean in, urgency threading my voice. "We've fought too hard for this. Our dreams don't have to mean we stop being a part of each other's lives."

His gaze locks onto mine, and for a moment, the world around us blurs. "So you're saying we can be supportive from a distance?"

"Exactly." I can feel the corners of my lips lift, the thought igniting a flame of hope within me. "I want to pursue fashion in Paris, but I also want to support you while you're abroad. We can share our experiences, grow together, and reconnect whenever we can."

"And what if we get so caught up in our own worlds that we forget to check in?" Nathaniel asks, his voice tinged with genuine concern.

"Then we set a reminder. Phone calls, texts, even goofy video messages. I'm not about to let you slip through my fingers that easily," I respond, my heart racing.

He smiles, that infectious, bright smile that always manages to light up my darkest days. "You always know how to pull me back in, don't you?"

"Someone has to keep you grounded," I tease, my playful tone a welcome reprieve from the weight of our conversation. "And if we both find our footing in this big, scary world, think about how much more we'll have to share."

The silence that follows is charged with unspoken promises, each of us envisioning a future filled with possibilities and challenges. I can almost feel the rhythm of our lives synchronizing, two melodies harmonizing beautifully, even as they play separately.

"Alright then," Nathaniel says, his tone more resolute now. "Let's do it. Let's chase our dreams and see where this takes us."

I smile, feeling a sense of freedom wash over me. "To our adventures, then. To the unknown."

"To our adventures," he echoes, and as we raise our imaginary glasses to toast our futures, the autumn breeze sweeps around us, carrying the laughter of children and the distant sounds of music from a nearby festival. It wraps us in a cocoon of warmth and hope, the air alive with potential.

In that moment, I feel a spark of something deep and unyielding. With each passing second, my heart swells with the knowledge that while we may be stepping onto different paths, our journey together is far from over. In fact, it's just beginning.

The air was thick with the mingled scents of fresh pine and damp earth, a reminder that nature, like life, could be beautifully unpredictable. As Nathaniel and I sat on that weathered park bench, the sounds of laughter and distant chatter from families enjoying the day drifted to us, weaving a tapestry of normalcy that felt almost surreal in the wake of our recent revelations. His hands were tucked in his coat pockets, a habit he'd picked up during colder days, and I couldn't help but notice how his brow furrowed slightly as he considered his next words, the way his lips pressed into a thin line before he finally spoke.

"You know, the world is much bigger than either of us." His voice was low, gravelly like the path beneath our feet, and yet it held an edge of warmth that made my heart flutter with both excitement and dread. "I've always wanted to explore. It's just... I never thought I'd have someone like you to think about leaving behind."

The sincerity in his tone was like a balm, soothing the pang of anxiety that had been building in my chest. I turned to face him fully, the late afternoon sun casting a golden glow that illuminated the subtle freckles across his nose. "And I never thought I'd find someone who understands my dreams as deeply as you do. It's terrifying to think of chasing them alone, but isn't that what life is about? Taking those leaps?"

Nathaniel shifted, his posture relaxing slightly. "You're right, but it's different when you're not just risking your own heart. I'm afraid of losing what we have." His gaze drifted to the horizon, where the sun began its slow descent, a vivid tapestry of orange and pink painting the sky.

"Losing what we have?" I echoed, trying to digest the weight of his words. "It's not lost if we choose to grow, is it? It's like... the leaves falling off the trees. They make way for new growth, for spring to come again. Maybe this is our autumn, and we're just making room for what's next."

A small smile tugged at the corners of his mouth, and I reveled in the softening of his features. "You always find a way to put a positive spin on things, don't you?"

"Only when it matters," I replied, allowing a playful tone to creep into my voice. "Besides, someone has to be the optimist in this relationship. You're the one with plans to run off to Europe and become the next great designer."

"I'm not going to Europe to become the next great designer," he corrected with mock seriousness, raising an eyebrow. "I'm just going to throw my sketches at the wall and hope something sticks."

"And here I thought you had it all figured out." I laughed, shaking my head. "Well, you'll have to keep me updated on your wall-throwing adventures. I expect nothing less than a full report of every rejected design."

He chuckled, and the sound washed over me like warm honey, bringing a lightness that had been missing for far too long. But as the laughter faded, I felt the weight of reality pressing in again. "So, what now?" I asked, the question lingering in the air between us like a cloud ready to burst.

He paused, clearly contemplating the implications of our next steps. "We go our separate ways for a while, but it doesn't mean we have to cut ties. I want you to pursue your fashion career, and I'll support you, even from a distance. But I also need to focus on my own path. It's not a goodbye; it's more of a 'see you later.'"

His words echoed through my mind, creating a rhythm that matched the thudding of my heart. "See you later," I repeated softly, savoring the notion of a future where our dreams didn't necessarily collide but rather danced around each other, intertwining like vines on a trellis.

"Ivy will want updates, of course," Nathaniel added, his voice teasing. "She'll probably show up with a notebook, demanding every detail."

"Like a fashion reporter on a mission!" I replied, a grin spreading across my face. "I can just picture her, taking notes like she's gathering intel for a secret mission. We should probably warn her about my questionable taste in fabric choices."

Our laughter filled the space around us, and for a brief moment, I allowed myself to forget the reality of our situation. It was easy to get lost in our banter, to imagine a world where we could chase our dreams hand in hand without the weight of distance hanging over us. But as the sun dipped lower in the sky, reality settled in, the inevitable tension creeping back.

"I guess the hardest part is that I really don't want to say goodbye," I admitted, the words tumbling out before I could stop them. "What if the distance changes us? What if we change?"

Nathaniel's expression softened as he turned to me, his eyes steady and reassuring. "Change is inevitable, but it doesn't have to mean losing each other. We're strong. We've weathered enough storms to know that love isn't confined by miles. It's about connection, trust, and... well, texts. Lots of texts."

I chuckled, feeling a sense of relief wash over me. "I'll send you pictures of every awful outfit I try on. You'll be my remote fashion consultant."

"And I'll be your cheerleader from across the pond," he replied, his voice warm and steady, promising something more than mere words.

Just then, a gust of wind rustled the leaves overhead, showering us with a cascade of gold and crimson. I closed my eyes for a moment, letting the crisp air fill my lungs, the scent of fallen leaves mingling with Nathaniel's cologne. It was a moment suspended in time, beautiful and bittersweet.

As we shared this space, I felt the certainty of our love, vibrant and resilient, promising that tomorrow would bring new adventures. I squeezed his hand gently, knowing that while our paths were diverging for now, they would surely converge again. With a heart full of hope and a spirit ready to embrace the unknown, I lifted my chin and smiled at Nathaniel, ready to embrace whatever awaited us, no matter the distance.

The sun began its final descent, casting long shadows and painting the world in shades of twilight. We sat there, suspended between two worlds, ready to leap into the next chapter, whatever it may bring.

The sun dipped lower, casting a golden hue that bathed the park in a warm glow, wrapping us in a cocoon of lingering possibility. The crisp air danced around us, a playful reminder that change was in the air, just like the rustling leaves that swirled in gentle eddies. I leaned back on the bench, allowing the moment to wash over me, feeling as if the universe had paused, waiting for the next act in our unfolding story.

"You know," Nathaniel began, breaking the comfortable silence, "I always imagined I'd take that leap alone. It's kind of terrifying to think of doing it with someone else's heart in my pocket." His gaze was serious, yet there was a hint of mischief in his smile, the way he always managed to balance gravity with levity.

"Are you suggesting I'm too heavy to carry?" I shot back playfully, nudging him with my shoulder. "I may not be as light as air, but I can assure you I come with all sorts of delightful baggage. Stylish baggage, mind you."

He chuckled, a rich sound that filled the space between us with warmth. "No, not heavy—more like... well, an exquisite collection of limited editions. A bit delicate, maybe. I wouldn't want to crack a precious vase while racing to catch a flight."

"Ah, I see. So I'm a rare find, but you're worried I might shatter?" I raised an eyebrow, feigning indignation.

"Not at all," he countered, leaning closer, his voice a conspiratorial whisper. "More like a Picasso. You can't rush the masterpiece; it needs time to breathe, to come into its own."

I rolled my eyes, trying to suppress a grin. "You do realize that Picasso is known for his abstract work, right? Are you saying I'm a little confusing and hard to understand?"

"Only to the untrained eye," he replied smoothly. "To those who know how to appreciate fine art, you're a breath of fresh air, a masterpiece in motion."

His words were a soothing balm, yet they also carried the weight of truth. I could feel the stakes rising, the uncertainty threading its way into the fabric of our conversation. "And what if I don't live up to the masterpiece you envision? What if I fall flat in this grand pursuit of fashion?" I asked, my tone shifting, revealing the vulnerability I often kept hidden behind a curtain of wit.

Nathaniel's expression softened. "Then we adapt. We paint over the mistakes, create new layers. Every great artist knows the value of a good edit." He paused, his gaze penetrating, and I could feel the gravity of his conviction wrapping around us. "But you need to promise me one thing: don't let fear stifle your creativity. Fear is a thief of dreams."

I nodded, absorbing his wisdom as if it were the final piece of a puzzle. "I won't. I promise." But as I said the words, a flicker of doubt tugged at my mind. Could I really navigate this journey without him by my side?

The chatter of the park patrons began to fade into the background as the two of us fell into a comfortable silence, the kind that was filled with unspoken understanding. We watched as children chased one another, their laughter a soundtrack of innocence, contrasting sharply with the weight of adult decisions looming over us.

But just as the moment seemed idyllic, my phone buzzed in my pocket, jarring me from my reverie. I pulled it out, my heart racing as I glanced at the screen. Ivy's name lit up, and an urgent wave of curiosity washed over me. I opened the message, her words flying across the screen like a bolt of lightning.

You won't believe what I just found out. Meet me at the café. It's important!

My brow furrowed, a sense of unease settling in my stomach. I looked at Nathaniel, who raised an eyebrow, clearly sensing my shift in mood. "What's up?" he asked, concern lacing his voice.

"Ivy's text... She said it's important," I replied, anxiety creeping into my tone. "I have to meet her."

Nathaniel sat up straighter, his expression turning serious. "Want me to come with you?"

"No, I think this is something I need to handle on my own." I could feel a knot tightening in my chest. I wasn't quite sure why, but something about Ivy's urgency felt ominous. "But I'll be back soon, I promise."

He nodded, though I could see the reluctance in his eyes. "Just be careful, okay? And call me if you need anything."

"I will," I assured him, rising from the bench with determination, though the flutter of uncertainty remained in the pit of my stomach. As I walked away, I could feel Nathaniel's gaze on my back, his concern wrapping around me like a shadow.

The café was a short walk away, its quaint façade a comforting sight amidst my mounting anxiety. As I stepped inside, the aroma of freshly brewed coffee enveloped me, mingling with the sweet scent of pastries. But there was no time to indulge. I scanned the room, spotting Ivy in a corner booth, her hands animatedly gesturing as she spoke to someone just out of sight.

I approached, heart racing. "Ivy! What's going on?"

She turned, her eyes wide, a mix of excitement and urgency etched across her features. "I've got news. You won't believe it!"

Before I could respond, the person seated across from her turned slightly, revealing a face I recognized all too well. My breath caught in my throat as my pulse quickened. There, looking every bit as enigmatic and magnetic as I remembered, sat Blake—my ex, the one who had slipped away without a trace, leaving nothing but questions in his wake.

"Surprise!" Ivy said, beaming, oblivious to the storm brewing in my heart.

I stared at Blake, an array of emotions swirling inside me. "What are you doing here?" I managed to croak out, a mix of disbelief and anger igniting like a fuse.

His gaze met mine, and for a moment, the world around us faded. "I had to see you," he said, his voice steady yet filled with an unspoken weight.

And just like that, the once-clear path ahead became shrouded in confusion and uncertainty, leaving me to wonder if the past had finally come to reclaim its hold on my future.

Milton Keynes UK
Ingram Content Group UK Ltd.
UKHW042241011124
450424UK00001BA/149